They need fiancés in a hurry…

Convenient Engagements

Three feel good romances from one beloved award-winning Mills & Boon author!

Jessica Hart was born in West Africa, and has suffered from itchy feet ever since, travelling and working around the world in a wide variety of interesting but very lowly jobs, all of which have provided inspiration on which to draw when it comes to the settings and plots of her stories. Now she lives a rather more settled existence in York, where she has been able to pursue her interest in history, although she still yearns sometimes for wider horizons. If you'd like to know more about Jessica, visit her website www.jessicahart.co.uk.

Convenient Engagements

JESSICA HART

DID YOU PURCHASE THIS BOOK WITHOUT A COVER?
If you did, you should be aware it is **stolen property** as it was reported *unsold and destroyed* by a retailer. Neither the author nor the publisher has received any payment for this book.

All the characters in this book have no existence outside the imagination of the author, and have no relation whatsoever to anyone bearing the same name or names. They are not even distantly inspired by any individual known or unknown to the author, and all the incidents are pure invention.

All Rights Reserved including the right of reproduction in whole or in part in any form. This edition is published by arrangement with Harlequin Enterprises II B.V./S.à.r.l. The text of this publication or any part thereof may not be reproduced or transmitted in any form or by any means, electronic or mechanical, including photocopying, recording, storage in an information retrieval system, or otherwise, without the written permission of the publisher.

This book is sold subject to the condition that it shall not, by way of trade or otherwise, be lent, resold, hired out or otherwise circulated without the prior consent of the publisher in any form of binding or cover other than that in which it is published and without a similar condition including this condition being imposed on the subsequent purchaser.

® and ™ are trademarks owned and used by the trademark owner and/or its licensee. Trademarks marked with ® are registered with the United Kingdom Patent Office and/or the Office for Harmonisation in the Internal Market and in other countries.

First published in Great Britain 2011
Harlequin Mills & Boon Limited,
Eton House, 18-24 Paradise Road, Richmond, Surrey TW9 1SR

CONVENIENT ENGAGEMENTS
© Harlequin Enterprises II B.V./S.à.r.l 2011

Fiancé Wanted Fast!, *The Blind-Date Proposal* and *A Whirlwind Engagement* were first published in Great Britain by Harlequin Mills & Boon Limited.

Fiancé Wanted Fast! © Jessica Hart 2003
The Blind-Date Proposal © Jessica Hart 2003
A Whirlwind Engagement © Jessica Hart 2003

ISBN: 978 0 263 88431 9

05-0211

Printed and bound in Spain
by Litografia Rosés S.A., Barcelona

FIANCÉ WANTED FAST!

CHAPTER ONE

'MALLORY left you?' Josh lowered his water bottle and stared at Gib in surprise.

'Ironic, isn't it?' said Gib with a somewhat crooked grin, shifting his back against the ice wall and putting on his jacket. It had been hot work climbing the last pitch, but at this altitude you soon lost heat. 'The boot's usually on the other foot!'

Josh grimaced. 'I'm sorry to hear that,' he said slowly. 'I always liked Mallory. You seemed really good together too.'

'That's what I thought,' said Gib wryly. 'Mallory's a very special lady. Smart as anything and beautiful and independent...I really thought she was going to be different.'

He tapped the side of his crampons with his ice pick to loosen the balled ice. 'But then the old C word started cropping up and I knew that was the beginning of the end.'

'The what word?' asked Josh, diverted.

'Commitment.' Gib stared morosely out at the spectacular view.

They had stopped for a rest on a frozen ledge, high up on the mountain. It was still some way to the summit, but you could look out at the hills stretching off to the hazy horizon. Gib loved the mountains. The air was clean and pure and the only sound was the wind cutting icily through the brilliant sunlight.

He was glad that Josh had called him up and suggested a climb. It was good to be up here where everything was simple and there was not a tearful woman in sight.

It certainly made a nice change.

'Why are women so obsessed with commitment?' he demanded. 'They all start off pretending that they're independent and just want a good time, but you're lucky if you get to a third date without them planning their wedding dresses!'

'You and Mallory had been together a bit longer than three dates,' Josh pointed out reasonably. 'It's nearly a year now, isn't it?'

'Exactly!' grumbled Gib. 'We were getting along great, everything was fine...why did she have to go and spoil it?'

'What did she say?'

'Apparently I am completely unable to "commit" or to "relate".' Gib hooked his fingers in the air to add sarcastic emphasis to the inverted commas. 'According to Mallory, I just thought of her as part of some kind of smorgasbord of women!'

Josh looked blank. 'A smorgasbord?'

'You know, one of those buffet affairs where all the dishes are set out along a big table and you go round to help yourself to whatever you fancy.'

'Right,' said Josh, none the wiser.

'Mallory's theory is that I treat women like so many different dishes, so that even if I find one I really like, I won't be content to stick with one because I'll always be wondering if there might not be one I might like even better further along the table.' Gib gave an exclamation of disgust. 'Don't you hate it when women analyse you?'

Josh didn't answer directly. Behind the dark glasses that protected his eyes from the glare, his expression was unreadable as he studied the view and considered Mallory's theory.

'She's right, though, isn't she?' he said at last.

'Listen, whose side are you on?' demanded Gib.

'You're the one who said that she's a smart lady.'

'I just happen to like women,' said Gib defensively. 'What's wrong with that?'

'Nothing.'

'And women like me.' He scowled. 'I love women! It's ridiculous to say that I can't relate to them properly!'

'Is that what Mallory says?'

'She says I've got no idea how to be friends with a woman.' Gib sounded outraged. 'Can you believe that?'

'Yes.'

'What do you mean?' he asked, taken aback by the typically quiet, uncompromising reply. Josh was so...so...so *British*...sometimes!

Josh was checking the ropes. 'Have you ever had a platonic relationship with a woman? A good one?'

'Sure.'

'When?'

'When? Well, let's see...when...when...' Gib searched his mind frantically. 'OK, I can't think of anyone right this moment,' he was forced to acknowledge, 'but I'm sure there must have been someone. I bet you can't think of anyone either,' he added, going on the offensive.

It didn't faze Josh. 'Yes I can,' he said calmly. 'Bella is one of my best friends, probably the best friend I've got, in fact. We were students together, and we've been close ever since.'

'And you've never slept with her?'

'No.'

'I bet you wanted to!'

Josh shook his head. 'No, that would spoil our friendship. Bella's always got some man in tow, and I have girlfriends, but it's different with her. I prefer what we've got. I can talk to Bella in a way I can't talk to anyone else. We understand each other.

'It's nothing to do with sex,' he went on. 'You could never be friends with a woman in the same way.'

'Want a bet?' said Gib, ruffled.

'OK.'

'OK?'

Josh tied off the end of the rope and sat back against the rock. 'I'll bet you...let's say ten thousand dollars?...to the charity of your choice that you can't be friends with a woman.'

Gib laughed. 'Ten *thousand* dollars? You're kidding, right?'

'You can afford it.'

'Yeah, but can you?'

'I don't think I will have to,' said Josh with annoying calm.

Well, Gib wasn't a man who could turn down a challenge like that! His eyes narrowed.

'Being friends is a bit subjective, isn't it? How would we decide if I'd succeeded or not?'

Josh unwrapped an energy bar and chewed meditatively for a while. 'How would you feel about spending a few weeks in London?' he asked at last.

'It wouldn't be a problem, I guess,' said Gib, a bit thrown by the apparent *non sequitur*. 'It's easy enough to keep in touch with what's happening here wherever I am.'

Absently he took the bar Josh handed him out of his rucksack. 'As a matter of fact,' he went on slowly, 'it might suit me quite well. I've been thinking about developing more European connections and with this whole Mallory thing, I wouldn't mind leaving the country for a while. I could do without all those scenes about who takes what!'

'OK.' Josh nodded briskly. 'Here's the deal. Bella shares a house in south London with three other girls, but one of them is getting married soon, so they're going to have a spare room. I reckon I could arrange it for you to live with them for a while.' He grinned. 'I think it would be a real test for you! If at the end of six weeks Bella and Kate and Phoebe all describe you to me as a real friend, you name the charity and I'll send the cheque!'

'Hhmmnn.' Gib looked a bit dubious. 'What are these girls like?'

'They're just three very nice, very ordinary English girls.'

'And that's it? I just live with them for six weeks and be their friend?'

'There's one more condition,' said Josh. 'You have to go incognito. You've had too many attractive, successful women falling over themselves for you here. Mallory's a psychologist and before that there was the TV presenter and that model...what was her name? The one with the legs up to her armpits?'

'Verona?'

'That's the one.' Josh allowed himself to remember her legs for a moment. They really had been spectacular.

'Anyway, the point is, you're spoilt!' he went on. 'It'll be different in London. The girls won't know anything about you, so you won't be able to buy their affection or impress them the way you do here. You'll just have to be yourself and if you can't be friends with them under those circumstances then you'll just have to accept that Mallory is right!'

Gib's face was inscrutable behind the dark glasses that cut out the mountain glare as he studied the horizon.

He was thinking about his father, who was now on his fourth wife. Gib got on with his father fine, but he didn't want to be like him. He had seen too many women in tears because his father's idea of commitment turned out to be very different from theirs.

Gib, on the other hand, prided himself on never making

promises he couldn't fulfil. He always made it clear to girlfriends that he wasn't offering happy ever after, and frankly couldn't see what was so wrong with being honest about wanting to live in the present without tying yourself to a future you weren't ready for.

But that didn't mean he couldn't be friends with a woman! No way was Gib prepared to accept that his attitude was anything like his father's. If he didn't have a female friend like Josh, it was just because most of the women he knew were more interested in being wives than friends.

Well, he would show Josh and Mallory and his father that he was perfectly capable of building a relationship with a woman that was based on friendship rather than sex. He would take the bet.

'Ten thousand dollars?' he said.

'Ten thousand dollars.'

'And I get to choose the charity that gets the money?'

'Only if you win. Otherwise I do.'

'OK, then.' Gib grinned as he held out his hand to Josh. 'You're on!'

Phoebe collapsed onto the sofa, kicking off her shoes and swinging her legs up with a sigh of relief. 'My feet are killing me! Next time I go to a wedding, remind me not to wear stilettos!'

'They are fab, though,' said Bella, handing out mugs of tea. It had been a sad moment when they all realised that after drinking champagne all day tea was all they really wanted. 'Sometimes you just have to suffer for style.'

Kate took her tea gratefully. She was lolling on one of the deep chairs, with her legs dangling over one arm.

'Personally I'd be exhausted if I had to be that stylish all the time. I'd no idea it was going to be such a smart wedding. Did you *see* some of those women there? It must be a full-time job looking like that! I felt so dowdy, like I was one of those embarrassing relatives you have to invite but nobody wants to talk to.'

'I know,' Phoebe agreed gloomily. 'You could tell they weren't at all surprised that we couldn't muster a single boyfriend between us.'

'Oh, come on, it wasn't that bad,' said Bella. 'I thought it was excellent! I love smart weddings like that. If I ever get married, I'm going to do it like Caro—the posh church, reception at some classy club, hundreds of guests all looking incredibly stylish.'

'Better get some new friends then,' said Phoebe rather indistinctly through a mouthful of chocolate digestive. 'If you're going to impose a fashion code, half of us won't be able to come. Kate and Josh and I will be camped out on the church steps just to get a glimpse of you as you sweep by!'

Bella grinned. 'Oh, Josh brushes up pretty well, and I'm sure I'll be able to find a dark corner to put you two in!'

'Better tell your father to start saving now,' put in Kate. 'That wedding today must have cost a packet.'

'I think Anthony must have contributed. It's not as if he can't afford it!'

'Well, I'd rather have a traditional country wedding,' said Kate. 'Just family and good friends and a marquee in my parents' garden so we can walk back from the village church. I'm going to have my two little nieces as bridesmaids,' she went on dreamily. 'They'd look sweet in taffeta with puffed sleeves and—'

She stopped as she saw Phoebe and Bella looking at her. 'Not that I've given it much thought, of course,' she said, but had the grace to blush.

'Of course not!' said Bella. She turned to Phoebe who

was saying 'What about you, Phoebe? Would you go for urban chic or the perfect country wedding?'

Phoebe concentrated on brushing biscuit crumbs from her dress. 'Neither. I think the best option would be to run away and get married on the quiet so that you don't have to plan anything. At least that way you would know the bridegroom was going to turn up!'

'Sorry, Phoebe,' said Bella contritely. 'I forgot you'd already been through all this.'

Phoebe attempted a careless shrug. 'Oh, well, it's been over a year now.'

Sixteen months, three weeks and four days, in fact.

Not that she was counting.

'And we didn't really get as far as planning the wedding before Ben changed his mind.'

Kate and Bella preserved a tactful silence. They knew quite well that she and Ben had been childhood sweethearts and that the chances of her not having spent most of her life thinking about the day they would get married were remote to say the least.

At least her parents hadn't sent out any invitations. She had been spared the humiliation of returning presents and answering sympathetic notes, although everybody had known, of course.

Phoebe picked up her tea. 'Anyway,' she said, 'I don't think any of us need panic about planning our weddings just yet. It's not as if hordes of men are desperate to sweep us off to the altar!'

'No,' Bella and Kate sighed.

'I'm beginning to think there's something wrong with this house,' she went on gesturing with her mug around the kitchen where they were sitting. 'It's as if it's cursed with a special man-repelling aura! Do you think I should sell it?'

The other two sat up in alarm. 'No!'

'I like it here,' Kate insisted.

'So do I,' said Bella, adding more practically, 'and we'd never be able to afford anywhere nearly as nice to live.'

'I know what you mean about the aura, though,' Kate reassured Phoebe. She brightened. 'Maybe that explains why Seb has been so funny recently?

'I think we should try feng shui before you do anything drastic,' she hurried on before Phoebe could start on the other possibilities for Seb's defection. 'I've got a friend who does it. Apparently you can change your luck just by shifting your furniture around a bit and keeping the loo seat down so that bad spirits can't get into the house.'

'Well, that shouldn't be a problem with no blokes around,' observed Phoebe glumly.

'Kate's right,' said Bella. 'Well, not about the feng shui maybe, but about not selling. It's a lovely house, and I certainly don't want to move. I must admit it's not going to be the same without Caro, though,' she added. 'I can't believe she'd be selfish enough to leave us just to get married!'

'I know,' agreed Phoebe. 'I mean, what's in it for her?' She gestured expansively with her free hand around the kitchen which was in its usual state of shabby chaos.

'Why would she want to leave all this for a big house in Fulham, a cleaner and an adoring husband?'

'I can't imagine,' said Kate loyally. 'You wouldn't catch me doing anything like that! Maybe she'll miss us so much she'll come back?'

'I don't think we should count on it,' sighed Phoebe. 'I know it's going to be hard to replace her, but I'm afraid I'm going to have to find someone else for her room or I won't be able to pay the mortgage. Neither of you have heard of anyone who's looking for somewhere to live, have you?'

They shook their heads. 'Not anyone I would want to share with anyway,' amended Bella.

'It looks like I might have to advertise then.'

'I'm not sure that's a good idea,' said Kate nervously. 'We could get all sorts of weirdos. Remember that film where the new flatmate murders the first girl and takes over her life? We could get someone like that.'

'Or worse,' said Bella. 'We could get someone obsessed with country dancing.'

They were all silent for a moment, brooding on the thought.

'Or we might get someone obsessed with cleaning,' suggested Phoebe. She looked ruefully around the kitchen. 'That wouldn't be too bad. She'd have plenty to keep her busy, anyway.'

'I shared with a girl like that once.' Bella shuddered at the memory. 'She was completely neurotic about cleaning. There were Post-its all over the flat with instructions about taking out the rubbish or reminders about the dusting rota, and the moment you made yourself a mug of tea she would whip out a coaster and follow you around until you put it down.'

She grimaced. 'It was seriously spooky! I think we'd be better off with a serial killer or a country dancer.'

'I think I'd rather sell the house,' sighed Phoebe.

'What about that guy Josh was talking about?' asked Kate suddenly. 'Did he mention him to you, Phoebe?'

'Briefly.' Phoebe drained her mug. 'What did he say his name was again?'

Kate tipped her head back and contemplated the ceiling while she searched her erratic memory. 'Gus?'

'Gib,' Bella corrected her.

'That was it.' Phoebe remembered her conversation with Josh as she helped herself to another biscuit. 'Doesn't he only want somewhere temporary, though? We need to find someone permanent.'

'Yes, but if he was here for a while it would give us time to find someone we really like,' said Kate.

Phoebe munched doubtfully. 'We don't really know anything about him, though,' she pointed out.

'We know he's a friend of Josh's.'

'But why does he only want to be here for a few weeks?' she asked Bella, who as Josh's best friend could be presumed to know more than the rest of them.

'I'm not sure. Josh was a bit vague about that. I know he lives in California, but that's about all. I got the impression he might be in a bit of financial difficulty, which is why he wants somewhere relatively cheap.'

Phoebe looked dubious. 'If he's that short of cash, why fly all the way from the States to London?'

'Maybe he just wants to get away from home for a bit,' suggested Kate, brightening perceptively at the idea of someone else to take under her wing. 'Perhaps his heart has been broken, and he needs some time and space to lick his wounds?'

'Oh, yes, that's *so* likely!' said Phoebe, rolling her eyes. 'There you are in California, with all that sunshine and spectacular scenery, and you think, "I need to cheer myself up, what can I do? I know, I'll go and spend six weeks in Tooting!" I mean, nothing against Tooting—I know we like it—but you've to admit that a suburb in south-west London isn't top of everybody's top ten tourist destinations.'

'It doesn't matter why he's coming, does it?' said Bella practically. 'Josh wouldn't have recommended him if he hadn't been able to pay the rent, and he can't be too awful if he's a friend of his. Why not think about it, Phoebe? Quite apart from anything else, it would be fun to have a man around the house again!'

Kate sat up straighter. 'And maybe Seb will hear about it and be jealous,' she added hopefully.

Privately, Phoebe thought it extremely unlikely that Kate's on-off, but more usually off, boyfriend, known to the rest of the world as Slimy Seb, would care one way or the other, but she knew that Kate lived in daily hope of hearing from him again. She was the only person Phoebe knew who actually believed that if you kept kissing a frog you'd eventually end up with a prince.

'You never know,' she said, avoiding Bella's eye. 'All right then, we'll give this Gib a go!'

Gib's mouth pulled down at the corners as he looked up at his home for the next six weeks. It was part of a terrace of identically narrow, faintly shabby Victorian houses that lined the street, and in the dank drizzle of that April evening even the tub of flowering bulbs at the front door failed to relieve the atmosphere of gloom.

Gib couldn't help thinking about his home on the Pacific coast, with its huge, light, open rooms and its view of the ocean, and he sighed. He was beginning to wonder if he might regret taking up the challenge Josh had thrown him.

Behind him, the taxi driver cleared his throat meaningfully, and Gib stepped up to the door and pushed the bell, his most charming smile at the ready. A bet was a bet, and it was too late to change his mind now.

He hadn't heard the bell ring inside, and pushed it again just as the door jerked open and he found himself looking at a tall, slender girl with the fiercest green eyes he had ever seen. She had a swing of straight dark hair, straight dark brows and a generous mouth that belied the severity of her expression.

Gib's smile blinked off in surprise. Had he got the right address? He distinctly remembered Josh saying that all three girls were very ordinary. They're just nice, friendly girls, he had said.

This girl didn't look at all ordinary to Gib, and she didn't look very friendly either.

'Yes?' she snapped.

'I'm John Gibson.' Gib put his smile back on, but it bounced right off her. 'Gib to my friends. And you must be Phoebe, Bella or Kate?'

'I'm Phoebe,' she acknowledged reluctantly, and frowned. 'We weren't expecting you until tomorrow.'

'Tomorrow was the original plan, but I was all ready and an earlier flight came up, so I thought I might as well just come on over and turn up.'

He had the bluest eyes Phoebe had ever seen, and they danced in a way that instantly made her feel boring and repressed for not being the kind of spontaneous person that changed arrangements at a whim and breezed across the Atlantic with about as much fuss as she would make popping down to the shop on the corner.

Less, probably.

Phoebe had had a bad day. Her boss, Celia, had been in a vile mood, nitpicking and throwing tantrums with an even greater regularity than normal. Escaping at last, she had spent more than forty minutes waiting for a bus which turned out to be only going as far as Clapham Junction anyway. Too fed up to hang around in the rain, she had set off to walk the rest of the way, without thinking about the fact that it would take her nearly an hour and that she was carrying two heavy folders and wearing quite unsuitable shoes, and when she finally hobbled into the kitchen she had discovered that the pilot light on the boiler had gone out, so there was no hot water for a bath.

And now there was this Gib on her doorstep.

Sod's law, thought Phoebe morosely. Be at your best with your hair perfectly in place and your lipstick perfectly applied, and you could be sure that when the doorbell went unexpectedly it would be someone doing market surveys or that man who kept trying to get them to change their electricity supplier.

Look and feel like a limp rag, however, and you could guarantee that the most attractive man you had ever seen in the flesh would turn up on the doorstep!

When she looked at him properly, she could see that he wasn't actually that handsome—his features were too irregular for classic good looks—but he had a quirky, mobile face with eyes so blue and so alive that somehow that was all that you noticed.

Phoebe was distinctly unnerved by the sheer vibrancy of the man. He had that relaxed yet vivid air of someone who spent his life in the sun. Just looking at him was like getting a blast of ozone. He was the sort of man who ought by rights to be at the helm of a yacht or plunging into the ocean waves with a surfboard under his arm, not standing in this grey south London street evidently wondering why she was staring at him.

Recollecting herself, Phoebe stepped back and held open the door. 'You'd better come in,' she said awkwardly.

Gib stayed where he was on the doorstep. 'The thing is, I've got a bit of a problem,' he admitted, and turned to indicate the taxi which was waiting in the street with its meter ticking at a rate of knots.

'I lost my wallet somewhere between LA and the arrivals hall at Heathrow. I think someone might have lifted it in the baggage hall, but anyway it's gone. I reported it to the police and have cancelled all my cards but I thought the best thing I could do would just be to get a taxi here and hope someone was in.'

He looked back at Phoebe with a rueful smile that she was sure was perfectly calculated to have most females swooning at his feet. 'You wouldn't have some cash to pay the taxi driver, would you? I'll pay you back, of course, as soon as I've sorted something out.'

Phoebe forced herself to resist the smile. It was just a little too like Slimy Seb's, who only ever came round when he wanted something and who was always patting his pockets and discovering that he had 'forgotten' his wallet, knowing quite well what a soft touch Kate was.

This Gib looked as if he was out of the same mould, one of those cocky, charming types that thought all they had to do was smile and everyone else would fall over themselves to do whatever they wanted. Phoebe didn't trust men like that. She had met too many of them, and seen too many friends like Kate hurt by their selfish behaviour to ever succumb herself.

Gib was watching her expression and reading her lack of enthusiasm without difficulty. 'Hey, it's no problem,' he said. 'I'll just get the taxi to take me to Josh's office. I'm sure I'll find someone there to bail me out.'

It was lucky that he had mentioned Josh. As Bella's best friend, Josh spent a lot of time in the house, and Phoebe was very fond of him. If Josh vouched for Gib, she had better not leave him to sort out his own problems the way she was strongly tempted to do.

'There's no need for that.' She managed a brittle smile. 'I'll just go and get my purse.'

'Thanks, I really appreciate that,' said Gib as the taxi drove off. 'I'll let you have the money back tomorrow.'

That was what Seb always said to Kate, too.

'Everything's a bit of mess,' said Phoebe stiffly as she led the way to the kitchen at the back of the house. 'We were going to tidy up for you tonight.'

They had planned a special welcoming meal as well. Bella was doing the shopping on her way home, but of course spontaneous types like Gib never thought of how they might mess up anyone else's plans, did they?

'Hey, I didn't want anyone to go to any trouble,' said Gib, alarmed by her frosty manner. 'Josh said you'd just treat me like a friend and let me muck in with the rest of you.'

'Now that you've turned up early, it looks like that's what you're going to have to do,' said Phoebe, carrying the kettle over to the sink to fill it.

Gib eyed her warily, picking up on the hostility but not quite sure what he had done to provoke it. Maybe she was cross like this with everyone, which would be a crying shame with that warm, creamy skin and that lush mouth, he thought and then remembered that he wasn't supposed to be thinking like that. *All you've got to do is be a friend*, Josh had said. What could be easier than that?

Clicking on the kettle, Phoebe turned to face him, and Gib looked quickly away. 'Nice kitchen,' he said.

It was a big, cluttered room with fitted cupboards at one end and at the other a shabby sofa and deep armchair covered with an ethnic-looking throw. In the middle was an antique pine table submerged beneath a welter of half-read newspapers, magazine cuttings, recipe books and files with papers spilling out of them. Gib spotted an iron, a collection of nail varnishes, a sequin bag, and—he did a double take—yes, a huge tabby cat curled up in a nest of papers.

The kitchen run by his housekeeper at home had gleaming steel surfaces and was so intimidatingly tidy that Gib rarely ventured in there. This room was messier and a lot less hygienic, he thought, glancing at the cat, but infinitely more inviting. The kind of room where you could sit down with a bottle of wine and relax without worrying about what anyone else was thinking of you.

'It's the warmest room in the house,' said Phoebe, looking around and trying to see it through his eyes. 'We spend all our time in here, as you can probably tell.'

'Whose is the cat?'

'Kate's.' Phoebe regarded it without affection. 'She's got the softest heart in the world. She's always coming back with these poor bedraggled creatures she's rescued, and then we all have to run around finding homes for them, but no one will take that cat, worse luck. Anyway, it probably wouldn't go,' she sighed. 'It's much too comfortable here. Kate spoils it, and Bella and I are terrified of it. Which reminds me,' she added, 'be careful when you come down in the mornings. It bites your ankles until you feed it!'

Josh hadn't mentioned savage cats when he made his bet, Gib thought a little sourly. He hadn't mentioned Phoebe's frosty manner either. Gib just hoped that there weren't any other nasty surprises in store for him.

As if understanding that they were talking about it, the cat got to its feet and stretched. Seeing the size of it, and the ferocious-looking teeth, Gib gave it a wide berth, but it only gave him a contemptuous stare and jumped off the table to land with a thud on the kitchen floor.

Phoebe watched it stalk out of the room and for the first time ever she warmed to it. Here at least was one other creature unlikely to be impressed by Gib's smile and spontaneity. Kate and Bella were bound to fall for his charm, but Gib would find that she and the cat were made of sterner stuff!

CHAPTER TWO

PHOEBE had been pouring boiling water into a teapot, and now got out a couple of mugs. 'Kate and Bella will be back later,' she said. 'Would you like some tea?'

'Great,' he said with the suggestion of a smile. 'Now I know I'm back in England!'

'How long have you been away?'

Gib thought a bit. 'Nearly eighteen years now.'

'That's a long time,' said Phoebe, trying to calculate how old that made him. It was difficult to tell just by looking at him. He had the solidity of an older man, and there were definite creases around the edges of his eyes. He had to be in his late thirties at least, but he had a disconcerting mixture of dynamism and lazy good humour that seemed to belong to someone much younger.

She wished Kate or Bella would come home. Something about him made her feel tongue-tied and awkward and—worse—boring. It was a feeling that reminded her all too painfully of that terrible time when she had wept as she had asked Ben 'why?', and he had told her that Lisa was sweet and feminine and fun.

Not like her.

Gib was obviously fun, too.

'What do you do?' she asked stiltedly. Too bad if he thought it was a boring question. She was just being polite. That was what boring people did.

Gib didn't roll his eyes at the banality of her conversation, but he wasn't very forthcoming either. 'Oh, this and that,' he said vaguely as he picked up his mug.

Silence didn't seem to bother him at all. Phoebe stirred her tea unnecessarily and sought for something else to say. 'Are you going to be working while you're here?' she managed eventually.

'I'm looking into setting up a couple of projects.'

It all sounded a bit vague to Phoebe, but if he wanted her to think he had a flourishing business with projects on the go, let him. She knew how sensitive men were about their success or lack of it, and she wasn't that interested anyway.

Gib was looking around him with interest, apparently unconcerned by her awkward attempts to make conversation. Phoebe couldn't get over how blue his eyes were, and she studied him surreptitiously, wondering if he wore contact lenses to make them that colour, only to flush with annoyance when he caught her looking at him and smiled.

Phoebe jerked her gaze away. He obviously thought she couldn't keep her eyes off him. How smug could you get? Really, he was just like Seb.

Typical, she thought glumly. The one attractive man to swim into her orbit since Ben, and he turned out to rub her up the wrong way right from the start. Bella and Kate were always urging her to find someone new to help her get over Ben, and she knew that she ought to make more of an effort, but a man like Gib—always supposing he was available— was the last thing she needed. She wanted someone kind and reliable, someone she could trust, not someone who made her feel twitchy and inadequate just by sitting there, no matter *how* attractive he was.

'How do you know Josh?' she asked, when he made no effort to break the silence. 'You don't seem at all like him.'

'Don't I?' Gib looked amused. 'That depends how you think of Josh, I guess.'

'Josh is wonderful,' said Phoebe firmly. 'He's mainly Bella's friend, of course, but Kate and I love him. He seems so quiet, but he's one of the nicest people I know. He never shows off or boasts about how good he is at what he does. He's just steady and reliable and *safe*. Anything could happen, and you could always rely on Josh to know what to do.'

It was funny, she thought irrelevantly. Josh was just the kind of man she needed, but it had never crossed her mind to think of him as anything other than Bella's friend.

'Yes, he's very competent,' agreed Gib, reflecting wryly that he clearly hadn't made much of an impression so far. He wondered how Phoebe had decided that he was *not* quiet, or nice, or reliable like good old Josh. All he had done was admire her kitchen and accept a cup of tea.

'I met Josh in Ecuador,' he went on, thinking that this was not the time to challenge her for being unreasonable. 'He was leading an expedition up Mount Chimburazo, and I went along.'

She stared at him in surprise. 'You're a mountaineer?'

Gib smiled and shook his head, his blue, blue eyes looking directly into Phoebe's. 'No, I just like a challenge,' he said.

Trapped by the intense blue gaze, Phoebe felt a wave of heat wash through her, and she swallowed, jerking her eyes away with an effort.

There was something disconcerting about him, she thought with an edge of desperation. His presence seemed to fill the room, sucking in all the air until it was hard for her to breathe. His eyes were too bright, his teeth too white, and he was too vibrant, too unsettling, too everything.

Phoebe felt unbalanced, a bit dizzy, and, desperate for something to break the suddenly jarring atmosphere, she pushed her papers out of the way.

'Sorry about all this mess. I was just trying to do some work before the others got home.'

Gib twisted his head on one side to get a glimpse of the papers. 'What is that you do?'

'I'm a production assistant for a company that makes programmes for television,' said Phoebe, unable to keep the pride from her voice.

Of course, being little more than a dogsbody at her age wasn't that much to be proud about, but Phoebe had wanted to get into television production for as long as she could remember, and she was determined to make a success of it. Dogsbody was just the first step on the ladder, she reminded herself frequently. It was unfortunate that had ended up with a prima donna of the first order as her immediate boss, but Purple Parrot Productions was her big break, and it was worth putting up with Celia for that.

'We make documentaries mostly,' she told Gib.

'What are you working on at the moment?' he asked politely.

You never show any interest in my job, Mallory had complained. *You have no idea how to talk to a woman as a person in her own right. You only ever think about one thing.*

Which was absolute rubbish, of course, thought Gib. He was perfectly capable of talking to a woman seriously. Look at him now, asking Phoebe about her job and listening to her answer and not even thinking about the curve of her mouth or the silky sheen of her hair as she pushed it impatiently behind her ear.

Suddenly realising that he had lost track of what she was saying, Gib tuned in again to hear something about banking.

'You're making a programme about a *bank*?'

'I thought it was a pretty dull idea too,' said Phoebe, unsurprised by his reaction, 'but actually, it's more interesting than you'd expect. This isn't an ordinary bank. It was set up by some guy who made a fortune on the currency markets then took everyone by surprise by setting up an ethical bank.'

Gib put down his mug. 'What?'

'I know, it sounds like a contradiction in terms, doesn't it?' Phoebe had relaxed a bit in talking about her job. 'I think it just means that it only invests in community-based projects in developing countries. I've done some research on the internet, and it sounds really good. It should make an interesting programme.'

'Is that right?' said Gib in an odd voice.

'The only trouble is that my boss is insisting that the focus of the programme should be on the guy who set it all up.'

'Really? Who's that?'

'J.G. Grieve,' she told him. 'Everyone refers to him as JGG, and he's famous for not giving interviews to the media.' Picking up a printout from a website, she studied it ruefully. 'I've tried all these contact numbers, but I always get the same message: the bank is happy to support any publicity about the projects, but not about JGG himself.'

'So what else do you know about this guy?'

Preoccupied with her own problems, she failed to notice the oddly grim look around Gib's mouth. 'Not much,' she said. 'Just that he's very rich.'

'He's not that interesting then, is he?'

'That's what I think,' she agreed, 'but Celia—my boss— is insistent that I've got to arrange an interview somehow. Working on this programme is my big break, so I've got to track him down somehow. I'm just not quite sure how I'm going to go about it,' she confessed.

Gib looked at her across the table and suddenly his expression relaxed and his mouth quirked. 'Well, I've been in the States for a while,' he said. 'I know some people. Maybe

I could ask around and see if anyone knows anything else about him?'

Phoebe looked back doubtfully. She couldn't imagine that someone like Gib would have the kind of contacts she needed, but she supposed it was kind of him to offer.

'Well, thanks,' she said awkwardly, 'but I'm sure I'll get through to someone in the bank eventually.'

Gib grinned at her as he picked up his mug once more. 'Suit yourself,' he said.

There was a silence. Phoebe sipped her tea and tried not to feel rattled by the way he was sitting at her table, looking as if he had always sat there. His presence filled the kitchen, which seemed to have shrunk around them alarmingly.

'I gather from Josh that you're my landlady,' said Gib after a while. 'Thanks for letting me stay.'

When he smiled his eyes looked bluer than ever. Phoebe was more than ever convinced that they couldn't possibly be real. She looked away from them with an effort.

'That's all right,' she muttered.

'Are there any rules I should know about?'

Phoebe considered the question. 'Not really,' she said at last, 'but don't, whatever you do, tell Kate about any stray animal you've noticed unless you want to find it sleeping on your bed.'

'Is that it?'

'It's not a good idea to talk to me before I've had a cup of coffee in the morning, but that's advice rather than a rule,' she admitted. 'Kate and Bella don't take any notice of it.'

'Well, that seems easy enough,' said Gib. 'I ought to be able to manage that.'

He produced another of those unnervingly attractive smiles that seemed to linger in the air long after he had stopped, and Phoebe found herself getting to her feet abruptly. 'Shall I show you to your room?'

'It's not very big, I'm afraid,' she told him, opening a door off the upstairs landing.

'Not very big' was something of an understatement, reflected Gib, squeezing into the room behind Phoebe. It was not very big in the way the Sahara was not very wet, or the South Pole was not very hot.

An average cupboard might have been a better description, or possibly a large box. It had a four-foot bed, a built-in wardrobe, and a couple of shelves fixed to the wall. With the two of them standing on the only available floor space, there was absolutely no room for anything else.

'Out of interest, how long did your last room-mate live here?' asked Gib dryly.

'About a year. She was the last to move in, so she got the smallest room.'

Gib was glad to hear it. He would hate to think that anyone was sleeping in anything smaller!

'Caro didn't care,' said Phoebe a little defensively She could tell from his expression that he was less than overwhelmed with the room. 'She spent most of the time at her boyfriend's flat. They've just got married, which is why we're looking for someone to take her place.

'Obviously the rent is lower because you wouldn't have so much space,' she went on stiffly, 'but of course you don't have to take the room if it's too small.'

'No, no, it's fine,' Gib reassured her, perceiving that he had got off on the wrong foot. 'I haven't got much stuff. I travel light.'

Phoebe could believe it. He didn't look like the kind of man who bothered with baggage in any shape or form.

Part of her envied people like Gib who drifted carelessly through life avoiding commitment and responsibility and leaving others to clear up the broken hearts and disappointment they inevitably left in their wake, but another part was intimidated and more than a little irritated by them too.

'Yes, well, it's not as if you're staying for ever, is it?' she said briskly, wishing that Gib would move. The room was small enough at the best of times without him standing there vibrating with energy.

Short of climbing on the bed, which risked looking suggestive, let alone ridiculous, there was no way she could get past him without pressing intimately against him. The thought made Phoebe tense and shiver at the same time.

It was a sinful waste from one point of view, because it was a very long time since she had been this close to an attractive man, but there was something about the way he seemed constantly on the verge of exploding into action that made Phoebe nervous and edgy. Touching him, however inadvertently, seemed an action that would be downright rash.

She was just going to have wait until he moved.

Concentrating on breathing shallowly, she stood as close to the window as she could while Gib looked round. Given the size of the room, that didn't take long, but it felt like hours before he went back out onto the landing.

'Can I see the rest of the house?' he asked, and Phoebe was so relieved to be able to breathe properly again that she gave him a guided tour.

'It's a nice house,' said Gib as they went back downstairs. 'How long have you lived here?'

'A couple of years. I bought it with my fiancé, as he was then.' Phoebe was quite proud of the coolness in her voice. 'We lived here together for a year, and then Ben decided to move back to Bristol with someone he'd met, so I took over the mortgage.'

Gib didn't need to know about the anguish and the heartache and the long, long months of misery she had endured since Ben had left.

'I couldn't afford to live here on my own, so I had to take in lodgers, and it was just lucky that Kate was looking for somewhere at the same time. We were students together, and she knew Bella from school. Caro was a friend of Bella's, so it all worked out perfectly until Caro decided to get married. We're not sure where we're going to find anyone who fits in as well as she did,' she confessed as they went back into the kitchen.

'Can't you advertise?'

'We could, and that's probably what I'll end up doing, but it's hard to know what to put when you're really looking for someone who'll be a friend and not just a tenant.'

Mindful of his bet with Josh, Gib pricked up his ears at the key word. 'How do you know if someone is a friend?' he asked casually.

'That's just it, you don't,' said Phoebe. 'You can't tell who's going to be a good friend and who isn't. It's just something that clicks between you.'

Absently, she began piling her papers together to clear the table a bit, while she thought about Gib's question. 'I suppose a friend is someone who's easy to talk to, who laughs at the same things. Someone who's just going to fit in and be comfortable sitting around and talking all evening without wanting to organise us or worrying about how long it is since anyone got the hoover out.'

It was a bit vague, but Gib reckoned he could do all of that.

'Perhaps you should put that in your advert,' he suggested.

'I don't know that it would be much help. You could get someone who said they were able to do all those things, but you still might not get on. It's a funny thing, friendship,'

Phoebe mused. 'I don't think you can ever pin down the magic ingredient which makes you really like some people and not others.'

So much for picking up pointers from Phoebe! Gib sighed to himself. She was clearly *not* including him in her category of those with that special magic ingredient that would make him a friend!

Not yet, anyway.

Phoebe might be more of a challenge than he had anticipated, but challenges were there to be met. Gib wasn't giving up yet. He had a bet to win!

'How are you getting on with Gib?'

Josh and Phoebe were sitting on the sofa, while at the other end of the kitchen Bella and Kate busied themselves with the welcoming supper they had planned for Gib. Bella had told him that they were treating his welcome like the Queen's birthdays, so that he not only had the real one when he arrived, but the official dinner to mark the occasion a day later.

No effort was being spared. The table had been ruthlessly cleared of its clutter and ransacking the cupboards had revealed no less than four plates, in varying states of repair but with recognisably the same pattern.

'One of us can have the plate with the bunnies running round the edge,' said Bella breezily. 'We'll need to use one of the folding chairs from the garden, too.'

Now she and Kate were fussing over some elaborate starter, while Gib opened some wine and Phoebe and Josh, assigned to washing-up duty, had retired to a safe distance.

Phoebe looked over at Gib who was manipulating the corkscrew with practised ease. His head was bent and the lights gleaming on his hair made it look fairer than usual.

'Kate and Bella are completely smitten,' she told Josh.

'But not you?'

Phoebe looked away from Gib. 'I certainly wouldn't describe myself as smitten with him,' she said.

'Why, what's he done?'

That was the thing. Gib hadn't done anything. She couldn't even hold the taxi fare incident against him. He had repaid her in full without prompting that morning.

How could she explain to Josh how *unsettling* Gib was? He had only been in the house a day, but he was already firm friends with Bella and Kate, and lounged around the kitchen as if he had lived there for ever. Phoebe ought to have been relieved that he was fitting in so well, but instead she found herself edging nervously around him, as if afraid he was about to explode into action at any second.

'He's not very restful, is he?' she said to Josh, and he laughed.

'You just have to get used to him.'

Phoebe couldn't imagine ever getting used to Gib. Every time he came into the room she would catch her breath as if startled by the blueness of his eyes and the lazy good humour of his smile. Nobody had the right to be that attractive and that relaxed the whole time!

She wished she could be like Kate and Bella, and treat him like just another friend, but somehow she couldn't. You weren't aware of friends the way she was always aware of Gib.

It made Phoebe uneasy. There was nothing wrong with physical attraction, but it felt all wrong at the moment. She wasn't ready for another relationship, whatever her friends said. Ben had meant too much to her for her to get over him that easily. She might never get over him and, if she did, it certainly wasn't going to be with someone like Gib. He wasn't her type at all.

So why couldn't she get used to him as Josh suggested?

'I'll try,' she said.

Across the kitchen, Gib eased the cork out of the bottle with a satisfying pop and watched Phoebe talking to Josh. For the first time, he wondered if there might be something in this friendship thing. He had found himself envying Josh's uncomplicated friendship with the three girls, who were all patently delighted to see him. Even Phoebe's face had lit up, and she had given him an unselfconscious hug.

Gib sensed that she wasn't someone who hugged indiscriminately. It would be a real sign of acceptance if Phoebe hugged you, he thought. He could imagine with unnerving clarity what it would be like to feel her slender body in his arms, her silky hair against his cheek. He bet she smelt wonderful. He had noticed a faint scent lingering in the air after she had passed once or twice.

All right, every time.

Hugging Phoebe would be his goal, Gib decided. Just in a friendly way, of course, he added hastily to himself. It would be just like hugging Kate and Bella, both of whom had thrown their arms around him when they first met him.

They were both such warm, friendly open girls that it was impossible not to be friends with them. Gib already knew about Kate's obsession with someone referred to by Bella and Phoebe as Slimy Seb, and he had heard so much about Bella from Josh that she felt completely familiar.

But Phoebe…Phoebe was different. She was much more guarded and inclined to be prickly. Gib knew that he would have to work hard to earn her friendship and the prospect of a hug, but if he did, he thought it would be worth it.

Bella's Thai crab cakes to start were a huge success. Kate had roasted a chicken and Phoebe had been persuaded to make her trade mark strawberry torte in honour of the occasion. By the end of the meal, they were all replete and relaxed, and Gib felt as if he had been living there for ever.

'I'll make some coffee.' Phoebe pushed back her chair as Gib polished off the last of the torte. Unsettling he might be, but you had to admit that there was something very appealing about a man with a good appetite.

'How was Celia today?' asked Bella, sitting back with the air of one anticipating a good story.

Phoebe filled the kettle under the tap. 'Oh, the usual nightmare,' she sighed.

'Phoebe has the boss from hell,' Bella leant over to fill Gib in. 'Kate and I love hearing about her. It's sort of therapeutic. When you realise what Phoebe's going through with her immediate boss, it makes you realise that your own isn't that bad.'

'What's she done now?' Kate asked across Bella.

'She's completely obsessed with the man who runs this ethical bank we want to make a programme about. Now she's threatening to dump me from production work altogether if I can't fix up an interview with him!'

'She can't do that, can she?'

'It's such a small company, and so many people are desperate to work in television that she can pretty much do whatever she wants,' said Phoebe despairingly. 'Personally, I don't see why we can't just concentrate on the community projects which are the whole point of the bank, but Celia keeps banging on about the personal angle, and how this guy is the real story.

'I'm afraid she wants to do one of those horrible, cynical hatchet jobs,' she went on, opening and closing cupboard doors in search of the cafetière. 'Her theory is that nobody could make that kind of money and be truly altruistic, so if this J.G. Grieve is setting up a bank, it's because he's getting something out of it for himself. So I not only have to arrange an interview with him, I also have to dig up any dirt I can find on him so that Celia can challenge him with it and make herself look like a fearless investigative reporter.'

'Maybe there's no dirt to dig up,' said Gib lazily.

'It's beginning to look that way,' Phoebe agreed. 'All I've found out about him so far is that he goes climbing occasionally. It's hardly the stuff of which award-winning documentaries are made, is it?'

She poked through the debris on the counter. 'Where's the coffee gone?'

'In the fridge,' said Bella before reverting to the problem in hand. 'Maybe climbing is just the first clue you need to track him down,' she suggested. 'Mountaineering's quite a small world, isn't it, Josh? Someone might have come across him. These rich guys always need someone to nanny them when they do dangerous sports like that,' she added authoritatively, as if she had years of experience of dealing with the rich and famous.

'That's a good point.' Phoebe straightened from the fridge and turned back to the table. 'You're always running up and down mountains, Josh. Have you ever come across a J.G. Grieve?'

'I can't say the name means anything to me.' Josh looked across the table at Gib. 'What about you, Gib? You've done some climbing. Do you know anything about him.'

Tipping back in his chair, Gib pulled down the corners of his mouth. 'Bankers aren't the kind of guys I want to spend much time with,' he said. 'They're usually pretty boring.'

'Well, this guy can't be that boring, or why would he refuse all interviews?' Phoebe pointed out. 'Most people in his position would do anything for publicity. The fact that he won't even consider it does make it seem as if he's got something to hide. Maybe Celia's right about that.'

'There might be lots of reasons why he doesn't want to

talk to journalists,' objected Gib, still balanced precariously on his chair.

'Yes, maybe he had a terrible accident that left him scarred for life,' Kate put in. 'His wife died in the same accident, and their only child, and probably their dog as well.'

'Oh, no, not the dog as well!' said Gib, much struck by the story unfolding.

Kate nodded firmly. 'Yes, a little terrier. Called Ruffy,' she added as an afterthought. 'And you see that's why he's never been able to forgive himself. He's shut himself away from the world ever since then, unable to face anyone.'

There was a moment's silence, interrupted by Phoebe bringing the coffee back to the table.

'Kate has a very rich fantasy life,' she explained kindly to Gib. 'You'll get used to it.'

'Well, she convinced me,' he said. 'I think you should leave the poor guy alone and stop hassling him for an interview!'

'I wish I could,' sighed Phoebe. 'I'm sure that in reality he's really dull and avoiding interviews is just a way to try and make himself interesting. I think I'll tell Celia that I'm following leads, and hope that eventually she'll forget him.'

She held up the cafetière. 'Who's for coffee?'

'Any messages?' Kate asked hopefully, dropping her bag onto the table. It was over a week since their welcoming dinner for Gib, and she had come home to find Phoebe and Bella draped over the armchairs and nursing a glass of wine each as they grumbled about their respective bosses.

'No,' said Phoebe. 'And before you ask, yes, the phone *is* working! No post has been discovered under the doormat, there have been no emails or telegrams or bunches of flowers that accidentally got delivered to the wrong address six weeks ago. You've got to face it, Kate,' she said more gently. 'Seb's not going to ring.'

'But why is he being like this?' wailed Kate.

'Because he's vile,' said Bella firmly. 'Phoebe's right. Seb is never going to love anyone but himself. It suited him to string you along for a while, but he's obviously found someone new to exploit.'

Kate slumped into the sofa with a sigh. 'You don't think he was knocked over by a bus and lost his memory?'

'No.'

'Or had to go to his grandmother's funeral on a deserted island where all the phone lines are down and they're cut off because of storms?'

'What, for six weeks?'

'Well, maybe he's part of some top secret government programme where he's not allowed to contact anyone and—'

'No, Kate.'

She sighed again. 'I know, I know, it's probably not that. You're right, he's not going to call.'

Her eye fell on the cordless phone that was lying half buried under a pile of papers at the end of the sofa, and Phoebe and Bella both jerked upright as she reached for it.

'Kate, you are *not* going to ring him!'

'I'm just checking to see if anyone else called,' she said with dignity, pressing 1471. She listened to the number on the recorded message and her mouth drooped. 'No, it wasn't Seb. Some Bristol number I think.'

Phoebe dropped her head back with a groan. 'That'll be my mother. She wants to talk to me about Ben's wedding.'

'You're not really going to go to that, are you?' asked Bella curiously.

'I've got to,' she said. 'Ben's family and mine are so close, it would be like his sister not being at his wedding.'

'Still, they can't expect you to celebrate your fiancé marrying somebody else,' said Kate.

'They don't know it wasn't a mutual decision to break up,' Phoebe confessed. 'They were all so happy when Ben and I got engaged, I just couldn't bear to tell them. I love Penelope and Derek. Ben's parents are closer than any of my own aunts and uncles. They would have been devastated if I hadn't pretended that Ben and I had both agreed that it wasn't going to work.'

'They must have had a clue when he told them he was going to marry Lisa, surely?'

'He didn't tell them immediately. They might have suspected something, but I think they'd prefer to believe that I'm quite happy with the situation, so if I don't turn up they'll realise immediately that's not exactly the case.'

Phoebe ran her fingers through her hair in a hopeless gesture. 'Then *they'd* be upset, and it would spoil the wedding for them, and I can't do that to them. As it is, Penelope and Mum are desperately worried in case I'm embarrassed, or Ben is embarrassed, or Lisa is embarrassed...'

She sighed. 'I think they're secretly afraid that I might make some kind of scene when it comes down to it. I'm dreading going to the wedding on my own. It's bad enough at the best of times. You know what people are like about single women in their thirties, and it's going to be worse at this wedding since there'll be so many old friends there who all knew me when Ben and I were together.

'I know I'm going to end up looking like Glenn Close in *Fatal Attraction*. Either people are going to be edging warily around me and making sure any stray bunnies are safe, or they'll be desperately sorry for me. I'll spend my whole time being told cheerily that it will be my turn next,' she finished gloomily.

'It's dire, isn't it?' said Kate with heartfelt sympathy. 'It's either that or being asked if it isn't time you were thinking of getting married—like you've got some kind of choice in the matter!'

Bella had been pondering the problem. 'What you need,' she said, 'is a man.'

'Tell us something new!'

'No, I'm serious. You should take a fabulous lover to show off at the wedding.'

'Oh, yes, and fabulous lovers are *so* easy to find!' said Kate sarcastically. 'Didn't you hear the announcement? It's now official: there are now no single, straight men over thirty at all in London, let alone any with a modicum of intelligence and financial stability. And as for trying to find one not suffering from a morbid fear of commitment...forget it!'

'Maybe not,' said Bella, 'but there's nothing to stop Phoebe inventing one.'

CHAPTER THREE

For a moment there was utter silence, and then Kate looked at Bella with new respect. 'That's a brilliant idea, Bel!' she said.

Phoebe was less impressed. 'I don't see that an imaginary lover is going to do me much good, however fabulous he is!'

'The whole point is that he doesn't *seem* to be imaginary,' said Bella. 'All you need is to hire someone to pretend to be a lover as fabulous as you want!'

'You don't mean hire a male escort?' Phoebe stared at her, appalled. 'I couldn't do that!'

'I'm not suggesting that you pick up some gigolo,' said Bella reasonably. 'I bet you're not the first woman to need an escort in this kind of situation. There must be some reputable agencies that supply presentable types who are used to going along to weddings and official dinners. You'd have to pay for it, of course, but there wouldn't have to be any funny business.'

'Yes, and since you're paying him, you could get him to say whatever you wanted,' Kate added eagerly, picking up the idea and running with it with typical enthusiasm.

'He's bound to be good-looking if he works for an escort agency, so you could pretend he's incredibly rich and successful, too. You can tell everyone that he utterly adores you, and asks you to marry him every day, but you're not sure whether he's *exactly* what you want, so you're keeping him dangling.'

'Why would I want to do that?'

'So everyone will envy you, of course. The other women at the wedding, anyway,' Kate qualified. 'And the best thing is that if anyone meets you in the future and asks what's happened to him, you can say that you just got bored with his insatiable sexual demands!'

Phoebe couldn't help laughing. 'That doesn't sound very likely!'

'OK, he can't satisfy *your* insatiable appetite!'

'Oh, yes, I can see myself telling Mum that when she asks why I don't bring my nice young man down for the weekend!'

'Kate's just complicating things,' said Bella, bringing them back to order. 'All you need is someone attractive who will brush up nicely in a suit and look suitably adoring so that instead of everyone pitying you or making their husbands and boyfriends cover their eyes whenever you go near them, they'll all be madly jealous!'

Phoebe let herself imagine what it would be like to turn up at Ben's wedding with someone apparently rich and good-looking on her arm. She had to admit that as an idea, it had its advantages. Her mother and Penelope would relax and enjoy the wedding for a start, and there was no doubt that it would be easier to meet Ben and Lisa if she wasn't quite so obviously left on the shelf.

'I'm not sure I would have the nerve to carry it off,' she said doubtfully.

Bella was having none of that. 'Of course you would,' she said briskly. 'Now, the first thing is for you to start dropping a few hints to your mother that you've met someone special, and then we've just got to find you a man and get him primed up with your story.'

'I don't know...' said Phoebe feebly, half dazzled and half terrified by the way Bella and Kate were sweeping her along on the tide of their enthusiasm.

They were always doing this, pushing her into doing things and then holding up their hands in innocence when the said things turned out to be a terrible mistake.

The colour of the bathroom paint—a lurid pink they had assured her would look fantastic—was a case in point.

Ignoring her feeble attempts to come up with some sensible objections—Phoebe was sure there had to be thousands, if she could only think of them—Kate and Bella were discussing how best to track down a reputable escort agency.

'I suppose we could try the obvious and look in the Yellow Pages,' said Bella eventually. 'Where are they, anyway?'

She started hunting through the pile of clutter on the table. 'I'm sure I saw them here the other day. God, we must tidy up soon, I can't find anything—oh, that's where my glove is!' She fished it out triumphantly and tossed it onto the sofa, where it promptly slipped down out of sight once more.

'Aha!' she cried, spotting the directory, dragging it free of a welter of paper and beginning to flick through it without much system. 'What do I look under? A for agency or E for escorts?'

'Hold on,' said Kate slowly. 'I've got a better idea.'

Bella looked sceptical. 'Not another of your elaborate fantasies?'

'No, no, this is so simple and so obvious I don't know why neither of you thought of it,' she insisted. 'Why go through an agency when we've got the perfect candidate living right here in the house?'

'Who?'

'Gib, of course!'

Kate sat back and beamed, delighted with her own brilliance.

'Gib?'

The other two stared at Phoebe's outraged tone. 'I never knew you could do such a good Lady Bracknell impression!' said Bella, diverted.

Phoebe shot her a look. 'I'm not asking Gib!'

'Why not? You've got to admit, he's incredibly attractive.'

'He's not that special,' she protested, unwilling to admit anything of the kind.

'Oh, come on, Phoebe!' Kate rolled her eyes in disbelief. 'He's gorgeous, and you know it!'

Phoebe's mouth set in a stubborn line. 'He's too pleased with himself,' she said, 'and I'm sure he must wear contact lenses. Nobody has eyes that blue!'

'Don't be silly, of course they're real,' said Kate. 'You're not doing much of a job of not finding him attractive if the only thing you can think of to say is that his eyes are too blue!'

'I can see that he's quite good-looking,' Phoebe allowed grudgingly. 'I just think he would be more attractive if he didn't know it.'

Kate shook her head. 'I don't understand why you don't like him,' she said, puzzled. 'I think he's great. He's good fun, he's easy to talk to, he does his bit around the house, and he doesn't roll his eyes at the mess or insist on correcting you if you say it's about five hundred miles to somewhere when in fact he knows it's four hundred and ninety-seven.'

'Well, don't you think that's a bit fishy?' countered Phoebe. 'He's just a little *too* perfect, if you ask me. Why hasn't he got a girlfriend if he's that wonderful?'

'Maybe he's gay,' said Bella dubiously.

'He's definitely not that.' Phoebe's voice held a tart edge as she thought of the way Gib flirted with everyone from the plump checkout woman at the supermarket, to the elderly lady who lived next door and the newsagent's shy wife. Flirtation obviously came as naturally as breathing to him, an automatic response to any female that crossed his path.

Except her, of course. He never flirted with her.

'I'd prefer him if he was,' she said.

'I don't think he's gay either,' said Kate. 'Maybe he's got a broken heart like the rest of us,' she added with a sigh.

'He's doing a good job of concealing it, then,' said Phoebe, unconvinced. 'He's always smiling, even when he's not.'

They blinked at her curiously. 'What?'

'You know.' Too late, she heard how obscure she sounded.

'No.'

'Yes, you do,' she insisted, a little embarrassed now. 'Even when he's got a perfectly straight face, you get the feeling he's laughing at you.'

'Phoebe, it's called having a sense of humour,' said Bella as if explaining to a child. 'And how many men do we know who need one of those? If only they were all like Gib, life would be a lot easier!'

Phoebe was beginning to get frustrated. Her friends just didn't seem to be able to understand how jittery Gib made her feel.

She picked morosely at the arm of her chair, trying to find the words to explain. 'He's just so *vague* about everything,' was the best she could come up with. 'We don't really know anything about him, do we? I mean, what does he *do* all day? He talks about these unspecified projects of his, but as far as I can see he spends his entire time lounging around here.'

'Well, he's got a laptop and a mobile phone,' Kate

pointed out in an infuriatingly reasonable voice. 'He can probably work just as effectively from here as going in to some office.'

'He doesn't look like he's working to me. I've never met anyone as lazy!'

'He's relaxed. That's a good sign.'

'No one's got the right to be that relaxed,' grumbled Phoebe, determined not to be convinced.

'Look, aren't we getting from the point?' Bella interrupted, chinking a teaspoon against her glass for their attention. 'Say what you like, Phoebe, but the fact is that Kate's right. Gib would be ideal. He looks good, he's got the confidence to carry the whole thing off, and the best thing is that he's actually living here, so if your mother or anyone rings and he answers phone, it would be dead convincing!'

'Maybe, but—'

'And I'm sure he would be willing to help you,' Kate chipped in before Phoebe had a chance to think up any more objections. 'You could always offer to pay him if that made you feel better. I get the impression he could do with some extra money and it would be a way of helping him out without hurting his pride.'

'Oh, yes, let's worry about Gib's pride!' said Phoebe sarcastically. 'What about *mine*?'

'Just think of it as a business arrangement,' said Bella. 'It's all it would be, after all. You were prepared to go to an escort agency, and who knows what kind of psychopath you could end up with there? At least Gib would be a better option than that!'

Phoebe opened her mouth to point out that she hadn't in fact got anywhere near agreeing to the idea of hiring an escort, but the sound of the front door banging made her stop.

Bella smiled triumphantly as if she had just won the argument. 'Here's Gib now,' she said unnecessarily. 'You can at least ask him, Phoebe.'

A few moments later, Gib himself breezed into the kitchen. As usual, he brought with him a surge of energy that swirled around the room as if a fresh wind had blown in with him, and as usual Phoebe found herself braced against the impact of his smile.

'Hey, girls,' he said and lifted a carrier bag in their direction. 'I bought more tonic.'

'You see!' whispered Kate. 'How can you say he's not perfect?'

Phoebe pretended not to hear. Draining her glass, she began to get to her feet. She was *not* going to let Kate and Bella push her into this stupid idea. There was nothing wrong with going to Ben's wedding on her own!

'Gib, we were just talking about you,' said Bella.

'Oh?' Gib turned from the fridge where he was stacking the bottles of tonic.

'Phoebe's got something to ask you.'

Jerking upright, Phoebe glared at her friend. '*Bel*-la,' she said warningly.

'Look Phoebe, you've been going on and on about how much you're dreading this wedding,' Bella said in a firm voice. 'You were worried about your pride. Well, here's a way to get through it with your pride intact. What's the harm in at least asking Gib?'

Gib looked from one to the other. 'Ask me what?'

'Come on, Kate, we'll let Phoebe ask him herself,' said Bella, getting up. 'We'll leave you two alone, and then she can tell you it's all our fault,' she added kindly to Gib, who raised an amused eyebrow and turned to Phoebe with an enquiring look.

She put up her chin. 'I don't want to ask you anything,' she said bravely, but Kate and Bella had already whisked out of the door, and she couldn't follow them because Gib was standing in front of it, his blue eyes alight with that disturbing laughter that never failed to send the air leaking out of her lungs.

'Yes,' he said.

Phoebe looked blankly at him. 'Yes, what?'

'Yes, I'll do whatever it is you want me to do.'

'But you don't know what it is yet!'

'Is it illegal?'

'Of course not!'

'Immoral?'

'No!'

Gib shrugged. 'Then why would I refuse?'

To her chagrin, Phoebe realised she had been manoeuvred into beginning to talk about Kate and Bella's idea with Gib, *exactly* the thing she hadn't wanted to happen! But she could hardly walk out in mid-conversation.

'Because it's embarrassing,' she muttered.

'For you or for me?'

'For both of us.'

'This is beginning to sound like fun!'

Gib strolled over towards her, and Phoebe found herself backing down into her chair once more. 'Come on,' he said encouragingly, sitting on the arm of the sofa. 'You've got this far, so you might as well tell me the worst!'

He wasn't anywhere near her, but Phoebe was desperately aware of him. She wished he'd go back to the fridge. If only he wasn't so...so *overwhelming*.

'It was just a silly idea,' she mumbled.

'All the best ideas are silly to start with,' said Gib. 'If they were sensible, somebody else would have thought of them before.'

'Well, this one really is silly,' she told him almost belligerently.

He smiled. 'Why don't you let me be the judge of that?'

Phoebe tore her eyes away from the warm blue eyes and scowled at the mess on the table.

'All right,' she said, giving in. 'I need a lover.'

There was a tiny silence. 'In that case, I'm glad I said yes,' said Gib, and although she wasn't looking at him, she could hear him smiling and the colour deepened in her cheeks.

'Not a real one! Don't be stupid,' she snapped.

'Right,' he said, humouring her.

'The thing is...' Somehow Phoebe stumbled through the whole sorry saga of Ben's wedding and her attempts to keep everyone in the family happy. 'So we were wondering—it was Kate's idea, I'd never have thought of it—and it's entirely up to you, of course—you can say no, it won't be a problem at all....'

She floundered to a halt, lost in a morass of sentences, and looked a little helplessly at Gib, who was studying her with a disconcerting half-smile.

'Well, I've already said yes, so I'm sure it won't be a problem,' he agreed, 'but I'm still not entirely clear what it is you want me to do, other than *not* be a real lover.'

Wasn't it *obvious*? Phoebe was hating this. If she had to spell it out for him, she would, but she couldn't help resenting Gib for not being able to make immediate sense of her incoherent ramblings.

'OK.' She drew a breath. 'I wondered if you'd be interested in earning some extra cash, that's all.'

Gib's brows rose. 'You're offering me a *job*?' he said blankly.

'We had the impression that things weren't very easy for you at moment,' said Phoebe stiffly, borrowing Kate's comment. 'In the circumstances, I'd be prepared to pay you to come to wedding with me and pretend...well, pretend...'

'That I'm in love with you?' he finished for her, a smile lurking around his mouth, and she let out a breath that she hadn't been aware until then that she had been holding.

'Yes.'

His lips twitched. 'You want me to be a male escort?'

'Yes.'

There, it was out. Phoebe sat back, oddly relieved. Maybe Kate and Bella were right. He could only say no, and when it came down to it, all she had done was offer him a chance to earn some extra money. What was so embarrassing about that?

'Well, I've never been offered a job like that before!' Gib shook his head, but he was grinning.

'It would be just a job, of course,' said Phoebe hastily. 'There wouldn't be any...any of the reason why you might normally pay for a male escort.' She could feel the treacherous colour creeping back up into her cheeks. So much for not being embarrassed! 'I'd be paying you to be an actor, that's all.'

Gib didn't answer immediately. 'You know, Phoebe, you don't need to pay me,' he said carefully at last. 'We're friends, aren't we? If Josh was sitting here now, you wouldn't even think of offering him money to help you, would you?'

It was true, of course. Phoebe wished that she *had* been able to ask Josh. He was so nice and reliable, he would have been ideal, but unfortunately her parents had already met him and knew about his friendship with Bella. They would never believe that she had come between those two.

Gib wasn't like Josh. He wasn't calm and he wasn't *safe*. He didn't make her feel comfortable the way Josh did. Phoebe couldn't think of him as a friend like Josh when all her nerves jangled and twitched the moment he walked into the room. Friends were people you could relax and be yourself with, not people who made you feel as if the earth was unsteady beneath your feet.

'I'd feel more comfortable if we both thought of this as a financial transaction,' she said firmly. 'That way I'll be able to ask you to do things I wouldn't want to ask if you were just doing me a favour.'

'Like what?'

'Like...' Phoebe didn't really want to get into what she might have to ask him to do to convince her family they really were in love. 'Well, I can't think of anything right now,' she prevaricated, 'but there's sure to be something. Anyway, it's already asking a lot for you to give up a whole day to spend it at a wedding with a load of people you don't know.'

'I'll know you,' Gib pointed out, unperturbed by the prospect.

'You'll have to get to know me a lot better before you can face an interrogation by my mother!' she warned him.

Gib's mouth quirked in a smile. 'I'll look forward to it.'

There was an odd little silence.

That was the thing about Gib, Phoebe thought edgily. He would say something perfectly innocuous like that, and suddenly the whole atmosphere had changed without you realising how or why it had happened.

She cleared her throat and strove for a businesslike tone. 'Well, as I say, I'd prefer to keep it a business arrangement. I'll pay you for your time, and also for the hire of a suit and anything else you might need.'

Her face was scarlet by this stage. Gib hesitated. The last thing he wanted was to take money from Phoebe, but he could see what it had cost her to ask him to help her. Paying him was a way of saving her pride, and if he argued with her, it would only prolong her embarrassment. It wasn't as if he had to do anything with the money, and he could always find a way to give it back to her later.

Meanwhile, here was the perfect opportunity to prove to all those Doubting Thomases like Mallory and Josh that he was just as good a friend as the next person. Phoebe needed him, and he wouldn't let her down. He would be doing this for her.

The fact that helping her would mean spending a day in close proximity was purely incidental. If he had to touch her, maybe even kiss her, as part of the pretence, well, that was hardly his fault, Gib reasoned virtuously. It was just a lucky side effect of being a friend, and Josh wouldn't be able to claim that he had broken the terms of their bet.

'OK, if that's what you want,' he said briskly, deciding that it would make things much easier for her if he played along with the idea that he needed the money. At least that way, she could think that she was doing him a favour too. 'You're the boss. How much were you thinking of paying me?'

'Well, I don't really know...' Phoebe was a bit taken aback by his abrupt volte-face. 'I suppose I could ring an agency and find out how much one of their escorts would cost,' she offered awkwardly, conscious of a quite unfair sense of disappointment that he had turned out to be interested in the money after all. He must need some extra cash very badly. 'I could pay you the same.'

'It's a deal,' said Gib and leant forward to offer his hand to seal the bargain.

Phoebe looked at it, stupidly reluctant to put hers into it, but she couldn't think of a good reason to refuse, and it would only look rude if she ignored it. So instead she put her hand out, bracing herself against the cool strength of his grasp and the tingling warmth of his palm pressed against hers.

'Right.' Gib released her just as she began to think that it didn't feel that bad after all. He was abruptly all business. 'Tell me again exactly what it is you want me to do.'

'I'm going to tell my mother that I've met someone special,' said Phoebe, marvelling at how easily she had been swept along into the whole idea. Hadn't she decided only a few minutes ago that she wanted nothing to do with it? Oh, well, she might as well go with the flow. Resisting the combined will of Bella, Kate and Gib would be just too exhausting.

'If I know Mum, she'll be straight on the phone to Penelope—that's Ben's mother—and you can bet your bottom dollar that an invitation to the wedding will be dropping through the door for you five minutes later.'

She hesitated. 'The thing is, if my mother rings up in the meantime, and you answer the phone for some reason, you'll have to be prepared to be cross-examined by her. Would you mind that?'

'That's what you're paying me for,' said Gib cheerfully.

Phoebe knew that she ought to be reassured by his down-to-earth approach, but somehow the fact that he was treating it as a job, just as she had insisted he should, was a bit disconcerting.

'Yes...well...' she said, somewhat at a loss. 'Then, obviously, there's the wedding itself. That's when the real pretence comes in.'

'The pretending to be in love with you?'

'That, too, but I was thinking more of you pretending to have a proper job or something. After all, if I'm going to make up a lover, I might as well make up an incredibly successful one.'

'Ah,' said Gib, looking down at himself, his would-be regretful expression marred by the twitch of his lips. 'That might be more of a problem,' he sighed. 'I can see why it would be good for you to have a wealthy and successful lover, but do you think I'd be able to carry off an image like that?'

Phoebe surveyed him with a critical eye. He was lounging on the arm of the sofa, wearing jeans and a battered leather jacket over a plain white T-shirt that stretched across his broad chest. Laughter lines fanned his eyes and creased his cheeks, and the blue, blue eyes danced. He looked vibrant and physical and—OK, Kate—attractive, and absolutely nothing like a businessman.

Her mouth turned down at the corners. 'Maybe if you cut your hair,' she suggested doubtfully, 'and generally brush up a bit. A suit would make a difference, too. You'd better hire one before the wedding.'

'It's going to be a smart wedding, then?' asked Gib, not unduly put out by her critical appraisal.

'Yes,' said Phoebe without enthusiasm. 'The wedding party is taking over an entire castle. It's been turned into a hotel, where all the rooms have panelling and four-poster beds, you know the kind of thing.'

'Aren't they getting married in a church?'

'No, the ceremony is at the castle as well, so that everyone moves straight on to the reception in the gardens. And then close friends and family are staying on for dinner and dancing in the evening. This will be a more intimate affair, according to my mother, and they've booked all the rooms in the castle, so I've got to get through all of that and breakfast next morning, as if the wedding itself wasn't going to be bad enough,' she finished glumly.

Gib raised an eyebrow. 'So we'll be spending the night?'

'I'll have to, but we can think of some excuse for you. I'll tell them you have to get back that evening because you've got a meeting the next day.'

'On a Sunday?'

'Not everyone has your relaxed attitude to work,' Phoebe retorted. 'It's a well-known fact that all successful businessmen are workaholics! I don't think anyone would be surprised to hear that you had a weekend meeting.'

'Right, well, I'll bow to your superior knowledge on that one,' said Gib. 'What sort of businessman am I supposed to be, anyway, in case anyone asks?'

'We hadn't got that far,' she admitted. 'What would you like to be?'

'Perhaps I could say that I'm in...oh, I don't know...' He scratched his chin thoughtfully. 'What about banking?'

Phoebe looked doubtful. 'You don't think you should pretend to be something less...ambitious?' she said carefully.

'What do you mean?' Gib pretended to be affronted. 'You don't think I look like a banker?'

'Not really.'

'Hey, I can put on a suit and poker up with the best of them!' he reassured her, but Phoebe was unconvinced.

'I don't know that it's such a good idea,' she said. 'Ben works for one of those big international tax consultancy firms, and the reception will be choc-a-bloc with City types. You know what men are like about sniffing out each other's status. If you say you're in banking they're bound to ask who you work for, what kind of bonuses you earn and how many Ferraris you've got sitting in your garage, and what are you going to say then?'

'I'll say I've been working for some American bank,' said Gib easily. 'Relax, it'll be fine.'

Phoebe wasn't so sure, but she told herself that she could always tell her mother that he had come down with an acute case of food poisoning if necessary and go on her own as she'd planned.

'When is this wedding?' he asked, still in businesslike mode.

'In three weeks.'

'That's fine then,' he said. 'I'll have plenty of time to prepare my role.'

He seemed so casual about the whole thing, as if women asked him to pretend to be in love with them every day of the week. Phoebe chewed her thumb nervously.

'Are you *sure* you don't mind doing this?' she asked, abruptly attacked by doubts.

'Why would I mind?' said Gib. 'It's a chance to earn some extra cash and drink champagne at someone else's expense. It'll be fun.'

It wasn't Phoebe's idea of fun. She felt tense at the mere thought of carrying off the deception. 'Frankly, at the moment sticking pins in my eyeballs seems like more fun,' she said.

'Then don't do it.'

Phoebe thought about turning up at the wedding on her own, and how awkward it would be for her family and for Ben's. 'No, I want to do it,' she said, making up her mind. 'It will make everyone happy if they see that I seem to have found someone else.'

'Everyone except you,' Gib pointed out.

She looked at the cat curled up on the sofa. 'I've got used to not being happy since Ben left,' she said bleakly.

There was a pause. 'You're still in love with him,' said Gib, sounding oddly flat.

Phoebe kept her eyes on the cat. 'Ben's part of my life,' she answered him after a moment. 'We were toddlers together. I planned to marry him when I was four, and I never wanted anyone else. I suppose I took it for granted that he would always be there for me, and now I can't get used to the fact that he isn't.'

In spite of herself, her voice wobbled treacherously, and Gib saw her lift her chin to an unconsciously gallant tilt. 'I know Ben didn't want to hurt me but I've accepted the fact that he loves Lisa, not me. Now I just want him to be happy, and if that means pretending to be in love with someone else at his wedding, that's what I'll do.'

Most of the women Gib had known would have given in to bitterness or rage at their disappointed dreams, but not Phoebe. He wanted to tell her how brave he thought she was, but he was afraid that she would be mortified if she thought that he had glimpsed her distress.

'If that's what you want,' he said, getting to his feet instead, 'I'm happy to do my bit to help. I won't let you down.'

Caught unawares by the sincerity in his voice, Phoebe glanced at him and saw that the blue eyes were warm with sympathy, almost as if he could see the painful lump of unshed tears in her throat. 'Thank you,' she said with difficulty.

'Hey, no problem.'

Murmuring something about a shower, he left her alone with the cat.

Phoebe looked after him with a curious expression. 'What do you think about that?' she asked the cat, who deigned to open one yellow eye in case food was in the offing. 'Who would have thought Gib would be that tactful?'

The cat yawned hugely, uninterested. Phoebe reran the conversation with Gib in her mind. He had been surprisingly understanding. He hadn't probed for details about her break up with Ben or made fun of her predicament, and now her resistance to asking him to help her was beginning to seem a bit churlish.

She wasn't sure how he was going to carry off being a banker, but otherwise Kate was right, he was the perfect person to help her. He had been nice about it, too. Phoebe watched the cat stretching and remembered how Gib had smiled. *I'm glad I said yes*, he had said when she told him that she needed a lover. *I'll look forward to it.*

The memory sent an odd feeling snaking down her spine, and she got abruptly to her feet. Anticipating the chance of being fed, the cat jumped down and headed purposefully to its bowl, where it sat and fixed Phoebe with faintly menacing yellow eyes.

'Oh, all right,' she sighed, fully aware that any movement towards the fridge would mean her ankles passing well within biting range. It went against the grain to give in but she cravenly shook some biscuits into its bowl. It was obviously her night for giving in.

What would it be like, spending the whole day with Gib? Phoebe was uneasily conscious of a tremble of anticipation uncurling somewhere deep inside her at the prospect. Ridiculous, of course. OK, so he had been nicer than expected, and at lot less irritating than usual, but that was no reason to forget that the arrangement they had made was a strictly businesslike one.

'Don't worry, I'm not going to do anything silly,' Phoebe informed the cat as if it had objected. 'There's no question of me getting involved with Gib.'

And there wasn't, she reassured herself. Gib wasn't the sort of man sensible girls like her fell in love with. He might be fun for a while, but he would move on eventually, and it would hurt. When Phoebe thought about the pain of the past year since Ben had left, she knew that she wasn't prepared to risk that again. If she did ever let herself fall in love again, she would have to be very, very sure that it would be for ever, and Gib just wasn't a for ever kind of guy.

'No, I'm grateful to him for helping me out,' Phoebe told the cat firmly, 'but that's all.'

CHAPTER FOUR

IN SOME ways, that conversation with Gib left Phoebe feeling even more unsettled than ever. It had been easier when he was irritating, she thought, and when the days passed with no sign that he was doing anything about preparing for his role, she was almost relieved to find herself getting quite cross again.

It was all very well for Gib to lounge around the kitchen joking with Bella and Kate, but he seemed to have no idea of how easily he could be revealed as a fraud, Phoebe fretted, her gratitude eking away with each fresh onset of nerves. Of course she appreciated how understanding he had been, but when it came down to it, she *was* paying him, and the least he could do was make an effort to seem convincing at the wedding.

Kate and Bella pooh-poohed her worries, but then *they* weren't risking humiliation in front of their family and oldest friends, were they? If anyone at the wedding discovered that Gib was not in fact the banker he claimed to be, her cover would be blown too. She would be revealed as a sad, pathetic spinster who was reduced to paying a man to pretend to be in love with her.

Phoebe cringed at the prospect. She couldn't stop thinking about everything that could go wrong, and had lived through each potentially disastrous scenario so many times that she could picture every one down to the last detail.

There was the banker who quizzed Gib about exchange rate mechanisms and investment portfolios with increasing puzzlement until he exclaimed, 'Damn it, I don't think you're a banker at all!' just as a hush fell on the gathering. Phoebe shuddered at the thought of everyone turning to stare at Gib, who would be left blustering unconvincingly.

Or one of the other guests might know Gib. It was all very well for him to say that he had been in the States for the past few years, but people travelled and coincidences happened all the time. What was the betting one of his old surfing pals would be there, only too ready to throw back his head and hoot with laughter at the idea of Gib being a banker?

Sometimes Phoebe varied the theme, and imagined one of his ex-girlfriends turning up at the wedding with one of Ben's friends, and spotting an ideal opportunity to wreak her revenge on him. There would be champagne thrown in his face, tears and tantrums and accusations as Gib's past caught up with him...oh, yes, she could see it all.

But the scenario Phoebe dreaded most was the one where it gradually dawned on her parents that the man masquerading as their daughter's lover knew nothing about her and cared even less. If they guessed that she was deceiving them, they would be desperately hurt. Her mother would tell Penelope, who would tell Ben, who would obviously tell Lisa, and before she knew it, word would go round the reception like wildfire. Already Phoebe could picture the whispered asides, the pitying glances, the way the conversation would fall awkwardly silent as soon as she approached, and she cringed as if it was already happening.

After nights spent churning over one humiliating scenario after another, she had just decided to call the whole thing off when she let herself into the house one evening to find Gib chatting cosily to her mother on the phone in the kitchen.

'To tell you the truth, Mrs Lane,' he was saying in a confidential tone, 'I knew the moment I saw Phoebe. It was like a bolt from the blue. I just looked at her and knew that she was the woman I wanted to spend the rest of my life with!'

Phoebe's mouth dropped open before she recovered sufficiently to snatch the receiver from Gib's hand. 'Mum!' she said on a gasp. 'Sorry, I've just got in.'

'That's all right, dear. I've been having a nice little chat with Gib. I must say, he sounds absolutely charming!'

Her voice was clearly audible, and Gib sent Phoebe a smug grin. Pointedly, she turned her back on him.

'We can't wait to meet him,' her mother was burbling happily on. 'Penelope was thrilled when I told her, and she said she would send an invitation off straight away. Did Gib get it?'

An embossed white card had dropped through the door practically the day after Phoebe had rung her mother to drop Gib's name into the conversation for the first time. She must have been straight on the phone to Penelope. Phoebe could picture Ben's mother frantically gesturing for a pen so that she could write out the invitation there and then.

'Yes, we got it,' she said. 'I'm not sure Gib will be able to spend the night, though,' she went on quickly, anticipating her mother's next question. She might as well knock that idea on the head right now. Her nerves were going to be in shreds as it was, without the prospect of spending the night with Gib as well.

'Oh, what a pity!' Her mother was clearly disappointed. 'You know what receptions are like. We won't get a chance to relax and talk to him properly until the evening.'

Relaxing and talking properly was precisely what Phoebe didn't want. That would be the very time they were likely to let slip a comment that brought the whole pretence crashing down around them. No, much better to get Gib firmly out of the way.

'I know, but Gib's got to work the next day, I'm afraid,' she said, trying to force some regret into her voice.

Her mother clicked her tongue impatiently. She had no time for the tedious business of actually earning a living. 'I'm sure he can work another time,' she said, and then to Phoebe's acute embarrassment lowered her voice. 'You know it's not a problem about you two sharing a room, don't you? Penelope's absolutely fine about it. We know things are different for your generation.'

'It's not that, Mum,' said Phoebe, squirming and hoping Gib couldn't hear. He hadn't even had the decency to leave the kitchen to let her talk to her mother in peace, and she was very conscious of him lounging on the sofa behind her, hands behind his head and long legs crossed.

'It's just that he's got a meeting in…um…' Oh, God, where did bankers have meetings? '…in…er, in…yes, Switzerland,' she remembered triumphantly after a nasty moment where her mind went completely blank. 'It's first thing the next day, so he'll have to get back.'

'Oh, well, if he must, he must.' Her mother made no attempt to hide her disappointment, and Phoebe sighed inwardly, spotting a fresh attack of guilt coming on.

'But do try and see if he can change his meeting,' her mother went on, working up to the emotional blackmail. 'We're all so looking forward to getting to know him. It's not just your father and I. Lara's very keen to meet him, too.'

Phoebe closed her eyes briefly. Lara was her younger sister. She had a sweet, pretty face and could be disconcertingly perceptive at times. Phoebe would have to keep her well away from Gib. She would see through him in a second.

'I'll ask him,' she lied. 'I'm sure he'll see what he can do.'

'This is turning into a nightmare,' she sighed as she switched off the phone and threw it onto a chair. 'I wish I'd never mentioned you to my mother!'

'Why?' said Gib. 'It seems to be working perfectly. You wanted your mother to be happy, and she is.'

This was unanswerable. Phoebe made a show of looking through the post she had brought in from the hall. A credit card bill, two circulars and a letter from the gym asking plaintively why they hadn't seen her for a while.

'Why did you tell Mum all that stuff about love at first sight?' she demanded instead.

'I thought I was supposed to be a besotted lover,' said Gib.

'Not that besotted! Nobody's going to believe you if you carry on like that!'

'Why not?'

'Well, because it doesn't happen like that in real life, does it?' she said, a bit thrown by the directness of Gib's question.

'What doesn't?'

'All that bolt from the blue stuff. You have to know someone before you can fall in love with them.'

Gib looked at her, one corner of his long, mobile mouth curling upwards in a crooked smile. 'That might be true for you, but it isn't necessarily the same for everyone else.'

'Don't tell me you've ever fallen in love at first sight!' said Phoebe, tearing up the letter from the gym and dropping the credit card bill onto the table unopened.

'Why shouldn't I have done?'

It was a fair enough question. 'You don't seem the type,' was the best she could do for an answer.

'That's what I thought until it happened to me.'

'Oh.' She eyed him a little uncertainly, wishing, not for the first time, that she could tell whether he was joking or not. He could keep his mouth perfectly straight as now, but it always seemed on the verge of twitching upwards, and as for those eyes...Phoebe risked a glance only to find herself skewered by a blue gleam that was impossible to interpret but which for some reason sent the blood surging into her cheeks.

She jerked her gaze away. 'Are you sure was it was love and not lust?' she said, trying to be ironic but succeeding only in sounding tremulous.

'I think it was a bit of both,' said Gib.

He smiled then, a reminiscent smile that turned up the corners of his mouth and creased the edges of his eyes. No doubt thinking of some long-legged, sun-streaked blonde he had met lazing around on a Californian beach, thought Phoebe, inexplicably irritable.

Turning her back on that smile, she headed over to the fridge, her dignified demeanour rather spoilt by falling over the cat who had been waiting to ambush the next human who approached his bowl.

'The point is, I'm trying to convince my family here,' she said coldly, disentangling herself from the weaving cat with difficulty and opening the fridge door, relieved to see a bottle of wine that had been chilling overnight. She could do with a drink! 'We need to stick to a realistic scenario, or they won't believe a word you say. And the fact is, I'm just not the kind of girl men fall in love with at first sight.'

'Your mother didn't seem to have any trouble believing me.' Gib watched her scrabbling through the drawers in search of a corkscrew. 'She told me that I sounded like a dream come true,' he went on virtuously.

Phoebe muttered under her breath as she located the corkscrew at last and attacked the foil at the top of the bottle. 'You're not taking this seriously!' she accused him.

'And you're taking it too seriously,' said Gib. 'You need to lighten up, Phoebe! Everything's under control.'

'Easy for you to say,' grumbled Phoebe, twisting the corkscrew. 'Have you organised a suit yet?' She bet he hadn't.

'Yes.'

Oh.

'Well, that's something, I suppose.' The cork popped out and she poured the wine into a glass, pausing for a second to savour its pale golden beauty before she went back to her fretting.

'What about this job you're supposed to have?' she demanded as she carried her glass over to the armchair next to him. 'I've told Mum you're a banker now, so you'd better be able to carry it off.'

'Relax,' said Gib lazily. 'I've been doing some research. Look.' He picked up a brochure from the floor by the sofa and waved it at her.

Phoebe took it with her spare hand. 'This is for the Community Bank,' she said blankly.

'I know.'

'Where did you get it?'

'It was lying on the table with some of the other stuff you brought home with you,' said Gib, and Phoebe was too busy studying the brochure to notice the faint hesitation in his voice. 'I thought I might as well take advantage of the research you've been doing for your programme, so I had a look through it. If anyone asks, I'll say I work in their development section. I ought to be able to bluff my way through on that.'

'That's not a bad idea.' She looked at him with grudging respect. 'It's a bank, but not a real bank.'

'What do you mean, it's not a real bank?' For once Gib was roused out of his lazy good humour and he sat up to object. 'It lends money, it supports its customers, it's an integral part of the financial infrastructure of the countries where it operates…'

Phoebe looked at him in surprise. 'You *have* been reading the brochure, haven't you?'

There was a tiny silence, and then Gib lay back down. 'I told you I'd been doing some research,' he said.

'I'm glad to hear you're getting into your role so well,' she said dryly. 'Anyway, I just meant that because it's an ethical bank, if you meet any other City types there, they won't expect you to be flash and boast about bonuses. They'll probably make allowances if you seem a bit…'

'A bit what?'

'I don't know,' said Phoebe with a touch of irritation. Why did Gib have to pick her up on everything? 'A bit different, I suppose.'

She sipped her wine reflectively, trying to spot the flaws in Gib's idea, but the more she thought about it, the better it seemed. 'No, I think it might work,' she said with gathering excitement. 'We could say that's how we met,' she went on, getting into the idea.

'Exactly,' said Gib.

Phoebe ignored his smugness. 'People know that I've been working on the programme. I'm so desperate that I've asked most of Ben's City friends if they've got any contacts in the States who might know about the Community Bank, but hardly any of them had even heard of it—which is good news for you,' she added as an aside. 'We can pretend that someone put me in touch with you, and you were so impressed by me on the phone that we arranged to meet and… Bam!'

'Ah, so it *was* love at first sight?' said Gib provocatively.

Phoebe rolled her eyes. 'Yes, all right, it was love at first sight, if that's what you want! If you've already told Mum that's how it was, there's not much I can do about it anyway.'

She might be reassured that Gib was getting ready to play his part, but as Ben's wedding approached, Phoebe grew more and more apprehensive. By the time the following Saturday came round, she was so jittery with nerves that she could hardly speak.

'You've got to calm down,' said Bella that morning. 'You're wound so tight, you're going to snap! Here, give me that,' she added, seeing Phoebe lay her dress onto the ironing board. 'You'll just burn it if you try and iron it in that state. Sit down and relax for a minute.'

'I can't relax,' said Phoebe, hugging her arms together edgily as Bella tested the iron with the tip of her finger. 'I keep thinking of all the things that could go wrong.'

'Like what?'

'Like Gib forgetting who he's supposed to be,' she said with a pointed glance at where he sat reading the paper at the table in jeans and a T-shirt, long legs stretched out before him and quite unperturbed by all the activity around him.

'Hey, I resent that!' he said, without looking up from his paper. 'I'm John Gibson, Gib to his friends, development manager at the Community Bank with special responsibility for setting up funding programmes and links between Europe and sub-Saharan Africa, and I can now bore for England *and* the States about development strategies, ethical investment opportunities and interest assessment.'

'See?' said Bella, impressed. 'He'll be fine.'

'I don't know,' said Phoebe fretfully, rummaging through her make-up bag in search of a mirror. 'It would just take one little slip, and they'll all know that my fantastically successful lover is in fact my unemployed lodger!

'I didn't sleep a wink last night thinking about it,' she

went on, opening the mirror and contemplating her face glumly. 'Excellent, bug eyes and puffy skin! Just what I need this morning!'

'Nothing a bit of make-up won't cure,' said Bella reassuringly. 'Put on some lippy and you'll be fine.'

'I think it's going to take more than lipstick this morning,' said Phoebe, refusing to be comforted. 'God, I look a mess!'

'No, you don't,' said Gib, lowering his paper to study her. 'You look absolutely beautiful.'

It was so unexpected that Phoebe's jaw dropped, and Bella looked up from her ironing in surprise.

'Blimey! She hasn't even got her make-up on yet!'

'Phoebe doesn't need make-up. She always looks beautiful to me,' Gib said soulfully, and belatedly Phoebe realised that he was just proving that he had his role down pat.

Mortified by her blush—what if he thought she had taken him seriously?—she lifted her chin and retreated behind her haughtiest air. 'You'd better not say anything like that today, or they'll know you can't be serious,' she said.

'Why?'

Phoebe glanced back at the mirror. Her face stared uncompromisingly back at her. 'I accepted a long time ago that I'm not beautiful, and I never will be,' she said flatly.

Gib looked across the table at her. She wasn't pretty, it was true. Her face was too full of character and her features too strong to be anything as insipid as pretty. Instead she was vivid and dramatic, with those fierce eyes and that mouth that hinted at a passionate nature well hidden behind her prickles.

'I don't agree,' he said.

Phoebe saw Bella's hand still and the sharp look of interest she gave Gib. 'All right, you can drop the act for now,' she said hastily. 'Save it for later, and don't overdo it,' she warned. 'Everyone there has known me for ever, and they know I hate all that gushy lovey-dovey stuff.'

'You might not if you were in love,' said Gib.

'Ben never went in for that kind of thing,' she told him, and he folded his paper and got deliberately to his feet.

'Well, I'm not Ben,' he reminded her, and when Phoebe met his eyes she saw with something of a shock that the familiar laughter was quite gone. 'You're in love with me now, remember?'

Phoebe moistened her lips, wondering why the kitchen was suddenly so airless. 'Just for today,' she managed.

There was an unpleasant silence for a moment, then Gib smiled. It wasn't his usual smile, though. There was something almost grim about it. 'Of course, just for today,' he echoed in a voice empty of expression. He turned for the door. 'Excuse me, I'll go and get ready.'

Phoebe didn't realise that she had been holding her breath until he left and she was able to let it out at last, very carefully. When she glanced back at Bella, she saw that her friend was watching her with a speculative expression.

'I wouldn't push Gib, if I were you,' was all she said, slipping the dress onto its hanger and handing it to Phoebe. 'Here you are. Go and have a shower, and I'll do your make-up for you afterwards.'

'You look fantastic!' she said later when Phoebe was glossed and mascaraed and dusted with Kate's special shimmering powder that promised a radiant golden glow. She made her turn and look at herself in the mirror. In heels and a flame-red suit with a dramatic necklace, Phoebe looked taller and more vivid than ever.

'All you need now is your hat,' said Bella. 'And a smile.'

Phoebe couldn't manage the smile, and wrung her hands together instead. 'Oh, God, Bella, do you think I'm doing the right thing?'

'Yes,' said Bella, who had no time for doubts. 'You're going to be able to go into that wedding with your head held high. Gib will be beside you, and he won't let you down.'

'He'd better not,' said Phoebe tensely.

Bella smoothed the short-sleeved jacket over Phoebe's shoulder. 'He was pretty convincing when he said he thought you were beautiful,' she said, carefully expressionless. 'I wondered how much he was pretending.'

'Of course he was pretending.' Phoebe didn't quite meet her eyes. The last thing she needed was Bella knowing that she had wondered the same for an embarrassing moment or two. 'That's what I'm paying him to do.'

Bella picked up Phoebe's hat. 'You seem to have been getting on better recently,' she commented in the same studiedly casual tone.

'I suppose so,' was all Phoebe would admit.

'I think he really likes you, Phoebe. So does Kate. We think he's just what you need,' she went on when Phoebe could only gape at her.

'No.' Phoebe found her voice at last. 'No, he's not what I need at all.' She shook her head firmly to emphasise the point, although it wasn't clear whether she was trying to convince herself or Bella. 'He's nothing like Ben.'

'Exactly,' said Bella. 'I know you loved Ben, Phoebe, but it's time you moved on. You need someone you can have some fun with, and I can't imagine anyone better than Gib for that.'

'I'm not sure I'm ready to have fun,' Phoebe confessed in a low voice. 'I'm scared of being hurt again, Bella. I don't want to get involved with anyone, let alone Gib. Anyway,' she went on, lifting her chin, 'I think you're wrong about him. Pretending to be in love with me is just a job to him. He was quite happy for me to pay him. He wouldn't be interested in money if he really liked me, would he?'

She needed to remember that, Phoebe told herself as she went downstairs carefully on her high heels.

They found Kate in kitchen, and by the time she had exclaimed over the outfit and heard Bella's account of Gib's unexpected acting ability, Phoebe's nerves were back in full force and her stomach was churning furiously.

She looked at her watch. The ceremony was at two-thirty, and they would need to allow at least two hours to get to the castle. Getting out of London on a Saturday could be a nightmare.

'OK, I've got my bag, got the present, got my hat...what else do I need?'

'Car keys?'

'God, yes, car keys! Where are they?'

Phoebe began scrabbling frantically through the piles of junk on the table. 'I had them yesterday,' she said fretfully. 'I'm sure they're here somewhere. Kate, can you see whether the cat is sitting on them? And where's Gib? We've got to go.'

'I'm here.'

All three girls looked up from where they were burrowing down the sides of the sofa or sifting through the clutter of papers on the worktop, and there was a moment of thunderstruck silence. Kate and Bella frankly stared, and Phoebe froze, breathless as if from a blow.

She couldn't believe how different Gib looked. He had showered and shaved, and changed into a beautifully cut grey suit with a classic white shirt and a pale grey tie. He looked much older, much more respectable, even distinguished, but his sudden grin at their expressions was exactly the same as before.

'Well!' whistled Bella, the first to recover. 'Who'd have thought you'd brush up so nicely!'

Kate walked round him critically. 'Ten out of ten!' she agreed. 'There's just something about a man in a suit, isn't there? What do you reckon, Phoebe? Will he pass?'

Why couldn't she be as easy with him as Kate and Bella were? Gripped by a ridiculous shyness, Phoebe couldn't meet Gib's eyes.

'He looks fine,' she said curtly.

'Are we ready to go?' His voice was warm with that unsettling undercurrent of laughter, so much so that Phoebe began to wonder if she had imagined the formidable look she had glimpsed earlier.

'When I've found my car keys,' she snapped.

'Here.'

To Phoebe's annoyance, Gib spotted them immediately on the sideboard and dangled them from his finger. Snatching them from him, she stalked out to the car, her exit only marred by the fact that she forgot to pick up her hat and her overnight bag.

'Are you OK to drive?' Gib asked when she had stowed them in the boot of her old Peugeot.

'Of course I am.' Phoebe bridled as she opened the driver's door. 'Why shouldn't I be?'

'You seem a bit...tense,' he said carefully.

'Of course I'm tense! I'm going to watch the man I love marrying someone else while lying to my family and friends about having a relationship with my unemployed lodger who's pretending to be a hotshot businessman, and knowing that if anyone even suspects what I'm doing it'll ruin the whole day for everyone!'

And that was quite apart from knowing that her friends thought she should get involved with a man who was only pretending to be nice because she was paying him.

Suddenly Phoebe felt close to tears.

'That's what I meant,' said Gib. 'I know it's going to be difficult for you today. If you want to drive, that's fine by me, but if you want one less thing to think about, I thought it would be something I could do for you.'

Phoebe hesitated, chewing her lip. She didn't want to give in, but she knew that Gib was right. She wasn't in a fit state to drive, and an accident was the last thing she needed right now. Usually, she loved being driven, but she wasn't sure she trusted Gib. He looked like the kind of man who burned along the highways in an open-topped sports car, one hand on the steering wheel and the other on a blonde, not one who would drive her old banger safely and sedately down to Wiltshire.

Gib came round the front of the car to her door. 'You're not really intending to drive in those, are you?' he said, nodding down at her strappy shoes with their delicate heels.

Of course she couldn't drive in them. She could dig out her driving shoes from the boot...or she could just let Gib drive.

Reading the decision in her face, Gib held out his hand and Phoebe put the keys into his outstretched palm.

'As long as you drive carefully,' she said with a flash of her old self as she got into the passenger seat.

Gib inserted the key into the ignition and pushed back the seat to allow room for his longer legs. 'You don't trust me, do you?' he said as he pulled out into the street.

'If I didn't trust you, I wouldn't be exposing you to my family,' said Phoebe, grabbing at the door as a taxi swerved in front of them.

'If you trusted me, you wouldn't be sitting there clutching the door and jamming your foot on an imaginary brake,' said Gib in a dry voice. 'If you're going to do that all the way to Wiltshire I'd rather you drove after all!'

Phoebe made a conscious effort to relax. 'Sorry,' she muttered.

Contrary to all her expectations, Gib was a calm, competent driver, quite unflustered by the London traffic. It was odd seeing him in the driving seat, his hands sure on her steering wheel. Phoebe's eyes kept sliding sideways, and every time the sight of him was like a tiny shock that made her look quickly away.

For a while the conversation was limited to Phoebe's attempts to direct Gib through the labyrinth of back streets to get out onto the M4, but once they hit the motorway, he put his foot down and settled back comfortably into his seat with a wriggle of his shoulders that sent a peculiar little shiver down her spine.

'Do you want to fill me in on a bit more background before we get there?' he said with a sideways glance. 'I know the situation with Ben, and I've got the job covered, but am I likely to meet anyone else I should know about?'

Phoebe looked out of the window at the speeding traffic. 'There'll be various friends who knew me when Ben and I were together, but I suppose we could say that our relationship is too new for me to have mentioned them to you.'

'Ah, yes,' said Gib with a wicked smile. 'When you're as much in love as we are, you've got better things to think about, haven't you?'

Faint colour touched Phoebe's cheekbones. 'Exactly.'

'So it'll just be your family I really need to worry about?'

'Yes.' Phoebe was glad of the chance to move onto a safer topic. 'Mum and Dad are pretty much what you'd expect, and my little sister will be there, too. Lara's the baby of the family. She looks like butter wouldn't melt in her mouth, but don't be fooled. She's sharp as a tack.'

'What does she do?'

'Drives my parents to distraction mostly,' she said wryly.

'She's incredibly bright, but she gets bored so easily. She keeps starting courses and not finishing them, or walking out of perfectly good jobs, and she's always got some unsuitable boyfriend in tow.'

'Not like big sister, then?' said Gib with another of those disconcertingly blue glances.

'No, I'm the boring one of the family.' Phoebe gave an unconscious sigh as she stared through the windscreen and thought about her sister. 'I've had such a conventional life. Fell in love with the boy next door, got a degree, saddled myself with a mortgage... Giving up my job to work for Purple Parrot Productions is the riskiest thing I've ever done, and that's not exactly living dangerously, is it?'

'Is that what you'd like? To live dangerously?'

'Sometimes,' she admitted, 'but I don't think I'd be very good at it. I'm too sensible.'

That was what Ben had said. *You're so sensible, Phoebe. I know that you'll understand that it's not that I don't care for you. It's just that we know each other so well that things aren't that exciting, are they? We can't surprise each other any more.*

'I wish I could be more like Lara sometimes,' she told Gib, pushing away the memory. If she had been, maybe Ben wouldn't have fallen in love with Lisa, who wasn't predictable and familiar. 'She decides she wants to do something, and she does it. She'll try anything. She doesn't stop to think about the consequences, or what might happen if something goes wrong, she just goes for it.'

Gib slid her another glance. 'I'll look forward to meeting her.'

'You'll like her.'

Phoebe was conscious of a faint wistfulness. Her sister had exactly the same streak of recklessness that seemed so much part of Gib. It didn't matter that he was rattling along in the slow lane in her battered old car, or that he was dressed in the most conventional of grey suits, he still exuded an air of danger and excitement that alarmed and intrigued her in equal measure.

Gib would find a kindred spirit in Lara, she thought. Lara was reckless and funny and open, the complete opposite of her big sister in fact.

CHAPTER FIVE

WITHOUT meaning to, Phoebe sighed.

'What's the matter?' Gib was watching her more closely than she realised.

'Nothing,' said Phoebe quickly.

She could feel his blue gaze sharpen assessingly as it rested on her averted profile, but after a moment he evidently decided to let it go.

'OK,' he said. 'What about us?'

'What *about* us?'

'We ought to agree on how we met,' he suggested.

'I thought we'd already decided that.' Phoebe pulled herself together. 'We met when I contacted you about the programme we're making.'

'You don't think that sounds a bit dry?' said Gib. 'I mean, won't they want to know a few more details?'

'Like what?'

'I don't know,' he said, lifting one hand from the steering wheel to gesture vaguely. 'Like whether it was love at first sight for both of us, or did I have to work really hard to win you?'

'Oh, that last one, I think,' said Phoebe crisply. 'I don't want to be a pushover.'

Gib cast her a wry look. 'I can't imagine you ever being that,' he said. 'Still, you obviously didn't play *too* hard to get since I've moved in with you already. In fact,' he went on with one of his swift, sidelong grins, 'I think you'd better just admit it! You couldn't resist me, could you?'

She hated his habit of being right about things like that.

It *would* sound odd if she was claiming to be keeping her distance when Gib had apparently moved into her house barely a week after she had supposedly met him.

'I suppose we'd better say I was swept off my feet,' she agreed stiffly.

Gib's eyes rested thoughtfully for a moment on her averted profile before he looked back at the road. 'What would it take to do that, Phoebe?' he asked.

'I don't know,' she said. 'It's never happened to me. I always knew I loved Ben, so it wasn't something that happened overnight. I can't imagine ever doing anything as rash as falling in love with someone I don't really know,' she admitted. 'I mean, being swept off your feet is all very well in theory, but in practice, how would you be able to trust a man who overwhelmed you and persuaded you into changing your life before you'd had a chance to think about what you were really doing?'

'I thought you wanted to live dangerously?'

'Not that dangerously,' said Phoebe. 'Falling in love like that seems like a sure way to get yourself hurt.'

Gib signalled and then moved out to overtake. 'I think if you fell in love you might change your mind. If you really loved someone, you'd be prepared to take that risk.'

'I've been in love,' she said flatly. 'I took that risk, and I got hurt. I'm not going through that again.'

There was silence for a while. Gib concentrated on driving, and Phoebe looked out of the side window and thought about Ben and the look in his eyes when he had told her that he had fallen in love with Lisa. He was the last person she had ever expected to hurt her. They had been so comfortable together, so gentle, so *safe*. She had thought that was what he had wanted too, but she had been wrong. Perhaps she hadn't known him as well as she had thought.

And then for some reason she found herself remembering

what she had said to Bella about Gib. It would be hard to find a man more different from Ben. Safe was the last word you would use about him! Phoebe could imagine *him* sweeping a girl off her feet all right. He was the type who saw what he wanted and went for it, and if what he wanted was you, you would have little choice in the matter, she thought with a tiny shiver. He would turn your life upside down, spin you around, subject you to a roller coaster of adrenalin and excitement—and then drop you back down to earth with a thump when he was bored and wanted to move on.

No, thank you, thought Phoebe. She could do without that kind of excitement. Living dangerously like that would not be worth the pain and humiliation you would have to endure afterwards. She had had enough of both of *them* in the last year.

'What shall I call you?' Gib broke the silence at last, and she turned to look at him in surprise.

'What's wrong with my name?'

'I was thinking more along the lines of endearments. Do you want to be "darling" or "honey" or what?'

Phoebe grimaced. 'I'm not really a "darling" kind of girl.'

'Why not?'

'Because darlings are soft and sweet and pretty, not sharp and intimidating.'

'Hey,' said Gib with a grin, 'you don't intimidate me, baby!'

She shot him a look. 'I'm not a "baby" either!'

'Shall I call you bunnikins then?'

'Not unless you want to spend the next month with your jaw wired,' said Phoebe evenly, and he threw back his head and laughed.

'But we're so in love!' he pretended to protest.

'We're not that in love,' she said, more unnerved than she wanted to admit by the way Gib looked when he laughed like that. He had obviously taken advantage of American dentistry because his teeth were very white and strong, and the creases starring his eyes deepened in what was—OK, she was prepared to concede this—a disturbingly attractive way. The sound of his laughter rolled around the car and seemed to linger, reverberating over her skin so that she shivered slightly.

If only he wasn't quite so overwhelming. He was so vivid, so vital, that she was left feeling pale and drab and somehow vulnerable in comparison.

Gib was still talking. 'I thought I was supposed to be the perfect man for you?'

'Exactly,' said Phoebe, pulling herself together with an effort. She really must get a grip. 'And everyone knows that I wouldn't let a man who would even *think* about calling me bunnikins within a mile of me!'

'So if they heard me calling you bunnikins, they'd know it had to be true love,' he pointed out.

'Listen, who's paying you here?' she said crossly, feeling herself being drawn into a ridiculous argument that would, on past form, end with her not only agreeing but begging Gib to call her bunnikins. That was how she had ended up in this mess in the first place! She had been determined not to be talked into asking him to act as her imaginary lover, but somehow, here she was, heading down the motorway towards the wedding with Gib beside her.

'If I hear the word bunnikins cross your lips, I'll cut that fee we agreed in half, so don't say I didn't warn you!'

'OK, bunni-boss!'

'Very funny,' she said with a frosty look.

'Perhaps I just call you madam and be done with it, if

you're going to be that stand-offish,' said Gib, pretending to sound aggrieved.

Phoebe gritted her teeth. 'Look, I don't care what you call me, as long as it's not bunnikins, all right? You're supposed to be perfect!'

'If I'm so perfect, how are you going to explain the fact that our fantastic, perfect relationship is going to end shortly after this wedding?'

'Well, I haven't quite decided yet,' she admitted. 'Perhaps I'll discover that you've got a deep dark secret. Everyone knows that I could never love a man who lied to me.'

'Oh?' he said carefully. 'Why's that?'

'I've always had a thing about lying. I hate it.'

'But you lie,' Gib pointed out with a cool glance. 'You've lied to your mother about our relationship and you're going to carry on lying today.'

'That's different,' she protested.

'How?'

'My lies aren't going to hurt anyone.'

'Things aren't always as straightforward as you want them to be,' said Gib, choosing his words with care. 'Sometimes the truth can hurt as much as a lie.'

Did he think she didn't know that? Phoebe thought about Ben, insisting on telling her about Lisa as soon as he knew that he was in love. That was one thing about Ben, he was always absolutely honest. He had never pretended, and if the truth had been unbearably painful, at least it had been better than discovering it from someone else much later.

Gib glanced sideways. Phoebe's face was sad and he cursed himself inwardly for triggering what were obviously unhappy memories. He was supposed to be supporting her today like the good friend he was trying to prove that he was, not making her even more miserable.

'So the idea is that in a couple of weeks' time you're

going to tell your mother that I lied to you and dump me without hearing my side of the story, is that right?' he said, deliberately keeping his voice light and upbeat.

'I'll probably have found out by then that there are lots of other things about you that have begun to irritate me,' said Phoebe loftily, but Gib saw the effort it cost her to reply in kind. 'Your lies will just be the final straw.'

'Wouldn't it be simpler to forget about the whole lies thing?' said Gib. 'Why don't you just say that I'm a bastard who's dumped you?'

'Because I've already been dumped once,' she said with a slight edge to her voice. 'This time I'm the one who gets to do the dumping. And what's more,' she went on, pointing at him for emphasis, '*you* are going to devastated! I'm going to tell Mum that you're making a real nuisance of yourself, sending me flowers every day, showering me with diamonds, and ringing up every five minutes to beg me to give you another chance.'

That was better. Gib pretended to look disconsolate. 'If I'm going to humiliate myself to that extent, I think you should give me one.'

'No way!' Phoebe shook her head definitely and he heaved a sigh.

'You're a hard-hearted woman!'

'You deceived me,' she pointed out.

'Yes, but I couldn't help myself,' said Gib. 'You drive me crazy. I haven't been able to think of anyone but you since I met you.'

Primming her mouth, she tried hard not to laugh. 'You should have thought of that before you abandoned your wife and six children in the States, shouldn't you?'

'Six children? Cut me a break! Wouldn't two be enough?'

'Nope. You've got six little darlings depending on you.' There was a twitch at the corner of Gib's mouth. 'I'm surprised I'm in any state for a passionate affair with you in that case! I must be quite a guy!'

'No, you're not,' said Phoebe firmly, realising with an odd start that she was actually enjoying herself. 'It turns out that you're a low, treacherous, lying creep.'

He considered the matter, but after a moment shook his head. 'I don't think that's going to work,' he decided.

'Why not?'

'I don't believe that you would ever be taken in by someone with so little integrity,' he said coolly. 'You're too...' He stopped, searching for the right word.

Too *what*? Phoebe found herself wanting to know, when really she shouldn't be caring one way or another what he thought.

'...too perceptive?' Gib wondered, almost as if she had asked out loud. 'Too honest? Too intelligent, maybe? Anyway, I can't see it happening.'

Hhmmnn. How was she supposed to take *that*? On the surface, being thought intelligent and honest and perceptive ought to be a compliment, but as usual it was impossible to tell from Gib's voice whether he was being serious or not.

In the end, Phoebe chose to ignore his comment altogether. 'All right, maybe there's some ex-girlfriend you forgot to mention,' she offered as an alternative. 'She gets in touch with me, weeping and wailing and complaining that you've broken her heart, and I feel so sorry for her that I break it all off with you.'

Gib lifted an eyebrow. 'Would you really do that?'

'I might if you were annoying me anyway and I was looking for an excuse to end the relationship.'

That disconcerting crease was back at the corner of his mouth. 'But what could I possibly do that would annoy you enough to kick out a man like me—wealthy, successful, a passionate lover—on the say-so of some neurotic ex?' he asked, assuming an aggrieved air.

Phoebe tried to think of all the ways he irritated her, but it was hard to put her finger on exactly why she found him so unsettling. It wasn't so much anything he *did*, she realised. It was just the way he was.

'You're too possessive,' she offered eventually.

'Oh, come on, you'll have to do better than that!'

'And you snore.'

Gib's expression showed how much he thought of that suggestion.

'You don't get on with Kate and Bella.'

He snorted. 'No one's going to believe *that*! I can't imagine anyone not getting on with those two.'

It was true, Phoebe thought, startled by the pang of envy that shot through her. Everybody loved her friends. They were bright and bubbly and fun in a way she could never quite manage. Of course Gib got on with them. It would be a lot easier for him to pretend to be in love with Bella or with Kate than her with her prickles and her sharp tongue.

Still, it was too late to start being sweet now. 'If you're going to be difficult about it, I'll tell everyone I was just using you as a sex toy and got bored with your technique,' she said crisply.

'Ouch!' Gib winced. 'I think I'll take the vengeful girlfriend, thanks!'

He glanced at Phoebe, who was sitting straight in her seat, her fine cheekbones tinged with colour and the smooth dark hair slipping silkily around her face. As he watched, she hooked a swathe behind her ear and he glimpsed the pulse beating nervously in her throat before he made himself look back at the road. She was trying hard, but she must be dreading the day ahead.

'Of course, you realise that *she'll* turn out to be the one who's lying, don't you?' he said, wanting to distract her, to stop her thinking about Ben and the fact that another bride was going to be standing in the place that should have been hers. 'You'll find that out too late, though, and realise that I was perfect after all, and then you'll be sorry!'

'Hah! I am *so* not going to have any regrets,' said Phoebe, shaking back her hair, but Gib was glad to see that she was laughing.

His tomfoolery had diverted her and for the first time she felt able to relax. For a while they talked easily, and it was only when they turned off the motorway that the butterflies started to swoop and flutter around her stomach once more.

Smoothing the map nervously over her knees, Phoebe directed Gib through the lush Wiltshire countryside with one part of her mind, while the other was fully occupied reviewing all the potentially disastrous scenarios that might unfold when they arrived.

'You won't forget that you're going back to London tonight, will you?' she fretted.

'What, and miss that meeting in Zurich? Impossible!'

Phoebe was too dithery by this stage to pick him up on his sarcasm. 'Right, so we'd better order a taxi to the station when we get there. It can pick you up after the reception. If we say half past six, that ought to be fine—oh, next on the left!'

Gib muttered under his breath at the lateness of the instruction and swung the car round the bend with a squeal of tires. 'Thanks for the warning! Do you think you could concentrate on the map and forget how you're going to get rid of me for the moment?'

'Yes, sorry...' Phoebe bent her head diligently over the map, only to be struck by another thought. Gib looked so much the part in his suit that it was easy to forget that he didn't have a real job. She chewed her lip, eyeing him under her lashes.

'Um...have you got enough cash to get you back to London?' she asked awkwardly. 'I brought some extra with me, just in case, so if you need it...'

Gib's smile twisted as she trailed off uncomfortably. 'Don't worry about it,' he said. 'I'll be fine.'

'I don't want you to be out of pocket.'

'I tell you what,' he said briskly. 'I'll keep an account of everything I spend today and we can tally it up at the end. You can add it to the fee we agreed.'

Phoebe went back to her map-reading. 'Oh. Right. Yes, of course. If you're happy with that.'

Now that the subject had come up, perhaps it might be an idea to sort out a few other things, she thought. Things she had deliberately avoided thinking about so far.

She cleared her throat. 'Maybe we should talk about what happens when we get there,' she said stiltedly. 'Lay down a few rules of engagement, so to speak.'

'Engagement?' Gib lifted his brows. 'I thought we were just lovers?'

'Engagement as in a battle,' she said with a frosty look. As if he didn't know.

'Battle? I didn't know things were going to get that serious,' he said, not bothering to disguise the undercurrent of laughter in his voice. 'Perhaps I should have negotiated danger money?'

'You might think so after today,' said Phoebe, unamused. 'I should warn you that you are going to be kissed a lot by people like my mother and Penelope who are going to fall on your neck for rescuing me from dreary spinsterhood.'

'I don't mind a few kisses,' he said equably.

'Good.' Phoebe bit her lip. 'And, er, I might have

to...you know...hold your hand or something. Just for show,' she added hastily.

'Holding hands, eh?' said Gib. 'Passionate stuff!'

'Nobody's going to expect you to throw me down and ravish me in front of the bridesmaids just to prove your affection,' she retorted in a tart voice. 'You're back in England now!'

'Still, I think we could do a bit better than holding hands,' he said, amused. 'Maybe we could go wild and have a little kiss every now and then, just to show them how much in love we are?'

Phoebe's colour deepened. She wished she could treat it as lightly as Gib. It was all just a big joke to him. 'If you don't mind,' she said stiffly.

Gib slid her one of those unsettling sideways looks. 'No, I don't mind,' he said.

'Just so long as you realise that it doesn't mean anything if...if...'

'If you kiss me back?'

'Yes,' she said, grateful to him for putting it into words but obscurely resentful of his casual attitude. He might at least *pretend* to find the prospect of kissing each other as awkward as she did!

She would just have to convince him that she was equally businesslike about the whole affair, Phoebe decided. 'So that's the first rule of engagement for today,' she said briskly. 'No getting involved, or misinterpreting any form of physical contact that we may have today.'

'Fair enough,' said Gib with a slight smile. 'What's the second rule?'

Good question. Phoebe wracked her brains for something suitable. 'Stick to the story we've agreed, and keep it simple.'

'And the third?'

'Two rules is quite enough,' she said a little crossly. She couldn't think up any more.

'OK,' he said. 'I should be able to remember those.'

'You'd better,' said Phoebe, rather proud of her rules now that she came to think of them. She had made it clear that their relationship today was to be a purely businesslike one, and ensured that there would be no misunderstandings between them. How cool could you get?

Even so, as they left the main road and cut across country towards the castle, she found herself fiddling with the map on her knees, turning over the corner until it was dog-eared and tatty.

Gib glanced at her. 'Nervous?'

'Yes.' What was the use of pretending, after all? 'Terrified might be a better word, if you really want to know!'

'What's the worst that could happen?' he asked, wanting to make her feel better but not sure how. Weren't friends supposed to know this kind of thing instinctively?

Phoebe was still mangling the page between her fingers. 'I suppose that we won't seem convincing together,' she said eventually. 'People like my sister pick up on body language. They'll be watching us so closely, I'm afraid they'll see that...you know...that we aren't really lovers.'

'You mean they'll be able to tell just from looking at us that we haven't even kissed?'

'Well...yes.'

Gib checked his mirror before pulling over into the entrance to a farm gate. This was one thing he *could* do to help her. 'Let's kiss now, then,' he said as he put on the handbrake and switched off the ignition.

'What?'

Calmly, he unclipped his seat belt and reached across to undo hers. 'You're the one who's worried people are going to guess that we haven't kissed,' he pointed out reasonably. 'If we kiss now, they won't be able to do that, will they?'

'You're not serious!' Astounded, Phoebe struggled to sit up straight, but that only brought her closer to him as he leaned over towards her, so she hastily retreated, shrinking back into her seat.

Gib paused. 'Don't you think it's a good idea?' he asked. 'Personally, I think it would be easier to kiss you for the first time when there are just two of us and not in front of an entire wedding reception, but it's up to you,' he said, as casually as if they were discussing whether or not to stop for a coffee. 'Of course,' he added with a look at Phoebe's face, 'if you don't want to, that's fine. I don't want to force you. I just thought it might help.'

'No...no,' she said, abruptly changing her mind as he made to sit back. 'You might have a point there.'

The idea of a first kiss under the interested gaze of assorted family and friends had been enough to make Phoebe blench. Ben might be watching too, and if anyone would be able to tell that she and Gib had never kissed before, he would. No, Gib was right. It was far better to have a go here. At least then she would know what to expect.

'No,' she said a little breathlessly. 'Let's do it.'

'OK.'

'OK,' Phoebe agreed, moistening her lips nervously.

Gib was disconcerted to discover just how much he wanted to kiss her. Of course, kissing like this wasn't really what friends did, he reminded himself, and a friend was all he was supposed to be. On the other hand, pretending to be Phoebe's lover was just a way of helping her out, so he was *being* a friend. A kiss under these circumstances wouldn't really count, would it? And it wasn't even as if it would be a real kiss, he reminded himself, remembering her rules of engagement. Surely even Josh couldn't object?

Lifting his hand, he pushed the silky hair away from her face. The green eyes staring back at him were wide and distinctly wary, in spite of her decision.

Gib smiled. 'Relax,' he said. 'Think of it as a dress rehearsal.'

He laid his palm against her soft cheek and tipped her chin up with his thumb. Then, very slowly so as not to alarm her, he touched his mouth to hers.

The feel of his warm, firm lips sent a jolt through Phoebe. She had been bracing herself against his touch, but when it came she was still unprepared for the clutch of her heart or the wash of sheer pleasure that lapped along her veins.

It was just pretending, of course. Gib was right, this was only a practice. Still, it did feel nice, she thought hazily. It felt very nice, so much so, in fact, that when his fingers slid into her hair and his kiss deepened persuasively she didn't try to resist. Instead, she let him push her back into the seat and kissed him back, her lips parting eagerly and her arms winding around his neck, enjoying the tightness of his hands in her hair, holding her still, enjoying the taste of his mouth and the feel of his hard body pressing against hers. Oh, yes, it was very, very nice...

And then, somehow, nice wasn't the word. Something indefinable changed, banishing niceness, as their kisses became hungrier and more demanding. Lost in the pounding of her heart and the surge of sensation, Phoebe was half-intoxicated, half-scared by the heat flaring between them. It was darkly, secretly exciting, it was dangerously intoxicating, it was much, much more than nice, and it was out of control.

This isn't what they were supposed to be practising, the thought drifted elusively through Phoebe's mind, but she was too far gone to care, and it was only when Gib broke the kiss reluctantly that her brain cleared enough for her to think that it shouldn't have been like that at all. It should have been a chaste little peck on the lips not...not *that*.

For a long, long moment they could only stare at each other, both breathing raggedly. Gib's eyes were very blue, their mocking gleam for once entirely absent.

Phoebe's heart was jerking frantically. She couldn't have spoken if she had tried. She could only think how close he still was and how easy it would be for them to kiss again. The same knowledge was reflected in Gib's eyes, and the possibility shimmered tantalisingly in the air between them until he pushed himself abruptly away with a muttered exclamation.

Raking his fingers through his hair, he sat back in the driving seat. 'Well,' was all he could say.

'Well,' Phoebe agreed unsteadily.

'I'm glad we didn't do that in front of your parents.'

'God, yes,' she said, appalled at the very thought.

Gib ran a hand over his face and tried to calm his pounding heart. So much for kissing her like a friend! But how had he been supposed to know how warm and exciting and *right* she would feel? How hard it would be to let her go?

'Sorry, I got a bit carried away,' he said after a moment.

'It's all right.' Phoebe drew a shaky breath. She mustn't let him see how that kiss had affected her. 'Lucky we agreed that first rule of engagement, isn't it?' she said, trying for bright, breezy unconcern but failing utterly to carry it off.

Gib didn't look at her. 'Very lucky,' he agreed dryly.

There was another uncomfortable silence.

Phoebe concentrated on breathing—in, out, in, out—until the deafening boom of her pulse receded and she was able to risk a glance at Gib, hoping to see that he was in a similar state. Of course, that *would* be the moment he looked at her, and to her annoyance he looked exactly the same as he always did. The lurking laughter was back in the blue eyes, as if they had never held that disturbing expression, as if they had not stared wordlessly into hers barely moments ago. Phoebe could almost believe that she had imagined the way they looked then.

'You've got lipstick on the corner of your mouth,' she said, surprised at how steady her voice sounded.

He wiped casually at his mouth with his thumb. 'Better?'

'Yes.' She twisted the driving mirror round to face her and made an attempt to repair her lipstick, hoping he wouldn't notice how her hands were shaking.

He did, of course.

'Are you OK?' he asked in concern.

Phoebe snapped the top back on her lipstick and summoned a brilliant smile. 'I'm fine,' she lied. 'Absolutely fine.'

When they pulled up in the courtyard, a number of wedding guests were milling around by the great doorway to the castle, brushing cheeks and clashing hats together as they caught up with old acquaintances.

Gib switched off the engine.

The silence in the car was very loud. Phoebe didn't move. For the last few miles she had been so preoccupied with trying not to think about that shattering kiss, and failing utterly, that she had forgotten to worry about the wedding. Now the full realisation of just how completely she was going to lie to her family and her friends hit her and she sat staring rigidly ahead, consumed by panic.

'Phoebe?'

'This is crazy,' she said, swallowing nervously. 'I'm terrified of getting out of the car and meeting my own family and people I've known and loved for years!'

For answer, Gib got out of the car and put on his jacket. He wasn't going to think about that kiss any more. He was

Phoebe's friend, not her lover, and he was going to see her through this. Straightening his tie, he collected Phoebe's hat from the boot and came round to open her door so that she had little choice but to swing her legs out and stand up.

'Now, listen,' he said, setting the hat on her head, 'it's going to be great. You're going to keep everyone happy and save your own face by getting through this day with your head held high. I think you're brave and you're beautiful, so get in there and knock 'em dead.'

Phoebe looked into his face and saw that the blue eyes were serious again, just as they had been after he kissed her, and for a moment she felt quite giddy with the memory of what it had felt like.

'I'll be right beside you,' said Gib, and suddenly it was easy for her to square her shoulders and walk across towards the others.

'Smile,' he murmured under his breath, and Phoebe, who had been thinking about the light touch of his hand against her back, quickly pasted on a smile.

Just in time, too.

'Phoebe!'

Lara spotted her first, and came running over to hug her. 'You look fantastic!' she exclaimed.

Very aware of how many pairs of eyes had swivelled in her direction at the sound of her name, Phoebe hugged her sister back. 'Thank you,' she said. 'You don't look so bad yourself!'

'I don't have that extra glow that comes from being in love!' said Lara, turning to smile at Gib with frank curiosity. 'You must be Gib,' she said. 'We've all been dying to meet you!'

In spite of herself, Phoebe tensed and a faint colour tinged her cheeks. Her sister had never been anything but totally upfront. 'This is my sister, Lara,' she said, a little disturbed to find that she was jealous of the appreciative smile Gib gave Lara and the easy way they hugged as if they had known each other for ever.

They were so alike, she thought with a pang. Both completely irresponsible, both blessed with that carefree charm that carried them through life. It was obvious already that they were going to get on like a house on fire.

And yes, there was Lara tucking her hand through his arm as if she owned him. 'Come and meet Mum and Dad. I know they can't wait to see you.'

Gib held out his free hand to Phoebe as if it was the most natural thing in the world, and she was alarmed at how comforting she found his warm grip as Lara led them through the crowd, talking excitedly. In fact, she rather missed it when he released her to let her kiss her parents.

Her mother had obviously been on the lookout for them, as she dragged her father over to meet them halfway. Phoebe made the introductions nervously, but she needn't have worried. Gib judged the handshake with her father perfectly and let her mother kiss him enthusiastically.

'We're all *so* pleased you could come,' she said. 'Phoebe told us how busy you are at the moment.'

Fortunately there was no time for much more as the guests were starting to drift towards the room where the ceremony would be held, but Phoebe knew her mother would be planning a detailed interrogation later. She just hoped Gib would be able to keep up the pretence under *real* pressure!

CHAPTER SIX

WELL, if he couldn't, there wasn't much she could do about it now, she realised. A certain fatalism crept over Phoebe. It was too late to change her mind, and confess that she had invented herself a lover. That would really spoil everyone's day, hers most of all.

And she had to admit that Gib was doing a great job so far, being amusing without being too pushy. Her mother was obviously charmed, and Phoebe could tell that her father was impressed too, which surprised her. With his military background, she would have expected Gib to be exactly the type to set his moustache bristling.

Perhaps it was the suit? Gib certainly looked different today. Phoebe studied him surreptitiously as they made their way into a charming circular tower room. It was hard to believe this was the same irritating man who lazed around her kitchen all day. He looked broader, and more solid somehow, and while the suit might be conventional it would take more than that to make him look like the serious, sensible men her father approved of. His face was too mobile, his eyes too full of laughter, his mouth too ready to twitch into a smile. Even straight faced, there was a daredevil quality about him, a reckless edge that set him apart from all the other identically dressed men in the room. Phoebe was amazed that her father couldn't see it.

Lara was beckoning, and Phoebe and Gib edged past others in the row to sit next to her.

'Are you OK?' Lara whispered to her.

'I'm fine,' said Phoebe. 'Why?'

Lara nodded towards the front of the room where the groom was waiting nervously with his best man. 'I was afraid it might be difficult for you seeing Ben again,' she explained tentatively.

Ben. Phoebe stared at him, confused. He was the love of her life, her soul mate, the man she had dreamed of marrying as long as she could remember. Shouldn't she have noticed him as soon as she came in?

She shook her head a little as if to clear it. This was the moment she had been dreading for months. She couldn't believe that his presence hadn't even registered with her until Lara had pointed him out. Something was wrong somewhere, surely?

'No...no, I'm fine,' she said again to Lara, but she didn't feel fine really. She felt disorientated and unnerved, as if the one certain thing in her life had suddenly vanished.

'I'm not surprised,' Lara whispered back. 'I'd be fine if I had a man like Gib,' she added enviously. 'He's a bit gorgeous, isn't he?'

Involuntarily, Phoebe's eyes returned to Gib on her other side. He was talking to a couple on his left, and making the girl giggle. His head was turned away so that all she could see of his face was the lean line of his jaw, but her heart dipped and lurched anyway. She swallowed.

'He's all right,' she said, knowing that Lara wouldn't expect her to gush, but her sister only laughed.

'You're not fooling anyone, Phoebe! It's obvious you can't keep your eyes off him.'

After that, of course, Phoebe tried everything not to look at Gib again, but it was impossible when she was sitting right next to him. She tried to concentrate on the ceremony, but no matter how fiercely she stared ahead, her eyes kept drifting sideways, distracted by ridiculous details, like the length of his thigh, or the whiteness of his collar against his brown skin, or the laughter lines fanning the corner of his eyes, and the memory of how it had felt to kiss him flared along her veins all over again.

Once, Gib caught her looking at him. His eyebrow lifted in a faint question, obviously wondering why she kept staring at him. Terrified in case he thought that she had already forgotten their first rule of engagement and was reading more into that kiss than the practice it had been, Phoebe jerked her gaze away so abruptly that her dark hair swung beneath her hat.

At the front of the room, Ben and Lisa were about to exchange rings. Shifting upright in her chair, Phoebe's brows drew together in an effort of concentration. This was *Ben*, she reminded herself. Ben, whom she had loved and wanted as long as she could remember. It had felt so right and so comfortable to be with him, that she had never imagined that he would be making those vows to somebody else. She should be thinking about him, not about Gib and the way they had kissed in the car.

As Ben promised to love and to honour Lisa 'so long as we both shall live', Phoebe found herself remembering when he had told her that he would love *her* for ever. They had been so happy together for so long. Impossible not to think about the times they had shared or to feel a pang as she watched him slide the ring onto Lisa's finger.

But it was just a pang. She had dreaded this moment for months, expecting to feel a terrible, tearing pain in her heart, not this wistful sadness for the dreams she had nurtured for so long.

So this was it. Ben was married and there was no way to turn back the clock. No more pretending that he might, maybe, change his mind, or that somehow Lisa would disappear and everything would be the way it had been before. It was time to stop wishing and hoping and dreaming that things could be different, time to start accepting that she was on her own and making the best of it.

Phoebe wasn't aware of her expression changing, but she suddenly found her hand gathered into Gib's. He held it in a warm, strong clasp that was amazingly comforting, and although she didn't dare look at him, she didn't pull her hand away either. Instead, she watched Ben kiss Lisa and felt Gib's fingers tighten around her own and wondered how it was possible to feel aware of every tiny millimetre of his skin pressed against hers.

The string quartet in the bow-window struck up a suitably celebratory tune and the bride and groom turned, beaming, to their guests, who stirred in anticipation of the champagne to come.

It was over, thought Phoebe, and knew that she ought to feel relieved while feeling only a curious sense of deflation when Gib let go of her hand. People were standing up and pressing forward to congratulate the happy couple, but Lara was already nudging them towards the door.

'Might as well get a head start on the champagne,' she said. 'We can do the kissy-kissy bit later.'

They weren't the only ones to have the same idea, and the walled garden, romantically lined with herbaceous borders and climbing roses, was soon crowded with little groups of guests clutching flutes of champagne and, in the case of the women, trying not to get their heels stuck in the grass.

This was the big test, thought Phoebe, her stomach clenching with nerves again. Gib was going to be exposed to some pretty expert questioners, beginning with her mother, who was making a beeline for them. She would have to stick beside him until she could manoeuvre him over to Ben's tedious uncle, who could be relied upon not to talk about anything but sport, or if things got really bad to

Penelope and Derek's neighbour who was about ninety-seven and unlikely to cross-examine him on the detail of banking or be able to hear much about his supposedly passionate affair with Ben's ex-fiancée.

Not that you could ever tell with old ladies, of course. In Phoebe's experience they were much sharper than they let on, and could hear perfectly well when it suited them.

'Careful,' she said in an undertone as her mother rushed up. 'You're about to be exposed to advanced interrogation techniques. The SAS send soldiers to Mum for practice on withholding information if they're captured by enemy forces, and very few of them pass the test!'

Gib only sent her a glimmering smile before he turned to greet her mother. For a while they chatted easily, and Phoebe could see her mother's smile broadening as she ticked her way through a mental check-list, obviously awarding Gib full points.

Now they had moved on to discuss the wedding. 'It's a beautiful setting,' commented Gib, glancing around him at the battlemented walls with their mullioned windows, spectacular doors and worn old stone.

'Ye-es.' Her mother clearly wasn't convinced. 'Ben and Lisa were very keen on the idea of having the wedding at a castle, but personally I prefer a more traditional setting. I'm hoping Phoebe will choose to have a church wedding.'

'*Mu-um!*' Phoebe shot her an agonised look.

'Oh, don't worry, dear, I'm not hinting,' said her mother airily.

Not much! Phoebe thought bitterly.

'It's just that there's such a pretty church in the village, it seems a shame not to make the most of it.'

'Well, maybe we'll bear that in mind,' said Gib, unable to resist the opportunity of putting an arm around Phoebe. 'What do you think, darling?'

'I think it's too early to be talking about weddings,' she said tightly, acutely aware of his arm around her and of her mother's eyes bulging with interest at that carelessly dropped 'darling' and the even more casual way he had suggested that they were thinking about getting married.

'It's never too early to start making plans,' her mother said eagerly. 'Sometimes you have to book the church months in advance.'

'Yes, well, we're nowhere near that stage yet,' said Phoebe firmly. She tried to move out of the circle of Gib's arm but he held her against him without any apparent effort and, short of an undignified struggle, it looked as if she would have to stay where she was.

She could see her mother's mind already flickering to dresses and flowers and coordinating table arrangements, and hastened to nip the very idea of marriage in the bud before her mother got out a megaphone and announced it to the entire county.

'Now, hold on, Mum,' she said firmly. 'We haven't decided anything definite yet. Have we?' she added to Gib with a look that dared him to contradict her.

Gib met it blandly before turning back to her mother. 'I've asked Phoebe to marry me every day since we met,' he confided. 'She won't give me an answer one way or another, so I'm just going to have to keep on asking until she does.'

'Well, it's not like you to be coy, Phoebe!' said her mother, clearly thrilled.

'I'm not being coy,' snapped Phoebe, shooting a dagger glance at Gib. What had happened to the second rule? Stick to the story and keep it simple: it wasn't *that* hard to remember, was it? Still, in one way she was relieved at the rush of nervous irritation. It was much easier to be cross with Gib than to be burningly aware of him the way she had been since he kissed her. That kiss had seemed a good idea at the time, but Phoebe wasn't so sure now.

'I just think that marriage is an important step,' she told her mother. 'It's not something to rush into.'

'I'm the last person to suggest that it was,' her mother said, bridling. 'But if you know you've found the right person for you, there's no reason to wait, is there? And you don't want to wait too long, dear,' she added with a pointed look.

Phoebe rolled her eyes. 'Go ahead, Mum, why not say it? You're thirty-two, time's running out, beggars can't be choosers?'

'Don't be so silly, Phoebe,' her mother tutted. 'Having a man like Gib want to marry you hardly makes you a beggar! I'm sure there would be thousands of girls who'd be more than happy to have him if you don't want him.'

Gib laughed. 'I don't think so, but even if there were, it wouldn't make any difference to me.' His arm tightened around Phoebe and he smiled down into her indignant face. 'I knew the moment I saw Phoebe that she was the only one for me, and I'm just going to keep on asking her until she gives in.'

Of course, her mother was delighted. 'That's right, don't you listen to her, Gib dear,' she said, patting his arm. 'She's always been so stubborn! She just doesn't know what's good for her sometimes.'

'Mum, I think I see Penelope over there,' said Phoebe through gritted teeth. 'I want her to meet Gib. We'll catch up with you later.'

She practically dragged Gib away. Yes, this was excellent. She really *was* cross with him now. 'I don't know who I want to kill first,' she muttered furiously out of the side of her mouth like a gangster. 'You or my mother!'

Gib was all outraged innocence. 'Why, what have I done?'

'You know perfectly well! All that stuff about getting married!'

'I didn't say that we were getting married. I said that I wanted to marry you.'

'It's the same thing! Now everyone will be on at me to announce our engagement!'

'I was just being creative,' Gib objected. 'I made it obvious that I'm in love with you, and your mother will remember the fact that you were hesitating when you tell her you've dumped me. It'll make you look much better in the end. I thought that was what you wanted.'

'What I *wanted* was for you to do what I'm paying you to do!' snapped Phoebe, only to press the heel of her hand against her forehead a moment later. 'Sorry, sorry, I'm sorry,' she sighed. 'I'm just on edge. I shouldn't have snapped at you. I know you're doing me a favour by coming along today.'

It was Gib's turn to feel guilty. 'No, it's my fault,' he apologised. 'I just thought it would be more convincing if I seemed to be thinking about marriage.'

'Maybe you're right.' Phoebe helped herself to a glass of champagne from a passing waiter and took a gulp. She would need it to get through today! 'We may as well go with the idea that we're getting married now,' she went on, resigned. 'After all, if we can fool Mum, we can fool anyone, and she's bound to tell everyone that we are engaged anyway. She's probably been on to the vicar already, checking out which Saturdays are free!'

Spotting Ben's mother bearing down on them, she gave Gib a nudge. 'Careful now, this is Penelope.'

'Hello, darling.' Penelope enveloped her in a warm embrace before turning with undisguised interest. 'So this is

Gib? We're so glad you could come,' she told him, giving him a hug for good measure. 'We were all thrilled when Sheila told us that Phoebe had met a gorgeous man! She seemed to think it sounded quite serious?'

She looked hopefully between them, and Phoebe bowed to the inevitable.

'Well, we're thinking about following Ben and Lisa's example,' she said. Snuggling against Gib in a suitably besotted pose, she felt his arm close around her with disturbing speed.

Penelope clapped her hands together. 'Oh, that's marvellous news! Your mother must be thrilled! She's been so worried about you.'

'It's just maybe at the moment,' Phoebe stressed. 'We haven't made any definite plans yet,' she hurried on before Gib could jump in and invent a date. She wouldn't put it past him. Left to his own devices, he would no doubt be dressing her up in a meringue and saddling her with a string of little bridesmaids in matching taffeta dresses!

Distracted by someone waving at her behind Phoebe's shoulder, Penelope clicked her tongue in frustration. 'Look, I must go. It's hopeless trying to talk to anyone at this stage, but we'll have a proper chat later tonight. It's just family and close friends staying, and we're all dying for the chance to get to know you properly,' she added, beaming at Gib.

'Oh, Gib won't be here,' Phoebe put in quickly, straightening out of his hold. She had had enough of being winsome. 'He's got to get back to London tonight. In fact, we were just saying he should get the receptionist to book him a taxi, weren't we, Gib?'

'We couldn't talk about anything else,' he agreed.

'Oh, but why?' cried Penelope, looking from one to the other in disappointment and missing the irony in Gib's tone.

Phoebe nudged Gib. 'An important business meeting, I'm afraid,' he said obediently.

'Not on a Sunday, surely?'

'It's first thing on Monday. In Switzerland,' Phoebe added with an edge of desperation. 'So he'll have to fly there tomorrow.'

'Still, it's only a couple of hours to London from here, so even if the flight's at lunchtime, you'd have plenty of time to catch the plane,' Penelope pointed out.

'That's true,' said Gib slowly.

Phoebe stared meaningfully at him. 'What about all the preparation you've got to do?'

'I've done most of that,' he told her with an easy smile. 'I just need to read through a report, and I could do that on the flight.'

'Oh, *do* stay!' Penelope implored him. 'I'm sure it would mean a lot to Phoebe if you were here tonight, and we all want a chance to meet you properly. It's not as if we can't squeeze you in, either,' she added with a twinkling look. 'Phoebe's got a huge room over in the tower, and she'll be rattling around in it all on her own. You'd much rather Gib was with you, wouldn't you, Phoebe?'

What could she say? Phoebe gritted her teeth and managed a smile. 'I just don't want to affect Gib's work. I know he's under a lot of pressure at the moment,' she added with a look that she hoped would remind Gib just what work he was supposed to be doing today.

'You're more important than work,' said Gib, ignoring it completely.

Penelope beamed at him, delighted. 'So you'll stay tonight?'

'Yes, I'd like to. Thanks.'

'Wonderful! Oh, there's Ben.' His mother waved him

over excitedly. 'Look who's here,' she told him, 'and with the most marvellous news!'

Ben had become separated from his bride somewhere in the crowd, so he had to face Phoebe unsupported while his mother bustled happily off. He looked a bit uncomfortable—as well he might, thought Gib sourly as he watched the other man plant an awkward kiss on Phoebe's cheek.

'Thank you for coming,' he told her. 'I hoped you would.'

'Of course I came,' said Phoebe, feeling very poignant as she returned his kiss. Once they had been everything to each other, and now Ben couldn't quite meet her eyes. 'I couldn't miss your wedding.'

Gib watched her narrowly. She was smiling, but he thought he could see a strained look around her eyes and a sadness in her smile. He wanted to punch Ben on the nose and gather her into his arms and make everything better. As it was, all he could do was stand there and watch her being brave.

'I hope you and Lisa will be very happy,' she was saying to Ben. 'I'm sure you will.'

'Thank you,' said Ben, which Gib thought was a bit inadequate. He could at least have acknowledged what a difficult moment this was for Phoebe, or said how much he appreciated her efforts to pretend that everything was absolutely fine and that he hadn't broken her heart.

As it was, the other man looked distinctly ill at ease. Gib studied him, unimpressed. What did Phoebe see in him? He looked pleasant enough, but dull, Gib decided dismissively. Not enough character in his face to deal with Phoebe. She needed someone with a bit more fire to appreciate her.

'This is Gib,' Phoebe introduced him awkwardly, and the two men shook hands without any noticeable enthusiasm.

'Congratulations,' said Gib.

There was a tiny pause. Phoebe kept her smile pinned to

her face and tucked her hand in Gib's arm. 'Congratulate us, too, Ben. Gib and I are thinking about getting married.'

'Really?' Ben looked taken aback for a moment.

Gib could practically see the relief warring with surprise and a touch of chagrin in his face. No doubt Phoebe was supposed to stay broken-hearted for ever, not find someone else.

'That's great news,' Ben recovered, kissing Phoebe again. 'Congratulations, Phoebe.' He looked warily at Gib. 'You're a lucky man.'

'I know,' said Gib discouragingly.

The moment Ben had moved on to greet other well-wishers, Phoebe rounded on Gib. 'Did you have to be quite so unfriendly?' she demanded. She had never seen him behave like that before. For a moment there he had looked quite grim. 'This is Ben's wedding day. You're supposed to be nice to him!'

'You can't expect me to fawn all over the man who hurt the woman I love,' said Gib with a slight edge.

'I don't think there's any need to take your role that seriously! Ben looked as if he were afraid you were about to punch him.'

'It might have livened him up a bit,' Gib beckoned a waiter over and exchanged his empty glass for a full one. 'What do you see in that guy, anyway? He's not exactly a ball of fire, is he?'

'Ben is a very nice man,' said Phoebe defensively. 'He's kind and honest and...and reliable—unlike some people I could mention! Why on earth did you tell Penelope you would spend the night when we had already agreed you would go back to London?'

'Because no self-respecting fiancé would leave you on your own the very night you most need support. Even if you were madly in love with me, it would be hard for you to see Ben getting married, and Penelope obviously knows that. If I'd gone back to London making some lame excuse about flying to Switzerland on Monday it really would have looked suspicious.'

Gib told himself that he was only trying to offer her support. He did think it would be easier for Phoebe if she had a friend with her tonight. He had hated the idea of getting on a train and leaving her to cope on her own. She might not want him, but he thought that she would need someone, and it might as well be him. The fact that he had leapt at the opportunity of staying had absolutely nothing to do with knowing that this might be the only chance he would have to get this close to her.

Of course not.

Phoebe eyed him with some frustration. It *sounded* reasonable enough, and the only argument she could really come up with was that he wasn't doing as he was told, which would come across as a bit childish.

Feeling rattled, she sipped edgily at her champagne. How could she tell Gib that she was far more bothered by the prospect of spending the whole night with him than she had been about coming face to face with Ben? She wasn't even sure that she was ready to admit it to herself.

'It'll certainly look suspicious if you leave now!' she said crossly. 'Then Penelope really would think we'd had a row. I suppose we'll just have to make the best of it.'

Suppressing a sigh, she looked around her, and forced a smile as she caught the eye of an old friend of Ben's family. 'We'd better circulate. From now on, could you *please* not introduce any more variations on the story we agreed? If we get separated, say as little as possible, and when you do, stick to neutral topics. Talk about cricket or something.'

Gib snapped into a mock salute. 'Whatever you say, boss.'

* * *

Phoebe picked up a plate and joined the queue for the buffet. Round tables had been set out where the guests could sit down or move around informally, and she looked around as casually as she could, trying to spot Gib, who had drifted from her side in far too relaxed a fashion. She didn't trust him now.

A girl who had known her when she was going out with Ben was standing next to her, rabbiting on about some skiing holiday, but Phoebe was too busy wondering where Gib was and what he was saying to concentrate. She nodded and put in an occasional 'yes' or an 'oh, really?' while her eyes scanned the crowd with increasing nervousness.

There he was! Phoebe's gaze did a double take and swung back to where she had spotted Gib sitting at a table with—oh, God!—her parents and Lara, and they all seemed to be getting on famously.

Typical, she fumed. There must be a hundred strangers here Gib could have picked to sit and make small talk with, but no! He had to choose the three people who were most likely to interrogate him closely and pick up on any weaknesses in their story!

Hastily grabbing a couple of vol-au-vents and a chicken leg, Phoebe muttered an excuse and, leaving Vanessa still yapping about drag lifts and chalet girls, fought her way across the room towards him to try and stop him before he embellished any more aspects of their supposed relationship. It took ages, though, as people kept hailing her, all delighted to see her again and eager to tell her how much they liked Gib.

He was so charming, they told her.

So funny.

So interesting.

'So attractive!' sighed more than one girl enviously. 'You are lucky, Phoebe.'

Hadn't she told Gib very clearly to stick to neutral topics? It didn't sound as if he had listened to a word she had said, Phoebe thought furiously. Far from lurking quietly on the sidelines talking about the weather or the lack of hold-ups on the motorway, he had obviously been in the thick of things, circulating breezily and talking to everyone who knew her!

Smile fixed, she agreed for the umpteenth time that Gib was wonderful and struggled on through the tables to her family.

'Ah, there you are!' her mother waved gaily and Gib turned quickly to see Phoebe suck in her breath to squeeze in between two chairs, holding her plate high to clear the heads. She looked hot and flustered, and beneath her hat he could see that her jaw was gritted and her smile decidedly brittle.

He got to his feet and pulled out a chair for her to sit down beside him. 'I lost you,' he said, taking the plate from her as a precautionary measure. Now that she was close, he could see that her eyes were flashing an unmistakably irate message, and he didn't want vol-au-vents all down his suit. 'I was hoping you'd find me eventually.'

'Gib's been keeping us entertained,' Lara told Phoebe, who was half tempted to refuse to sit next to Gib but couldn't think of a reason that wouldn't make her look childish.

'So I saw,' she said rather grimly instead as she sat down in the chair he still held.

'He's been telling us all about how you met,' Lara went on. 'You never told us it was quite that romantic, Phoebe!'

Romantic? What had he been telling them? Phoebe looked at Gib with foreboding, which only deepened when she saw his eyes dancing. She wished they wouldn't *do* that. It only made her more nervous.

'I didn't tell them *everything*,' he assured her, straight faced, and to Phoebe's consternation her family laughed merrily, as if he had already told them more than enough.

'Perhaps I should know what he *did* tell you,' she said, holding on to her temper with difficulty.

'He said it was a very easy mistake to make.'

'And that it was wonderful to meet someone without any preconceptions about him.'

'Yes, and that one of the reasons he loves you is that you just don't care what he does.'

They beamed at her.

Phoebe looked at Gib. 'Is that right?' she said, unable to think of anything else, other than the obvious option which was that she had no idea what any of them were talking about.

'I didn't tell them what an idiot you felt when you realised that I was the president of the bank and not the layabout you thought I was when you were trying to get an interview.' Gib's eyes gleamed with appreciation as he saw her struggling to come to terms with the sheer nerve of him. 'You were expecting the president to be someone a lot more formidable, weren't you, darling?'

Somehow Phoebe managed to stretch her mouth into a ghastly smile. 'It was quite a surprise,' she said.

'I must say, darling,' said her father, 'you might have told us what Gib did. You just told your mother he worked for a bank, as if he was some teller. I felt a complete fool when I realised!'

'It sounds wonderful, too,' said Lara, equally impressed. 'It's not as if an ethical bank is something to be ashamed of. Not like…I don't know…being an arms dealer or a politician or something.'

Gib put a consoling arm around Phoebe's shoulders. 'But that's exactly what I love about Phoebe. She just doesn't care what I do or how much money I have.' He smiled teasingly into her eyes. 'You love me for what I am, don't you, bunni—' He pretended to catch himself up guiltily. 'Don't you, *honey*?'

'You know exactly how much I love you,' she said, meeting his gaze directly, and he laughed and released her.

'What did you feel when you found out that Gib was actually the president?' Lara asked eagerly. 'You must have felt a bit stupid, didn't you?'

'To tell you the truth,' said Phoebe, a decidedly crisp edge to her voice, 'I didn't believe a word of it!'

'*President*!' she bit out the moment the door to their bedroom closed behind them. The guests had begun to drift away from the reception and they had a couple of hours to recover before they had to go back down for dinner and dancing. 'Couldn't you have chosen something a bit more likely, like Chancellor of the Exchequer or Director General of the United Nations?'

'I always fancied myself running a bank,' said Gib by way of an excuse.

'Why stop at a bank? Why not pretend you were President of the United States?'

'They would have known that wasn't true.'

Phoebe ground her teeth at the reasonableness of his tone. 'Whereas, it's so believable that you should be running your own bank?'

'They did believe me, didn't they?' he replied, unanswerably.

'I thought we agreed that you would stick to our story?' she accused him, wrenching off her hat. She had a massive tension headache, and the champagne she had been reduced to gulping to cope with the stress of Gib's increasingly ridiculous lies hadn't helped any.

'No more variations, we said. Now I'm not only supposed to be engaged to you and spending the night with you, I'm an accessory to illegal impersonation! Have you thought what will happen if J.G. Grieve hears that you've been impersonating him?'

'I don't think that's very likely,' said Gib soothingly. He hadn't been able to resist the temptation to tease Phoebe a little by elaborating on the basic outlines they had agreed. 'How's he going to know what goes on at an obscure English wedding?'

'These people have lawyers, you know,' said Phoebe with a dark look. 'If he sues you, you needn't think I'm going to support you. God, what a day!' she sighed, sinking down onto the edge of the vast four-poster bed and easing off her high-heeled shoes so that she could rub her sore feet.

Flopping back across the bed, she stared tensely up at the embroidered canopy. 'And we've still got tonight to get through!'

CHAPTER SEVEN

'OH, COME on, it hasn't been that bad.' Gib loosened his tie with a sigh of relief as he wandered around the room, inspecting the wood panelling and the magnificent stone fireplace.

'Not for you, maybe,' she grumbled, 'but it's been a nightmare for me, not knowing what ridiculous story you're going to make up next, and just waiting for someone to turn round and spot that you're here under false pretences. I'm going to feel great when that happens, aren't I?'

'Relax,' he said soothingly. 'Everything's fine. You're just tired. What you need is a nice bath.'

Without waiting for her to reply, he disappeared through a door in the panelling, and the next minute Phoebe heard the sound of water gushing into the bath. 'I'll bring you a drink, and you can unwind,' he shouted over the noise. 'You'll feel much better then.'

Phoebe was tempted to tell him that she would be the judge of what would make her feel better, but a wonderful fragrance of foaming bubbles was drifting through into the bedroom and, when it came down to it, the thought of a long hot soak with a long cool drink was immensely appealing. No point in cutting off her nose to spite her face.

So she leant back against the pillows and let Gib run the bath for her. 'Your bath awaits, madam,' he said grandly at last, holding the door open with a flourish.

The bathroom turned out to be almost as impressive as the bedroom. It was panelled throughout, apart from a deep stone window, just wide enough to stick your bow and arrow through. A stuffed bear's head was fixed to the wall. There was a selection of imposing antique chests and, in the middle, a vast claw-footed tub, filled to the brim with scented foam. Averting her eyes from the bear, Phoebe saw that Gib had put fluffy towels conveniently to hand on a wooden chair and set out the tempting array of luxurious freebies provided by the hotel along the side of the bath.

'Thank you,' she muttered, touched in spite of herself by the trouble he had taken.

He smiled at her, that unsettling, daredevil grin that never failed to make her nerves jump alarmingly. 'It's my way of saying I'm sorry,' he said disarmingly. 'I didn't mean to wind you up today.'

'That's OK,' Phoebe said awkwardly, feeling as if the wind had been rather taken out of her sails.

'Now, what would you like to drink?'

'Really, you don't need to—'

'I'll add it to my expenses if that will make you feel better,' Gib offered.

Phoebe wasn't sure whether being reminded that he was only doing his job made her feel better or worse, but decided in the end that the most dignified course of action would be to relent.

'Something long and cold would be wonderful,' she said.

'You get in,' said Gib. 'I'll be back in a minute.'

When he had gone, Phoebe got undressed and stepped into the bath. It was enormous, more of a swimming pool than a bath, and she lay back with a luxurious sigh, immersing herself completely beneath the scented water. Maybe Gib wasn't so bad after all, she thought as she emerged, blowing bubbles out of her mouth, and smoothing the wet hair back from her face.

Perhaps she *had* been overreacting. Gib was right, everyone had accepted him without question and there had been no need for her to be so nervous. She had been wound up about the whole situation, she realised, but in the end it hadn't been the wedding or meeting Ben or fooling her family that had made her nervous. It had been Gib himself, Gib with his glinting, unsettling smile, and his warm hand on her back.

You're beautiful and you're brave, he had told her, and it had been the look in his eyes she had been thinking about when she watched Ben getting married, not the ache in her heart. The look in his eyes and touch of his mouth and the feel of his palm against her cheek.

It would have been much easier if he hadn't kissed her. Really, there had been no need for it, Phoebe scolded herself. If she'd thought, it would have been obvious that no one would expect them to kiss like that in the middle of Ben's wedding. She should have told Gib that it was a stupid idea and pushed him firmly away.

Instead of which she had wrapped her arms around him and pulled him closer and kissed him back. A wave of heat that had nothing whatsoever to do with the bath tingled through her as she remembered how it had felt, and when a sharp knock fell on the door her heart jerked painfully.

'I've got a long, cold G&T here for you,' came Gib's voice. 'If I promise to keep my eyes closed, shall I bring it in to you?'

'Just a minute,' she said on a gasp as she slid decorously beneath the deep layer of bubbles. 'OK,' she called.

Gib handed her the drink with a flourish. It looked wonderful, satisfyingly full of chinking ice cubes, a slice of lime bobbing merrily as the tonic fizzed. Her fingers touched his as she took the glass from him. It was so cold that condensation was trickling down the side, making it hard to hold.

That was the reason Phoebe gave herself for the unsteadiness of her grasp anyway. Nothing whatsoever to do with the warmth of Gib's hand.

'Got it?'

'Yes. Thanks,' she added, and then made another mistake of looking up into his face.

He was studying her with appreciative blue eyes, taking in her bare shoulders rising out of the foam. Her hair was slicked back from her face, unconsciously emphasising her bone structure, and the dark lashes were wet and spiky around the green eyes.

'My pleasure,' he said, smiling.

To her fury, Phoebe felt a blush rising up her throat and seeping into her cheeks. 'I thought you were going to keep your eyes closed?' she said as severely as she could.

'I was afraid I would drop your drink if I did that,' said Gib. 'I'll close them now.'

Shutting them virtuously, he proceeded to make a big show of bumping into things on his way out of the bathroom.

'Idiot!' sighed Phoebe, shaking her head, but in spite of herself she was smiling.

She didn't know whether it was the bath or the gin that did the trick, but she was feeling a million times better when she emerged from the bathroom some time later to find Gib stretched out on the four-poster bed.

He had loosened the shirt at his neck and rolled up his sleeves and was lying with his hands behind his head. He looked lean and lazy, and somehow disturbing, and Phoebe's nerves, which had calmed down while she was in the bath, instantly sprang to the alert again at the sight of him.

Gib turned his head as she came out of the bathroom, wrapped in a towelling robe supplied by the hotel, her skin pink and glowing. There was a tiny pause.

'Better?' he asked after a moment.

'Yes, thank you,' said Phoebe stiffly. She felt ridiculously shy of him again all of a sudden. 'You can have the bathroom now if you want.'

'I'll have a shower in a bit.' He yawned, and suddenly it was as if that moment of tension had never been. 'I'm just enjoying this bed. It's very comfortable. You should try it,' he added, patting the cover beside him and pulling up some pillows invitingly.

Phoebe hesitated. Every instinct told her that climbing into bed next to Gib was asking for trouble, but it was too soon to get changed and the only other place to sit was a wooden chair which was no doubt authentic but which didn't look at all comfortable.

And anyway, she wasn't getting *into* bed with him, she rationalised. She was just getting *onto* it, which was a different matter entirely. Gib just happened to be sitting there as well. What could possibly be awkward about that?

So she clambered up beside him, trying not to expose too much leg beneath the towelling robe. The bed was huge and, as Gib had said, very comfortable. Phoebe leant back against the pillows with a sigh. After the accumulated tensions of the day, it was good to relax for a moment.

'I've always wanted to sleep in a bed like this,' said Gib, breaking the silence that was really quite companionable.

Phoebe, who had been almost asleep, jerked back to attention. It was going to be bad enough getting through the rest of the evening without the prospect of actually getting into bed with Gib to cope with!

'I hope you're not planning on sleeping in one tonight!'

'Where else am I going to sleep?' he asked in a mock injured tone. 'That floor is made of stone!'

Phoebe looked around the room, which was authentically furnished with an austere wooden chair and absolutely no modern innovations like a sofa or even an armchair where she could reasonably expect Gib to make himself comfortable. There were good reasons why they didn't live in the Middle Ages any more.

She sighed inwardly. She supposed the idea of getting married in a castle had seemed very romantic to Ben and Lisa but, when all was said and done, there was nothing wrong with a nice, characterless motel room. Preferably with twin beds.

'You don't think sharing a bed might be a bit intimate given that we're not...that we don't...?' Phoebe trailed off uncomfortably.

'I won't forget you're my boss if that's what you're worried about,' said Gib with one of those lurking smiles of his.

'That's good coming from someone who's spent the entire day forgetting that I'm boss!' she retorted, nettled by his refusal to take the situation seriously.

'Oh, that's a bit of an exaggeration, isn't it?'

'We agreed that you would stick to the story and keep it simple. The second rule of engagement, if you remember? I'm not sure how claiming to be president of an international bank was keeping it simple!'

Gib looked at her and wondered if she had any idea how desirable she looked with her damp, dark hair and her vivid face and her eyes bright and green with irritation.

'I stuck to the important thing, which is that I'm in love with you,' he pointed out. 'You can't get simpler than that. I've kept my side of the bargain, haven't I?' he challenged her.

Phoebe dropped her eyes first. She couldn't deny that he had been very convincing. He was certainly a much better actor than her.

'Yes,' she acknowledged.

'And I said I was sorry,' Gib reminded her, his eyes dancing. 'And I ran you a bath. *And* I bought you a gin and tonic!'

'On expenses!'

'It's the thought that counts,' he said virtuously. 'I'm trying to do my job as best I can, and if you were a caring employer, you wouldn't even *consider* making me sleep on a stone floor! Besides,' he said, patting the expanse of cover between them, 'this bed could sleep a family of six easily! And we can always put a pillow down the middle if you don't think you'll be able to keep your hands off me otherwise,' he added in what Phoebe considered was a spirit of sheer provocation.

'I don't think *that* will a problem!' she said in a tart voice.

'And I'll keep my hands off you,' he promised, which somehow didn't make her feel quite as good as it should have done.

'Please make sure you do!'

'So, can I sleep with you tonight?' asked Gib. 'I know it won't mean anything and it won't be setting a precedent. See,' he told her, grinning. 'I haven't forgotten that first rule of engagement, either!'

'Oh, all right,' said Phoebe, who couldn't be bothered to argue any longer. 'But I don't want to hear any more stupid stories this evening,' she warned him, 'or you'll be sleeping on the floor after all. I don't care how cold it is!'

They only had a couple of hours before they had to return for dinner and dancing but, to Phoebe, lying next to Gib on that big bed, it was quite long enough. It wasn't that he was restless or said anything she could object to, and the bed was so wide that there was no danger of brushing against him accidentally.

It was just that whenever she closed her eyes all she could see was his smile dancing behind her eyelids, and the moment she snapped them open, they would stray sideways to where he lay beside her, managing to fill all the available space with the sheer force of his personality even when he was at his most lazy and relaxed.

All in all, it was a relief when Gib went off to have a shower. Phoebe took the opportunity to scramble off the bed and change into the dress she had brought specially for that evening. It was very simple, a slim sheath the colour of a tropical lagoon that brought out the green in her eyes and left her shoulders bare. Phoebe had worried that it might be a little too dramatic for her to carry off, but Kate and Bella had been unanimous in their approval.

'It's perfect! No one would ever think you were broken-hearted in a dress like that!'

'That,' Kate had agreed, 'is a dress worn by a woman in control of her life.'

There was irony for you, thought Phoebe, wondering what to do with her hair. She *never* felt in control when Gib was around.

The bathroom door opened and Gib came out, a towel wrapped around his hips. He whistled when he saw her, and she span round, the breath drying in her throat. His blonde hair was dark and damp from the shower, and she couldn't help noticing how lean and brown and compactly muscled his body was. Quickly, she turned back to the mirror where she was fixing slides into her hair.

'I hope you're not planning to go like that,' she said, horrified by the shake in her voice.

'I wish I could.' Gib contemplated his suit without enthusiasm. 'I suppose I'll have to put that on again. I've got nothing else to wear, and before you say it, yes, I know it's my fault! I hate wearing suits,' he grumbled as he retrieved his shirt from the hanger. 'I can't stand the feel of a tie around my neck.'

'I'm surprised you're not used to it, running that bank of yours,' said Phoebe, taking refuge in sarcasm to distract herself from view of his smooth brown back in the mirror.

He glanced at her over his shoulder with a glimmering smile. 'Maybe mine's a different kind of bank where you don't have to dress like a dummy all day!'

'That sounds about as likely as you being president,' she said, mumbling through the clips she was holding in her mouth while she secured her hair in place. 'Don't you want your staff to look professional?'

'In my bank we're more concerned with what people do than how they look,' Gib informed her loftily.

Phoebe smoothed the last hair into place. 'Right,' she said, her voice laced with irony. 'I'm sure it's a great success! Now look, can you please keep off the subject of banks this evening? We don't want to be rumbled now we've got this far. I'd appreciate it if you'd remember what you're here to do!'

'To show everyone how in love with you I am?'

'Yes,' she said, not quite able to meet his eyes directly. She busied herself looking for the necklace Bella had insisted on lending her instead.

'That shouldn't be a problem with the way you look tonight,' said Gib. 'You look sensational!'

Startled, Phoebe's eyes flew involuntarily to meet his in the mirror. He was smiling, obviously joking, but there had been something in his voice that made her suddenly, acutely, aware of him, of the breadth of his shoulders and the long, muscled legs and the easy way he moved.

'There's no need to start pretending yet,' she said, tearing her gaze away with an uncertain laugh. 'There's nobody else here.'

'I know,' said Gib.

The air leaked out of Phoebe's lungs, and in the taut

silence that followed, she fumbled around on the chest of drawers for her jewellery. She was intensely relieved when Gib went back into the bathroom. He reappeared wearing trousers, which was something, she thought. Shrugging on his shirt, he looped the tie round his neck and knotted it loosely.

The casual intimacy of dressing threw Phoebe completely. She was trying to fasten Bella's spectacular necklace, and Gib's presence only made her fingers even clumsier at the fiddly catch, until she muttered under her breath in frustration.

'Here, let me have a go,' he offered, having watched her struggling for a few moments.

It would be childish to refuse, Phoebe decided. She bent her head, tensing as Gib moved towards her and brushed her hair gently out of the way. The graze of his fingers against her neck made her shiver involuntarily, and she stood mouse-still as he fastened the necklace and smoothed it into place.

There it was done. But instead of stepping back with the flip comment she half expected, Gib let his hands rest for a moment on the curve of her shoulders. Slowly, almost unwillingly, Phoebe lifted her head and met his eyes, blue and serious, in the mirror. They had held the same expression after he had kissed her in the car and her heart began to slam in her chest. She couldn't move, could just stand there feeling the warmth of his hands on her skin, while an answering heat uncoiled inside her at an alarming rate.

With an enormous effort, she moistened her lips. 'We'd better finish getting ready,' she managed, appalled at the huskiness of her voice. Clearing her throat, she tried again. 'We'll be late.'

Gib dropped his hands and stepped back. 'We don't want that,' he agreed dryly. 'They might think that two people as much in love as we are have got better things to do alone here with a four-poster bed than get dressed up in uncomfortable clothes to spend an evening making more small talk!'

'Making small talk was part of the deal,' she reminded him, still not quite as steadily as she would have liked.

'Ah, yes, the deal, we mustn't forget that!'

They walked across the courtyard from their tower in silence. Phoebe was desperately aware of Gib, close beside her but not touching. There was a strange, jittery feeling just below her skin, and her stomach was looping and churning in a way that made her wish she could go back to simply worrying about whether anyone would spot that Gib wasn't really a banker and wasn't really her lover. That had seemed bad enough at the time, but this new consciousness of Gib was much, much worse, this was a whole new level of nervousness and Phoebe didn't like it at all.

For dinner the remaining guests were divided up among five round tables. Phoebe and Gib were sitting with Lara, who spent most of her time moaning about her parents and their unreasonable behaviour in disapproving of her latest boyfriend.

'He's got his own band,' Lara confided. 'Some guy in the music business came to listen to one of their gigs, and he thinks they've got a great future. They're going to London soon to make a recording, not that that cuts any ice with Mum and Dad! They're so conventional,' she grumbled. 'They can't bear the fact that Jed lives in a squat. They don't understand that he's an artist. He'd be stifled in an ordinary environment. That's why he didn't get an invitation to come to the wedding, even though we've been going out for *weeks* now! They want me to find someone like Gib, with a proper job.'

Involuntarily, Phoebe glanced at Gib. 'Nice to know that

someone appreciates how hard I work,' he murmured provocatively.

'Oh, they think you're great,' said Lara, missing the irony. 'Mum can't wait for you to spend the weekend so she can interrogate you properly! You'd better brace yourself, Phoebe. She's bound to get out the baby photographs and tell Gib about the time you took your knickers off in the middle of their sherry party.'

'I was only three,' said Phoebe as Gib raised an enquiring eyebrow.

'At least Jed is spared that,' said Lara, cheering up at the realisation. 'You should have been a rebel, Gib, then they wouldn't be so keen on inviting you to stay.'

Oh, dear, Phoebe sighed inwardly. She should have foreseen that her mother would start planning intimate family get-togethers. Now she would have to think up endless excuses as to why they couldn't go down for the weekend until their supposedly perfect relationship had had time to fall apart convincingly.

But how could she think when Gib was sitting next to her, and she was aware of every time he lifted his glass or gestured, every time he turned his head towards her and his smile burned at the edge of her vision. Her shoulders were still tingling where his hands had rested. The image of how he had looked when he came out of the bathroom with his powerful shoulders and his bare, brown chest and his straight, strong legs shimmered in front of Phoebe's eyes no matter how hard she tried to blink it away so that she could see the medallions of lamb on her plate.

Not that she could eat, anyway. She pushed the food distractedly around her plate and tried to decide whether she longed for the evening to end, or dreaded, because it would mean being alone with Gib again.

And that bed.

Phoebe gulped at her wine. She must stop thinking about Gib like this! Stop thinking about his mouth and his hands and his lean, hard body. If Kate and Bella were here, she was sure they would tell her that she was simply projecting her feelings for Ben onto Gib because he was handy.

Yes, that was all it was. She was trying to turn him into some substitute for Ben. Ridiculous, really. So all she had to do was concentrate on Ben and maybe her pounding pulse would calm down and the twitchy feeling would fade and the tight knot in her stomach would relax.

It was hard to think about Ben when she couldn't see him, but once the pudding had been removed, the music struck up and bride and groom took to the little dance floor to much sentimental sighing from the other guests. This gave Phoebe the opportunity she needed, and she turned her chair like many of the other guests so that she could watch Ben holding Lisa close. He looked very contented, she thought. Not the most exciting man in the world, perhaps, but contented.

Where had *that* thought come from? Phoebe caught herself up with a frown. She had never found Ben at all dull before, so there was no reason to start thinking it now, just because he was so different from Gib, Gib with his gleaming blue eyes and his unsettling smile and his ability to make her furious and want to laugh at the same time.

Turning her back deliberately on him, she made herself focus on Ben, and after a while, as people were starting to move around, Gib got up and went over to talk to her parents. Phoebe was still staring determinedly at the dance floor, but she might as well have been looking straight at him, so acutely was she aware of every move he made. She was watching Ben, but all her senses were attuned to Gib as he sat down next to her parents. She didn't need to see him to know that his alert, mobile face was lit with laughter, or that his hands were gesticulating as he talked.

'Phoebe!'

She started as her mother came to take Gib's empty chair. 'Phoebe,' she demanded in an urgent undertone, 'what on earth do you think you are doing?'

From the other side of the room, Gib saw Phoebe stiffen and her chin came up at a combative angle. He didn't know what her mother was saying to her, but it obviously wasn't going down at all well. Phoebe's face was flushed and there was a dangerous glitter to her eyes.

Murmuring an excuse, he got to his feet and went over. 'Come on, Phoebe,' he said as he held out his hand. 'Let's dance.'

Phoebe went without a word. She let him pull her into his arms and was glad of the excuse to hide her face in his throat. She felt ridiculously shaky all of a sudden. Gib held her tightly in a way that was at once comforting and disturbing. She was very aware of the hardness of his body, of the masculine scent of his skin, of the warmth of his hands through the silky material of her dress.

Gib could feel her trembling, and his expression was wry. Seeing Ben dancing with his new bride must have been the final straw for her today, and whatever her mother had been saying to her obviously hadn't helped. Pulling her onto the dance floor had been an instinctive act to offer her an escape, but he hadn't counted on how hard it would be for him. She was so warm and so slender, and her dress slipped distractingly over her skin beneath his hands. He could smell her perfume and feel her soft breath and the tickle of her eyelashes against his throat, the silky hair beneath his cheek.

A friend, he reminded himself. That was all he was supposed to be. A friend was what Phoebe needed right now, and he should be thinking about how much she was hurting rather than about how much he would like to take her back to that four-poster bed and make her forget all about Ben, and make her smile again.

In the meantime, she needed him to carry on the pretence, Gib told himself. If nothing else, it was a pretext to pull her closer, to kiss her ear and smooth his hand down her spine, feeling the dress shift tantalisingly over her bare skin.

It was just part of the act, after all. If he was really her lover, he wouldn't want to let her go when the music stopped, would he? He wouldn't want to take her back to the table and share her with everybody else. He would take her out into the summer night where he could kiss her properly in the darkness.

Almost without thinking, he found himself steering Phoebe out through the open French windows and onto the terrace. She didn't resist, but when they came to a halt at last in the shadows, she pulled back to look at him, her eyes huge and dark in her pale face.

'Thank you for that,' she said with a crooked smile. 'Mum and I were about to come to blows!'

Gib made himself let her go. 'What was she saying to you?'

'Oh, she came over to tick me off for ignoring you.' The shadows hid the flush that crept up Phoebe's cheeks as she remembered what her mother had said. She had been furious with Phoebe for sitting and mooning openly over Ben, as she thought.

'You told us that you were over Ben,' she had accused her. 'You said that you were in love with Gib. It certainly doesn't look that way from where we're sitting,' she had swept on when Phoebe had tried to protest. 'It looks as if you've just been using Gib as a way to get back at Ben somehow. That's not fair, Phoebe. It's not fair to Ben and it's not fair to Gib.'

There had been a lot more along the same lines. Trapped, Phoebe had been unable to explain that watching Ben had only been a way of not watching Gib.

'Mum thought we'd had a row,' she told him. 'She's afraid I'm going to lose you by being too uncompromising.'

'Shall I tell her I like you that way?' said Gib.

Her smile glimmered in the dusky light. 'I'm not sure she would believe you. In Mum's world, women are sweet and subservient and agree with everything their husbands say.'

'Sounds like a parallel universe to me,' he commented dryly.

'Exactly. Anyway,' Phoebe went on awkwardly after a minute, 'I owe you an apology.'

'Oh?'

'After everything I had to say about you sticking to the script, I'm the one that's made Mum suspicious,' she said with difficulty. 'She thinks I'm just using you and that I'm still in love with Ben.'

Sheila Lane was no fool, Gib thought, and she must know her daughter better than anyone. If she thought Phoebe was still in love with Ben, it was probably true.

'We'd better convince her that's not true, then, hadn't we?' he said, deliberately brisk. 'What do you want to do? Another smoochy dance?'

Phoebe looked at him then away. This was her chance. 'No,' she said, and then had to stop and take a breath. 'I want you to kiss me.'

It came out more abruptly than she had intended. 'If you don't mind,' she added hastily.

Gib looked at her with rather a twisted smile. 'Sure, if that's what you want,' he said.

He didn't sound exactly thrilled at the prospect, Phoebe

noted with a sinking heart. It had seemed reasonable enough when she had first thought of it, sensible even. What was the point of obsessing about that kiss this morning, when she could just get the whole thing out of her system by kissing him again? she had reasoned. It wouldn't be the same this time, and it might at least keep her mother quiet. It wasn't that she *wanted* him to kiss her particularly. It was just part of the act.

'I don't want to force you,' she said defensively. 'Of course you don't have to if you don't want to.'

He shrugged. 'It's no big deal. I'm getting paid, remember?' he pointed out. 'You might as well get your money's worth.'

Well, there was one way of taking any romance out of the situation.

Phoebe wished she had never started this, but it was too late to back out now.

And, as Gib had so coolly reminded her, she was paying him good money for this. Why shouldn't she ask him to kiss her? The fact that she had been thinking about it all evening was neither here nor there.

'Shall we move back where your mother can see us more clearly?' Gib was saying briskly.

Without waiting for an answer, he took her by the waist and manoeuvred her as if she were a rather unwieldy piece of furniture until they were on the edge of the light spilling out from the French windows, where they would be visible while looking as if they had meant to conceal themselves in the shadows.

In spite of his deliberately prosaic attitude, Phoebe's senses jolted with anticipation as Gib's hands tightened against her. Her heart was thudding in slow, painful strokes, and the excitement building inside her was so intense that she abruptly lost her nerve.

'M-maybe this isn't such a good idea after all,' she croaked, but she didn't move and her hands seemed to be creeping up his arms as if they had a will of their own.

'Oh, I think it is,' said Gib in an odd voice. He pulled her close, and when his mouth came down on hers Phoebe's momentary hesitation evaporated in a rush of sensation.

His lips were warm and sure and persuasive as they explored hers. He might not have been too keen on the idea initially, but it certainly didn't seem to be too much of a hardship for him now. That might be a sign of a man expert in dealing with women, but Phoebe was beyond caring one way or another. She gave herself up to the sheer pleasure of being held hard against him and, as his hands drifted enticingly down her back, she wrapped her arms around his neck and kissed him back.

God, it felt wonderful! It was all Phoebe could do to hang on to the last vestiges of her self-control but somewhere she found the will-power to unhook her arms from round his neck. Reluctantly, she broke the kiss, and took a ragged breath.

'I think that should do the trick,' she said.

CHAPTER EIGHT

FOR a split second, Gib looked blank, and then his hands dropped. 'Right,' he said tonelessly.

The momentary blaze of expression in his eyes gave Phoebe pause but, just as she was about to apologise, she saw him smile again, and the words dried on her tongue. He was a little too expert at this kissing business, she told herself. A little too cool in the way he took her in his arms, as if she was just the latest in a very long line of women who had begged him to kiss them.

'Thanks,' she said instead, steadying her voice with an effort. 'That was fine.'

Gib's smile faded. Fine? he thought savagely. She had melted into his kiss and kissed him back as if he was the only man in the world she wanted. She knew damn well it had been more than fine for both of them!

He couldn't believe that she had really just been acting to convince her mother that they hadn't had a row. Still, if that was the way she wanted to play it, it was up to her. He shrugged.

'It's all part of the service,' he told her.

The coolness in his voice rather daunted Phoebe. He might at least pretend that it had been more than a rather tiresome part of his job!

Now he actually had the nerve to glance at his watch. 'Do you think we've spent long enough out here, or do you want to kiss again?' he asked in a bored tone.

Phoebe couldn't help flinching. He obviously couldn't wait to get inside. Probably terrified she was going to insist on being kissed again. Oh, God, what if he thought it was all an elaborate ruse to get her hands on him? After the way she had kissed him back, he must think that she was absolutely desperate and was probably even now making up excuses in case she threw herself at him in the night!

Mortified, she retreated behind an air of prickly hauteur. 'No, I think that was quite enough,' she said.

Back in the banqueting hall, it was obvious that her mother had seen the kiss and was looking satisfied. She didn't even raise her eyebrows when Phoebe went to talk to friends on another table, leaving Gib with Lara.

On her mettle, Phoebe was on sparkling form. She was determined to show Gib that she was quite as unaffected by that kiss out on the terrace as he was. That meant keeping an eye on whether he was noticing or not but, infuriatingly, he hardly seemed to be aware of her at all.

He had loosened his tie and was relaxed in his chair, chatting easily to the others on the table. If nothing else, his part required him to look as if he cared where she was and what she was doing, thought Phoebe piqued, and when she saw him take to the floor with Lara, her eyes narrowed dangerously. They didn't need to look as if they were having quite such a good time!

She was so busy trying not to watch Gib dancing with her sister that she hardly noticed when Ben joined the table where she was sitting. He and Lisa were obviously circulating. Phoebe listened with half an ear, laughing at all the right points, but her mind was on Gib, and Ben had to ask her to dance twice before he could gain her attention.

'For old-time's sake,' he said.

Over his shoulder, Phoebe could see Gib laughing with Lara as they went back to their table, and she smiled brilliantly at Ben as she got to her feet. 'That would be lovely!'

It was odd to be dancing with Ben again. Phoebe felt

awkward and unfamiliar in his arms, as if he were a stranger rather than the man she had once planned to spend her entire life with, and she couldn't help comparing it with the way she had felt when she was dancing with Gib. The thought wiped the glittering smile from her face and made her stumble.

The next instant Gib was beside them. 'I think it's my turn now,' he said. He was smiling, but something in his face made Ben release Phoebe with alacrity.

'What do you think you're doing?' she demanded as Ben made good his escape and Gib calmly pulled her into his arms to continue the dance.

'My job,' he said. 'You're paying me to act like a besotted lover, and believe me, no lover could sit and watch you looking at your ex-fiancé like that.'

'We were just having a dance for old-time's sake,' Phoebe protested. 'There was no need for you to barge in and embarrass me!'

'Oh, you think that was embarrassing, did you? You want to try making jolly conversation with the other wedding guests while your supposed fiancée makes it blatantly obvious that she's still in love with the bridegroom! What was the point of us going through this whole pretence if you're going to dance with Ben like that?' he demanded furiously.

Phoebe opened her mouth and then shut it again as it hit her for the first time that she wasn't in love with Ben any longer. She had got so used to him being part of her life, that she hadn't even realised that he wasn't there any more.

But she couldn't tell Gib that. She had made such a fuss about Ben and how desperate she was to save face that she couldn't admit now that none of it had been necessary. He would think that it had just been an excuse to spend time with him, and Phoebe wasn't having him wondering why she had responded so eagerly to the kiss that she had ordered if *that* was the case.

She didn't even want to wonder about it herself.

No, much better for Gib to think that she was still in love with Ben.

'I can't help how I feel,' she said.

'He's married,' said Gib brutally, 'and you're supposed to be in love with me.'

'Just for tonight!' Phoebe reminded him.

She felt oddly detached. Here they were, both wearing fixed smiles and arguing through clenched teeth as they moved mechanically in time to the music, and all the time a part of her couldn't help noticing how good it felt to have his arms around her, how oddly familiar his body felt after Ben's.

If Gib was conscious of a similar sense of recognition, he gave absolutely no sign of it. For once the lazy good-humour was entirely absent. His jaw was taut and a tell-tale muscle twitched tensely in his cheek.

'Yes, I know,' he gritted. 'I'm only being paid for twenty-four hours! Any longer and I'll start asking for a bonus.'

'Don't count on it—twenty-four hours will be more than enough!'

They glared at each other for a moment before Gib pulled her roughly against him. 'Might as well make it look as if we can't keep our hands off each other,' he said, laying his cheek against her hair. Phoebe held herself rigid at first but, realising how ridiculous she must look, she succumbed to temptation eventually and let herself relax against him.

Just for show, of course.

Only it wasn't that easy. His closeness was having a strange effect on her insides, which felt as if they were un-looping and unravelling with an alarming momentum while her heart had set up a slow, irregular thudding that drowned out the music and the laughter around them and left nothing but the smell of Gib's skin, and the faint roughness of his jaw and the solid strength of his body where he held her against him.

'What was he saying to you anyway?' Gib asked as if the words had been forced out of him.

'Who?' said Phoebe, momentarily disorientated by his abrupt question.

'Ben,' he said impatiently. 'I saw him whispering sweet nothings in your ear. You'd never guess that he'd only been married a few hours!'

'If you must know, he was telling me that he thought you and I were made for each other, and that he was glad that I was so happy. Ironic, don't you think?'

Gib snorted dismissively. 'He's only saying that because it suits him to believe it. If he knew you at all, he wouldn't think you were happy. Even I can see you're miserable.'

'Well, that's where you're wrong,' said Phoebe, putting up her chin. 'All I wanted was for this to be a happy day for everyone, especially Ben, and it has been. That's enough to make me happy.

'I should thank you,' she went on as she spotted an opportunity to convince Gib that she had just been using him and that when she had responded to his kisses, it had been strictly according to their first rule of engagement. 'I don't think I would have been able to convince everyone on my own, but I have to say you played your part to perfection. You should take up acting if your business plans don't take off.'

'There's no need to thank me,' he said shortly. 'You're paying me.'

'Still, I appreciate it,' she persevered, rather proud of her casual tone. 'There were a lot of little touches that really made a difference, like that kiss out on the terrace.'

A 'little touch'? Was that all it had been to her? Gib's jaw clenched. *He* was the one who was always first to back out of a relationship the moment it threatened to get too emotional. It was a new experience to be given the brush-off at this stage, and Gib didn't like it much.

Had his attitude rankled with all those women he'd dated the way Phoebe's coolness was grating on him? he found himself wondering with a trace of compunction. Not getting involved was the sensible option, but when you were on the receiving end, it wasn't a nice feeling.

'It's OK,' he said in a curt voice. 'I'm not expecting a tip! Anyway, it wasn't difficult.'

Right, what was a heart-shaking kiss here and there to a man like Gib? thought Phoebe with a touch of resentment.

'Good,' she said a little stiffly.

'It's easier when you're not emotionally involved,' Gib went on with a shrug.

Yes, all right, she had got that point. Phoebe pressed her lips together in a thin line.

'I'm glad it's been such easy money for you,' she said, unable to keep an acid edge from her voice.

Gib thought about kissing her, about the way she felt in his arms now, about the night to come when he was going to have to lie next to her in that damned four-poster bed and not touch her.

'I wouldn't put it quite like that,' he said.

Using Gib's flight to Switzerland as an excuse, they left early the next morning before anyone else was up.

Getting up early wasn't a problem, at least not for Phoebe. She had hardly slept the night before. The evening had seemed interminable. Part of her had longed for it to be over so that she could escape, while another part dreaded being alone with Gib.

When they got back to the room, the bed had been turned down invitingly in the light of a bedside lamp, the perfect setting for romance. Gib closed the heavy door with a clunk of the old-fashioned iron key, and silence settled like a blanket around them, stifling all the oxygen from the air and making it hard to breathe.

Phoebe's heart was battering in her throat and her breath was coming in short, jerky gasps. She was appalled by her spiralling thoughts. This was absolutely not the time to start obsessing about Gib's mouth and Gib's hands, not the time to think about his body or what it would be like if they were the lovers they had pretended to be all day, but she couldn't help it.

Gib had continued to play his part in front of the others, but as soon as they were alone he had become cool and distant. Phoebe was confused by how much she missed the gleaming mockery in eyes and the slow smile that had so unsettled her before. It seemed like a lifetime since she had found him irritating.

Now she stood just inside the door, her eyes skittering frantically around the room in an effort not to look at him. There was a quivering deep inside her, a certain knowledge that if he turned to her now and smiled she wouldn't be able to resist him, so when he did turn, she caught her breath.

He even smiled, but it was a perfunctory smile at best and he was thinking not of romance but of the practical arrangements about how they would sleep. She didn't need to worry, he told her. They would put a pillow down the middle of the bed in time-honoured fashion and she could sleep easy. 'I haven't forgotten those rules of yours,' he said, and Phoebe reminded herself that she had better not forget them either.

The bed was huge and there was plenty of room for both of them, but that didn't stop Phoebe being agonisingly aware of Gib all night. Not that her closeness seemed to bother *him*, she realised resentfully. He simply stretched out and went to sleep without any problem, leaving her to toss and turn restlessly all night.

By the time morning came, Phoebe was gritty-eyed, but she had given herself a good talking to during those long, sleepless hours, and she was determined to get back to normal. From now on she would be as brisk and businesslike as Gib had been.

'Perhaps this is an appropriate time to pay you,' she said when Gib emerged from the bathroom, dressed once again in his suit. 'Is a cheque all right?' she added, picking up her handbag. 'Or would you prefer cash?'

The muscle in Gib's jaw tightened momentarily. 'A cheque's fine.'

'Good.' Phoebe made big deal of finding her cheque-book and then a pen. 'Now, who should I make it out to?'

'J. Gibson,' said Gib, after only the tiniest of hesitations.

Scribbling her signature, Phoebe handed the cheque to him. He gave it a cursory glance, and then frowned. 'This is more than we agreed.'

'Well, it all went according to plan,' she said carelessly. 'I thought you deserved a bonus.' There, if that didn't show him that she had been treating the whole weekend as a purely business arrangement, nothing would!

Gib looked at her for a moment, then tucked the cheque into the pocket of his shirt. 'Thanks,' he said in a voice empty of all expression.

It was a largely silent drive back to London, with conversation limited to stilted comments about the traffic. Unable to think of a good reason why she should be tense or nervous, Phoebe said that she would drive, but perversely she felt both. It was something to do with the fact that Gib was sitting beside her, not frowning, not sulking, just looking neutral. Phoebe was horrified at how much she missed his smile. She couldn't help comparing this trip with the drive down, only the day before, when they had laughed as they invented explanations for the ending of their supposed romance.

Now it seemed all too obvious that even an invented romance between them was doomed to disaster. No one seeing them together this morning would have any trouble in believing that it would all end in tears.

A sigh escaped Phoebe as she waited to turn onto the main road and, hearing it, she pulled herself up sharply. There was no reason for her to feel this depressed. She had got through Ben's wedding better than she could have hoped, Gib had played his part, she had paid him as agreed, and that was the end of the matter. The sooner she got back to London and normality, the better.

Phoebe had hoped that their early start would mean that they could sneak into the house while Kate and Bella were still asleep, thereby avoiding instant interrogation, but a traffic jam near Heathrow meant that by the time they got back, the other two girls were drinking coffee at the kitchen table, yawning and bleary-eyed but definitely awake.

Gib disappeared, muttering about changing out of his suit at last, so Phoebe was left alone to undergo a detailed cross-examination about the wedding. The girls began easily enough, insisting that she describe key outfits, especially the bride's dress, and wanting to know whether there had been any hats to rival Phoebe's, but any hope she might have had that they might leave it at that was soon quashed. Kate told her severely that they were just warming up. She was to tell them about Ben, about how he had been with her and how she had felt, and how Lisa had treated her, but all the time Phoebe could feel them building up to the key question.

It was Bella who voiced it in the end. 'So,' she asked in an oh-so-casual kind of way, 'how did you and Gib get on?'

'Fine,' said Phoebe brightly.

'He ended up spending the night then?'

'Mmmnn,' she said, getting up to pour herself some more coffee.

'Did you have to share a room?'

'What?' Phoebe busied herself finding some milk in the fridge. 'Oh...yes, yes we did.'

'And?'

'And nothing,' she said. 'What did you expect? A night of wild passion?' She even managed a laugh, as if she hadn't spent half the night wondering *exactly* what that would be like. 'You don't really think I would have felt like that, having just seen the love of my life get married, do you?' she went on, making sure that they got the point. 'Honestly, it was just a perfectly straightforward arrangement for both of us, and before you ask, yes, we *did* kiss a couple of times, and it didn't mean anything at all. It was just part of the act.'

'That's right,' Gib's voice came from behind her, and Phoebe span round, slopping coffee.

He had changed into jeans and a T-shirt, so he looked more like the Gib she remembered, but she noticed that his smile had the faint edge it had worn since the night before, and her heart, which had lurched at the sound of his voice, sank inexplicably.

Gib came over to the table and dropped a careless hand on Phoebe's shoulder. 'Yes, it was all just an act, wasn't it, Phoebe? The easiest money I've ever earned,' he added to Kate and Bella, while Phoebe was burningly conscious of the warmth of his hand through her shirt. 'I've even got the cheque to prove it,' he said.

* * *

It was all just an act. They had been her own words, but over the next couple of weeks, Phoebe found herself resenting them more and more. If it was all just an act, why couldn't she forget about those kisses, the way Gib so obviously had? She kept thinking about how he had taken her cheque and put it in his pocket. Easy money, he had called it.

Phoebe couldn't understand what was wrong with her. She was usually so good at being sensible. She was famous for her ability to pull herself together and get on with things. Even at her lowest point, when Ben had told her that he didn't love her any more, she had clamped down on the hurt and listened while everyone told her how well she was dealing with it. She was doing just the right thing in putting on a brave face, they said, but it had seemed to Phoebe that she didn't have any choice in the matter. She had to just carry on. It was that or fall apart altogether.

So if she had been able to get on with her life then, why couldn't she do it now? There was no point in endlessly reliving the feel of his lips and the touch of his hands and the taste of his mouth. No point in thinking about how good it had felt to be held against him. And certainly no point in wishing that he hadn't overheard her telling Kate and Bella that his kisses had meant nothing to her and that Ben was still the love of her life.

Gib wasn't wasting his time remembering that weekend. He had reverted to his old self, and was as laid-back and lazily cheerful as ever. Once or twice, Phoebe felt his blue eyes on her, but when she glanced at him she saw only the familiar, mocking gleam. He was charming, friendly and funny, and he treated her exactly like Kate and Bella.

Phoebe knew that she should have been relieved. That weekend at Ben's wedding might never have happened for all Gib referred to it. Anyone would think, she thought sometimes, that he had never kissed her at all. Which was just what she wanted.

Only it didn't stop her feeling vaguely disgruntled about it all the same.

Restless and on edge, Phoebe threw herself into her job. To her relief, the programme about the Community Bank had been put on the back-burner while they worked frantically to finish another film, and she spent long days in the edit suite, watching it being cut together before rushing back to the office to sort out the fact that all the sound turned out to be distorted and to arrange for extra footage for one of the key interviews.

Tired as she was at the end of the day, the moment she walked back in the door and saw Gib, he was all she could think about. Matters were not helped by her mother who kept ringing up to tell her how much everyone had liked Gib, and to ask when she was going to bring him down for the weekend.

'I do wish you would, Phoebe,' she pleaded. 'We'd so like to see him again, and maybe you could talk to Lara when you're here,' she added with a sigh. 'She's being so *difficult* about this ghastly boy she's seeing at the moment. He's got rings through every available part of his anatomy, as far as I can see, and his hair is so *dirty*! It makes your father feel ill just to look at him. Why can't she find someone like Gib?'

Phoebe prevaricated as best as she could. Her mother was obviously so worked up about Lara, that she couldn't bring herself to tell her that her supposed engagement was off and that Gib had turned out to be not so wonderful after all. Also, that would have meant discussing the whole matter with Gib, and somehow Phoebe hadn't been able to bring herself to do that.

'I've told Mum there's a crisis at your bank and that

you're very busy,' she told him stiltedly, just in case her mother got him on the phone next time. 'You haven't forgotten that you're president of your very own bank, have you?' she asked with a hint of her old spice.

'Ah, yes, so I am.' Gib tipped back in his chair with his arms behind his head, and his eyes glinted. 'I must find out how they're managing without me!'

'I can see that you've been in a real fret about it!'

'No point in fretting,' he said. 'I trust my staff. There's no point in paying them good salaries if I have to do all the working and worrying myself.'

'I can't imagine you doing either of those things,' said Phoebe. 'Don't you ever get bored lazing around all day?'

Gib let his chair legs drop back to the floor. 'What makes you think I do that?'

'Observation!'

'You haven't been watching me closely enough, Phoebe,' he said with one of his gleaming smiles. 'It just so happens that I work while you're out.'

'Doing what?' she asked suspiciously.

'I've been setting up a project,' he told her. 'It's all looking pretty good, as a matter of fact. I'm hoping to finalise everything before too long, and then I'll be out of your hair.'

Phoebe felt as if she had walked into a wall in the dark. 'You're leaving?'

'I have to leave some time,' said Gib.

'Oh.' Phoebe tried to swallow the desolate feeling in her throat. It was almost as if she wanted to cry, which was ridiculous. 'When?' she asked, and then, afraid that it sounded too abrupt, 'I mean, I'll have to find another lodger.'

'I'm not sure yet,' he said. 'I'll let you know.'

'Fine.' She looked down at her hands. 'We'll miss you,'

she said, and it was as if the words came out of their own accord.

'Will you?'

'Of course,' she said brightly, suddenly nervous. 'We've got used to having you here.'

'No, will *you* miss me?'

Something in his voice compelled her to meet the intense blue gaze, and when she did it was as if the air was evaporating around her, shortening her breath and making her heart batter against her ribs. She wanted to laugh and give him a flip answer, the way he would have done in the same situation, but somehow she couldn't.

'Yes,' she admitted. 'Yes, I will.'

Gib's chair scraped over the tiles as he got to his feet. 'Phoebe,' he began urgently, only to break off as the doorbell pealed imperatively.

'I'll get it,' Bella's voice shouted as she clattered down the stairs. 'It'll be Josh.'

Gib hesitated. Bella was never ready to go out, which meant that Josh would come into the kitchen and have a drink while he waited, the way he always did.

Phoebe was waiting expectantly, but he couldn't talk to her now. 'It doesn't matter,' he said flatly, and turned towards the fridge instead. 'I'll get Josh a beer.'

But it wasn't Josh. It was Lara, carrying a bulging bag and wearing a defiant expression.

Bella showed her into the kitchen, grimacing warningly at Phoebe from behind Lara's shoulder.

'Lara!' Phoebe hurried over to hug her sister. 'What on earth are you doing here?'

'I've come to stay.'

'What?' She did a double take as she stepped back from the hug.

'Jed's come up to London with his band,' said Lara.

'They've got some gigs lined up, and they're going to make a recording. This could be their big break. Mum and Dad are delighted, of course,' she added bitterly. 'They're hoping that I'll forget all about him now that he's left, but I won't, I *won't!*'

Her voice rose alarmingly. She looked exhausted, thought Phoebe in concern, making her sit down in the armchair.

'Of course, you won't,' she said soothingly. 'I know Jed's important to you...but wouldn't you rather stay with him in that case?'

Lara sniffed dolefully. 'He doesn't know I'm coming,' she was forced to admit. 'He thinks I'm too spoilt and that I wouldn't be able to live rough the way he does, but I wouldn't mind if only I could be with him.'

Her blue eyes swam with tears as she looked at her sister. 'He didn't believe me when I said I'd give up my course and follow him to London, but if I turn up at the gig tomorrow night, he'll have to take me seriously, won't he?'

Remembering what her parents had told her about Jed, Phoebe wasn't so sure. Pierced he might be, but it sounded like Jed had her little sister sussed. Lara was just as spoilt as he had said, and Phoebe didn't think she would enjoy living in a squat at all, whatever she said now.

'I won't stay long,' Lara was saying earnestly. 'Just until I can convince Jed that I really want to be with him.'

'The thing is, there's not that much room with Gib living here now,' Phoebe prevaricated, hoping that Lara wouldn't remember the layout of the house, and be instantly disappointed.

'You must still have that little spare room that Caro had before she married,' she pointed out immediately.

'Yes, but—' Phoebe stopped. She had been about to say that Gib was sleeping there, but of course Lara would assume that she and Gib would be sharing a room since she still hadn't broken off their mythical engagement. They could always tell Lara the truth, of course, but it was all too complicated to go into at the moment.

'I won't be any trouble,' Lara was pleading. 'It'll only be for a few days and then I'm sure I'll be able to move in with Jed. 'Oh, *please*, Phoebe!' she wailed as Phoebe still hesitated. 'You don't know what it means to me!'

Harassed, Phoebe found herself looking helplessly at Gib. Lara might think that Jed was all she wanted to make her happy, but Phoebe wasn't so sure, and she knew that she shouldn't encourage Lara to abandon yet another course. But, short of turning her little sister out onto the street, she didn't see what else she could do.

'What do you think?' she appealed to Gib. If they really were engaged, she would ask his opinion, wouldn't she?

'I think it's too late for Lara to go anywhere else tonight, so she might as well make herself comfortable and we'll sort something out in the morning,' he said sensibly.

Lara gave him a grateful hug. 'I knew you'd be cool.'

The doorbell went again. 'That really will be Josh,' said Bella, who had been following it all with interest.

Phoebe jumped up to follow her as she went to open the front door. 'Gib, can you get Lara a drink? I'll be back in a second.'

In the corridor, she seized Bella's arm. 'Bel, you've got to go and get everything out of Gib's room,' she whispered urgently. 'Just chuck it all in my room for now, but make it look as if his hasn't been slept in for a while. I'll keep Lara in the kitchen as long as I can.'

'Where's Gib going to sleep? Hi,' she said as she opened the door to Josh and kissed him on both cheeks. 'With you?'

'He'll have to—hi, Josh—Lara thinks we're practically engaged, and she's got to go on thinking it. Right now, I can't cope with my mother going into mourning because there's no wedding to plan!'

Josh stepped into the house. He was used to arriving in the middle of conversations like this. 'What's going on?'

'Bella will tell you,' said Phoebe with a harried look. 'I've got to get back to Lara.' She turned to head back down the corridor to the kitchen, and then thought better of it. 'Oh, Josh, if it comes up in the conversation, can you remember that Gib and I are engaged? Nothing official yet, but we're looking at rings and thinking about a date—you know the kind of thing.'

'Congratulations,' said Josh. 'I always thought you were exactly the kind of girl Gib needed!'

Phoebe looked at him uncertainly. Like Gib, it was often hard to tell whether Josh was joking or not. Either way, she decided that it would be more dignified just to ignore his comment.

She hurried back to the kitchen, where she found Lara sobbing in Gib's arms, her head burrowed into his chest while he held her comfortingly close and murmured soothingly into her blonde curls. The sight was enough to make Phoebe stop dead, her stomach wrenching with what she recognised to her horror as sheer, unadulterated jealousy, but the next instant Gib had lifted his head, and the naked appeal in his expression was enough to unknot her insides and send relief spilling through her veins instead.

'I was just trying to be nice,' he said apologetically.

Lara was overwrought by this stage, and it took some time to calm her down. She kept telling Phoebe tearfully how lucky she was to have Gib. 'Mum and Dad think he's wonderful. Mum's always boasting about him in the golf club.'

Phoebe's heart sank. Keeping up with her golfing friends was a point of pride with her mother. She would have loved telling them all about her daughter's fantastically successful fiancé. Phoebe could practically hear her. No announcement yet, but there *is* a slot at the church in September, and I'm sounding out the best caterers... She was going to be mortified when Phoebe told her that it was all over.

Oh, dear, it was all so complicated, Phoebe sighed to herself. That was the trouble with lying. There was never any end to it. All she had wanted was to make Ben's wedding easier for everyone, and now if she wasn't careful she was going to spend her entire life inventing imaginary lovers to keep her mother's end up at the golf club.

CHAPTER NINE

PHOEBE was exhausted by the end of the evening. Kate had come home with some smoked salmon that she had spotted on special offer, so they had ended up having an impromptu dinner party. Normally, sitting round the kitchen table with her friends, talking and laughing, was what Phoebe liked doing best, but the prospect of sharing a room with Gib again left her feeling edgy and she was terrified that someone would spot that beneath her discomfort lurked a drumming sense of anticipation.

Nor were matters improved by the relish with which Bella, Josh and Kate threw themselves into the pretence. Bella had rung Kate's mobile to warn her of the situation, so she played along with gusto when she got back. In fact, all three of them had an excellent time asking Phoebe and Gib awkward questions about the fictional wedding, allotting themselves key roles as bridesmaids and best man, and inventing stories to prove to Lara how in love the two of them were.

Phoebe's smile grew increasingly brittle, and the moment Lara yawned, she leapt up and offered to show her to her room. 'You must be tired,' she said eagerly, ignoring the meaningful looks the others were exchanging.

There was no sign that Gib had ever been in the spare room. Relieved, Phoebe made up the bed, kissed her sister goodnight, and made her way wearily along to her own room, where it was immediately obvious that Bella had taken her instruction to chuck Gib's stuff in there quite literally. The floor was strewn with clothes, papers, bedding and assorted bits and pieces, although his laptop had been placed—Phoebe hoped—on her bed.

Wearily, she bent to start picking things up, and she was just gathering together various papers when Gib put his head round the door. 'Can I come in?'

'This is your room now,' said Phoebe, not meeting his eyes. 'You don't need to ask.'

'Maybe I'm a very polite fiancé.' Gib came into the room, only to still as he saw that she held his passport in her hand. 'I should put that somewhere safe,' he said, and to his relief she passed it to him without insisting on looking at his photograph the way some people would.

'I'm afraid Bella was in a bit of a hurry when she cleared out your room,' she apologised. 'I hope you haven't lost anything.'

Trying desperately to remember if he had left anything incriminating out, Gib bent to help her pick up the last few papers. Fortunately he kept most of his work on his laptop, but there had been some paperwork involved with the latest project which should be here somewhere...

'Oh, here's something about the Community Bank,' said Phoebe in surprise, smoothing out a brochure on her knee. 'Where did you get this?'

'It must have been in all those papers you had,' said Gib after the tiniest of pauses. 'I probably found it when I was researching my part for the wedding.'

Phoebe studied the brochure, a slight frown between her brows. 'I don't remember this one,' she said, puzzled. 'It looks interesting, too. I'm sure I haven't seen it before.

'You had a lot of papers there. Perhaps it was caught up with everything else?'

'It must have been, I suppose.' Her shrug was baffled. 'I might as well take it back, anyway,' she decided. 'It might give me some new ideas for the programme, and it's not as if you need it any more, is it?'

'No,' said Gib. 'Of course not.'

Quickly he gathered the rest of the papers together and tidied them into a pile. 'I'll sort these out later,' he said firmly and began picking up his scattered clothes.

'I'm sorry about all this,' said Phoebe awkwardly as she handed him a shirt.

'Don't worry about it. I can see that Bella was in a hurry, and it's not as if anything's broken.'

'No, I meant about acting as my fiancé again,' she made herself explain. 'Sharing a room, all of that...you know.'

'You weren't to know Lara was going to turn up,' Gib pointed out in a reasonable voice.

'No, but I should have put a stop to the whole business ages ago,' Phoebe confessed guiltily. 'It's just that Mum's been so worried about Lara, and so thrilled at the idea that I might get married, I haven't had the heart to tell her that it's all over.'

Gib, continuing to retrieve clothing from the floor, made a non-committal sound.

'The thing is,' she struggled on, 'I don't want her to hear from Lara that we're not really a couple. She'd be devastated if she found out I had made it all up, so I wondered if...well, if you wouldn't mind getting back into your role while Lara's here?' she finished in a rush.

'No, I don't mind,' said Gib, but Phoebe, already acutely self-conscious, was convinced that his twisted smile meant that he did.

'You don't have to if you don't want to,' she said hastily.

'No, it's OK,' he said. 'I really don't mind.'

'Oh. Well...good. Thanks.'

There was an uncomfortable silence. At least, Phoebe found it uncomfortable. Gib seemed quite happy to carry on with the business of tidying up the mess Bella had created. Realising that she was just standing there, she bent to retrieve the duvet.

'It should only be for a few days,' she said as she attempted to roll it neatly, unsure whether she was trying to reassure Gib or herself. 'As soon as Lara's gone, I'll ring Mum and tell her that we've broken up.'

'I thought you were worried about disappointing her?' he said with one of his sharp blue glances.

'I am, but I suppose she's got to be disappointed some time,' sighed Phoebe. 'Otherwise we'll end up getting married for her, and then there'll be grandchildren, and before we know where we are we'll be spending our entire lives together!'

'And we can't have that, can we?' Gib murmured, but there was something in his voice that made Phoebe look at him in puzzlement.

'I can't imagine you'd want to impersonate the president of an international bank for ever! It wouldn't take long for even Mum to start wondering why someone so successful was driving around in my old car, and living in my old house which we could never afford to do up.'

'I guess that would be a bit of a give-away,' he agreed.

After another puzzled look, Phoebe turned away to start clearing a space in her wardrobe. 'Um...would you be happy with the same terms as last time?' she asked, putting his shirts onto hangers.

'You mean the same rules of engagement?' asked Gib sardonically, and her face burned.

'Those, of course, but I was thinking more about money.'

'Oh, that,' he said. 'No.'

She hadn't anticipated such a flat response. 'You want more?'

'I don't want any money, Phoebe!' For the first time, Gib

sounded really angry. 'How can you even ask me that? I thought we were friends now?'

Phoebe was taken aback. She had never seen him look so forbidding. 'We are,' she said but Gib pounced on the uncertainty in her voice.

'You don't sound very sure,' he accused her. 'You said you would miss me earlier. Did you mean it, or were you just saying it?'

She swallowed. 'Of course I meant it.'

'I'm going to miss you, too,' he said deliberately. 'I think that means we're friends, and you don't offer to pay friends for helping you out.'

To her amazement, Phoebe realised that he wasn't angry, he was hurt. 'Sorry,' she muttered.

'No, I'm sorry.' Gib was instantly contrite. 'I shouldn't have shouted at you. I hated the idea that you might not think of me as a friend after all. I guess I just…wanted you to like me,' he finished, appalled at how gauche he sounded, he who was so famous for his charm and his smooth talking.

Phoebe had been in the middle of putting one of his shirts on a hanger, but at that she paused, clutching it to her chest. She couldn't believe how unsure of himself Gib sounded. It was hard to remember now how irritated she had been by his confidence and charm.

Now all she could think about was the fact that he wanted her to like him.

There was a tight feeling in Phoebe's chest, and her breath had shortened uncomfortably. 'I do,' she said.

'You didn't like me when I arrived,' Gib accused her.

'No,' she admitted. There was no use in pretending that she had. 'I thought you were cocky. You reminded me of Slimy Seb, who was so horrible to Kate. He used to think that all he had to do was smile and everyone would fall over themselves to do whatever he wanted, which they usually did, of course. He hurt her so badly, I didn't like the thought that you might come in and do the same.'

She paused, trying to understand herself the point at which her attitude towards him had changed. 'And then you...you changed everything,' she said slowly. 'You hang around the house, not doing anything, and half the time you drive me nuts, while the other half I spend feeling jittery because I don't know what you're going to do or say next, but yes, I do like you,' she told him, as if goaded. 'I don't really know why, but I do.'

A smile started in Gib's blue eyes and spread out, illuminating his face. 'I like you, too,' he said.

Taking the shirt and hanger from Phoebe's nerveless hands, he tossed them onto the bed. 'Come here,' he said and enfolded her in a warm hug. Almost of their own volition, her arms crept round his back to hug him back.

It felt so good to be held against him again. It felt warm and safe and somehow right, like coming home. Phoebe rested her face against Gib's neck and breathed in the scent of his skin with a giddy rush of pleasure. *He liked her.*

And then the pleasure congealed in her veins as it dawned on her that she didn't like Gib at all. It was much, much more than that.

She loved him.

The world seemed to rock around Phoebe as the realisation seeped through her, and instinctively she clung to him even as she stiffened in his arms, and Gib's hold tightened in response. She felt his lips brush her hair and her heart began to batter relentlessly, so convinced was she that he would turn his head and kiss her.

But Gib didn't kiss her. He released her instead and smiled down into her face. 'I like you a lot,' he told her.

Like, not love.

Phoebe stepped back, shaken by the terrifying new

knowledge that was churning around inside her. 'I don't know why,' she muttered, hugging her arms together. 'I've been horrible to you.'

'I know,' said Gib, but he was teasing her. The blue eyes were alight with laughter and one corner of his mouth curled irresistibly. 'There's no accounting for it at all!'

'Perhaps you don't really like me at all,' she said unsteadily.

There, that was his cue. Say I don't like you, Gib, she willed him mentally. Say I love you.

The smile faded from his eyes and he was suddenly serious. 'I do,' he said. 'I like your strength and your loyalty. I like your sharpness and the way you put up your chin sometimes and the bravery in your eyes. You can put up your prickles all you like, Phoebe, but I know there's a very nice person hiding in there.'

Phoebe looked away. She didn't want to be a very nice person. She was sick of being strong. She wanted Gib to think of her as warm and desirable, not just *very nice*.

He was only two steps away. More than anything, she longed to close the gap between them, to press her lips into his throat and feel his arms around her once more. She wanted him to kiss her and tell her that he wanted her the way she suddenly, desperately wanted him.

Terrified that her body would move towards him of its own accord, Phoebe made herself turn away. She picked up the shirt and hanger from the bed where Gib had thrown them. He would be aghast if she suddenly threw herself at him like that, but tonight…tonight they would be sharing a bed, and there were some things that were easier said in the dark.

She cleared her throat. 'Well, at least now we know that we like each other it should make it easier than last time. Sharing a bed, I mean.'

'Do you think so?' Gib's voice was very dry. She had been so warm and tempting in his arms. He could still feel the silkiness of her hair underneath his cheek, still smell her tantalising fragrance. 'I don't. I think I'd better sleep on the floor tonight.'

Phoebe looked at him in dismay. 'On the floor? Why?'

'Your bed is much too small for a start,' he said, nodding at where it was pushed up against a wall. 'It was hard enough last time, Phoebe,' he went on with a crooked smile, 'and you remember how big that four-poster was.' He glanced back at her bed. 'If I had to sleep with you in that, I wouldn't be able to keep my hands off you!'

The air evaporated around Phoebe. 'Would...would that be such a bad thing?' she asked breathlessly.

Gib steeled himself to stay where he was and keep his hands fixed firmly to the pillow he was holding. 'It would be for you,' he said. 'Ben's been married less than a month. I know how much he meant to you, and that you're not over him yet.'

She had told him that she was still in love with Ben, Phoebe remembered. She had let him believe it, even when she had known that it wasn't true any more. How could she tell Gib now that he was the one she loved? Even if she were to convince him that she wasn't just on the rebound from Ben, telling him would just spook him. He might like her, but he had said nothing about love.

Love implied commitment and staying and settling down. Those weren't words she associated with Gib at all. He was a free spirit, too restless and open to new experiences to want to tie himself down to one girl. Phoebe imagined a succession of beautiful blondes telling him that they loved him only to hear a casual goodbye in return. She would only be the latest in a very long line.

If only it made a difference. If only knowing that he

would be leaving soon would stop her being in love with him, but now that she had admitted it to herself, it had taken her over completely. Cool reason stood no chance against the way her body ached for him. All Phoebe cared about was being with him that night, being able to hold him and touch him. At least then she would have something to remember.

'Maybe,' she said in a low voice, 'sleeping with you is what I need to help me to get over Ben.'

Gib's jaw tightened. Part of him was furious at the idea that he might be just a way of helping her to get over Ben, but it was all he could do to keep the rest of him from reaching for her. It was only by reminding himself that it wasn't what Phoebe really needed that he managed to stay where he was.

Was this what Josh had meant when he had challenged him to be friends with a woman? Putting her needs over his own desire? Josh believed that you couldn't mix sex and friendship, and Gib thought he knew what he meant now.

He wanted Phoebe very badly, but it would be different with her. It would *mean* something. Instinctively he knew that making love to her would be important in a way it had never been for him before, and after that there would be no retreat. He would find himself involved, would get tangled up in caring and commitment and all those things he had spent his entire adult life avoiding. Gib wasn't sure that he was ready for that.

No, far better to keep things as they were, he decided. Phoebe was a friend, a dear friend but still just a friend, and that was how she would stay.

'Only time will do that, Phoebe,' he said, sounding strained. He might think that he was doing the right thing, but it didn't make it any easier. Was it this hard for Josh not to reach out for Bella? he wondered bleakly.

'Perhaps,' she said, and then gathered her courage as she saw her chance slipping away. She swallowed. 'But in the meantime, I might need some comfort,' she said, going as far as she dared.

Comfort? Gib set his teeth. He didn't want to be a comfort to her! He wanted more than that.

'I don't think that's a good idea,' he said with difficulty.

Phoebe moistened her lips. 'Why not?'

Yes, why not? Why not take her in his arms and draw her down onto the bed and make love to her all night?

'I don't want to lose your friendship.'

'It wouldn't have to be like that,' said Phoebe, gripping her hands together and unable to believe how forward she was being.

'I think it would,' said Gib. 'Sex and friendship don't go together.' If he said it often enough to himself, he might even believe it. 'If I slept with you, I'd lose you as a friend, and you're too important to me for me to want to do that. I'll play my part for Lara, of course, but at night I think it's better if I sleep on the floor.'

Well, she wasn't going to beg.

'Fine,' said Phoebe stiffly. 'Whatever you want.'

She hung the shirt in her wardrobe and reached for another.

'Phoebe—' Gib began, hating to see her retreat behind her prickly mask once more.

'Yes?'

He was a little daunted by her brittle smile. 'Phoebe, you do understand, don't you? Sex always ends up complicating things, and it doesn't last. Sooner or later one of you gets bored, and then you can't go back to being friends.'

'No, I'm sure you're right,' Phoebe said, proud of how cool she sounded. 'It would have been a bad idea. It would have spoiled everything.'

Everything was spoiled anyway, though, she thought dismally. Falling in love had done that. She couldn't believe how it had happened, with Gib of all people, too! He wasn't her type at all. Really, it was such a cliché, falling for good looks and charm! Phoebe had always expected herself to be more discriminating.

She tried everything to talk herself out of it. She told herself it was just a reaction to Ben getting married, that it was a purely physical attraction that would disappear as soon as Gib left, that it wasn't really *love*. It was just wanting him and needing him and feeling more vivid and alive just because he was there.

Never had Phoebe thought that she would be grateful to Celia, but her boss's increasingly manic demands at least gave her an excuse to put in long hours at the office and avoid going home to be *friends*. She didn't want to be friends. Friends wasn't enough.

Phoebe was mortified by Gib's rejection. She couldn't have made it more obvious that she wanted to sleep with him, but he clearly didn't want her.

Why should he? She studied her reflection gloomily. She was too prickly, too fierce, too intimidating. Of course Gib would prefer sweet, pretty, winsome girls who knew how to flutter their eyelashes and smile seductively, and do all the things she could never do. It was absolutely stupid for a girl like her to fall in love with a man like him. It would never work. For the umpteenth time, Phoebe told herself to stop it at once.

Only it wasn't as easy as that. Lara was still pursuing Jed to his gigs, but they tended to start later in the evening, so she was at home when Phoebe got back. That meant that Phoebe had to smile and pretend to be happy, to let Gib touch her lightly the way a lover would do, knowing all the time that at night she would lie alone in her bed, watching his lumpy outline on the floor and wishing she could crawl under the duvet with him and put her arms round him and kiss him and make him love her.

Phoebe didn't know whether to be glad or sorry that Lara was still hanging around a week later, not having had much success in persuading Jed to let her move in with him. On the one hand, it was torture having to pretend that everything was nice and normal, but at least as long as Lara was there, Gib couldn't talk about leaving.

The thought of the house without him now was unbearable, but Phoebe knew that he would go eventually. 'I'll stay as long as you need me,' he had said, talking about the situation with Lara and she had wanted to shout at him and tell him in that case he would have to stay for ever. Instead she had nodded and thanked him politely and said that she didn't think that Lara would be staying for much longer.

Love, she thought, wasn't suiting her at all. Her eyes were dull from lack of sleep, and she had lost her appetite. Kate and Bella were beginning to look at her in concern. 'Is something the matter, Phoebe?' Kate asked one day. 'You don't look well.'

Aware of Gib's suddenly narrowed stare on her, Phoebe straightened her shoulders instantly. 'I'm fine,' she insisted. 'Just a bit tired.'

'Is Celia still giving you a hard time?'

'She keeps hassling me about this bank film and how we have to have an interview with the president,' said Phoebe, clutching at the excuse. 'I hoped she'd forgotten all about it, but now the other programme is in the can, she's back to obsessing about J.G. Grieve. She's hinting that she'll bring in someone else if I don't arrange some kind of personal interview. I think I could talk her into accepting an interview with someone else, since we're obviously not going to get J.G. Grieve, but I can't get anyone at the

Community Bank to talk to me at all.' She sighed. 'I don't know what I'm going to do—unless it's start looking for another job!'

The next evening, when she came wearily into the kitchen after another frenzied day at Purple Parrot Productions, they were all waiting for her, sitting around the table and evidently bursting with anticipation.

Phoebe looked from one to the other. 'What's going on?'

'Gib's got something for you,' said Lara, beaming.

'Oh?' As always now, her heart squeezed whenever her eyes rested on him. 'What is it?'

Getting to his feet, Gib dug a business card out of his shirt pocket. Not a diamond ring or a surprise trip to Paris, then.

'Yesterday I happened to bump into a friend of friend who turns out to work for the Community Bank,' he said. 'I didn't tell you yesterday as I wasn't sure if it would work out, but I went to see him today and asked if he would speak to you. He doesn't know if he could get you an interview with J.G. Grieve, but he might have some contacts in the organisation who could help you.'

Phoebe stared down at the card in disbelief. All this time she had been desperately trying to find a contact, and Gib *just happened* to bump into someone! She knew she ought to be delighted. This was the lead that could well save her job. Before she knew that she loved Gib, she would have been thrilled, but now it was all she could do to summon a smile.

'Thank you,' she said, and then saw the others at the table looking surprised at her muted response. They were obviously expecting her to demonstrate her gratitude in a more affectionate way.

There was nothing for it but to widen her smile. 'That's

fantastic!' she tried to enthuse and kissed Gib on the cheek. That was fair enough, surely?

His arm came round her automatically, and he held her close against him, tightening his hold when she would have stepped back and turning his head so that his mouth met hers, sending an instant, intense flare of response through her.

This might be her last chance to kiss him, Phoebe thought hazily. Lara would be leaving any day now, and then he would be gone. But for now he was here, and his arm was around her and his mouth was warm and persuasive on hers. Phoebe let herself melt into him and kissed him back, uncaring of what he or anyone thought. Her arm slid around his waist to hold him closer, while her other hand, still clutching the business card, crept to his chest and twisted in his shirt as if to anchor herself against the intoxicating rush of pleasure.

When Gib lifted his head, there were tears stinging Phoebe's eyes. She blinked them away fiercely to see Lara watching her with interest, and Bella and Kate wearing identically speculative expressions. Swallowing, she made herself step away from him.

'I'll ring this guy first thing tomorrow,' she said.

'He's on his way back to the States,' said Gib quickly. 'I'd give him a couple of days—and don't forget to tell him I gave you his number.'

Lara went out soon afterwards, announcing that Jed had a gig in Hackney and that she wanted to get there early so that she could offer to help with setting up.

'Hackney's the other side of London,' Phoebe pointed out. 'How are you going to get home?'

'Don't fuss, Phoebe. I'll be fine. Anyway, I'm hoping tonight will be the night Jed and I get back together. He mentioned something about a party later, so don't worry if I don't come back at all.'

Phoebe was left to avoid eye contact with Gib and her friends. She escaped to the bath and then, pleading tiredness, straight to bed. The tiredness was real, but she couldn't sleep for thinking about that piercingly sweet kiss and whether it would be the last time Gib held her. If Lara moved in with Jed, she would have no excuse but to ring her mother and tell her that the 'engagement' was off, just as she had promised.

Much later, Gib let himself quietly into the room. 'Phoebe?' he whispered, but she squeezed her eyes shut and pretended to be asleep, afraid he would only want to justify the kiss and explain that it wasn't meant to spoil their friendship. After a while, Gib lay down and rolled himself in his duvet, and Phoebe was left to another sleepless night alone with her aching heart.

There was no sign of Lara the next morning. Jed must have relented after all. Phoebe wanted to be glad for her sister, but all she could think was that now there would be no excuse for Gib not to go, and she felt leaden inside as she walked along to the tube.

Still, when the receptionist rang through to tell her that Lara was on the line, Phoebe forced a smile to her face as she asked her to put her sister through. At least one of them should be happy.

It certainly wasn't Lara. Her voice crowded with sobs, she told Phoebe that she was going home.

'What's happened?' Phoebe demanded in concern, but Lara was crying in earnest by that stage and it was impossible to get anything out of her. 'Where are you?' she asked instead, and Lara managed to tell her that she was back at the house.

'Stay there,' said Phoebe. 'I'm coming.'

'You can't go home in the middle of the morning!' Celia objected. 'You've got too much to do. You haven't got me an edit suite yet and I need you to book those lights and when are you going to email Dave about that tripod...'

Phoebe walked out on the rest of it.

She found Lara weeping miserably, face down on the bed that had once been Gib's. For once he was out. Phoebe tried to remember the last time she had come back and he hadn't been there, and couldn't think of a single occasion. The house felt oddly empty without him, and she thought bleakly that she had better get used to it.

Sitting down on the edge of the bed, she stroked her sister's hair and coaxed the whole story out of her. She was terribly afraid that something awful had happened, but it turned out that the worst hurt was to Lara's feelings. She had finally received her much-longed-for invitation to party with the group after the gig, and when she was asked back to where they were living, she was ecstatic. It was only when she got there that she realised that Jed had been annexed by an intimidatingly cool girl and that she herself was evidently intended for the least prepossessing member of the group.

'And I'd spent all my money buying them all drinks at the club so I didn't have any left to get back here,' Lara sobbed. 'I had to stay there all night fighting this guy off, and everything was so dirty it was *horrible*! And the worst thing is that Mum and Dad are going to say 'I told you so' and I gave up my course and everything and I feel such a *fool*. They're going to be furious with me!'

Privately, Phoebe thought her parents would be so glad to see Lara safely home that they would forgive her anything, but in the end she said that she would drive her back to Bristol and face them with her. Of course, her mother insisted that she spend the night rather than driving straight back—'You'd better ring Gib, dear, and let him know where you are or he'll be worried'—so she left very early the next morning and went straight to work.

She half expected Celia to sack her there and then for walking out the previous day, but there was so much to do that even her notoriously irrational boss had realised that this was not the time to lose a key member of the team. Either that or she had realised just how much Phoebe did.

By the end of the day, Phoebe was tired and frazzled and wanted nothing more than to be at home with a strong drink. But going home would mean facing Gib and keeping her promise to ring her mother and end the pretence, so she was still sitting at her desk when she remembered the contact Gib had given her at the Community Bank.

Taking out the card, she studied it. California. It was almost seven o'clock in London by then, which meant that there was a chance that Brad Petersen would be at work. She could try, anyway.

Phoebe dialled the number before she had a chance to lose her nerve and sat listening to the foreign ringing tone. The way her luck was going at the moment, there would be no one there—but no! She was through.

'Could I speak to Brad Petersen, please?' she said, reading his name from the card.

That was as far as her luck went. Brad, it appeared, was sick and wouldn't be in for another couple of days. Was there anyone else who could help?

'I'm not sure,' said Phoebe doubtfully. 'I'm calling from London, and I was given his name by somebody called John Gibson—' She broke off as the man at the other end of the phone gave a shout of recognition.

'You don't mean Gib, do you?'

'Er...yes.' She held the receiver away from her and stared at it in puzzlement. 'Do you know him?'

He laughed. 'We certainly do! How the hell is he?'

'He's fine,' she said in a frozen voice. 'I didn't realise he knew anyone other than Brad at the Community Bank.'

'I'd say he knows just about everybody,' the man said, sounding amused.

'Really? How's that?' Phoebe couldn't believe her own control. 'Does he work for the bank as well?'

'You could say that.' Yes, that was definite amusement. 'Listen, are you likely to see him soon?'

'I'm going to see him tonight, as it happens.'

'Well, say hey from all of us in Development, will you? Tell him we've all been missing him!'

'Oh, I will,' said Phoebe. 'I'll tell him *exactly* what you've said.'

Very carefully, she put the phone down. For a while she sat, just staring at it while hurt and humiliation built gradually inside her into a white-hot fury. It was surging invigoratingly along her veins by the time she got to her feet, but she was outwardly uncannily calm as she picked up her bag, put on her coat and retrieved the car from the car park where she had left it all day. Then she drove home, her knuckles white against the steering wheel.

Kate and Bella were out, Phoebe was glad to see, and Gib was alone in the kitchen. His face lit up in a way that made her heart crack when he saw her.

'Hey!'

'Hey,' she echoed, but enunciating it very clearly. 'Oh, that's from everyone in Development, by the way!'

Gib stilled. 'Development?' he repeated cautiously.

'Surely you haven't forgotten those guys, have you?' Sarcasm dripped from her voice. 'I gather they all miss *you* a lot!'

'You didn't talk to Brad Petersen,' said Gib flatly as he realised what must have happened.

'No, Brad's sick, but it turns out that wasn't a problem, because everybody knows good old Gib!' Phoebe's eyes flashed dangerously green. *'I just happened to bump into him!'* she quoted his words back to Gib furiously. 'I couldn't believe it! All this time I've been going on and on about the Community Bank and how hard it is to contact anyone there and *you*, you actually work for them! Why didn't you tell me?'

Gib sighed. 'I didn't want to get involved with the programme. It's the bank's policy not to give personal interviews and to make sure that any publicity concentrates on the projects. You told me yourself that Celia wanted to do a hatchet job on the president. Of course I wasn't going to help you do that!'

'You lied to me!' Phoebe was too hurt and angry to listen to him. 'I hate liars!'

'I didn't lie outright,' Gib tried to defend himself.

'You said you didn't have a job!'

'I never said that. *You* assumed that I didn't, but I told you myself that I was working on various projects while I was over here.'

'Community Bank projects?'

'Yes.'

Too angry to stand still, Phoebe was striding around the kitchen like some kind of caged beast. 'No wonder you thought you'd be in banking when I wanted you to pretend that you had a job! *I know, I'll say I work for the Community Bank! I'll do some research.* Oh, good idea, I said. How stupid can you get?' she demanded bitterly. 'All you had to do was promote yourself a bit, make yourself President, because why not? Phoebe's too dense to work it out! She'll never know.'

It was all so obvious when you knew the truth, she

thought savagely. Of *course* he had been able to convince everyone that he was a banker at the wedding!

'No wonder I always thought you were laughing at me! You must have had a very amusing time seeing me make an idiot of myself, all that worrying about how you'd cope at the wedding, all that scratching my head about how to contact someone at the Community Bank—what a laugh you must have had!'

'Phoebe, it wasn't like that,' Gib tried, but Phoebe was in no mood to listen to him.

'Oh, wasn't it? What was it like then, Gib? Why couldn't you just tell me if it wasn't like that?'

Gib hesitated, then mentally threw his cards on the table. Only complete honesty would help him now, he thought.

'I couldn't tell you,' he said, 'but not because I was laughing at you. It was because of a bet.'

CHAPTER TEN

'A BET?'

Stony-faced, Phoebe listened as Gib, opting for a full confession, told her what Mallory had said, and explained how he and Josh had come to make the bet.

'So that's what all this has been for, a *bet*?' she said when he had finished, her voice shaking. 'All that stuff you were spouting about friendship and how important it was to you, and all the time it was just some stupid joke!'

'No! It wasn't a joke,' Gib protested, raking his fingers through his hair in frustration. He thought he had explained all this. 'It started out as a challenge but that's not how it ended. I never expected...I hadn't counted on you.'

'Oh, I'm sure you hadn't! I must have been a big disappointment! Bella and Kate are pushovers, of course—they'll be friends with anybody—but I was a harder nut to crack, wasn't I? I've got to give it to you, though, Gib, you worked hard on me,' said Phoebe, raw with hurt. 'And I fell for it in the end.'

Her cheeks burned with humiliation as she remembered that scene in her room. 'That was very clever, the way you pushed me into admitting that I thought of you as a friend! I suppose you were taping the whole conversation so that you could prove to Josh that you'd won the bet. Look, here's Phoebe saying that she'll miss me! What more do you need?'

'Phoebe, you've got it all wrong—'

'Oh, yes, it's all falling into place now!' Phoebe thought that she had been angry when she found out that he worked for the bank, but it was nothing compared to the rage that seized her now. 'Then I nearly spoilt everything by getting too keen. That must have been a nasty moment when I wanted to sleep with you, because you couldn't have that, could you? Sex wasn't part of the bet! I don't blame you for insisting on the floor—I'd have done the same if I got ten thousand dollars for it! And I suppose that kind little gesture of putting me in touch with your "friend" was by way of being a consolation prize?'

'Of course it wasn't!' Gib was having trouble keeping his own temper under control by now. 'I just didn't like seeing you so tired. I wanted to help you keep your job.'

'Oh, very noble!' she jeered. 'And no doubt Brad Petersen wasn't supposed to let on that he knew you?'

'No,' he admitted. 'I wanted to keep it secret a bit longer.'

'Well, now that the cat's out of the bag, you might as well set up an interview for me,' said Phoebe, glaring at him. 'As I understand it, you've got lots of friends at the bank, so it shouldn't be too hard. It's the least you can do after the way you've used me!'

'You used me too,' said Gib angrily, losing his precarious control on his temper. 'You went on and on and *on* about your precious Ben, making it crystal clear that I was only there as substitute for him. How do you think that made me feel? I didn't sleep with you, not because of the bet, but because I knew I would only ever be second-best to him.

'Well, sorry, Phoebe,' he swept on as she opened her mouth, not giving her a chance to speak, 'but that's not enough for me. You claim that you want to live dangerously, but you don't. You want to keep things right as they are. You'd rather stay obsessed with a man you can't have than look around to see if there might be someone else for you. You'd rather work ridiculously long hours than relax and enjoy yourself, and if work's not enough of an excuse not to try something new, there's always your family!'

'Leave my family out of this!'

'Why? You never do,' Gib retorted, equally angry by now. 'They're all perfectly capable of looking after themselves, but no, Phoebe knows best! You're the one that claims not to like lying, but that's exactly what you've been doing because you think you know how everyone feels and you think it's up to you to make it all better. Well, I've got news for you, Phoebe. You can't. You need to learn to trust people to sort out their own problems.'

'You've got a nerve, lecturing me about trust when you've spent the last six weeks pretending to be my friend!'

His jaw set. 'I wasn't pretending.'

'Friends don't lie to each other—oh, sorry, you weren't lying, were you? You just omitted to fill me in on a few little details like the fact that you've been living a double life!'

'Well, you can go and live your other half now,' Phoebe told him, green eyes a-glitter with tears. 'You can stay with Josh, and give him his ten thousand dollars while you're at it. You're going to have to come to terms with losing for once, Gib. Your girlfriend was quite right. You've got no idea what women really want from a man, but I can tell you it's a lot more than a bit of superficial charm and ability to lie, which is all that you've got to offer. Sorry, but you just don't have what it takes to be a friend!'

When Bella and Kate came back later that night, they found Phoebe raging around the house, close to tears and incoherent with fury.

'What do you mean, Gib's gone?' Bella demanded blankly, latching onto the only part that she could understand.

Phoebe poured out the whole story all over again, and

was outraged to discover that her friends were a lot less concerned about Gib's deception than she was. 'How can you be so calm about it?' she asked furiously. 'He lied to you, too!'

'Oh, I don't know,' said Kate, considering the matter with infuriating reasonableness. 'The worst thing he did was to make me think that he was unemployed when in fact he apparently has a perfectly good job. It's not the end of the world, is it?'

It felt like it to Phoebe. Angrily, she brushed the tears of rage from her eyes. She was *not* going to cry over Gib. That would be the final humiliation!

'What about the bet? Don't you feel like you've been used?'

'Not really,' said Bella apologetically. 'It's not like Gib was just pretending to like us. I'm sure that he did, and we liked him.' She sighed. 'It won't be the same without him!'

'Oh, I'm *so* sorry!' fumed Phoebe, offended. 'I should have been the one to leave so that the three of you could carry on being such good friends! I mean, I'm obviously being completely unreasonable to object to someone living in my house under false pretences. I can't think *why* I'd have a problem with that!' she added sarcastically.

'Can't you?'

Phoebe was taken aback by Kate's quiet question. 'What do you mean?' she said defensively.

'Oh, Phoebe, it's so obvious! You're upset because you're in love with Gib.'

'I am not!' Phoebe spluttered furiously and then faltered as she met Kate's unwavering eyes. 'Not any more, anyway,' she said.

'No?'

'How can I be in love with someone I can't trust?' she said with an edge of desperation. 'Now I don't know if anything he told me is true. I feel as if I don't know him at all.'

'You do know him, Phoebe. He's exactly the same guy he was before. You just know that there's more to him than you thought.'

'Yes, a whole life I know nothing about!'

'That's not important,' said Kate, choosing her words with care. 'What's important is that there was something special between you. It was obvious to all of us. We could see it in Gib's face when he looked at you, and in yours when you looked at him. That wasn't a lie. Gib wasn't pretending then. He was in love with you too.'

'No, he wasn't,' Phoebe gulped back the tears. 'He wouldn't even sleep with me!'

Bella rolled her eyes. 'He would have done if he hadn't really cared about you. As it was, of *course* he didn't want to be just a substitute for Ben. He never struck me as the kind of guy who'd like being second-best, and that's what you made him feel.'

'Bella's right,' said Kate, putting her arm round Phoebe's shoulders. 'I know you're hurt, but I think you should give Gib a second chance. It's rare to have the kind of connection you had with him, and it would be a shame to throw it away without even trying to see if you could make things right.'

'I don't know how,' Phoebe confessed miserably.

'There's no point in doing anything while you're in this state,' Kate said, and even in the depths of her despair Phoebe couldn't help being amused by the reversal of their usual roles. Normally Kate was the one in floods of tears over her love life, while Phoebe stuck to being sensible. Bella was good on sympathy, but Phoebe was the one they both turned to for comfort and practical advice. All that was changed now!

'Leave it a few days until you calm down,' Bella added.

'I'm sure Gib will ring before then anyway, and if he does, give him a chance and listen to what he's got to say.'

But Gib didn't ring.

Phoebe spent the next week lurching between bitterness and despair. One minute she was furious with him for not getting in touch, the next she missed him so acutely it was like a physical pain.

She tried telling herself that any relationship would have been doomed anyway. It could never have worked. Gib had made it clear that he wouldn't be staying in London long. Presumably he would have to go back to his job at some point. It couldn't be a very important one if he had been able to spend nearly two months hanging around in London. Whatever he said about the projects he had been setting up, he had hardly been in a frenzy of activity that a top executive would have generated. Perhaps he had taken unpaid leave so that he could take up Josh's challenge. It was exactly the sort of thing Gib *would* do.

Whenever Phoebe thought about that bet, her guts twisted painfully with the memory of that conversation in her room. 'Your friendship is important to me,' Gib had said. Had that been a lie too, and if it wasn't, *why*, *why*, hadn't he been in touch? It didn't matter how much she hated him for using her to win his bet, all she wanted was to hear his voice.

The silence of the phone mocked her. Soon she was as bad as Kate, constantly ringing 1471 to see if anyone had called and not left a message, and checking her email obsessively, but there was nothing from Gib.

Her only glimmer of hope was a message from the Community Bank responding to their long-standing request for an interview. The head of Development would be available after all to talk about the history of the bank and the projects in which it invested. Celia bitched about not getting the president, but it was a huge coup.

Phoebe could only think that Gib had pulled some strings for her. He might not have a particularly responsible job, but she knew to her cost how charming and persuasive he could be and, judging by the phone call she had made, he had plenty of contacts in Development.

However it had happened, she wanted to believe that he had done it for her, and it gave her the excuse she needed to call him. She could thank him for his help without sounding as if she was desperate to talk to him, couldn't she?

'I'm sorry, Phoebe,' said Josh when she rang. 'He's gone.'

'Gone? Gone where?'

'Back to the States.'

'Oh.'

Phoebe almost staggered beneath the wash of desolation. Gib had gone, and he hadn't even bothered to say goodbye. With a huge effort, she swallowed the tears in her throat. 'The thing is, I think he might have helped to arrange an interview for me,' she said unsteadily. 'I just wanted to tell him that I appreciated it.' Stumbling over her words, she asked Josh if he could give her a contact number or an email address.

'I can't give it to you, I'm afraid.' Josh sounded acutely uncomfortable. 'Gib was very angry when he left. He made me promise that I wouldn't.'

So that was it.

Bella and Kate were wrong. Gib didn't love her, and he didn't want to hear from her. Wearily, Phoebe put down the phone. Her heart felt as if it had been crushed into a small, cold stone in her chest. She would survive, she knew that. She had survived Ben's rejection, and she would survive without Gib, but never had life seemed so bleak or the future so empty.

She lost all interest in her job. Even the fact that she had arranged an interview at last seemed a hollow victory, not that Celia gave her much credit for it, although even she had to accept that it was more than anyone else had been able to get.

Ten days later, the two of them flew to California with a cameraman. It should have been a thrilling experience for Phoebe, the high point of her career in television that far, but all she could think about was Gib and the dull, persistent ache in her heart.

The headquarters of the Community Bank was a light, airy building, all wood and windows and the last word in technology, set in beautiful grounds far from the smog and bustle of the city. Phoebe was desperately nervous. She presumed that Gib had come back, and she didn't know whether she longed to bump into him or dreaded it.

At the very least she might meet someone who would be able to give him a message, she told herself, but even if she did, what would it say? The only thing she could think of to tell him was that she loved him and missed him and that all she wanted was to see him again, but how could she ask anyone to pass *that* on?

Dave, the cameraman, raved about the setting, and they had to hang around for ages while he shot the exterior before at last persuading him inside.

'Phoebe Lane?' They were met by a pleasant-looking man who held out his hand with a warm smile. 'I'm Brad Petersen. I'm *very* pleased to meet you!'

Phoebe was a little surprised at the warmth of his welcome, but she reminded herself that Americans were notoriously friendly. So this was Brad, she thought, studying him surreptitiously as she shook his hand. He was the contact who had been sick when she had phoned, and she wondered how different things would have been if he had been there and had kept Gib's secret for him.

She longed to ask if he had seen Gib, but her tongue seemed stuck to the roof of her mouth and, in any case, Celia was there looking impatient at all the attention Phoebe was getting and pushing forward to introduce herself as producer and director so that Brad knew exactly who was in charge.

Brad shook hands civilly enough, but apparently didn't understand Phoebe's lack of status, turning back to her immediately and asking her if she had had a good trip and urging her to let him know if there was anything that he could do for her.

'Thank you, no,' said Phoebe, with a nervous look in Celia's direction. 'We're just very grateful to you for agreeing to be interviewed.'

'Oh, I should have mentioned,' said Brad. 'I can't make this afternoon. A meeting that I can't miss, I'm afraid.'

'That's absolutely typical of you, Phoebe!' Celia exploded, already irritated by being effectively ignored. 'You were supposed to confirm all of this! What on earth is the point of us coming all the way out here if we're not even going to get any interview? If you'd done your job properly, we could have sorted this out before we left London and arranged a different date. As it is the whole trip is going to turn out to be a complete waste of time and money thanks to you!'

Brad shot her a look of dislike before carrying on talking to Phoebe as if Celia hadn't spoken. 'However, the president is available this afternoon, and he wondered if you'd like to interview him instead.'

Their jaws dropped in unison. 'The *president*?' said Phoebe blankly. 'Not J.G. Grieve, the president?'

'Yes.'

'But...I thought he didn't give interviews!'

Brad smiled. 'He doesn't normally, but he's prepared to make an exception in your case.'

Phoebe thought that she would long treasure the expression on Celia's face at that moment. For once even she had nothing to say.

Hardly able to believe their luck, they followed Brad through spacious open-plan offices with views out over the spectacular grounds. To Phoebe, it didn't feel like a bank at all. Everyone was smiling and relaxed, and they were all dressed very casually. With a pang, she remembered how Gib had pretended to be the president at Ben's wedding.

'Mine's a different kind of bank where you don't have to dress like a dummy all day,' he had told her and she had rolled her eyes in disbelief. How was she to have known that he was describing a real place?

Forcing down the memory, she smiled at Brad as he stepped aside to usher her into a private office. A man rather more smartly dressed than the others was sitting behind a desk, but he got up to shake hands when they appeared.

'Thank you so much for agreeing to see us, Mr Grieve,' said Phoebe politely, and he grinned.

'I'm not Mr Grieve, I'm afraid. I'm just his assistant, but he is expecting you.'

He knocked on a door behind him, and opened it in response to a muffled 'come in' from inside. 'The film crew from London are here,' he said and held open the door so that they could file past him.

They found themselves in a vast office with glass walls on two sides and a polished wooden floor. The desk was bare except for a computer and a telephone, and two cream sofas faced each other over a low glass table. A man was lounging on one of them, but he laid the report he was reading aside and stood up as they came in.

'Welcome to the Community Bank,' he said, and smiled.

A very familiar smile.

It was Gib.

Phoebe stopped dead so that Celia, following close on her heels, bumped into her.

'Do look where you're going, Phoebe,' she snapped and pushed past her to shake Gib's hand and introduce herself.

She ignored Phoebe, who stood as if riveted to the spot. It was as if the floor was shifting dangerously beneath her feet, and she didn't dare move in case she fell over.

There was a roaring in her ears and she swallowed convulsively to wake herself up, because clearly she had fallen asleep on the plane and this was just a dream—a nightmare!—where everyone else was treating a surreal situation as completely normal. Any minute now a flight assistant would prod her to ask if she wanted a meal, and she would wake up with a start.

'Where do you want Mr Grieve sitting?' Celia asked Dave, and they started conferring about light and angles, while Gib strolled over to where Phoebe still stood by the door.

'Hello, Phoebe,' he said softly.

'You're not the president of this bank,' said Phoebe very carefully, to show that she knew this was a dream.

'I'm not?' Gib looked down at himself in mock dismay. 'Well, don't tell anyone else! They all think that I am, and we don't want them to know I've just been pretending all this time!'

For a dream, this was going on a little too long, and Gib himself was uncannily real.

And achingly familiar. The laughter lines creasing his face. The devilry dancing in the blue eyes. The shape of his jaw and the line of his throat and the way the long, mobile mouth curled into that smile that cracked her heart.

Phoebe moistened her lips, not sure now whether she

wanted it to be a dream or not. 'You can't be,' she said hoarsely.

Gib went over to the door and called for his assistant. 'Mark, am I president of this bank?'

'Er...yes, sir.'

'There you go,' said Gib, turning back to Phoebe. 'Mark says I am, so I must be.'

This couldn't be happening! 'So who is J.G. Grieve?' she managed to ask. 'Or was your name another lie?'

'J for John and G for Gibson, I'm afraid, Phoebe.'

'Phoebe!' Celia was snapping her fingers irritably. 'Don't just stand there! Dave needs you to sort out the cables and get the boom organised.' Pasting a smile on her face, she turned to Gib. 'Mr Grieve, if you'd like to sit down over there, I'll run through the questions I'd like to ask you while they're setting up.'

Numbly, Phoebe moved cables around and tested for sound, oblivious to Dave's curious looks. When he judged they were ready, Celia started on the interview. She might be a prima donna of the first order, but she could switch on the professionalism when it counted.

Not that Phoebe took in any of it. She couldn't take her eyes off Gib. She saw him talking, smiling, looked relaxed in front of the camera, but his words were drowned out by the hammering of her heart and the whirl in her head where disbelief jostled with humiliation at this final deception, but neither was as strong as the sheer joy beating along her veins, telling her that this was real after all and that he was there, he was there, he was there!

Celia was winding up. 'Why did you decide to break with precedent and talk to us this afternoon?' she asked at last.

Gib took his time before replying. He seemed to be picking his words carefully, and Phoebe found herself leaning forward to hear what he had to say.

'I've always believed that what we do here is not about us, but about the projects around the world that we support. But support is the keyword. The people who are really making a difference are those who set up the projects and devote their time and energy to making them a success. I used to think that by giving interviews that focus on me or the Community Bank, we would divert attention away from what really matters, which are the communities who are working to improve their own lives.'

'So what made you change your mind?' asked Celia.

He looked directly at Phoebe, who was holding the boom out of camera shot. 'I spent some time away from the bank recently,' he said, 'and I realised that believing something doesn't always make it true. I know now that it's not a sign of weakness to change your mind, or to admit that you were wrong.'

His eyes held Phoebe's and she looked back at him, knowing that he wasn't talking about giving media interviews any more. 'I was wrong about a lot of things,' he went on. 'Doing this interview was the only way I could think of to put things right.'

'Ah,' said Celia, evidently baffled. She exchanged a glance with the cameraman, who shrugged.

'I hoped that it would be a chance to explain,' said Gib without taking his gaze from Phoebe. 'I had something very special, and I didn't realise what it meant to me until I had thrown it away. I wanted a chance to say that I was sorry, and that I didn't understand until too late that my life had changed without me knowing it.'

'Er...right. Well, thanks very much,' said Celia, having obviously decided that Gib had lost it completely. 'Have you got all the shots you need, Dave?'

The cameraman, more perceptive, was looking at Phoebe.

'For now,' he said, and gently took the boom from her nerveless hand. 'I'll take this, love.'

Phoebe couldn't move. She could just look back at Gib, while Dave deftly packed up the kit and propelled a confused Celia out of the office. The door closed on her demand to know what on earth was going on, and why Phoebe was just *standing* there like an idiot...

Gib got up from the sofa, but he made no move to touch Phoebe. 'I hurt you,' he said. 'I'm sorry.'

'Josh said you were angry,' she found her voice at last.

'I was, but mostly with myself. I'd been selfish and arrogant and stupid, and all the things I swore I never wanted to be. I hadn't thought about you or how you might feel when you found out that I wasn't who you thought I was.'

He paused. 'I should have told you, Phoebe. I know that now. The bet wasn't important, but there never seemed to be a good moment, and I was afraid that if I did tell you it would spoil everything—which it did when you found out anyway.

'So of course I found excuses for myself,' he said. 'I told myself that I didn't mean anything to you, that I was a free spirit and that the last thing I wanted was to tie myself down. I was the guy who ran a mile at the first hint of commitment. Why would I want to give up my freedom for a girl who wasn't even in love with me? A girl who as far as I could see didn't even like me?'

'But I told you I liked you,' said Phoebe.

'I know, but you didn't sound very sure.'

'Well, I suppose that's because I wasn't. I'm afraid that I was lying too. I didn't like you.'

Gib's face fell ludicrously. 'You said that you did!'

'I didn't mean it,' said Phoebe, shaking her head sorrowfully, but the expression in the blue eyes made her stop teasing then. 'I do much more than like you, Gib,' she told him softly. 'The truth is that I love you.'

He stared at her for a long moment and then reached out to take both her hands. 'You love me?'

'Yes.' It was a release to say it at last. 'I was just too scared to admit it.'

'You love me,' he said again, trying out the words with a different intonation as if he couldn't take them in.

A smile wavered on Phoebe's lips. 'Yes.'

'Phoebe...' Gib drew her closer. 'Say it again.'

'I love you.'

'And I love you.' Gib let go of her hands to cup Phoebe's face, and she thought that she would dissolve with happiness at the warmth in the blue eyes. 'I never thought that I would say that, but it's true. You must believe me.'

'I do,' she said, and he kissed her then.

Phoebe melted into him, winding her arms around Gib's neck as the grey misery that had settled in her since he left was washed away in a tumbling tide of happiness and relief. Adrift in enchantment, she clung to him and kissed him back, again and again, deep, sweet, hungry kisses that said more than words could ever do.

'I've been so unhappy without you,' she mumbled, pressing kisses into his throat. It was much later by then, and she was sitting on his lap on one of the cream sofas. 'Why didn't you tell me you loved me?'

'Sheer jealousy,' Gib confessed, stroking her hair. 'You kept telling me that you were still in love with Ben, and I thought I would only ever be second-best for you. I tried telling myself that I would forget you quickly enough when I came back here, but I didn't. I missed you.' His arms tightened around her. 'I missed you more than I can say. I've always had a great life here. I've got everything I need—a fantastic job, a great house, wonderful friends—but none of them meant anything without you.

'And I felt guilty, too, about the way I had hurt you. I remembered what you'd said about making myself useful, and I decided that you were right. The least I could do for you was to let you have the interview you needed, and to hell with policy as long as you kept your job.'

'I wondered if it was you that had arranged it,' said Phoebe, snuggling closer. 'But I imagined you pulling strings with your superiors, not being the one who made the decision! I thought we were coming to interview Brad Petersen, though.'

'I asked Brad to do it at first because I was still feeling raw, but when it came down to it, I couldn't bear the idea that you might be in the building and I wouldn't see you. As soon as you walked in here, I knew it was hopeless,' said Gib. 'It wasn't enough just to apologise and retire with my pride intact. I knew that I had to tell you that I loved you.

'You know, Josh was right,' he went on thoughtfully. 'He told me that I was spoilt, and I was. I was bored with girls falling in love with me, and then going off in a huff when I didn't fall in love back. I never had to make an effort for any of them...and then I met you. The one person I wanted, the one person it seemed I couldn't have.'

Phoebe sat back in his lap and looked at him seriously. 'Gib, are you sure I'm not just another challenge for you, like climbing a mountain?'

'Climbing isn't a challenge,' Gib protested, pretending outrage. 'It's a passion! That feeling when you get to the summit and look out over the world...it's incredible, and it's the only thing that even comes close to the feeling I got when you told me you loved me just now.'

He smiled as his warm hand slid seductively up her thigh.

'And I have a feeling,' he said, dropping his voice until it was so deep and so low that it vibrated up and down Phoebe's spine, making her shiver with delicious anticipation, 'that the feeling I got then is only a fraction of what I'm going to feel when I finally take you to bed!'

'Are you sure you wouldn't rather stay just good friends?' asked Phoebe provocatively, even as her own hands were drifting teasingly over his body. 'Sex and friendship don't go together, you said. It just complicates things, you said. It would spoil everything.'

'Ah, yes, but that was when I thought a friend was all you'd ever be,' said Gib. 'Friendship is all very well, but when you're in love, it isn't enough. I need more from you than that. I need to know that you love me, that you will always be there, that I'll see you every morning when I wake up...and sex goes very well with all of that!'

Phoebe smiled. 'I suppose we could always try it and see,' she suggested, and Gib flipped her expertly beneath him and slid down until they were both lying horizontally on the sofa.

'We could,' he agreed, kissing his way along her jaw, 'but I think we should agree a few rules of engagement first.'

'Engagement as in battle?' she teased, breathless beneath the blizzard of kisses.

'Engagement as in getting married and living happily ever after,' said Gib into the curve of her neck so that she stretched and shivered with pleasure.

'What exactly is involved in these rules?'

'Oh, they're easy,' he murmured, continuing his delicious assault. 'First of all, you have to love me for ever.'

'I think I can manage that,' said Phoebe, not without difficulty as his lips drifted onwards.

'You might have to prove it by kissing me on a regular basis.'

She pretended to sigh. 'If I must.'

'And when we do kiss,' said Gib, 'we don't want any misunderstandings. It means everything.'

'Like this?'

Phoebe pulled him close and they kissed, a long, long kiss of promise with an undertow of dizzy, intoxicating desire.

'Exactly like that,' Gib managed raggedly at last.

'So what's the second rule?'

'I thought you'd guess this one,' he said. 'Stick to the story and keep it simple!'

She stretched luxuriously beneath his increasingly insistent hands. 'What is the story this time?'

'The same as it was before,' said Gib. 'We met, we fell in love, and we're going to spend the rest of our lives together. The only difference is that this time it's true. Do you think you can remember that?'

'Oh, I think so,' she said.

'No deviating from the script now!' he warned. 'That's the rule. You have to promise to marry me or the deal is off.'

'It doesn't sound *too* hard,' she allowed, smiling.

'I wanted to keep them simple so you know exactly what you're agreeing to,' said Gib.

'Hhmmn.' Phoebe pretended to consider.

'Just two rules,' he said. 'Love me for ever and marry me soon—what could be easier than that? It's up to you whether you accept them or not, but once you do, I have to tell you that they're not negotiable. Oh, that's the third rule!'

'In that case,' said Phoebe with a sigh of contentment, 'I accept.'

'All the rules?' said Gib, just to make sure.

'Every one of them!'

THE BLIND-DATE PROPOSAL

CHAPTER ONE

'WHAT time do you call this?'

Finn looked up, scowling, as Kate knocked on his door with some trepidation.

She looked at her watch. 'It's...er...nearly quarter to ten.'

'And you're supposed to start at what time?'

'Nine o'clock.'

Kate was horribly aware of her pink face. She was hot and flustered, having run up the escalator from the tube and all the way to the office, where she had panted past the surprised receptionist to fall into the lift. Somewhere along the line she had laddered her tights, and a tentative glance in the mirror was enough to confirm that her hair, a mass of wild brown curls hard to control at best of times, was tangled and windblown.

Not a good start to the day.

She was at a distinct disadvantage compared to Finn, too. In his grey suit and his pristine shirt, her new boss had always seemed to Kate buttoned up in more ways than one. He had a severe face, steely grey eyes and strong dark brows which were usually pulled together in a frown and whenever he looked at Kate, like now, his mouth was clamped together in a disapproving line.

'I know I'm late, and I'm *really* sorry,' she said breathlessly and, oblivious to Finn's discouraging expression, she launched into a long and convoluted explanation of how she had befriended an elderly lady confused by the underground system and intimidated by the rudeness of officials.

'I couldn't just leave her there,' she finished at last, 'so

I took her to Paddington and showed her where to find her train.'

'Paddington not being on your way here?'

'Not *exactly*...'

'One might even say that it was in completely the opposite direction,' Finn went on in the same snide tone.

'Not quite *opposite*,' said Kate, mentally consulting her tube map.

'So you got halfway here and then turned and headed off in a completely different direction, even though you must have known that there was no way you'd be able to get to work on time?'

'I had to,' Kate protested. 'She was so upset. There was no reason for everyone to be so rude to her,' she remembered indignantly. 'Her English wasn't that good, and she couldn't be expected to know where she was going and how to get there. How would that ticket collector like it if he had to find his way around...oh, I don't know...the Amazon, say...where he didn't know the language and nobody could be bothered to help him?'

Finn looked at her wearily. 'You're mistaking me for someone who cares,' he said. 'The only thing I care about right now is keeping this company going, and it's not that easy with a PA who turns up whenever she feels like it! Alison makes a point of arriving ten minutes before nine every day,' he added pointedly. 'She's always reliable.'

Not so reliable that she didn't break her leg on a skiing holiday, Kate thought, but didn't say out loud. She was sick of hearing about Alison, Finn's perfect PA who was discreet and efficient and immaculately dressed and who reputedly typed at the speed of light. She could probably read Finn's mind too, Kate had decided sourly after he had shouted at her for not being able to find a file that he himself had dumped onto her desk. Alison's desk, of course, was always tidy.

The only marvel was that Alison had been careless enough to break her leg, leaving Finn to get through eight weeks without her.

He wasn't finding it easy. Already two temps had left in tears, unable to cope with the impossible standards Alison had set. Kate was just surprised that she had hung in as long as she had. This was her third week and, judging by Finn's expression, it might well be her last.

She wasn't surprised the others had given up. Finn McBride gave a whole new dimension to the notion of grumpiness and he had an unpleasantly sarcastic edge to his tongue. If she hadn't been desperate for a job, she would have been tempted to walk out on him as well.

'I said I was sorry,' she said a little sullenly. 'Not that I should have to apologise for community spirit,' she went on, still too fired up by her encounter that morning to be able to summon up the correct degree of subservience that no doubt came naturally to Alison.

Finn was unimpressed. His cold grey eyes raked her from head to foot, taking in every detail of her tangled hair and dishevelled clothes and stopping with exasperation on her laddered tights.

'I encourage my staff to do what I pay them to do,' he said frigidly, 'and that's what they do. You, on the other hand, appear to think that I should pay you to breeze in and distract everyone else in the office all day.'

Kate gaped at the unfairness of it. She had made efforts to get to know the rest of the staff, but without any great success. They didn't seem to be great ones for gossiping and, on the few occasions she had managed to strike up a conversation, Finn had been safely shut in his office. He must have X-ray eyes if he had noticed her talking to anyone!

'I don't distract anyone,' she protested.

'It sounds that way to me,' said Finn. 'You're always out in the corridor or in the other offices chatting.'

'It's called social interaction,' said Kate, provoked. 'It's what humans do, not that you'd know that of course. It's like working with robots in this office,' she went on, forgetting for a moment how much she needed this job. 'I'm lucky if I get a good morning from you, and even that I have to translate from a grunt!'

The dark brows twitched together into a terrifying glare. 'Alison never complains.'

'Maybe Alison likes being treated like just another piece of office equipment,' she said tartly. 'It wouldn't kill you to show a little interest occasionally.'

Finn glowered at her, and Kate wondered whether he was so unused to anyone daring to argue with him that he was taken aback.

If so, he soon recovered. 'I haven't time to waste the day bolstering your ego,' he snapped.

'It doesn't take long to be pleasant.' Kate refused to be cowed now. 'You could always start with something easy like "how are you?", or "have a nice weekend",' she suggested. 'And then, when you'd got the hang of that, you could work up to trickier phrases like "thank you for all your help today".'

'I can't see me having much need of that one while you're around,' said Finn nastily. 'And frankly, even if I did, I don't see why I should change my habits for you. In case you haven't noticed, I'm the boss here, so if you can't cope without constant attention, you'd better say so now and I'll get Personnel to find me another temp for Monday!'

That was enough to pull Kate up short. She really couldn't afford to lose this job. The agency had been reluctant enough to send her as it was and, if she messed this up, she'd be lucky if they didn't drop her from their books.

'I can cope,' she said quickly. 'I just don't like it.'

'You don't have to like it,' said Finn tersely. 'You just have to get on with it. Now, can we get on? We've wasted quite enough time this morning.'

He barely allowed Kate time to take off her coat before she had to endure a long and exhausting session being dictated to at top speed without so much as a suggestion that she might like a cup of coffee before she started. What with befriending old ladies and diversions to Paddington, she hadn't had time to grab her usual cappuccino from the Italian coffee bar by the tube station, and the craving for caffeine did nothing to improve her temper.

She simmered as her pen raced over the page—at this rate she would get repetitive strain injury—and could barely restrain a sigh of relief when the phone rang. A breather at last!

Holding her aching wrist with exaggerated care, so that Finn might take the hint and slow down—although there was fat chance of that!—Kate studied him surreptitiously under her lashes. He was listening to the person on the other end of the phone, grunting the occasional acknowledgement, and absently drawing heavy black boxes on a piece of paper on the desk in front of him.

Doodling was supposed to be highly revealing about your personality. What did black boxes mean? Kate wondered. Probably indicative of someone deeply repressed. That would fit with his closed expression and that reserved uptight air of his.

Although not with that air of fierce energy.

Or his mouth, come to think of it.

Kate jerked her eyes quickly away. She looked instead at the framed photograph that stood on his desk, the only personal touch in the otherwise austerely efficient office. From where she sat, she could only see the stand, but she knew it showed an absolutely beautiful woman with dark hair and enormous dark blue eyes, holding the most gorgeous baby, and both smiling at the camera.

Finn's wife, Kate had assumed, marvelling that he had had enough social skills to ask anyone to marry him, let alone a beauty like that. It was hard to imagine him smiling or kissing or even holding a baby, let alone making love.

Bizarre thought. An odd feeling snaked down Kate's spine and she shook herself slightly, only to find herself looking straight into Finn's glacial grey eyes. He had finished his phone call while she was distracted and was watching her with an expression of exasperated resignation.

'Are you awake?'

'Yes.' Faint colour tinged Kate's cheeks as she sat up straighter and picked up her notebook once more.

'Read back that last bit.'

Please, Kate wanted to mutter, but decided on reflection that this might not be the day to try and teach Finn some manners. His brusqueness left her feeling crotchety and, when he finally let her go, she took out her bad temper on her keyboard, bashing away furiously until the phone rang.

'Yes?' she snapped, too cross to bother with the usual introductory spiel.

'It's Phoebe.'

'Oh, Phoebe...hi.'

'What's up? You sound very grumpy.'

'It's just my boss here,' Kate grumbled. 'He's so rude and unpleasant. I know you thought working for Celia was bad, but honestly, he gives a whole new dimension to the idea of the boss from hell.'

'As long as he's not a creep like your last boss,' said Phoebe bracingly.

Kate wrinkled her nose remembering her ignominious departure from her last job, where her boss hadn't even made a pretence of listening to her side of the story once

Seb had got in first. Seb, of course, was an executive, and she was just a secretary and by implication dispensable.

'No, I don't think you could call him a *creep*,' she said judiciously, 'but that doesn't make him any easier to deal with.'

'Attractive?' asked Phoebe.

'Quite,' Kate admitted grudgingly. 'In a stern sort of way, I suppose. If you like the dour, my-work-is-my-life type—which I happen to know that you don't!'

'I don't think anyone could call Gib dour, no,' said Phoebe.

They both laughed, and Kate felt a lot better. It was wonderful to hear Phoebe so happy. The transformation in her friend since she had married Gib a few months ago had been remarkable, and it made up for her own dismal love life since Seb had dumped her so unceremoniously. She didn't even get wolf-whistles in the street any more, Kate thought glumly.

'I was just ringing to remind you about supper tonight,' Phoebe was saying. 'You are coming, aren't you?'

'Of course,' said Kate, but Phoebe pounced on her momentary hesitation.

'What?'

'Well, it's just that Bella hinted that you might be setting me up on a blind date tonight.'

'She shouldn't have told you!' Phoebe sounded really cross. 'I only told her because I invited her and Josh as well so it would seem more casual, but she's met some new man who's taking her to some swanky club tonight instead. Josh is coming, though,' she added reassuringly, 'so it won't be too much of a set-up.'

'Why didn't you tell me?'

'Because I wanted you both to be natural, and I knew you wouldn't be if you were nervous about whether he liked you or not.'

'Hhmmnn.' Kate wasn't entirely convinced. 'What have you told him about me?'

'That you're a high-powered PA—which you could easily be if you put your mind to it!' said Phoebe. 'He's got his own consultancy or something, so I wasn't sure if he'd be that impressed by you temping, but apart from that we told him the truth, the whole truth and nothing but the truth,' she finished virtuously.

'Oh, the *truth*!' said Kate, her voice heavy with irony. 'And what's that, exactly?'

'That you're warm and funny and attractive and basically completely wonderful,' Phoebe said firmly.

Perhaps she should ask Phoebe to put in some PR for her with Finn McBride, Kate thought, and then frowned slightly as she realised that she had been unconsciously doodling in her turn as she listened to Phoebe.

At least she didn't go in for severe black boxes. She had done her favourite, a tropical sunset complete with leaning palm tree and a couple of wiggly lines to indicate the lagoon rippling gently against the shore. What did that indicate about her?

Probably that she was a hopeless fantasist, in which case she could save herself the cost of a professional analysis. She already knew that she was far too romantic for her own good. People had been telling her for years that she needed to shape up, get real, wake up and smell the coffee, and do all the other things that simply didn't come naturally to her.

Suppressing a sigh, Kate carefully added a bunch of coconuts to the palm tree. 'So won't he wonder why if I'm that perfect I'm reduced to being set up on blind dates by friends? Why aren't men falling at my feet wherever I go?'

'I don't know. Why aren't they?'

That was one of the things Kate liked about Phoebe. She really believed in her friends.

Kate put down her pen and forced herself to concentrate.

Perhaps all this was a sign to stop dreaming about Seb miraculously turning into a different person and to start making an effort to meet someone new. To wake up and smell the coffee, in fact.

'So what's he like, this guy?'

'I've never met him,' Phoebe had to admit. 'He's an old friend of Gib's.'

'How old, exactly?'

'In his early forties, I think.'

'Just coming up for his mid-life crisis then,' said Kate with an uncharacteristic touch of cynicism.

'He's already had more than enough crises,' said Phoebe soberly. 'He's a widower. His wife died when their daughter was just a toddler, and he's been struggling to bring her up on his own ever since.'

'Oh, how awful,' said Kate, her ready sympathy roused and feeling instantly guilty for her flip comment. 'It must have been terrible for him.'

'Well, yes, I gather it was. Gib says he absolutely adored his wife, but it's six years ago now, and he's thinking that his little girl is getting to the stage when she really needs a woman around. He's out of the way of dating, though, and since you were complaining about not meeting any men, Gib suggested a casual supper to introduce you. It's no big deal, but he thought you might get on.'

'I don't know that I'm really stepmother material,' said Kate doubtfully. 'I don't know anything about children.'

'Nonsense!' Phoebe wasn't having any of that. 'Look how good you are with animals, and children are just the same. They need someone to take them under her wing, and you know what a soft heart you've got for lame ducks.'

'Yes, but I don't want to go out with a lame duck,' Kate protested. 'I want someone sexy and exciting and glamorous.'

Like Seb.

The same thought was clearly in Phoebe's mind. 'No you don't,' she said firmly. 'You want someone kind.'

Kate sighed. 'Why can't I have someone who's kind *and* sexy and exciting and glamorous?'

'Because I married him,' said Phoebe smugly. 'Now listen, this guy's had a hard time, so be nice to him.'

'Oh, all right,' grumbled Kate. 'What's his name, anyway—' She broke off as Finn's door opened. 'Uh-oh, here comes Mr Grumpy! I'd better go—I'm not supposed to use the phone for personal calls. See you later.' She put the phone down hastily.

Finn looked at her with a suspicious frown. 'Who was that?'

Well, she wasn't going to tell him the truth and, although she could have made up something innocuous, Kate had an irrepressibly inventive streak and as a matter of principle resisted the simple option when she could complicate matters. She embarked instead on a long, involved and utterly untrue story, inventing an accountant who had met Alison skiing but who had subsequently been on a business trip to Singapore and had only just heard about the accident and, remembering that Alison had told him where she worked, now wanted to know where to send a card.

'I said it would be all right if he sent it here and we would forward it,' she finished, having embroidered the story with so many details that she almost believed it herself.

Finn's expression was glazed with irritation by the time she got to the end. 'I wish I'd never asked,' he sighed. 'You've just wasted a quarter of an hour of my life!'

'It's not as if we do brain surgery here,' said Kate, a trifle sullenly. 'I don't see what difference fifteen minutes here or there makes.'

'In that case, you won't mind staying late tonight to make up for the hour you missed this morning,' Finn said with an unpleasant look. 'We've got an extremely important project coming up and I need to get this done to fax to the States before tomorrow morning.'

'I can't, I'm afraid,' she said, not sounding at all regretful. 'I'm going out.'

Finn frowned. 'Can't you ring and say you'll be a bit late?'

For anyone else, Kate would have offered to do just that, but something about Finn McBride rubbed her up the wrong way. It wasn't as if he had made the slightest effort to be pleasant to her.

'Oh, I don't think my boyfriend would like that very much,' she said instead, trying for the unconscious smugness that so often seemed to accompany the words 'my boyfriend'.

'You've got a boyfriend?' Finn was unflatteringly surprised, and Kate bridled. It was bad enough putting up with his rudeness without knowing that he thought her incapable of attracting a man as well!

'Oh, yes,' she said, determined to convince him that while she might not be a perfect PA, *somebody* wanted her. 'In fact,' she went on, leaning forward confidentially, 'he's taking me somewhere really special tonight. I think he might be going to pop the question!'

'Really?' Finn raised a contemptuous eyebrow, not even bothering to try and hide his disbelief.

How rude, thought Kate indignantly. He clearly didn't think she was the kind of girl who would get a man at all, let alone one who wanted to marry her.

Her brown eyes narrowed. 'Oh, yes,' she said on her mettle. 'Didn't you know? That's why I'm temping. Ever since I met—'

She searched wildly for a name before remembering Bella's current and very glamorous man. Your best friend's boyfriend was normally out of bounds, but she didn't think Bella would mind her borrowing him mentally.

'—Will,' she carried on after the tiniest beat, 'we've both known that we were meant for each other. He's a financial analyst,' she went on breezily, deciding that she might as well take Will's career as well, 'so I didn't want to commit to a permanent job when he might be posted to New York or Tokyo at any minute. Of course, he keeps saying to me, "Darling, there's no need for you to go out to work every day," but I feel it's important to keep some financial independence, don't you?'

'I wouldn't have thought your earnings as a temp would make much difference if you're living with a financial analyst,' said Finn with something not a million miles from a sneer.

'It's a matter of principle,' said Kate airily, quite enjoying the thought of herself destined for a life of expatriate luxury.

Finn turned back to his office. 'Perhaps you could make it a matter of principle to turn up on time tomorrow,' he said nastily. 'That would make a nice change.'

It was a pity she wasn't as good at real life as she was at inventing it, Kate reflected glumly as the bus inched through the rush hour traffic, vibrating noisily. Wouldn't it be nice to be going home to a real adoring man with pots of money and to be told that she never had to go and work for the likes of Finn McBride ever again?

Kate sighed and rubbed the condensation from the window with her sleeve and peered down at the crowds hurrying along Piccadilly in the rain. They all seemed to know exactly where they were going. Why was she the only one who drifted along from one muddle to the next?

Look at her. Thirty-two and what did she have to show for it? No career, no home of her own, no relationship. The only thing she had gained over the last few years was twenty pounds. Even the misery diet hadn't worked for her. When their hearts got broken the weight fell off her friends, but comfort eating had been the only way Kate could deal with losing Seb and her job together before Christmas. A double whammy.

Fortified by Bella and Phoebe and a good deal of champagne, Kate had resolved that things would change in the New Year. She was going to sharpen up her act. She would get another, better job and another, better man, she vowed. She would lose weight and start going to the gym and get her life under control.

It was just that all those things seemed a lot easier to achieve after a bottle or two of champagne. It was February already, and her New Year resolutions were still at the talking stage.

She ought at least to have found herself a proper job by now, but nothing was being advertised—no doubt everyone was staying put while they paid off their Christmas credit card bills—and even temping hadn't proved to be the guaranteed fall-back position she had assumed. Nobody seemed to be getting flu this year, and Kate had been about to sign on as a waitress at the local wine bar when Alison had broken her leg.

Tomorrow, Kate told herself. She would buy a paper and check out the appointments page, go to the gym on her way home and cook herself something healthy and non-fattening for supper.

Tomorrow would see the start of the new Kate.

Bella was eating toast in the kitchen with her hair in rollers when Kate let herself into the house. Since Phoebe had married and moved in with Gib, the two of them and Kate's surly cat had had the Tooting house to themselves.

The cat was waiting, a brooding presence by the fridge, and Kate knew better than to try and sit down until he had been fed. He was more than capable of shredding her ankles, so she fished out a packet of the over-priced cat food that was all he would accept and forked it into his bowl before she had even taken off her coat.

'I thought you were going out?' she said to Bella, eyeing the toast enviously.

Bella could eat whatever she liked and still not put on weight. 'Metabolism,' she said cheerfully whenever she was challenged by her less fortunate friends. She was ridiculously pretty, a blue-eyed blonde with legs that went on forever and a sunny disposition. The worst thing about Bella, Kate and Phoebe had often agreed, was that it was impossible to hate her.

'I am, but Will's taking me to some incredibly cool restaurant where the portions are bound to be tiny. I thought I'd have something to eat now so I don't pig out when I get there. Anyway, I'm hungry,' Bella added simply.

Lucky Bella, going out with the gorgeous Will while she got some poor old widower who needed someone to be nice to him. Kate sighed to herself. Typical.

Without thinking she dropped a slice of bread into the toaster.

Bella pointed her piece of toast at her. 'You'll regret that,' she warned through a mouthful. 'Gib always cooks enough for an army. Anyway, I thought you were on a diet?'

'There's not much point in starting a diet when I'm going out to dinner,' said Kate, taking off her coat at last. 'And we've got to eat up all the fattening food before we can restock with the healthy stuff.'

It was a good enough excuse to slather butter on her toast as she told Bella about borrowing Will mentally. 'I wasn't going to tell Finn McBride that I was just going on a blind date with a sad widower.'

'A widower?'

Kate told her the little she had learnt from Phoebe. 'It doesn't sound like it's going to be a bundle of laughs, does it?'

'Come on, he might be gorgeous,' said Bella.

'Not with my luck,' grumbled Kate, but she did her best to talk herself into a more positive frame of mind as she got ready to go out. Perhaps Bella was right. Perhaps a fabulous hunk of manhood was going to walk into her life tonight and sweep her off her feet. It had to be her turn sometime soon, surely?

Just in case, she dressed carefully in a flounced dress whose plunging neckline showed off her best assets. At least there were some advantages to having a figure like hers. It was just a shame that a curvaceous bust came with equally curvy hips and thighs and tummy.

Wriggling her feet into high heels, she felt instantly taller and therefore better. Kate had often thought that life would be so much easier if only she had slightly longer legs. An extra couple of inches wouldn't have been asking too much now, would it? And a couple less around her hips, which would have balanced her out nicely.

She studied her reflection in the mirror. Amazing what a bit of make-up could do. In a dim light she might even pass for exotic. The warm red in her dress gave her a vaguely gipsyish look that went quite well with her tumbling brown curls and vibrant lipstick. Would the widower be into gipsies? Somehow Kate felt not. Perhaps she should have gone for a rather more demure look?

Could she carry off demure? Kate wondered, unaware that she had lost track of time. It was only when Will arrived to pick up Bella that she thought to look at her watch, and gave a yelp of fright. How could it be eight o'clock already?

It was little comfort to know that Bella wasn't ready either. Will was reading the paper resignedly in the kitchen, and he raised a laconic hand in greeting as Kate teetered down in her heels to ring for a minicab.

'It'll be another twenty minutes,' said the bored voice at the other end of the phone.

Oh, God, now she would be *really* late. Punctuality was another of Kate's New Year resolutions that didn't seem to be working out as planned.

'Sorry, sorry, sorry,' Kate gabbled when she finally arrived at almost quarter to nine, practically falling in the door when Phoebe opened it. 'I know I'm late, but I really didn't mean to be. Please don't be cross with me! It's just been one of those days.'

'It's always one of those days with you, Kate,' said Phoebe, trying to sound severe as she gave her friend an affectionate hug.

Kate hung her head. 'I know, I know, but I am trying to get better.' She lowered her voice conspiratorially. 'Is he here? What's he like?'

'A bit stiff—no, reserved would be a better word,' Phoebe corrected herself. 'But he's very nice when you get to know him, and he's got a lovely smile. I think he's quite attractive, too.'

'Really?' A hot widower after all! Kate perked up. Things were sounding promising. 'No beard?'

'No.'

'Beer belly? Wet lips?'

'No!' Phoebe was laughing now. 'Come and see for yourself.'

Maybe her luck had changed. Smoothing down her top, Kate took a deep breath and followed Phoebe into the sitting room.

'Here's Kate,' she heard her say, but Kate had already stopped dead as she saw who was standing by the mantelpiece with Gib and Josh. He had turned at Phoebe's words, and she had a nasty feeling that his expression of horror only mirrored her own.

It was Finn McBride.

Then he was blocked from her view temporarily as Gib came towards her, grinning. 'Kate!' he cried, sweeping her up into a warm hug. 'Late as usual!'

'I've already grovelled to Phoebe,' Kate said returning his hug and hoping against hope that she had been mistaken and that when Gib moved she would see that the stranger wasn't Finn at all, but just someone who looked like him and either didn't care for the gipsy look or disapproved of unpunctuality. Or both.

But no. Gib was turning with his arm still around her to face the others and there was no doubt about it. There stood Finn, looking as if he had been turned to stone to match the granite of his expression.

Clearly *not* enjoying discovering that he had been set up on a blind date with his own secretary.

Mortified beyond belief, Kate considered her options. Wishing that she had never been born came top of her list, closely followed by that old cliché, a bit tired but effective nonetheless, of wanting the ground to open up and swallow her.

Could she get away with pretending to faint? Probably not, she decided regretfully. She wasn't the fainting type.

Which just left brazening it out.

CHAPTER TWO

'HELLO.' Plastering on an artificially bright smile, she stared Finn straight in the eyes, daring him to acknowledge her. Finn looked back at her with a glacial grey gaze.

'Kate, this is Finn McBride,' said Gib. 'We've been telling him *all* about you.'

Great, thought Kate. Now Finn would know just how sad her life was.

She stuck out her hand and Finn didn't have much choice but to take it. 'Kate Savage,' she introduced herself in a brittle voice, trying not to notice the feel of his fingers closed around hers. In spite of his obvious reluctance, his clasp was firm and warm, much warmer than she had expected, and she snatched her hand away, oddly unsettled.

'You're being very formal, Kate,' said Gib amused. 'At least I don't need to bother introducing you to Josh.' He turned to Finn. 'Josh practically lives with Kate.'

'Oh?' said Finn coldly.

'Kate shares a house with a very good friend of mine,' Josh explained, and the quick smile he gave Kate was sympathetic. He had obviously been told that he was there to make it less obvious that this was a blind date, although his presence wasn't fooling Finn one little bit. 'How are you, Kate? I haven't seen you for a while.'

'I'm fine.' Apart from wanting to die of embarrassment, that was.

Phoebe handed Kate a glass of wine. 'Finn's just been telling us about his disastrous experiences with temps in his office,' she said cheerfully. 'We thought you could give him a few tips on how to handle them.'

Oh, yes, Gib and Phoebe had built her up into a top-flight PA, hadn't they? As if her humiliation wasn't complete enough!

'Really?' Kate produced an acidic smile. 'It does seem to be difficult getting good secretarial staff these days! What's wrong with the temp you've got?'

'She doesn't seem to have any idea of time-keeping for a start,' said Finn with a sardonic glance at the clock on the mantelpiece. No doubt he had been here on the stroke of eight, long before Phoebe and Gib would have been ready for him. 'She's completely unreliable.'

Unreliable, was she? Kate took a defiant gulp of her wine. 'It doesn't sound as if she has much motivation to work for you. Why would that be, do you think?'

Finn shrugged. 'Sheer laziness?' he suggested. 'She seems to have a very vivid fantasy life too,' he went on and Kate coloured in spite of herself, remembering how she was supposed to be sitting here being proposed to right now by a financial analyst called Will.

No doubt Gib and Phoebe had already filled him in on her disastrous relationship with Seb, and even if they hadn't he would still know that story wasn't true either. After all, if she had a financial analyst to go home to, she wouldn't be the kind of sad person who needed to be set up on blind dates by friends.

Kate suppressed a sigh. Could things get any worse?

'It can be just as bad on the other side of fence,' Phoebe was saying loyally. 'Tell them about your horrible boss, Kate. He sounds ghastly.'

Ah. They *could* get worse.

'Oh?' said Finn, thin-lipped. 'Why's that?'

Oh, well. In for a penny, in for a pound. She might as well take the opportunity to tell him what she thought, and it wasn't as if he had spared *her* feelings!

'He's just generally rude and unpleasant,' she told him.

'He doesn't seem to have even the most basic social skills. He can hardly be bothered to say "good morning" and as for "please" and "thank you"...well, I might as well ask him to talk Polish!'

A muscle had begun to beat in Finn's jaw. 'Perhaps he's busy.'

'Being busy isn't an excuse for not having any manners,' said Kate, meeting his gaze levelly.

'He's absolute death on personal calls in the office as well,' Phoebe put in, apparently unaware of the antagonism simmering between Finn and Kate. 'Kate's always having to put down the phone in the middle of a conversation when his door opens, and we can be in the middle of a really good chat when she suddenly starts putting on an official voice and telling us she'll get back to us on that as soon as possible. That's our cue to call back later when he's gone! It's very frustrating.'

She turned politely to Finn. 'You let people in your office use the phone, don't you?'

'I don't encourage it, no,' he said with a nasty look at Kate, who was almost beyond caring by now.

She was obviously never going to be able to use the office phone again—not that Kate could imagine going into work again after this. On the scale of embarrassment, being blatantly fixed up with your boss must rank pretty high, she thought. It was certainly one of the most excruciating situations Kate had ever found herself in and, let's face it, she had plenty to compare it to. Sometimes she seemed to spend her life lurching from one mortifying episode to another.

'Access to phones and email for personal business is good for staff morale,' she pointed out. 'If you treated your staff like human beings who have a life outside work, I think you'd see productivity shoot up.'

'There's nothing wrong with our productivity,' snapped

Finn, and this time his irritability did catch the others' attention. They looked at him a little curiously and he controlled his temper with an effort.

'There's a difference between dealing with a crisis, in which case of course staff can use the phones, and spending hours gossiping on my time,' he said in a more reasonable voice.

'Doesn't your temp get the job done?' Kate asked sweetly.

'In a fashion,' he admitted grudgingly.

'Perhaps you should go and work for Finn,' said Gib in such a blatant attempt to push them together that he might as well have shown them to the spare room and tucked them in to bed together. 'You might get on better with him than with the boss you've got at the moment.'

'Now, there's an idea!' said Kate as if much struck by the thought. 'Have you got any jobs going at the moment?'

'It's very possible that there might be a vacancy for a temp in my office coming up,' Finn said with something of a snap, 'but that wouldn't interest you, of course, you being such a high-flyer! Gib and Phoebe here were telling me that you practically run the company where you are at the moment. I'm not sure I could offer you anything that challenging.'

A hint of colour touched Kate's cheekbones at his sarcasm. 'No, well, I'm thinking of changing career anyway,' she told him loftily.

'Really?' the other three all said together.

'Yes,' she said, thinking that it wouldn't be such a bad idea, come to that. It didn't look as if she had much future in the secretarial world, anyway. 'I'm sick of being treated like a lower life form, so I've been thinking that I might...what's the word?...downscale.'

'Downscale?' Josh echoed doubtfully, clearly wondering how it was possible for her to downscale from her current position. Being a temp was hardly the giddy heights of a career, was it?

'Or do I mean diversify?' said Kate. 'Do something different anyway. Think out of the box. Use my talents.'

'What exactly are your talents?' Finn asked, the sardonic lift of his brows belying the apparent interest in his voice.

Yes, what *were* her talents? Kate's normally fertile imagination went inconveniently blank at the very moment she needed it most.

'She's a great cook,' Phoebe prompted, evidently still under the impression that Kate might make a suitable wife for Finn.

For some reason it was only at this point that Kate made the connection and remembered that his presence here meant that Finn was a widower. She had been so shocked to see him that she hadn't thought beyond the awkwardness and antagonism, and now she felt suddenly contrite. That beautiful, glowing girl in that photo on his desk was dead. No wonder he seemed so grim.

Kate was conscious of a twinge of guilt about all the times she had thought Finn abrupt and rude, but then, how was she to know that his brusqueness hid a broken heart?

The others were still madly promoting her. 'Kate's a communicator,' she heard Gib say. It was the kind of thing that made you realise just how long he'd spent in the States. 'She's got wonderful people skills.'

'Not just people,' said Josh dryly. 'She's pretty good when it comes to animals too. Remember that dog in the pub, Phoebe?'

'God, yes.' Phoebe gave an exaggerated shudder, and Josh grinned.

'I still wake up in a cold sweat sometimes thinking about it,' he told Finn. 'Kate confronted a skinhead with huge hands and no neck. He was covered in tattoos and snarling and swearing at his dog. Kate told him he wasn't fit to own an animal and took the dog away from him while the rest of us were dancing around in the background being mealy-mouthed and saying I'm not sure this is a good idea, Kate, why don't you let the RSPCA deal with it? Meanwhile Kate was about half the size of this guy, and giving him a piece of her mind, and the rest of the pub was squaring up for a good fight.'

There was a flicker of interest in Finn's eyes. 'What happened to the dog?'

'Oh, Kate got it,' said Josh. 'We knew she would. It was a savage Alsatian cross, and I wouldn't have wanted to go near it myself, but Kate had it eating out of her hand in no time.' He turned to Kate. 'What *did* happen to that dog?'

'I took him down to my parents,' she said, uncomfortable with all this blatant promotion. 'He's spoiled to death now, of course, and getting much too fat.'

Finn glanced at Kate. 'Do you think the dog really cared one way or another?'

'I don't know,' she said, meeting his eyes defiantly. Why did people like Finn always have to make you feel so stupid and sentimental when it came to animals? 'But someone had to.'

There was a tiny silence.

'A word of warning,' Gib confided to Finn. 'Kate might look sweet and cuddly, but don't ever try mistreating an animal when she's around, or you'll find yourself in big trouble! She's got a hell of a temper when roused.'

Finn's cold grey gaze flicked to Kate, whose cheeks were burning by this stage, and then away. 'I'll remember,' he said.

'What Kate really needs,' said Phoebe as she ushered them all through to the dining room, 'is a house in the country where she can make chutney and keep chickens and dogs and all the other stray people and animals that cross her path.'

'No, I don't,' objected Kate. A big house in the country sounded perfect, but also a bit too much like she was hanging out to get married. She wasn't having Finn thinking that she was desperate for a husband, certainly not desperate enough to consider him!

'I'm a metropolitan chick, really,' she said loftily. 'I don't think I'm ready to make jam yet. I was thinking more along the lines of PR—' She broke off as Phoebe, Gib and Josh burst out laughing, and even Finn managed a sardonic smile. 'What's so funny?' she demanded, offended.

'Kate, darling, you're not nearly tough enough for PR! You'd always side with the underdog regardless of what your client wanted. You might as well decide to be a brain surgeon!'

With that they were off, vying with each other to think up more unlikely careers that Kate could try. Josh's suggestion—pest controller—was voted the best.

'Kate would take all the rats home and make up little beds for them!'

Kate gritted her teeth. She could feel Finn watching her with a curling lip. He was probably one of those people who thought that a soft heart equalled a soft head.

She wouldn't have minded so much if the other three hadn't been so determined to push her as a homemaker. Couldn't they *see* that Finn wasn't the least bit impressed? Things got even worse over dinner when Phoebe manoeuvred the conversation, none too subtly, round to Finn and his daughter.

'What's her name?'

'Alex,' said Finn almost reluctantly.

Kate didn't blame him. He could obviously see the subtext—how much he needed to get married again to provide his daughter with a stepmother—as clearly as she could, and she was conscious of a treacherous twinge of fellow feeling. He couldn't be enjoying this any more than she was.

'She's nine,' he added, evidently recognising that the information was going to be dragged out of him somehow, so he might as well get it over and done with.

'It must have been very hard, bringing her up on your own,' said Phoebe.

Finn shrugged. 'Alex was only two when Isabel died, so I had various nannies to help. She never really took to any of them, though, and since she's been at school full time we've managed with a housekeeper who comes in every day. She picks Alex up from school and cooks an evening meal, and she'll stay with her if I'm late back from work.'

His voice was emotionless, as if his small daughter was just another logistical problem he had had to solve. It was Alex Kate felt sorry for, poor motherless child. Kate had never taken a phone call from her, or seen her at the office, so she clearly wasn't encouraged to disturb Finn there. Having grown up with four brothers, Kate thought Alex's life sounded very lonely. It couldn't be much fun growing up with just a housekeeper and Finn for company.

Certainly not if Finn was always as boring as he was tonight. He was driving, so he drank very little, and although Kate couldn't object to that, she did feel that he could at least *look* as if was enjoying himself.

He was obviously terrified that she was going to throw herself at him and force him to marry her. It was understandable, Kate supposed, after the way the others had built her up as a domestic goddess, but he needn't worry. Getting together with him was the last thing on her mind. She wasn't *that* desperate for a relationship!

Finn sat beside her at dinner, radiating disapproval as Kate laughed and drank rather too much wine and talked about clubbing and parties and generally made it clear that she was absolutely not in the market for uptight widowers, no matter how sorry she felt for his poor daughter. Of course, the more poker-faced and buttoned up he was, the more she she had to compensate for Phoebe and Gib's sake. They had gone to so much effort, she felt that the least she could do was try and make it a successful evening.

Defiantly ignoring the way Finn was looking down his nose, Kate held out her glass for more wine. Anyone with a sense of occasion would relax and have a drink as well. They would agree to call a taxi and come and pick up the car in the morning, but the Finns of this world evidently didn't do relaxing or having fun.

Of course, it was a bit tricky trying to impress her complete lack of concern on Finn and ignore him at the same time, especially when she was so aware of his austere presence beside her. It wasn't that he didn't contribute to the conversation, but he made it very clear that he thought Kate was too silly for words, which just made her nervous, and nervousness made her drink more until she was trapped in a vicious circle. As the evening wore on, she could hear herself getting louder and more outrageous, and had reached the owlish stage when Finn, obviously unable to bear any more, looked at his watch.

'I must go,' he said, pushing back his chair to forestall any objections.

'I think you should go too,' said Gib to Kate with a grin, 'or you'll never get to work tomorrow.'

Kate didn't want to think about going into work. 'Don't talk about it,' she groaned, closing her eyes, but that was a mistake. The room started to spin and she opened them again hastily, clutching her tousled curls instead.

'I don't suppose you could give her a lift home, could you?' Gib asked Finn. 'She can't be trusted to get home alone in this state!'

'I'm absolutely fine,' Kate protested instantly, lifting her head and trying not to sway at the sudden movement. 'I'm great!'

'You're fab,' agreed Phoebe soothingly, helping her to her feet, 'but it's time to go. Finn's going to take you home.'

'Why can't Josh take me?'

'Because I haven't got my car with me and I live in completely the opposite direction,' said Josh ungallantly.

'I'm very happy to give you a lift,' said Finn with a certain grittiness, clearly feeling far from happy but unable to think of a good excuse.

Outside, it was raining and making a determined effort to sleet, if not actually to snow. Finn watched, resigned, as Gib and Phoebe helped Kate into her coat like a little girl for the short walk to the car, buttoning her up and kissing her goodnight before consigning her into his charge.

Kate thanked them both graciously for supper, although she had a sinking feeling that the words might have come out a bit slurred, and set off down the path, very much on her dignity. Unfortunately, the effect was spoilt by stumbling on her heels, and only Finn's hand which shot out and gripped her arm stopped her landing smack on her bottom.

'Careful!' he said sharply.

'Sorry, the path's a bit slippy...slippery,' Kate managed, wincing at the iron grip of his fingers. She tried to pull her arm away, but Finn kept a good hold of her as he marched her along to his car.

'You're the one that's a bit slippy,' he said acidly and opened the door with what Kate felt was unnecessarily ironic courtesy.

Tired of being treated like a child, she got in sulkily, and he shut it after her with an exasperated click.

The car was immaculate. There were no sweetie wrappers, no empty cans, no forgotten toys or scuffed seats. It was impossible to believe that a child had ever been in it, thought Kate, wondering where poor little Alex fitted into Finn's efficiently streamlined life.

Still buoyed up by a combination of alcohol and nerves, and anticipating an uncomfortable journey, she leant forward and switched on the radio. Classical, of course. Pressing random buttons, she searched for Capital Radio, until Finn got in to the driver's seat and switched it off with a frown.

'Stop fiddling and do up your seatbelt.'

'Yes, sir!' muttered Kate.

Finn lay his arm along the back of her seat and swivelled so that that he could see to reverse the car along the narrow street to the turning place at the bottom. Kate was acutely aware of how close his hand was to her hair and she made a big deal of rummaging in her bag at her feet in case he thought that she was leaning invitingly towards him.

It was a relief when they reached the turning place and Finn took his arm away to put the car into gear. At least she could sit back.

Only it wasn't that much easier then. Finn was a fierce, formidable presence, overwhelming in the dark confines of the car while the rain and the sleet splattered against the windscreen and made the space shrink even further. The light from the dashboard lit his face with a green glow, glancing along his cheekbones and highlighting the severe mouth.

He was concentrating on driving, and Kate watched him under her lashes, daunted more than she wanted to admit by his air of contained competence. It was evident in the calm, decisive way he drove, and when her eyes followed his left hand from the steering wheel to the gear stick, something stirred inside her and she looked quickly away.

Her wine-induced high had shrivelled, leaving her tongue-tied and agonisingly aware of him. It was ridiculous, Kate scolded herself. He was still Finn. He was a disagreeable, if thankfully temporary, boss and an ungracious guest. She didn't like him at all, so why was she suddenly noticing the line of his mouth and the set of his jaw and the strength of his hands?

'Where am I going?'

His brusque question broke the silence and startled her. 'What?'

'Gib asked me to take you home. Presumably he knows where that is, but I'm not a mind-reader.'

'Oh...yes.' Kate huddled in her seat, too appalled by this new awareness of him to rise to his sarcasm the way she would normally have done.

She directed him through the dark streets while the windscreen wipers thwacked rhythmically at the sleety rain and the silence in the car deepened until Kate could bear it no longer.

'Why didn't you tell Gib and Phoebe that you recognised me?'

Finn glanced at her. 'Probably for the same reason that you didn't,' he said curtly. 'I thought it would make the situation even more awkward than it already was.'

His tone was so uninviting, that Kate subsided back into silence. Anyone else giving her a lift home would have made some attempt at conversation, even if only to talk about the evening or the food or even, if things were desperate, the weather, but Finn was evidently in no mood for idle chit-chat. His face was set in grim lines and when he glanced in the rear-view mirror, Kate could see that he was frowning.

'It's just along here.' She pointed out her street in relief. 'There's never anywhere to stop, so if you could drop me here, that would be fine, thanks.'

Finn ignored her, turning down the street she had indicated. 'How far down are you?'

'About halfway,' admitted Kate, surrendering to *force majeure*. She pointed. 'Just past that streetlight.'

As usual, the street was lined with cars bumper to bumper, so Finn had no choice but to stop in the middle of the road. Kate fumbled for the doorhandle as he put on the handbrake.

'Thank you for the lift,' she muttered. 'I hope I haven't brought you too much out of your way.'

A gust of sleet hit her full in the face as she opened the door, and instinctively she recoiled. 'Yuck, what a horrible night!'

'Wait there.' Cursing under his breath, Finn reached behind him for an umbrella and got out of the car. He'd managed to get the umbrella up by the time he made it round to the passenger door. 'I'll see you to your door.'

'Honestly, I'll be fine. You don't need to—'

'Just hurry up and get out!' said Finn through his teeth. It was hard to tell whether they were gritted with temper or with cold. 'The sooner you do, the sooner I can get home!'

Reluctantly Kate scrambled out of the car and into the shelter of the umbrella. The wind was bitter and the rain ran down her neck, but she was still able to notice how intimate it felt to be standing so close to Finn. He was tall and solid and she had a bizarre impulse to put her arms round him and lean into him, to feel how hard and strong he was.

'Right, let's move it before we both freeze to death out here!' said Finn, fortunately unable to read her mind. Or possibly telepathic and quick to take avoiding action. 'Which house is it?'

He set off towards the pavement with Kate teetering on her heels in an effort to keep up with his long stride. 'Why on earth don't you wear something more sensible on your feet?' he demanded, holding the umbrella impatiently above her.

'If I'd known I'd be going on a polar expedition, I might have done!' said Kate, her teeth chattering so loudly that she could hardly speak, but obscurely grateful to the vile weather for disguising the shakiness that might otherwise be obvious in her legs and her voice. She couldn't *believe* what she had been tempted to do just then!

Finn would have had a fit if she had thrown herself at him like that. Or might he, just possibly, have pulled her towards him and kissed her under the umbrella? What would *that* have been like? Kate swallowed, torn between relief and disappointment that she would never know.

Still blissfully unaware of her wayward thoughts, Finn protected her with the umbrella while she fumbled for her key. Her hands were shaking in time with her teeth by that stage, and she was shivering so much that she couldn't get the key in the lock.

Unable to bear it any longer, Finn put out his hand for the key, but his fingers brushing hers were enough to make Kate jerk back in alarm, dropping it into a puddle.

Mortified, she crouched down to retrieve it. Finn was holding out his hand with barely restrained impatience and meekly she dropped the wet and dirty key into his outstretched palm.

Without a word, Finn unlocked the door and pushed it open for her. 'Thank you,' said Kate awkwardly. 'And thanks again for the lift.'

That was Finn's cue to say that it had been a pleasure, an opening he pointedly missed.

'I'll see you tomorrow,' he said gruffly instead.

Fine, if that's the way he wanted to be, she wouldn't invite him in! Kate hugged her coat around her. 'Are you sure you still want me to come into work?'

'That's generally the idea behind paying you,' said Finn with one of his sardonic looks.

'But I thought I was a disaster?'

'You're not exactly a resounding success as a secretary,' he agreed, 'but you're the best I've got at the moment. We've got a big contract coming up, as you would know if you'd been paying attention, and I can't afford to spend the time explaining everything to yet another secretary. I'm better off sticking with you.'

'Well, thanks for that warm vote of confidence!'

'You didn't make many bones about how much you dislike working for me,' Finn pointed out, 'so I don't see why I should dance around saving your feelings! The fact is that you can't afford to lose this job just yet, and I can't afford the time to replace you.'

'You're saying we're stuck with each other?' said Kate, lifting her chin.

'Precisely, so we might as well make the best of it.' He looked down into her face from under his umbrella. 'I suggest you drink a litre of water before you go to bed,' he said dispassionately as he turned to go. 'We've got a lot to do tomorrow, so please don't be late!'

Groping blearily for the alarm clock, Kate forced open one eye to squint at the time, only to jerk upright with what should have been a cry but which came out more as a groan. The sudden movement was like a cleaver slicing through her aching head and she put up a shaky hand to check that it was still intact.

Unfortunately, yes. Right then death seemed preferable to the pounding in her head and the horrible taste in her mouth.

Not to mention what Finn would say if she was late again.

Kate grimaced as she looked at the clock. If she skipped

the shower and was lucky with the trains, she might *just* make it...

Somehow she got herself out of bed and along to the tube station, but regretted it deeply when she had to stand squashed in with thousands of other commuters, all wet and steaming from the rain above ground. Kate clung to the rail with one hand, swaying nauseously as the train lurched and rattled its way along the tunnels, and tried to ignore the queasy feeling in her stomach.

To make matters worse, her memory of the night before was coming back in fragments of intense clarity separated by the blurry recollection of having generally made a complete fool of herself.

The things she did remember were bad enough. The appalled look on Finn's face when the terrible truth dawned that his date for the evening was none other than his much-despised temporary secretary. The windscreen wipers thwacking in time to the beat of her heart as she fixated inexplicably on his mouth and his hands. Huddling under the umbrella, wondering what it would be like to touch him.

She must have been completely blotto.

God, what if she'd made a pass at Finn? Kate thought in panic. Surely she would remember *that*?

If she had, she would have been firmly repulsed. That was one thing she did remember. Her much loved top and favourite shoes had gone down like a lead balloon with Finn. Kate had always been told that she looked really hot in that top, but he had just looked down his nose and averted his eyes from her cleavage. If any pass had been made, it certainly wouldn't have come from him!

She got to the office with less than a minute to spare. Finn was already at his desk, of course. He looked up over his glasses as Kate held on to the doorway for support.

'You look terrible,' he said.

'I feel worse,' she croaked. 'I've got the most monumental hangover.'

Finn grunted. 'I hope you're not expecting any sympathy from me!'

'No, I don't think I could cope with any miracles today,' said Kate tartly before remembering a little too late that her job was very much on the line. Finn was obviously thinking much the same thing because his eyes narrowed slightly behind his reading glasses.

'You'd better be in a fit state to work,' he warned her. 'We've got a lot to do today.'

'I'll just have some coffee and then I'll be fine,' Kate promised, holding her head.

'You can have five minutes,' said Finn and picked up the report he had been reading once more, effectively dismissing her.

Kate groped her way along to the coffee machine and ordered a double espresso, trying not to wince at the sound of ringing telephones and clattering keyboards. There was a tiny manic blacksmith at work inside her skull, banging and hammering on her nerve endings.

Perhaps Alison would have some paracetamol, she thought, sinking gratefully down at her desk. That might help.

Any normal girl would keep hangover cures handy in her top right-hand drawer, but not Alison. Having rummaged through the desk, Kate was forced to accept that Alison didn't have hangovers. Alison probably didn't even know what a hangover *was*. She probably never got nervous or drank too much or showed off in front of Finn.

The coffee was only making her feel worse. Groaning, Kate collapsed onto the desk and buried her head in her arms. That was it. She was giving up. She was just going to have to die here in Finn's office. He would just have to decide what to do with her body although, knowing him, he'd get the next temp to deal with it. Just dispose of that corpse, he would say, and then come in and take notes at the speed of light.

'You didn't drink any water before you went to bed, did you?' Finn's voice spoke above Kate's prostrate form.

'No,' she mumbled, mainly because it was easier than shaking her head.

'You're dehydrated.' Somewhere to the right of her ear, she could hear the sound of a mug being set on the desk. 'Here. I've brought you some sweet tea, and a couple of aspirin.'

The promise of aspirin was enough to make Kate lift her head very cautiously. 'Thanks,' she muttered.

She took the pills and screwed up her face at the taste of the tea, but her mouth was so dry that she sipped it anyway. After a few minutes, she even began to feel as if she might live after all.

Finn was leaning against the edge of her desk, frowning down at the file in his hands. He always seemed to be frowning, Kate thought muzzily. Was he like this with everyone, or was it just her? The thought that it might be her was oddly depressing. Granted, turning up for work late or massively hungover probably wasn't the best way to go about getting him to smile, but still, you'd have thought there'd have been *something* about her he could like.

CHAPTER THREE

AS IF aware of her gaze, Finn glanced up. 'Feeling any better?' he asked, although not with any noticeable degree of sympathy.

'A bit,' croaked Kate.

'Good.' Closing the file, he dropped it onto her desk with a loud slap that made her wince, and he sighed. 'Why on earth do you drink so much if you feel this bad the next day?'

'I don't usually,' she said a little sullenly. 'Last night I was trying to have a good time, since *you* obviously weren't going to! Why did you come if you weren't going to make an effort?'

'I went because Gib asked me,' said Finn curtly. 'He said Phoebe had a friend he thought I might like to meet. I was expecting someone gentle and motherly, not a goer with a plunging cleavage, ridiculous shoes and a determination to drink everyone else under the table!'

Aha, so he *had* noticed her cleavage, Kate noted with a perverse sense of satisfaction.

'They've obviously got no idea,' she agreed sweetly, but with an acid undertone. 'They told *me* that you were really nice. How wrong can you be? I don't think I'll be letting them fix up any more blind dates for me!'

A muscle worked in Finn's jaw. 'I couldn't agree with you more.'

'Well, there's a first!' Kate muttered.

Finn got to his feet. 'If you're well enough to argue, you're well enough to do some work,' he said callously. 'I think we can both agree that last night was extremely awkward for both of us. Frankly, I'd rather not know about your personal life, and I don't believe in mixing mine with business. However, as I said last night—although of course you won't remember this!—I can't afford the time to explain everything to someone new at this stage, so I suggest that we pretend that last night never happened and carry on as before. Although it would help if you would turn up on time and in a fit state to work occasionally,' he added nastily. 'That could be different!'

Kate held her aching head with her hand. She just wished she was in a position to tell Finn exactly what he could do with his job. She had a hazy recollection of telling everyone last night that she was planning a major career change, which had seemed like a good idea at the time, and still did, frankly.

One of these days she would have to do something about it but, in the meantime, she had to live, and this crummy job was her best hope of paying her bills for the next few weeks. She had never been big on saving, and she had bailed Seb out too many times to have anything left to fall back on. It looked as if she was going to have to stick with Finn for now.

'Alison should be back in a few weeks,' he said as if reassuring himself.

'Meaning you won't have to put up with me for too long?' In spite of her own reluctance, Kate was obscurely hurt to realise that Finn couldn't wait to get rid of her.

'I was under the impression that the feeling was mutual,' he said coldly.

'It is.'

'Are you trying to tell me you want to leave now?'

'No,' said Kate, forced into a corner. 'No, I want to stay. I haven't got any choice.'

'Then we're both in the same boat,' said Finn. He turned for his office. 'And if you do want to carry on working here, I suggest you go and freshen up, and come back ready to start work!'

Three hours later, Kate was reeling after a barrage of complicated instructions and tasks which Finn rapped out, making no allowances for her hangover, before going out to an expensive lunch with a client.

'Have that draft report on my desk by the time I get back,' was his parting shot.

Kate pulled a face at his receding back and dumped the armful of files and papers onto her desk. Did she really want to hang onto this job that badly?

Finn's expression had been as grimly unreadable as ever, but she could have sworn that beneath it all he was enjoying the sight of her struggling to cope with a hangover and an avalanche of work. She was prepared to bet that a lot of this stuff could easily have waited and that he had only pulled it out to punish her. It was hard to believe that for a peculiar moment or two last night she had actually found him attractive!

Running her fingers wearily through her hair, Kate sighed as she contemplated the scattered piles of paper on her desk. She needed another coffee before she could tackle that lot!

In spite of everything Finn had to say about his staff not going in for gossip, Kate had noticed that the coffee machine was a favoured meeting place. Of course it was possible that the two older women from the finance department were talking about work, but somehow she doubted it. They stopped as she approached and moved aside politely to let her through to the machine.

'Thanks,' said Kate with a smile. 'I'm desperate!'

'Feeling rough?'

'Awful,' she admitted, searching her memory for their names. 'I am never, ever, going to drink again!'

Elaine and Sue, that was it. They had been polite if rather

cool with Kate in her few brief dealings with them, but she noticed they thawed slightly at her frank admission of a hangover.

'So, how are you getting on?' the older one—Sue?—asked.

'I don't think I'm ever going to live up to Alison's standards,' Kate sighed as the machine spat out coffee into her cup. 'What's she like? Is she as perfect as Finn makes out?'

Sue and Elaine considered. 'She's certainly very efficient,' said Elaine, but she didn't sound overly enthusiastic. 'Finn relies on her a lot.'

Kate sipped her coffee, still disgruntled by the amount of work Finn had thrown at her. 'She must be an absolute saint to put up with him!'

Wrong thing to say! The two women bridled at the implied criticism of Finn. 'He's lovely when you get to know him,' Elaine insisted, and Sue nodded.

'He's the best boss I've ever had. You want to count how many people have been here years and years. We don't get the same kind of turnover as in other companies. That's because everyone here feels involved. Finn expects you to work hard, but he always notices and comments on what you've been doing, and that makes all the difference.'

'He treats you like a human being,' Elaine added her bit.

It was news to Kate, thinking about that morning.

'Of course, Alison's absolutely devoted to Finn,' Sue said. She lowered her voice confidentially. 'Between you and me, I think she might be hoping to become more than a PA one day.'

'Oh?' Kate was conscious of a sudden tightening of her muscles. 'Do you think that's likely?'

'No.' Elaine shook her head definitely. 'He's never got over losing his wife, and I don't think he ever will.'

'Isabel was a lovely person,' Sue agreed. 'She used to come in to the office sometimes, and we all loved her. She was so beautiful and sweet and interested in what everyone did. There was just something about her. She made you feel special somehow, didn't she, Elaine?'

Elaine nodded sadly. 'Finn was different then. He absolutely adored her, and she was the same. She used to light up whenever he came into the room. Oh, it was such a tragedy when she died!'

'What happened?' asked Kate, hoping she didn't sound too ghoulish.

'Someone got into a car having had too much to drink, and poor Isabel was coming the other way...' They shook their heads at the memory of it. 'She never came out of the coma. Finn had to make the decision to switch off her life-support machine.'

Sue sighed. 'You can only imagine what it was like for him. He had Alex to worry about too. She was in the car as well, so she was in hospital too, although not so seriously hurt.'

'She wasn't much more than a baby,' Elaine added. 'Just old enough to cry for her mummy.'

Kate's hand had crept to her mouth as she listened to their story. 'That's...terrible,' she said, feeling hopelessly inadequate.

'Terrible,' Elaine agreed. 'Finn's never been the same since. He closed in on himself after Isabel died. Alex is his life now, and he won't let anyone else close. He kept the company going, but I've always felt that was more for all the staff here than for his own sake.'

'We all hope he'll remarry one day,' Sue said. 'He deserves to be happy again and Alex needs a mum. Maybe he'll miss Alison while she's away,' she added hopefully. 'I know she can be a bit cool, but that's just her manner, and she's very attractive, isn't she?' she demanded of Elaine, who nodded a bit reluctantly.

'She's always beautifully groomed.'

'And she must know him pretty well after working for him for so long. I think she'd be a good wife for him.'

It didn't sound to Kate as if Alison was at all the right kind of wife for Finn. He was quite cool and efficient enough by himself. What he needed was warmth and tenderness and laughter, not practicality and good grooming.

Not that it was anything to do with her, of course.

Still, she couldn't get Finn's tragic story out of her mind all afternoon. She kept imagining him by his wife's side, with the life-support machines beeping in the background, willing her to open her eyes, or trying to explain to his baby daughter why her mother couldn't come.

'No wonder he didn't approve of me drinking last night,' she said to Bella that evening, having told her about the disaster of her blind date and what she had learnt from Elaine and Sue. 'I feel terrible now. I've been so nasty about him, and all the time he's had to cope with all of that.'

'Don't do it,' said Bella, handing Kate a drink.

'Don't do what?'

'Don't get involved.'

'I'm not involved,' said Kate a little defensively. 'I just feel desperately sorry for him.'

Bella sighed as she contemplated her friend. 'You know what you're like, Kate,' she warned. 'One tiny tug at your heartstrings, and you're turning your world upside down to try and make things better, and sometimes you just can't. You were desperately sorry for Seb, too, and look where that got you!'

'This is entirely different,' Kate protested. 'Finn's not trying to get anything from me. He hasn't even told me about Isabel himself. I'm not sure he'd even want me to know.'

'I just don't want you jumping from feeling sorry for him to wanting to help him to falling in love with him,' said Bella with a warning look. 'You've got to admit it's a bit of a pattern with you, and this time you really could get hurt. It would be much worse than Seb. You'd never be able to live up to a perfect wife like that, Kate. You'd only ever be second-best.'

'Honestly, Bella!' said Kate crossly. 'Anyone would think I was planning to marry him! All I'm saying is that maybe I should be more understanding when he's grumpy with me.'

'Hhmmnn, well, just be careful. You didn't like him when you thought he was happily married, and he's exactly the same man. Being a widower isn't really an excuse for being unpleasant to you, is it? You said it's six years since his wife died, that's long enough for him to be coming to terms with it. Don't let him take advantage of your soft heart, that's all.'

Kate didn't say any more—*ER* was on, and there were more important things to do—but afterwards she thought about what Bella had said. Her friend might seem the quintessential feather-headed blonde at times, but she could be very pragmatic when it came to relationships.

Of course, it was nonsense to suggest that there was any chance of her falling in love with Finn. She had no intention of doing anything of the kind. What she *would* do from now on was make allowances for his brusque temper instead of getting cross about it.

It would be part of her new, professional image, Kate decided. She would be cool, courteous and discreetly efficient. If all she could do to help him was to create a calm atmosphere in which he could work, then that's what she would do.

That was nothing like falling in love with him, was it?

Changing the atmosphere in the office was all very well in theory, but in practice it was less easy.

Kate really tried. Sick of hearing about the immaculately

groomed Alison, she had made more of an effort to dress smartly. She was never going to look completely at home in a suit and her hair just didn't do neat, but at least she was showing willing. When Finn snapped at her, she bit her tongue and didn't answer back. She just got on with her work and waited for him to notice how much easier his life had become. She even practised an understanding speech for when he told her how grateful he was.

That was a waste of time! Far from being grateful, Finn seemed deeply suspicious of her new, improved attitude.

'What's the matter with you?' he demanded.

'Nothing,' said Kate, a bit taken aback.

'You're too polite,' he grumbled. 'It makes me nervous. And why are you dressed like that?' His expression sharpened. 'Have you got an interview for another job?'

Chance would be a fine thing. 'No,' she said. 'I'm just trying to look professional. I thought you would approve,' she was unable to resist adding.

Finn looked at her. Her attempt to tie back her hair had failed miserably, most of the soft brown curls escaping their confines to tumble around her face once more. Her one and only suit was a rather dull grey affair and the white shirt was creased. It was hard to believe they came from the same wardrobe as the vibrant dress with its swirling skirt and its daring neckline that she had worn to dinner at Phoebe and Gib's.

'I'm not sure you can carry off the professional look,' he said dryly.

There was no pleasing some people, thought Kate with an inward sigh.

Faced with a comprehensive lack of encouragement on Finn's part, she found herself slipping back into her old ways, especially after an interesting little chat with Phoebe one evening. Kate had braced herself to confess that she had known exactly who Finn was, and was a little peeved to discover that Finn had told Gib himself the very next day when he had rung to thank them for supper.

'Did he say anything about me?' Kate heard herself ask when Phoebe had finished telling her how amused they were by the whole situation.

'I think he was a bit thrown by seeing you dressed like that,' said Phoebe, carefully avoiding a direct answer. 'Presumably you don't usually wear quite such revealing tops in the office?'

'Of course not,' said Kate, miffed for no obvious reason. 'What was he expecting? Me to turn up to dinner in a suit?'

'I gather Finn told Gib that I wasn't his type,' she said when she reported the conversation to Bella.

She was cross that she hadn't spoken to Phoebe earlier so that she could have passed a message onto Finn that he wasn't Kate's type either.

'I don't think I'll bother being nice to him any longer,' she grumbled. 'He obviously doesn't appreciate it anyway.'

Still, that was no reason to give up her new cool image. Kate was determined to show Finn that Alison wasn't the only one who could be professional. Every morning she tried to be at her desk before he arrived, calmly going through the post. It meant getting up at the crack of dawn, of course, but it was worth it to see the disconcerted look on his face when he came in, and it wasn't as if she would have to do it for ever. She fully intended to go back to her slovenly ways the moment Alison returned.

She was nearly a week into her newly punctual mode when she emerged from the underground one day, turning up her collar against the cold. It was a dreary morning, with a sleety drizzle giving the pavements a slippery sheen, and Kate paused to put up her umbrella. Normally she wouldn't have bothered, but the rain made her hair even more uncontrollable than ever, and she was determined to achieve a style that would stay halfway neat for the morning at least.

She glanced at her watch. Just time to get a cappuccino from the Italian café on the way to the office.

Kate stood in line with all those others unable to face another revolting coffee from the machine at work. Accepting a perfunctory '*Bella, bella!*' from the Italian as he handed her the beaker to take away, she cradled it close to her chest for warmth. She would really enjoy this when she was sitting calmly at her desk, waiting for Finn to appear.

Putting up the umbrella with one hand turned out to be a tussle of wills, but after some wrestling, Kate won. It was raining more heavily now, and the wind was coming in gusts, so she had to hold the umbrella almost in front of her face to stop it blowing inside out. It made it tricky to see where she was going, but she set off, telling herself that there was only a block to the office. She might as well try and stay dry.

The next moment there was a yelp and she was sprawling full length, her fall partly cushioned by a pile of rubbish bags waiting to be collected.

'Are you all right?' someone stopped to ask reluctantly.

'I'm fine...I think,' said Kate, struggling to her feet and looking down at herself as she brushed the rubbish off her jacket in dismay. The cappuccino had ended up all the way down her skirt. Her hands were filthy, her tights torn, and as for her hair...well, she might as well forget it for today.

Relieved at not being roped into a scene, her reluctant Samaritan had hurried on. Kate bent stiffly to retrieve her umbrella, remembering the yelp and wondering what had caused it. She could see now that some of the pile of black bags had been torn open, so that rubbish spilt out onto the pavement, and in the middle of them, cowered a little dog with bony ribs and fearful eyes.

Her bruises forgotten, Kate crouched down among the bin bags and held out her hand. 'You poor sweetheart, did I tread on you?' she asked gently, holding out her hand, until the dog crawled closer to lick it. It was wet and shivering, and when Kate looked closer she could see that it had no collar.

'You're not much more than a puppy, are you?' she said, letting it smell that she was unthreatening before she stroked it behind its ears, one of which was cocked and the other flapping disreputably.

It was not perhaps the most beautiful dog she had ever seen. A dispassionate observer might even have thought it was ugly with its legs disproportionately short in relation to its long shaggy body, its pointed, whiskery nose and big ears, but Kate saw only the thinness of its ribs and the untreated sores, and her blood boiled.

There was no point in looking round for an owner. This was a business district, the streets lined with office blocks and no one would be walking a dog around here. This little dog wasn't lost, it had been abandoned, if indeed it had ever had a home in the first place. But something in the way its tail wagged feebly in response to her gentle pats made Kate's heart crack.

'Come on, darling, you're coming with me,' she told it firmly. She couldn't leave it here to starve if it didn't get run over first.

Very gently, she pulled the little dog towards her. It whimpered but didn't struggle when she lifted it up. When she examined it, it didn't seem to be badly hurt. 'I think you're just cold and hungry,' she decided.

There was a mini-market back by the tube station. Tucking the now useless umbrella under one arm and the dog under the other, Kate retraced her steps and bought some bread and milk, and a couple of newspapers in case of accidents. She would have to worry about a lead and collar later. This wasn't the kind of area you found a pet shop, even if she had time to track one down. By this stage she was almost as dirty and bedraggled as the little dog, and it was nearly half past nine.

So much for being early.

Well, it couldn't be helped. Ignoring the receptionist's appalled expression, Kate walked towards the lift with the precious burden under her arm. She could feel its little heart battering and her own didn't feel that steady at the prospect of facing Finn, but she was still too angry at the cruelty of anyone who could abandon a defenceless animal to care what she looked like.

The door of her office was open. Kate took a deep breath and walked inside, only to stop dead when she saw that there was someone sitting at her computer. For a heart-stopping moment she thought that she had been replaced, but a second look showed her that the occupier of her desk had quite a bit of schooling left before she had to think about getting a job.

The little girl stopped typing when Kate came in and stared at her with unfriendly eyes. She had thick glasses and a thin, guarded face, together with an air of self-possession quite intimidating in one so young.

'Who are you?'

'I'm Kate. Who are you?' countered Kate, although she had already recognised that steely expression. Like father, like daughter.

'Alex,' she admitted. 'My dad's angry with you,' she went on.

'Oh, dear, I was afraid he might be.' Kate put the little dog down and stroked it soothingly.

'He said a rude word.'

That sounded like Finn. 'Where is he now?'

'He's gone to find someone to look after me and to fill

in for you until you deign to turn up,' said Alex, obviously quoting verbatim. 'What does "deign" mean?'

'I think your father thought I was late on purpose,' said Kate, sighing. She took off her jacket and hung it up while she wondered what to do next. She really ought to find Finn and explain, but the little dog was still shivering with a combination of nerves and cold.

She knew how it felt.

Alex had been studying her critically. 'Why are you so dirty?'

'I fell into a load of rubbish.'

'Yuck.' Alex wrinkled her nose. 'You do smell a bit,' she informed Kate, who lifted an arm and sniffed the unmistakable odour of rotting rubbish. Eau de bin bag.

Great. That was all she needed.

Alex had come round the front of the desk and was regarding the quivering dog with some wariness. 'Is that your dog?'

'He is now,' said Kate.

'What's his name?'

'I don't know...what do you think I should call him?'

'Is it a boy or a girl?'

Good question. Kate lifted the dog gently. 'A boy.'

Alex came a little closer. She seemed cautious but fascinated by the dog, who was sniffing the floor with equal uncertainty. Kate waited for her to suggest Scruffy or Patch or Rover.

'What about Derek?'

'*Derek*?' Kate started to laugh, and Alex looked offended.

'Don't you think it's a good name?'

'It's a great name,' Kate recovered herself quickly. 'Derek the dog. I love it. Derek!' she called to the dog, snapping her fingers for his attention.

He pricked up his ears and sat down clumsily, which

made Alex smile for the first time. Her smile transformed her rather serious little face, and Kate wondered if a smile would have a similar effect on Finn's expression.

Not that she was likely to see him smile just for the moment.

Alex squatted beside her. 'Hello, Derek,' she said.

'Let him smell your fingers before you pat him,' said Kate, and smiled when Derek wagged his tail and licked Alex's hand.

'He's cute,' said Alex.

'I'm not sure your father will think so.'

The words were barely out of her mouth before Finn came striding into the room, scowling ferociously. 'Oh, there you are!' he said as he spied Kate. 'Nice of you to join us!'

Kate got to her feet, acutely conscious of her bedraggled state. 'I'm sorry I'm late,' she began but Finn interrupted her as he got a proper look at her.

'For God's sake, Kate, look at the state of you! What on earth have you been doing?'

'Please don't shout!' she said, but it was too late. Cowering at the sound of Finn's raised voice, the little dog had squatted and made a puddle on the carpet.

'Now look what you've done!' Kate accused Finn as she pulled one of the newspapers apart and spread a couple of sheets over the puddle to mop up the worst of it. 'It's all right, sweetheart,' she said, caressing the still trembling dog. 'I won't let the nasty man shout at you any more.'

She glanced up at Finn from where she was crouched. 'You're upsetting Derek.'

'Upsetting...?' Finn shook his head in baffled frustration. 'Who?'

'It's his name, Dad,' Alex told him.

'*Derek*?'

'Alex thought of the name,' said Kate quickly, before he

could say anything to upset his daughter. 'It suits him, don't you think?'

Finn ignored that. He looked as if he was counting to ten in an effort to keep his temper. 'Kate,' he said at last in a voice of careful restraint, 'what is that dog doing here?'

'I found him on my way to work.'

'Well, you'd better lose him pretty damn quickly! An office is a totally inappropriate place for a dog.'

'It's not that appropriate for a child either.'

His mouth thinned. 'That's a completely different thing,' he snapped. 'My housekeeper has been called away unexpectedly to look after her sick mother, and the school is having a training day. I didn't have any choice but to bring Alex in today. I couldn't leave her in the house on her own.'

'I couldn't leave Derek in the street on his own,' countered Kate. 'He would have been run over.'

Finn ground his teeth in frustration. 'Kate, this is an office, not Battersea Dogs Home! I thought you were trying to be more professional?'

'Some things are more important than being professional,' she said, and bent to pick up the dog.

'Where are you going?' he snarled. 'I haven't finished with you!'

'I'm going to dry him and give him something to drink,' Kate answered patiently, 'and when I've done that, I'll come back and you can be as cross with me as you like.'

'Can I come and help you?' Alex asked while her father was still spluttering in outrage.

'Sure,' said Kate. 'You can hold Derek while I dry him.'

'Now just a minute—' Finn began, unable to believe that he had lost control of the situation so easily.

Alex rolled her eyes in an impressively adolescent fashion. 'Dad, I'll be fine,' she said wearily, and followed Kate out of the room before he could assert his authority.

In the Ladies, they found some paper towels and wiped the worst of the dirt and wet off Derek, and then off Kate, who was in nearly as bad a state.

She pulled a face at her reflection as she washed her hands. 'I don't think I'm going to win any awards for glamour today,' she sighed.

Alex was cuddling the little dog, murmuring to reassure it about finding itself in yet more strange surroundings. 'You're not like Alison,' she commented.

Kate sighed and lifted her hopelessly tangled hair in despair. 'So your father is always telling me.'

'I don't like Alison,' Alex confided. 'She talks to me in a stupid voice like I'm a baby! She's soppy about Dad, too.'

'Is your dad soppy about her?' Kate couldn't help asking, although she knew that she shouldn't. She hoped she didn't sound too interested.

Alex shrugged. 'I don't know. I hope not. I don't want a stepmother. Rosa fusses, but I'd rather have her as a housekeeper than Alison.'

Poor old Alison, thought Kate. There was a very stubborn set to Alex's chin, inherited from her father no doubt, and she wouldn't like to bet on Alison's chances of winning her round.

Feeling more cheerful for some reason, she sent Alex in search of a couple of bowls while she made a bed of newspapers for Derek behind her desk where he would feel secure. He seemed quite happy to curl up there, but when Alex reappeared with a bowl of water and a saucer, he got up to investigate, and the offer of some bread soaked in milk got his tail wagging eagerly.

'He's so sweet!' said Alex, watching him adoringly. 'I wish I could keep him! Do you think Dad would let me?'

Kate thought the answer would be definitely not, but Finn could presumably deal with his own daughter. 'You'd have to ask him. I'd wait until he's in a better mood though,' she cautioned.

This looked like good advice when Finn emerged glowering from his office. 'Alex, you can go and sit with the girls at the reception desk for a while if you want. You know you like doing that sometimes.'

'Only when Alison is here,' muttered Alex. 'Anyway, I'm going to look after Derek. Kate says I can.'

'Yes, well, I want a word with Kate,' said Finn ominously.

'I won't disturb her,' Alex reassured him, misunderstanding. 'It'll make it easier for her to work because she won't have to check on Derek the whole time. You don't mind, do you, Kate?'

'It's fine by me.'

'It's not a question of what Kate minds,' Finn bit out, goaded beyond endurance. 'Come into my office,' he ordered Kate. 'If you've quite finished turning my office into a branch of Animal Rescue, that is,' he added sarcastically, standing back with mock courtesy so that she could go ahead of him.

'Would you like to explain what the hell is going on?' he said furiously as he sat behind his desk.

Kate wondered if she was supposed to stand in front of him with her hands behind her back, like being brought before the headmaster. She opted to sit anyway. Finn was so angry that one more thing wasn't going to make any difference. He certainly couldn't look any crosser.

'Nothing's going on,' she told him. 'I didn't mean to be late, but I couldn't just walk past that dog. You saw the state of him. Someone's just got bored of him and thrown him out. I don't know how people can be so cruel.' Her voice shook with emotion.

'They should bring back public flogging,' added Kate, who rescued spiders and stepped carefully round snails and loathed all forms of violence. 'That might teach them what cruelty feels like! I once saw—'

Finn cut her off. 'Kate, I'm not interested,' he said curtly. 'I've got a business to run here. It's distracting enough having to cope with Alex in the office, and now we've wasted half the morning on that dog.'

'Alex is quite happy looking after him, so I'd say that's solved your problem. In fact, it's all worked out very well,' said Kate, unrepentant. She waved her notebook at him and smiled brightly. 'I'm ready to start work whenever you are.'

CHAPTER FOUR

'DAD?' Alex waited until Finn had finished giving Kate a long list of orders which she was scribbling into her notebook.

Finn peered round the desk to where his daughter sat in the corner, Derek's head on her lap. 'Are you OK down there?'

She nodded vigorously. 'You know you said that I could have whatever I wanted for lunch if I was good this morning?'

'Yes,' he said with a certain wariness.

'I don't really want any lunch,' she told him. 'Can we go to a pet shop and buy Derek a lead and collar instead?'

'Alex, I don't want you getting too attached to that dog!'

'No, I won't,' she promised fervently. 'But please, Dad! You did promise.'

'I was thinking more of going out for a pizza.' Finn glared at Kate as if it was all her fault. 'Perhaps we should let Kate take responsibility for the dog. She rescued it, after all.'

'Kate hasn't got time to go out to lunch,' said Alex before Kate had a chance to speak.

How true, thought Kate, looking at her list. She had just been thinking that she would need to improvise a lead and collar. 'I'm sure I'll be able to find some string or something,' she said, opting for the martyr approach which she was fairly sure would annoy Finn. 'You go out and enjoy your lunch. Don't worry about me.'

Finn scowled. 'Oh, yes, that's going to do wonders for

our professional image, isn't it? My PA leaving the office with a dog on a piece of string!'

'I can wait until everyone else has gone,' Kate offered innocently.

'Oh, Dad, please say we can go to a pet shop,' Alex interrupted. 'I've been good—haven't I, Kate? And you did say just the other day that everyone should keep their promises.'

Kate suppressed a smile as Finn champed in frustration. Alex clearly needed no advice in managing her father.

'I don't know where we're going to find a pet shop in the middle of London,' he grumbled, but he had obviously given in on the point of principle.

'Most of the big department stores should have a pet department,' said Kate helpfully.

Not that Finn looked very grateful.

When Alex had gone off with her father, the dog crept closer to Kate, wriggling ingratiatingly. Really he wasn't very beautiful, but his liquid brown eyes were so trusting that her heart melted.

She knew that she shouldn't let herself get too attached to him either. She couldn't keep him and would have to find him a good home somewhere else but, still, she lifted him up, unable to resist the appeal of that tail. He was small enough to sit on her lap, where he licked her hands and curled up comfortably.

To hell with professionalism, Kate decided. It wasn't as if he was stopping her working. She could still type and email and make phone calls.

It was nearly half past two by the time Finn and Alex returned, laden with basket, toys, bowls, a pooper scooper, and dog food, as well as the lead and collar that had been the ostensible purpose of the exercise. Kate quickly put Derek on the floor before Finn spotted him.

He—Finn, not the dog—wore a resigned expression as

Alex proudly showed Kate what she had persuaded her father to buy.

'Here's his collar,' she said, producing it with a flourish.

Kate couldn't help laughing when she saw it. It was made of red velvet and studded with mock diamonds, the kind of nonsense that cost a fortune.

'Don't tell me!' she said. 'Your dad chose this!'

The irony went over Alex's head, but Kate saw the corner of Finn's mouth twitch, and felt as if she had conquered Everest. OK, it wasn't exactly a smile, but it was a response.

She forced her attention back to Alex, who was assuring her that it was a present. 'I used my own money,' she said proudly.

'That's very nice of you,' said Kate, looking doubtfully at the pile of goodies for Derek. Alex must have a very generous allowance.

'Dad paid for the rest,' Alex admitted, almost as if she had read her mind.

Kate glanced at Finn. That tantalising glimpse of humour had vanished, leaving him aloof and austere once more. 'I'll write you a cheque,' she promised.

'Please don't,' he said. 'I'd rather forget the whole business as soon as possible. I can think of better ways to spend a lunch hour than trailing around the pet department being subjected to emotional blackmail by a nine-year-old!'

'Well, thank you anyway,' said Kate, deciding to make it up to him somehow later. She stooped to fasten the collar around Derek, who shook himself at the unfamiliar feel of it. 'Look how smart you are now!' she told him, and smiled at Alex. 'It *was* kind of you to give up your lunch for him.'

'I had a pizza as well,' Alex had to admit.

Kate laughed, even as her own stomach rumbled with hunger. 'I didn't think your dad would let you go hungry.'

'Look, we brought you a sandwich,' said Alex to her

surprise, taking a bag from her father. 'Dad said you needed some lunch.'

Kate peered into the bag to find half a baguette temptingly stuffed with chicken and bacon and avocado. All of her favourite things in fact. How on earth had he known?

She lifted her eyes to meet Finn's, and something shifted in the air between them. 'Thank you,' she said, ridiculously breathless.

'I can't afford to have you passing out from hunger,' he said gruffly. 'We've still got a lot to do this afternoon.'

Still, he had thought of her. A little thrill went through Kate at the knowledge, at least until she managed to suppress it. Letting herself feel little thrills like that about Finn would be bad, bad, bad, and Bella's voice seemed to echo in her ears. *Don't do it, Kate.*

She moistened her lips and handed him a folder of letters for him to sign. 'I've made those appointments you wanted, and the final draft of the tender is being copied right now.'

'And the arrangements for next Thursday?'

'Yes, they're done.'

'You've been busy,' he grunted, and in spite of everything Kate felt herself warm at his grudging approval.

Oh, dear, careful, Kate, she warned herself.

She was busy all afternoon, and in the end Finn arranged for one of the girls from reception to go with Alex when she wanted to take Derek for a little walk. The rest of the time the little girl was quite happy to play with him and the two of them spent hours chasing balls up and down the corridor, but by five o'clock they were both flagging.

Kate knocked on Finn's door. 'I think Alex needs to go home,' she said, bracing herself for him to tell her to mind her own business. 'I'll stay and finish up here if you want to go.'

Finn looked at his watch and frowned. 'I didn't realise

the time. Yes, I'd better take her home.' He glanced at Kate. 'Are you sure?'

'Yes. I owe you extra time anyway after I was late this morning. Then we can call it quits,' she suggested. 'I don't mind staying, honestly. I don't want to take the dog home in the rush hour, and anyway, there's not that much more to do.'

'Well...thanks,' said Finn roughly as he got to his feet and shrugged on his jacket. He sounded deeply uncomfortable and Kate guessed that he didn't like having to be grateful to anyone for anything.

'It's nothing,' she said, brushing it aside. 'I'm sorry for all the hassle I've caused.'

Finn was patting his pockets for his keys. 'What are you going to do about that dog?' he asked abruptly as Kate turned for the door.

'My parents live in the country. They love animals and they've got lots of space, so I'm sure they'd take him, but they're away on holiday at the moment, and won't be back for a few weeks. I'll keep him with me in the meantime.'

She chewed her lip as she considered what it would mean. 'It would mean leaving him all day, but I could walk him as soon as I got home—unless I could bring him to the office with me?' She looked at Finn hopefully. 'He wouldn't be any trouble. You've seen how quiet he is.'

Right on cue came the sound of excited barking and Alex's laugh. Finn looked at Kate.

'Normally,' she added.

Finn sighed. 'I think Alex is going to be more of a problem than the dog. She won't want to be separated from it now.'

He was right. Alex was adamant that Derek should go home with her. 'He's just got used to me,' she protested. 'He'll be confused if I leave him now.'

'You trust me to look after him, don't you?' said Kate,

trying to defuse the imminent stand-off between Finn and his daughter.

'It's not that.' Alex's bottom lip stuck out mutinously. 'If I can't take him home, I won't see him again, and I want to keep him,' she wailed. 'Please, Dad! You know I've always wanted a dog.'

Finn raked his fingers through his hair in frustration. 'Alex, you know it's not possible for you to look after a dog. You're at school all day.'

'Rosa wouldn't mind looking after him during the day.'

'I'm not so sure about that, and anyway, Rosa's not there, so we can't ask her at the moment.'

The bottom lip wobbled. 'But what's going to happen to him?'

Patiently, Finn explained that Kate would look after the dog until she could take it down to her parents.

'Well, couldn't I keep him until then?' pleaded Alex desperately.

'He'll still need a walk during the day, Alex.'

Alex pounced on the flaw in her father's argument. 'How is Kate going to walk him then? She's at work longer than I'm at school.'

Finn gritted his teeth at the realisation that he had been boxed into a corner. He was going to have to give in to one of them. 'Kate's going to bring him into the office,' he said, succumbing to the inevitable.

'Then why couldn't you bring him in, Dad?' Alex persisted. 'You've got a car, so it wouldn't make any difference to you. I'd walk him in the morning and in the evening when you bring him home, and he could spend the day with you.'

Finn cast a meaningful look at Kate. It was crystal clear that he thought that it was her dog and her responsibility to knock the idea on its head once and for all. Kate met his eyes with a bland smile. She was rather enjoying seeing Finn comprehensively out-argued by a nine-year-old.

'I think that's a good idea,' she said, wilfully ignoring her cue and Finn's baleful glare. 'I could walk him at lunch time so your dad doesn't have to be bothered with him,' she offered to Alex, whose face brightened instantly.

'Oh, yes, *please!*'

'And what happens when Alison comes back?' demanded Finn, annoyed at being outmanoeuvred. 'She might not feel like walking a dog in her lunch break!'

Alex barely missed a beat. 'Rosa's mother might be better then and she can come back. I bet she wouldn't mind Derek.'

Kate suppressed a smile at Finn's expression. 'You've done a wonderful job of bringing Alex up,' she told him with mock seriousness. 'Not many girls of nine could argue so well! You must be very proud of her.'

'I don't think I'd choose proud to describe the way I'm feeling right now,' said Finn, exasperated, but it was obvious that he had decided that he was fighting a losing battle.

'Very well,' he said, turning back to his daughter. 'But—'

He was interrupted by Alex throwing herself into his arms with a shriek of delight. 'Oh, thank you, thank you, thank you!' she cried, almost drowned out by Derek who went into a frenzy of shrill barking as he picked up on the excitement.

For a moment, there was chaos, and Kate couldn't help laughing. At the same time she couldn't help being touched by the way Finn hugged his daughter back. He might hide behind a gruff exterior but it was obvious that they adored each other.

Kate even felt a little bit excluded, which of course was ridiculous. *She* didn't want to be gathered up and hugged and included in their little family unit with the dog. She was supposed to be a hip metropolitan chick, not yearning for security and love, right?

Right.

'*But*—' Finn managed to raise his voice above the commotion at last. 'On one condition. You're not to get too attached to this dog, Alex. You're at school, I'm at work, and it's not part of Rosa's job to walk a dog. You can take him home with you now, but only as long as Kate is working here, or until she can take him to her parents. That's the deal. OK?'

Alex looked up at him speculatively. Kate could practically hear her thinking that this was the best offer she was going to get for now, so she might as well accept and find another plan for when the first one came to an end.

'OK,' she said, and looking at the tilt of her chin, so like her father's, Kate thought that Finn was probably going to end up having a dog whether he wanted it or not.

Kate herself thought it had worked out pretty well. Her parents would take Derek, of course, but she didn't really want to ask them again, having landed them with so many other waifs and strays in the past. She wished she could keep Derek, but it was hopeless when you were temping and, anyway, she could already see the bond that existed between the dog and the little girl. Derek would be happier with Alex.

'I hope Alison never comes back,' Alex whispered when Finn went to get his coat, and Kate was disconcerted to realise that she didn't want Alison to come back either.

The next morning it was Finn's turn to be late. He came into the office with Derek prancing and chewing on his lead, to find Kate sitting behind her desk and looking innocently at her watch.

'Don't say anything!' he warned her, unamused.

Kate grinned. 'I wasn't going to.'

'I suppose you realise that you and this dog between you have completely disrupted my life?' grumbled Finn, letting Derek go as he recognised his saviour of the day before and went into frenzy of excitement.

Released, he dashed over to Kate, who picked him up, still wriggling ecstatically, but then had to turn her head away from his attempts to lick her cheek and chin, her face lit with laughter.

The suit had had to go to the cleaners after yesterday's encounter with a pile of rubbish, so she was back to wearing a long skirt in some vaguely ethnic pattern with a top that clung to her curves and was, in spite of its long sleeves and high neck, somehow much more disturbing than the more revealing one she had worn to dinner at Phoebe and Gib's.

She had given up on her hair as well, and it fell in soft brown curls to her shoulders. To Finn she looked vaguely scruffy but startlingly warm and vivid as she stood there with the squirming dog in her arms against the background of sterile office equipment.

'That dog is completely out of control,' he said, his voice very dry as if his throat was tight.

'Oh, but he's so sweet! How could he possibly be any trouble?'

'Have you ever tried taking him for a walk? He's got no idea how to walk on a lead and if you let him off he goes round in manic circles or runs off and won't come back. It's hard enough getting Alex to school on time as it is without coping with a miniature whirlwind on four legs. *And* he's chewed my best shoes!'

'Well, he's just a puppy,' said Kate. 'That's what puppies do. You'll have to be careful to keep things out of his reach.'

'That's not a puppy, that's a fully grown dog and uncontrollable with it!'

'Nonsense,' she said briskly, and Derek squirmed with pleasure as she kissed the top of his head. 'You just need a bit of training, don't you? We'll have you sitting and staying in no time.'

Finn snorted. 'You take him, then, and while you're at it, train him to do something useful like make breakfast or tidy the kitchen.' He sighed as he took off his coat. 'God, what a morning! It's bad enough Alison being away without losing Rosa as well.'

'When is she coming back?' asked Kate, putting the dog back on the ground and trying not to feel hurt at the knowledge that she was missing Alison.

'Not soon enough!' Finn picked up the letters Kate had opened for him and began to flick through them. 'I'm not the most domesticated of men, and there's only so much take-away food that you can stomach. But Rosa's mother is still in hospital and she doesn't know how long she's going to be away.'

'Couldn't you get someone to help temporarily?'

'It's a bit difficult not knowing how long it would be for. Besides, Alex hates change. She doesn't like having a housekeeper at all and would rather it was just the two of us. She tolerates Rosa, but that's about as far as it goes.'

'I can see it's difficult,' said Kate, and Finn frowned as if recollecting too late that he was confiding his personal concerns.

'Yes, well, I'd better get on,' he said abruptly. 'Any messages?'

'Mr Osborne's PA rang. Could you call him back?'

'What does he want?'

Kate consulted her notebook. 'I gather he wants you to go and see him this afternoon. There are some points he wants to clarify before they make their final decision. What's the problem?' she asked as Finn cursed under his breath.

'I'll have to go. We can't afford to lose that contract, but I promised Alex I'd pick her up from school today as it's Friday. She wants everyone to see the dog.'

He stuck his hands in his pockets and frowned worriedly at the floor. 'She's always been a very solitary child—inevitable I suppose—but I hoped she'd make more friends at this new school. This morning's the first time she's shown any interest in what the other children thought,' he went on reluctantly. 'I'm afraid that if she's told everyone about the dog and he doesn't appear they'll think she's been making it up.'

'Why don't I go and meet her with Derek?' Kate offered, and his head jerked up to stare at her.

'You'd do that?'

Kate couldn't quite meet his eyes. She wasn't quite sure what had prompted her impulsive offer herself. It couldn't be wanting to ease the lines of strain around his mouth or the worry from his voice...could it?

'I wouldn't mind,' she said. 'It's partly my fault anyway. If I hadn't landed you with a dog, you wouldn't be in this situation.'

Finn hesitated. 'I might not get back until after seven if Osborne's in a nit-picking mood.'

'That's all right.' She busied herself sorting the papers on her desk into neat piles. 'I'll stay with Alex until you get home.'

'Are you sure? It's Friday night. Haven't you got anything planned?'

'Nothing special,' said Kate, 'and anyway, I can always go out later.'

'No heavy date with a financial analyst then?'

'What? Oh.' Colour crept into her cheeks as she remembered the elaborate story she had made up to impress him. 'No, that's the advantage of a fantasy man,' she said, putting up her chin. 'He fits in with all your other arrangements. He's the perfect man, really.'

'I see.' A disconcerting gleam lit Finn's grey eyes. 'Well, if you're sure you don't mind, I'd really appreciate it if you could go and meet Alex. I'll give you a note for the school and arrange for a car to take you there and then on home.'

Why was she doing this? Kate wondered as she sat with Derek in the back of the limousine Finn had booked. She had been so determined to stay cool and professional, too. Bella would say that she was getting involved, but she wasn't really. She was just helping out in a crisis. She'd do the same for anyone.

It was nothing whatsoever to do with the warm glow inside her when she remembered the almost-smile in Finn's eyes and the approval in his voice.

Because that wouldn't be at all professional, would it?

Standing at the school gates with all the other mothers and nannies was an odd experience. Kate could feel their curious sidelong glances at the impostor. She was sure they were all wondering what on earth she was doing there. What would it be like to be one of them, a bona fide mother instead of a pretend one? To be waiting for your own children, to take them home to the warmth and security of a loving home?

Kate had never allowed herself to think about having children too much. Even in the depths of her obsession with Seb she had known that he would be aghast at the very idea of children. Seb needed the world to revolve around him, and he wouldn't want to share the attention with anyone else, least of all a baby who wouldn't blend in with his décor. He was much too fickle and unreliable to make a good father anyway, unlike Finn.

Just for instance.

When the children started pouring out into the playground, Kate wrenched her mind away from the thought of

Finn as a father and craned her neck to find Alex. She spotted her at last, searching the crowd in her turn for her father. Kate saw the moment when it dawned on her that he wasn't there, and sullenness masked the bitterness of her disappointment.

Pushing forward through the press of mothers and pushchairs with Derek, she waved to get her attention. 'Alex!' she called.

The terrible withdrawn look was wiped from Alex's face as she caught sight of Kate with the dog. It lit up instead and she rushed towards them.

'Dad's really sorry he couldn't come,' said Kate quickly, 'but he sent Derek instead. You don't mind, do you?'

'Not if Derek's here,' said Alex, crouching down so that the little dog could put his paws on her knees and greet her properly.

There was soon a circle of curious children staring at Derek. 'He's my dog,' said Alex nonchalantly, and Kate approved the careless way she dealt with the attention, as if it didn't matter to her whether anyone envied her or not.

Derek played his part brilliantly, greeting every child with enthusiasm and generally behaving in such an endearing way that none of them could resist asking Alex if they could pet him. He was clearly winning her lots of kudos in the playground, and her cheeks were pink with satisfaction when she finally left, holding tightly onto Derek's lead and waving a casual farewell.

The office was so modern and streamlined that Kate had somehow expected Finn to live somewhere similar, but it turned out to be a substantial Victorian house close to Wimbledon Common, with a large, safe garden. Ideal for a dog, in fact.

Inside, the house had evidently been decorated professionally, but it had a sterile, unlived-in air that Kate thought was rather sad. It was a house and not a home, and she wondered whether it had been that way since Isabel had died.

Alex led the way to a big kitchen with French windows opening onto the garden. 'I wanted Derek to sleep in my room, but Dad said he had to stay here,' she told Kate, pointing out the basket and bowls set out in the corner.

'He's probably better off in the kitchen,' said Kate tactfully. That must have been another battle of wills. No wonder Finn had looked harassed this morning!

She looked around the kitchen while Alex had a drink and then, remembering what he had said about being sick of take-away food, suggested that they walk Derek along to the shops and buy something to cook for supper.

'You can cook?' Alex looked at her strangely.

'Well, nothing very impressive, but I can knock up the basics. What do you like to eat?'

Alex was fascinated by the fact that Kate knew how to make her favourite meal, macaroni cheese. 'Rosa doesn't make it, I don't think they have it where she comes from,' she said. 'Can you make puddings too?'

'Yes, some. Why, do you want a pudding as well?'

'Dad likes puddings, but Rosa's not very good at them either.'

Kate liked the idea of Finn having a weakness, even if it was only a sweet tooth. 'Do you think he'd like a chocolate pudding?' she asked Alex.

'Oh, yes, he loves chocolate.'

Better and better.

'Well, let's see what we can do.'

When Finn came home, he found his daughter, his temporary secretary and the dog in the kitchen. Unnoticed by any of them, he hesitated in the doorway, taking in the scene. Normally Alex retreated to her room, but today she was sitting happily at the kitchen table, the dog panting at her feet, helping Kate cook. There was flour everywhere and the sink was piled with dirty bowls and cooking implements. Alex's face was smudged with chocolate, and Kate's was not much better.

It struck Finn that he had never seen the kitchen look messier or more welcoming.

Kate was wearing Rosa's apron. She looked warm and dishevelled, her cheeks pink and her brown curls tumbled. As Finn watched, she lifted a hand to push her hair back from her face, leaving a streak of flour on her forehead.

'Not much of a guard dog, is he?' Finn's sarcasm disguised the sudden dryness in his throat.

At the sound of his voice, Kate started and Derek leapt belatedly to his feet, barking and wagging his tail so furiously that it would have taken a much harder heart than Finn's not to feel gratified at the warmth of his welcome.

'He's pleased to see you,' Alex told him as he bent to kiss his daughter.

Kate bent her head over the bowl into which she was sifting flour and tried to get her breathing back to normal. The sudden sight of Finn in the doorway had sent her heart lurching into her throat, where it lodged, jerking madly.

Shock at seeing him so unexpectedly, Kate told herself, in which case she wished her heart would just calm down. There was nothing to get excited about. It was just Finn, Finn with his cool eyes and his stern mouth and dark, austere presence. Nothing to make her senses fizz, or the breath evaporate from her lungs. And absolutely no reason to suddenly feel so ridiculously, embarrassingly shy.

'Hello,' she croaked in return to his greeting and carried on sifting with a kind of desperation.

Under her lashes, she could see Finn taking off his jacket and wrenching at his tie to loosen it. 'Something smells good,' he said.

'Kate's made macaroni cheese.' Alex tugged at his sleeve excitedly. 'And I have to have some salad, but then there's a chocolate pudding. We made it especially for you.'

Finn glanced at Kate, who blushed hotly and made a big deal of banging the sieve against the edge of the bowl. 'Alex said you liked chocolate.'

'I do.'

'I hope you don't mind me taking over your kitchen like this,' said Kate awkwardly. 'I thought I might as well make supper for you since I was here.'

'Mind?' echoed Finn. 'I'm very grateful!'

He seemed less dour and formidable than usual, as if the rigidity had gone from his jaw and his spine. It was only natural, Kate thought. He was at home, so it wasn't surprising if he was more relaxed than at the office.

But it was more disturbing, too. She wasn't sure how to deal with Finn when he was being approachable like this, and it made her nervous in a way that his brusqueness didn't any more.

'I won't be long,' she said, uncertain as to what she ought to do now, 'and I'll tidy up before I go.'

'But you'll stay and eat with us, won't you?' said Finn, and Alex added her voice as well.

'Oh, yes, you must stay!'

He might be just being polite. Kate twisted the sieve between her hands. Part of her longed to stay, and the other part was apprehensive. She felt very odd, all jittery and jumpy and it was something to do with the way Finn was standing there, looking at her.

Don't do it. Wasn't that what Bella had said?

'Well, I—'

'You said you didn't have anything special on tonight,' Finn reminded her.

'No, but—'

'I'll get a taxi to take you home later,' he promised. And

then, almost as if the words were forced out of him, 'Please stay.'

What could she say? 'All right,' said Kate. 'Thanks.'

At which point Finn really threw her by smiling. A real smile. At her. 'I'm the one who should be thanking you,' he said.

Kate's hands were shaking as he went to change. She had imagined what he would look like when he smiled often enough, but she was still unprepared for how it transformed his face, illuminating those piercing grey eyes and softening the hard mouth. It had only been a brief smile, enough to glimpse the whiteness of his teeth and the way it creased his cheek and the edges of his eyes, but hardly enough to justify the sudden weakness at her knees or the bump and thump of her heart which had already been working overtime ever since he walked into the kitchen.

Guiltily, Kate faced the fact. She was doing exactly what Bella had warned her against. She had felt sorry for Finn since learning his tragic story, and now she was fancying herself attracted to him.

Which was just silly. She had had enough of falling for unobtainable men, and they didn't come more unobtainable than Finn. Not only was he utterly committed to the memory of his dead wife, but he was her boss. Getting involved when she had to see him every day at the office was a bad idea.

A *very* bad idea given that Alison would be coming back soon, and then where would she be? She was supposed to be out there meeting someone with whom she could have some fun, Kate reminded herself, not stuck in a Wimbledon kitchen with an apron on, all twitchy and flustered because Finn had smiled at her.

She was just going to have to pull herself together. She

had helped him out today, but that was as far as it was going to go. She would have supper, Kate decided, and then she would leave and she wouldn't even *think* about getting any closer.

CHAPTER FIVE

'THIS is a nice room.'

Alex had gone to bed and Finn had suggested to Kate that they had coffee in the sitting room. He had pulled the heavy red curtains across the window to shut out the cold, dark night, and had put on a lamp in the corner. Now he bent to switch on the fire. It was gas, but the appearance of real flames was very effective.

A bit *too* effective, Kate thought. The flickering light made the room dark and intimate, and now she was even more nervous about being alone with him. It hadn't been too bad while Alex was there, but now there was only Derek as chaperon and, in spite of all her efforts to keep up a flow of bright conversation, a tension was seeping back into the atmosphere.

It was Finn's fault, she had decided. He looked different tonight. It was the first time she had seen him out of a suit. He'd changed before supper and, in casual trousers and a warm shirt, he seemed younger, less austere, and Kate was disturbingly aware of him.

She tried not to look at him as he straightened from the fire and sat down at the other end of the sofa, which was when she was forced to make her inane comment about the room instead.

Finn glanced round as if he had never seen it before. 'I don't use this room very much,' he said. 'It's too big. I rattle around in it when I'm on my own. I usually sit in my study.'

Kate thought of this beautiful room sitting empty while Finn retreated to his study every night. 'It must get lonely sometimes,' she said, and felt Finn's eyes flicker to her face and then away.

'I'm used to it now,' he said.

Kate swirled the wine around the bottom of her glass. 'Do you miss her all the time?' she asked, emboldened by the darkness and the firelight.

'Isabel?' Finn sighed and stared into the flames. 'It was hell at first, but now...it comes and goes. Sometimes I think I've accepted that she's gone and others I miss her so much it's like a physical pain. I look at Alex and I get angry that she didn't get the chance to see her daughter growing up.'

'I'm sorry,' said Kate quietly, not knowing what else she could say.

Finn looked across at her again, his face unreadable in the dim light. 'You know what happened?'

'Someone at work told me it was a car accident.'

He nodded. 'She was in a coma for a week. I couldn't do anything, I could only sit there and hold her hand and tell her how much I loved her.' He turned back to the fire. 'The doctors said she couldn't hear me.'

Kate's throat ached for him. 'Maybe she could feel you.'

'That's what I told myself. I promised her that I would look after Alex, that I'd do on my own, for both of us, but I'm beginning to wonder if I can keep that promise.'

Draining the last of his wine, Finn leant forward to put the glass on the coffee-table in front of them. 'It's hard being a single parent. The worst bit is not having anyone to share your worries with. Alex can be difficult sometimes, and that's when I miss Isabel most. She was so calm and gentle. She would know how to handle her.'

'But Alex seems very happy,' said Kate, thinking of the way the little girl had chattered through supper.

'Thanks to you.'

Kate's jaw dropped. 'To me?'

'She's happier now than I've seen her for a very long

time, and it's because of that mutt you gave us.' He stirred Derek with his foot where he lay under the coffee-table, and ecstatic at the least bit of attention, the dog rolled over onto his back with a sigh of contentment.

'Alex doesn't make friends easily,' Finn went on. 'She's very reserved for a child. I worry that she's too possessive of me, too.'

'I suppose that's inevitable when it's just the two of you,' said Kate.

'Perhaps.' He leant forward, resting his elbows on his knees, and the firelight cast flickering shadows across his face, highlighting then concealing the lines of strain. 'She resents the fact that we have to have a housekeeper, and doesn't understand why it can't just be the two of us.

'I've thought about selling the company and staying at home,' he admitted, 'but what would happen to everyone who's worked for me so loyally, and what would I do with myself? Alex is at school all day. There's only so much cooking and cleaning I can do, and I'd still have to make a living somehow.'

Finn hunched his shoulders. He had obviously been over his options again and again. 'The other alternative, of course, is to marry again,' he said. 'Alex is growing up. She's going to need a woman around even more, but it doesn't seem fair to ask someone to marry me just to be a stepmother…'

He trailed off with a hopeless gesture. He sounded so tired that Kate had a terrifying impulse to put her arms around him, to draw his head down onto her breast and tell him that everything would be all right, that she was there.

Not the best way to go about not getting involved.

Swallowing hard, she stared at the fire instead. 'Is that why you came to dinner with Gib and Phoebe? Looking for a suitable stepmother?'

'Partly,' said Finn. 'I'd talked myself into making an

effort to go out and meet more people. I thought maybe if I actually met someone, things might change somehow, but...'

'But you just met me,' Kate finished for him.

'Yes,' said Finn after a moment. 'I met you.'

There was a silence. To Kate it seemed to last for ever, fraught with unspoken implications. That she wasn't the kind of stepmother he was looking for, that she hadn't changed anything for him. Or that she might have done if she hadn't turned out to be working for him?

Or if she hadn't been determined not to get involved, of course.

It was Finn who broke the silence. 'What were *you* doing there?'

'Phoebe's one of my best friends.'

'Did you know I was going to be there?'

'Yes. I didn't know it was *you* of course,' Kate added hurriedly, 'but I knew that they'd invited someone for me to meet.'

Finn looked at her curiously. 'I don't understand it.'

'What do you mean?'

'You're a pretty girl,' he said. 'You must know that. You're lively, intelligent—when you want to be, anyway—and you've obviously got lots of friends. I'd have thought men would be queuing up to take you out. Why would a girl like you need her friends to fix her up on a blind date?'

Kate shrugged. 'It's not as easy as you think, especially when you get past thirty. All the nice men are settled in relationships, usually with your friends, and you end up making a fool of yourself over the ones that are available.' A tinge of bitterness crept into her voice. 'That's what seems to happen to me, anyway.'

'Not Will the financial analyst?'

'No.' Kate half smiled. She might as well admit it. 'Will exists all right, but he's Bella's boyfriend, not mine. I just borrowed him for my little fantasy to try and impress you. Not that it worked.'

'I don't know,' said Finn. 'You had me convinced for a while.'

Without thinking, Kate had made herself more comfortable, putting her feet up onto the coffee-table and leaning back into the cushions so that she could rest her head against the back of the sofa. Finn's eyes rested on her face.

'So if it wasn't Will, who was it?'

'His name's Seb.' Kate looked up at the ceiling, remembering. 'I was mad about him. He was one of the junior executives where I used to work, and I used to fantasise about him from afar. He was so good-looking and charming and he had a terrible reputation—but of course, that was part of his appeal,' she said ironically. 'When he noticed me amongst all the other girls there, I couldn't believe my luck.'

She sighed a little. 'Phoebe and Bella never liked him, but I was in thrall to him. It's hard to explain now. He had this kind of sexual charisma. I couldn't think properly when I was with him.

'I told them they didn't understand him the way I did. I persuaded myself that his selfishness was a result of the way he'd been brought up and that there was a little lost boy inside him. I thought that all he needed was the love of a good woman, and that I'd be the one to change him, you know the sort of thing.' She laughed but there was an undercurrent of bitterness to it. 'I was such a fool.'

'We all make mistakes,' said Finn neutrally.

'Most people learn from theirs. I didn't.' Kate leant forward to pick up her coffee. 'We had what magazines call a "destructive relationship". I humiliated myself for months. I'd go out of my way just to bump into him, and wait desperately for him to call. I got obsessed with checking the phone and my email, and Seb knew it. He'd say that he would contact me, then he'd ignore my existence, until I'd just given up hope.

'He always timed it perfectly. He'd ring or drop round out of the blue, and I'd be so pleased to see him that I didn't realise until too late that he was only there because he wanted something. He wanted to borrow some money or get his washing done.'

Kate caught Finn's look. 'Oh, yes,' she said with a rueful smile. 'I'd wash and iron and cook and clean for him. I cringe when I think about it now, but at the time it seemed the only way I could keep him.'

She must sound completely pathetic. Finn would probably despise such spineless behaviour, but it was hard to tell from his expression what he was thinking.

'What made you change your mind about him?' was all he asked.

'I went up to his office one evening,' Kate told him. 'I'd found an excuse to work late as usual, knowing that he'd be there, and I found him shouting at one of the cleaners. I don't even know what she was supposed to have done, but the poor woman was terrified. English obviously wasn't her first language, and I just hoped that she couldn't understand half the things he was calling her.

'It was horrible,' she said with a shudder at the memory. 'I couldn't believe how unpleasant he was! When I told him he couldn't talk to people like, he turned on me, and we had a huge argument. I ended up saying that I was going to report him for verbal abuse.'

'And what did Seb say to that?'

'He told me not to bother, because *he* was going to report *me* for harassment.'

'And who do you think they're going to believe?' Seb had sneered. 'A not very efficient secretary or a rising executive?'

'That's exactly what he did,' Kate finished. 'And I lost my job.'

Finn was looking grim. 'Couldn't you fight it?'

'The trouble was that everyone knew I was mad about him, and the way I'd made excuses to see him made it easy for him to make everyone believe that I was practically stalking him. Of course he didn't tell anyone about the times he showed up on *my* doorstep.'

'Is that why you had to leave your job?' Finn sounded even grimmer now.

'Yes. Oh, I wasn't sacked. Nothing as crude as that. It was merely suggested that I might be happier elsewhere, and that if I stayed my position might become "untenable".' Kate hooked her fingers in the air to add extra emphasis to the pomposity of the phrases they had used.

Seb had been promoted. She didn't tell Finn that.

'You should have appealed,' he said, frowning.

She shrugged. 'By that stage I didn't want to work there any longer anyway. It was ironic, really. After all those months desperate to catch a glimpse of Seb, the moment I didn't want to see him any more, he seemed to be around the whole time. I was glad to leave.

'The only trouble was that they gave me a really grudging reference, which meant I couldn't get another job,' she went on. 'Joining the temp agency was my only option in the end, and working for you is my first job with them.' No harm in reassuring Finn that she hadn't forgotten that their relationship was strictly professional.

She smiled brightly at him. 'That's why I have to try and make a good impression and stick with you until Alison gets back.'

It was true. If Finn gave her a rotten report, she might find herself off the agency's list, but Kate didn't think there was any need to labour the point.

'Is that what you're doing now?' he said, putting his coffee-mug very deliberately back onto the coffee table.

'Now?' she echoed blankly.

'Picking Alex up from school, making supper, all of this.' There was a harsh note in his voice, almost as if he was disappointed.

'No,' said Kate. 'I didn't even think about it. Besides, the ability to make macaroni cheese isn't the kind of thing employers look for in a reference. I was just hoping you'd notice that I was being more punctual and efficient.'

'I see,' was all Finn said, but he sounded less hard.

'It's all part of my new attitude,' Kate went on to make sure he understood that she was in absolutely no danger of misinterpreting that they were alone in the dark and firelight.

'I've decided to sharpen up my act all round. Seb taught me a valuable lesson—two, in fact. From now on I'm going to keep my personal life quite separate from work, and I'm not going to get too serious about anyone. I'm going to take any opportunity to meet new people, even if it means going on a blind date. So when Phoebe rang and said they had invited someone to meet me, I thought "why not"? I wasn't interested in finding a deep and meaningful relationship,' she told him. 'I just wanted some fun.'

'But you just met me,' Finn quoted Kate's words back to her.

Something in his voice made Kate turn her head. He was watching her from the other end of the sofa, his expression unreadable, but his eyes trapped hers without warning, stopping the breath in her throat and holding her mousestill, skewered by the directness of his gaze. Kate wasn't sure how long they sat there with the air evaporating around them, and the silence stretching unbearably, broken only by the faint hiss and splutter of the gas fire and the booming roar of her pulse in her ear, but when Finn looked away it was like being released from a pinion-hold.

Now all she had to do was remember what they had been talking about before she turned her head.

Ah, yes. Impressing on him that she was just out to have a good time and not in the market for marriage or anything remotely serious. So he needn't panic.

'Yes, it was a bit of a shock.' She forced a smile. 'It's not much fun to find yourself on a blind date with your boss.'

'No,' said Finn, looking into the fire. 'I imagine not.'

It was all very well convincing Finn that she just wanted to have a good time, but Kate found it harder to live up to in practice. There was no problem about going out. Bella was relentlessly social, and Kate could always tag along with her. But somehow going out wasn't quite as much fun as it had used to be.

Kate was exasperated to find herself in the middle of a party, fretting about how Finn and Alex were managing with the housekeeper still away. It wasn't her problem, she reminded herself endlessly. She was supposed to be having fun and being cool, and worrying about grieving widowers and motherless children wasn't part of the plan.

Sitting in a bar with a City type baying at her about his bonuses and his flash car, or pretending to study the menu in a crowded restaurant, Kate would find her mind wandering to the house in Wimbledon. She thought about Alex and the little dog, but mostly she thought about Finn, sitting at the other end of the sofa in the firelight. She thought about the way his smile illuminated the severe face, about the line of that stern mouth and, whenever she did, which was too often for comfort, something twisted and churned inside her.

It was even worse in the office, though. She was jittery

and on edge in the same room as Finn, and if he came anywhere near her she would suddenly become clumsy, spilling her coffee or dropping papers, and colouring painfully when he looked at her in surprise.

Only three weeks until Alison was due back. Kate wasn't sure whether she longed for an end to the daily embarrassment of making a complete fool of herself, or dreaded it. Sometimes she tried to imagine working for someone else, in a different office, but she just couldn't do it. No dog to walk every lunch time. No willing her nerves not to jump whenever Finn walked into the room.

No Finn.

Ever since that evening when she had picked Alex up from school the atmosphere between them had been one of careful constraint. Finn was gruff but polite, and Kate found herself wishing more than once that he would go back to shouting at her and being grumpy and generally disagreeable. Things had been easier then.

Somehow Kate struggled through to the Friday, but by that afternoon she was in no fit state to deal with the long and complicated list of instructions Finn decided to give her. Sitting across the desk from him, she was supposed to be taking notes, but she kept getting diverted by the sight of his hands as he moved papers around, or letting her eyes rest on his mouth while he searched for a particular bit of information, and then when he looked up again, his eyes would be so piercing that she instantly lost track of what she was supposed to be doing.

'Are you all right?' Finn asked at last, after she had had to ask him to repeat himself for the sixth time.

'I'm fine,' stammered Kate, colour rushing into her cheeks. Honestly, it was getting to the point where she couldn't talk to him without blushing like an idiot.

'It's just that you seem even vaguer than usual today.'

'No, I'm a bit tired that's all,' she said. 'I had a late

night.' That was true enough, she had been out with Bella. 'We went out to a club, and you know what it's like when you're having good time,' she went on, spotting another opportunity to persuade Finn that, while she might be behaving like a love-struck schoolgirl, it was nothing whatsoever to do with him.

'You forget to look at your watch,' she told him, all ditzy brunette, the kind of girl who danced till the small hours and whose only aim in life was to have fun. The last kind of girl to waste her time even *thinking* about a man preoccupied with domestic problems.

'I'll take your word for it,' said Finn dryly.

He paused, shuffling papers unnecessarily. 'I told Alex that you had a very social life,' he said unexpectedly, 'but I promised her that I'd ask you anyway.'

'Ask me what?' said Kate, surprised into normality.

'She seems to regard you as an authority on dogs. God knows, you've got to know more than we do anyway! Anyway, she wanted to know if you'd come over and show her how to train Derek one afternoon this weekend. Apparently you told her that you would give her a few tips,' he went on almost accusingly, as if the invitation was her fault somehow.

She *had* promised Alex that she would show her how to train Derek, Kate remembered. That wasn't the problem. The problem was how much she wanted to go.

'I told her you'd be busy,' Finn said as she hesitated.

'No...no...I'm not busy,' said Kate, who had opened her mouth to take the let-out clause he offered and found herself saying something completely different instead.

'I mean, an afternoon would be fine,' she stumbled on, her mouth still operating contrary to strict orders from her brain which was telling her to do the sensible thing and not get any more involved than she was already. 'Perhaps we could go for a walk on one of the parks?'

'That's kind of you,' Finn said in such a stilted voice that Kate wondered if he had wanted her to refuse. 'Alex will be pleased.'

What about you? she wanted to ask him. Will you be pleased?

'Would Sunday afternoon suit you?' he was saying, still repressively polite.

'Sunday would be fine.'

'We'll come and pick you up in the car. About two o'clock?'

In spite of giving herself a good talking to on the way home, and reminding herself of all the reasons why she didn't want to get involved with Finn or his daughter or his dog, Kate was appalled at how much she looked forward to Sunday afternoon. Saturday night, another wild session orchestrated by Bella, was just an endurance test, and she left as early as she decently could, hoping that Bella wouldn't notice her lack of enthusiasm.

No such luck. 'What is up with you at the moment?' Bella accused her when she finally emerged, yawning and tousled, on Sunday morning.

'Nothing,' said Kate brightly.

'I lined up Will's friend specially for you, and you blew him off. I thought Toby would be just your type.'

'He was OK.' Kate fidgeted around the kitchen, putting jars and packets away, and wiping down the work surface with a cloth.

Bella looked at her in deep suspicion. 'And why are you tidying the kitchen suddenly?'

'No reason,' said Kate. 'It's just a mess.'

'It's always a mess and it never bothered you before. Who's coming round?'

'Finn and his daughter might come later.' Kate tried to sound casual, but she should have known better than to try and fool Bella.

'Finn as in the boss you hated and then felt sorry for? The one you had no intention of getting involved with?'

'Yes,' she had to admit.

'Explain to me how having him round to your house on a Sunday afternoon is not being involved?'

'If you must know, it's a date with his daughter. We're going to take the dog for a walk, and Finn's just going to drive us from A to B.'

'Right,' said Bella, obviously not believing a word.

'It's true. I'm only going because I feel a bit responsible for the dog.'

Bella filled the kettle at the sink. 'So what will I tell Toby if he rings and wants to see you again?'

'Absolutely,' said Kate firmly. 'I'm into fun, fun, fun.'

'That'll be why you're getting ready for a *walk* about four hours early! What are you going to wear?'

Oh, God, good point. What *was* she going to wear? Back in her bedroom, Kate rummaged through her clothes. She really must hang some of those skirts up some time.

It was all too difficult. She didn't want to look a mess, but she didn't want to look as if she was trying too hard either. Her jeans were a bit tight, but she squeezed into them and pulled on a red jumper which was one of her favourites. Not that Finn was likely to see it under her jacket, of course.

Unless she offered them some tea? And scones might be nice after a cold walk.

Kate galloped back down to the kitchen and began burrowing through the cupboards for flour and cream of tartar.

'Do you know if we've got any bicarb of soda?'

Bella looked up from the gossip pages in the Sunday paper. 'What do you want that for?'

'I thought I might make some scones,' said Kate carelessly.

'Scones?' Bella shook her head. 'You have got it bad!'

and then when Kate swung round to protest, 'try the cupboard above the toaster.'

Kate fidgeted around the kitchen for the rest of the morning, driving Bella mad by trying to tidy up around her.

'I wish this Finn would just come and put you out of your misery,' Bella grumbled as she gathered up the paper and her coffee and retreated to the sitting room.

By the time the doorbell rang, Kate had worked herself up to a pitch of nerves she couldn't remember since her very first date. Pulling down her jumper, she ran her fingers through her curls and took a deep breath before opening the door.

Finn was standing behind Alex, and Kate's heart gave a great lurch when she saw him. She looked quickly away at Alex, who greeted her with an unselfconscious hug. In similar circumstances Kate would think nothing of kissing a visitor like Finn on the cheek, but the thought of touching him, however briefly, seemed fraught with difficulty, and in the end she contented herself with smiling stiffly.

'Hello.'

Alex sat in the back seat with an over-excited Derek. She was in a chatty mood, so all Kate had to do was nod and smile and put in the occasional comment, which was just as well as she was having trouble concentrating with Finn's hand moving competently on the gears so close to her knee.

It was a relief to get out of the car and concentrate on Alex and the dog. She showed her how to offer little treats when Derek did as he was told, and before long he was sitting and waiting until he was called before he came lolloping towards her.

Alex was delighted. 'He's clever, isn't he, Dad?'

'Clever enough to know what it takes to get some food,' said Finn, who had been watching them with a resigned expression.

Afterwards they walked around the park. It was a cold, blustery day and the wind blew Kate's hair around her face. Alex ran ahead with Derek, while Kate tried not to be too conscious of Finn striding beside her, his head down, his hands thrust into the pockets of his jacket, his dark hair ruffled by the breeze.

Every now and then Alex would come galloping back, her cheeks pink and her eyes shining behind her glasses. 'I wish we could do this every weekend!'

'You never liked walking before,' said Finn.

'It's different if you've got a dog. I'm so glad you came to work for Dad,' she told Kate fervently. 'Aren't you, Dad?'

Finn glanced at Kate, who was trying unsuccessfully to hold her hair back from her face. Her brown eyes were bright in the sharp light and the exercise had brought colour to her cheeks.

'She's certainly changed my life,' he said, and Kate smiled uncertainly, not sure how to take that. Was changing his life a good thing or a bad thing, or was he just joking?

In the end, she decided it would be safer just to ignore it. She asked about the housekeeper instead. 'Will Rosa be coming back soon?'

'We don't know. She's been very good about keeping in touch and she's obviously anxious not to lose the job, but her mother's still very ill and she just can't tell when she'll be able to leave her. In the meantime, Alex and I are managing as best we can.'

'It's great,' said Alex. 'It's much better without a housekeeper at all.'

'You won't think so when your Aunt Stella arrives,' Finn said. 'She'll be horrified that there's no one to look after you properly.'

'You look after me,' Alex said loyally, tucking her hand into his, and Kate saw the rueful twist of his smile.

'Stella will tell me I'm not enough, and she'll be right.'

'Who's Stella?' she asked.

'She's Dad's sister. She's so bossy!'

'She lives in Canada,' Finn said, more measured. 'She comes over here every year to make sure Alex and I are all right.'

He hesitated. 'She's got a good heart, but she can be a bit...domineering.'

'Bossy,' said Alex.

'Overbearing,' Finn overruled her and turned back to Kate, ignoring the way his daughter muttered an insistent 'Bossy!' under her breath. 'Stella decided a couple of years ago that Alex needed a stepmother, and now whenever she's over she lines up a string of what she thinks are suitable women for me to meet.'

'They're always awful too,' Alex put in. 'Aren't they, Dad?'

'Let's just say that Stella has different ideas from us about the kind of stepmother Alex needs,' said Finn. 'I'm fond of her, and I know she means well, but I wish she'd just let me organise my life my own way.'

Kate was intrigued. 'I can't imagine you being bossed about by anybody,' she confessed.

'You don't know my sister! It's a pity, because now Alex and I dread her visits.'

'You know what we should do, Dad?' said Alex, skipping along beside them.

'What?'

'We should pretend that you've already got a girlfriend, then Aunt Stella wouldn't be able to say anything.'

'I don't think Stella is that easy to fool,' said Finn wryly. 'She'd insist on meeting any girlfriend, and we'd look a bit stupid if we couldn't produce one, wouldn't we?'

'Maybe we could ask Kate to pretend,' suggested Alex.

'Pretend what?'

'Pretend to be your girlfriend.' Alex bounced up and down as she realised the full potential of her idea. 'You could say that you were going to get married. That would shut Aunt Stella up!'

There was an uncomfortable silence. Kate's heart had lurched oddly at Alex's suggestion, but she knew that she had to treat it as a joke, so she forced a laugh to show that she wouldn't even *think* of taking the suggestion seriously.

'I don't think that's a very good idea,' said Finn after a moment.

'Why not? Kate wouldn't mind, would you, Kate?'

Kate made a noncommittal noise, which seemed the only option.

'It would be fun,' Alex went on. 'Imagine Aunt Stella's face when she comes in all ready to bully you into getting married and you told her that you'd found someone without her interfering! I think it would be great.'

'That's enough, Alex,' her father said sharply.

'But why not?' Alex insisted. 'We could have a nice time instead of spending our whole time trying to avoid those women Aunt Stella insists on inviting round.'

'I *said*, that's enough!'

Alex subsided, muttering sullenly, before working off her bad mood by throwing sticks for Derek.

'I'm sorry about that,' said Finn when she had run off. 'She gets a bit carried away.'

'That's all right.' There was another awkward pause. 'Is your sister really that bad?' Kate asked after a moment.

'Worse,' he sighed. 'I know it's just because she worries about Alex, and I know she's right, but she's a very...forceful personality.

'Really?' Kate was unable to resist murmuring. 'Fancy you being related!'

Finn shot her a sharp look but evidently decided to ignore her ironic interruption. 'She and Alex have clashed ever since Alex realised what Stella was trying to do. The thing about Stella is that she hasn't got a lot of tact and she thinks she can bully people into doing what she thinks is the right thing. She's always been the same.'

Kate tried to imagine a female version of Finn, and quailed at the thought. Stella sounded very scary.

'Can't you just tell her that you and Alex are happy with the way things are?'

'Believe me, I've tried,' said Finn. 'The thing is, I owe her a lot. It was Stella who kept things together when Isabel died. I don't know what I'd have done without her. She's a good person to have around in a crisis. She lives in Canada and has her own family, but she came straight over and looked after Alex—and me—until I could cope.

'I've told her that I can see that she's got a point, and I'll think about getting married again, but Stella thinks that unless she nags and bullies and introduces endless divorcees I'll never get round to it. And the truth is that it's hard to face up to trying to meet women when Alex is so against the idea, so in a way she's right. I just wish she wouldn't go on about it so much.'

CHAPTER SIX

'It's hard when people care about you,' said Kate. Her collar was turned up against the wind, and her hands were deep in her pockets to stop them wandering over towards Finn of their own accord.

'When I was going out with Seb, Bella and Phoebe used to go on and on about how bad he was for me. Deep down, I knew they were right, but it didn't make it any easier somehow. I couldn't be cross with them because I knew it was only because they loved me and wanted me to be happy, but sometimes,' she admitted, 'I wished they would just shut up and leave me alone.'

Their pace had slowed without either of them realising it, and now Finn stopped and looked down at Kate, a curious expression in his flinty grey eyes. 'Yes, that's just what I feel about Stella,' he said.

Clouds were scudding across the sky in the wind, and for a moment the sun broke through the greyness like a biblical picture. To Kate it was as if the two of them were standing alone in an intense beam of light that held them motionless, breathless, isolated from everyone else in the park. She was intensely aware of her heart beating, and the blood pulsing through her veins, of the flecking of silvery light in Finn's cool grey eyes and the dark ring around his pupils.

Then the clouds shut out the sun again, like someone switching off a light, and Alex was running back, calling to Derek, and Finn looked away. Kate felt oddly shaken and disorientated. Her heart was beating in her throat and there was a constricted feeling in her chest, so that she had to concentrate to breathe.

Finn cleared his throat and made a big deal of looking at his watch. 'Maybe we should think about going back.'

Kate was very glad of Alex's chatter as they drove back to Tooting. She felt very strange. Her body was thumping and there was a disturbing quiver deep inside her that made her excruciatingly aware of Finn, of his hand shifting gear, of his eyes flicking to the mirror, of the turn of his head.

She really *must* pull herself together! All he had done was meet her eyes for a few seconds, and for all she knew he was thinking about something else entirely. Anyone would think he had pulled her down on the grass and made mad, passionate love the way she was carrying on!

What had made her think of *that*? The image was so clear that Kate caught her breath and she had to stare desperately out of the side window, trying to force the picture of what it might be like if Finn did pull her towards him, did kiss her, did let his hands slide over her body, out of her mind. But it was as if the thought was lodged there now, so real and so vivid that Kate was terrified it was emblazoned across her face.

Finn found a parking space right in front of the house, and switched off the engine. 'Would you like to come in and have some tea?' Kate heard herself asking into the sudden silence. Her voice came out all funny, thin and high, as if she was really nervous or something. 'I've got some scones.'

'Proper tea!' said Alex approvingly. 'Can Derek come?'

'Of course.'

In fact, Derek got an extremely frosty reception from Kate's cat, who had been curled up comfortably on the sofa and was outraged to find himself nudged by a cold, wet nose attached to a tail wagged in tentative greeting. Arching his back, he puffed out his fur and hissed, adding a swipe of his paw to reinforce the message.

'What's his name?' asked Alex as Derek squealed and backed off hastily.

'We just call him Cat,' said Kate. 'He was a stray like Derek, but he was practically wild when I brought him back. He used to bite our ankles and scratch and Phoebe refused to let me give him a name because she said I'd want to keep him then. But I could never find a home for him, so we just got used to calling him Cat.'

'He wouldn't have gone anyway,' said Bella who had been lying in one of the chairs painting her nails when they came in. 'Say what you like about that cat, he's not stupid and he knows he'd never find a sucker like Kate anywhere else!'

She smiled at Finn and Alex. 'If you want to be spoiled to death and never do anything in return, Kate's your gal! I'm sure all the stray animals in London have passed the word around about what a pushover she is, because they're always turning up on the doorstep, holding up a paw and looking needy.'

'Bella, I'm sure they don't want to hear all those stories,' said Kate with a meaningful glare at her friend. Once Bella got started, there was no stopping her.

'Yes we do!' Alex piped up, and Bella grinned.

'Of course they do,' she said with an unrepentant wink at her friend, and proceeded to regale Alex and Finn with her repertoire of stories, each one more exaggerated than the last and all illustrating Kate's ridiculously soft heart and/or capacity to get herself into an unholy muddle.

Bella was outrageous, but knew how to lay on the charm, and she could be very funny. Alex was giggling and even Finn's mouth twitched occasionally.

Mortified, Kate fumbled around making tea and heating up the scones. She could feel Finn's eyes on her every now and then. Probably wondering how such an idiot could ever have been taken on by the temp agency, she thought gloomily.

'I hope you realise she's making most of these stories up,' she said as she carried the tray over to the comfortable chairs where they were sitting.

'I am not!' Bella protested.

'Grossly exaggerating, then. I notice you never tell any stories which show me as intelligent and sophisticated!'

'There aren't any of those, Kate!'

'Very funny,' said Kate mirthlessly, but at least Bella was diverted by the scones.

'I could tell loads of stories about what a good cook you are,' she offered.

'We already know that,' said Finn, glancing at Kate, who immediately started blushing and stammering that she wasn't really, honestly, she just muddled her way through recipes like everyone else...

A story that showed her as sophisticated? Dream on, Kate, she thought, listening to herself with a sinking heart.

Bella looked from Finn to Kate, blue eyes suddenly speculative. Kate could practically see her deciding to unleash the full force of her considerable charm on Finn, and just hoped he was ready for it. Bella on top form was hard to resist, and Kate wondered if Finn guessed quite how thoroughly he was being interrogated. Judging by his responses, which were civil but not exactly revealing, she guessed that he had a good suspicion of it anyway, and she didn't know whether to be glad or sorry that he was apparently impervious to her friend.

'This is a nice kitchen,' Alex said when Finn started to make a move. 'I wish ours was more like this, Dad.'

Kate could see Finn looking around the clutter, the empty bottles waiting to be recycled, the magazines strewn everywhere, Bella's nail polishes, the lingerie drying haphazardly on the airer. He didn't actually wince, but he might as well have done.

'It takes a lot of work to keep a room as messy as this,' she told Alex solemnly. 'I'm not sure your father's up to it.'

She felt quite giddy when Finn laughed. He actually laughed at something she'd said! 'You've obviously had years of experience,' he said, oblivious to the way her heart was somersaulting around her chest at the whiteness of his teeth and the deep crease in his cheeks and the humour crinkling the edges of his eyes.

'I like to practise at the office, too,' she said a little breathlessly, and then he smiled again.

'I can tell,' he said.

Bella was finishing off the last scone when Kate came back from seeing them all to the car, her elation evaporated by the mundane nature of Finn's farewell. She had hugged Alex and patted Derek, but Finn made sure that things were firmly back on a neutral footing.

'See you tomorrow,' was all he had said.

Well, what had she expected? That he would be flinging his arms round her or drawing her close for a passionate kiss? It would take more than a laugh for Finn to forget that they had to go back to work.

Back to reality.

'Yes, see you tomorrow,' Kate echoed flatly.

'Not very forthcoming, is he?' mumbled Bella through a mouthful of scone.

Kate didn't pretend not to know who she meant. Drearily, she began gathering up the tea things. 'He's... private,' she said.

'He's that all right. I've never met anyone that hard to read.'

Kate was conscious of a twist of disappointment. More

than a twist, if she was honest. A pang would describe it better. Or a knife turning in her gut.

She didn't want Bella to find Finn unreadable. Her friend was so much more perceptive than she was. She wanted her to confide that she had seen Finn watching Kate, perhaps, or that having talked to him it was obvious that he was in love with her. If there had been the slightest hint of anything like that, Bella would have spotted it.

But there hadn't been.

'It doesn't bother me,' she said, even managing a creditable shrug. 'As far as I'm concerned, he's just my boss, and only temporarily at that. I don't particularly want to know every last detail about his private life.'

The trouble was that Bella was just as perceptive about her as she was about everybody else. 'Sure,' she said, then she got up and put an arm round Kate's shoulders. 'Never mind,' she consoled her. 'There's always chocolate!'

'Finn McBride's office,' Kate answered the phone the following Tuesday.

'This is Alison, Finn's PA,' a cool voice told her.

'Oh...hello. How's your leg?'

'Much better, thank you. How have you been getting on?' There was a slight but distinct note of condescension in Alison's voice that made Kate bristle.

'Fine, I think,' she said, striving for equal coolness. 'Would you like to speak to Finn?'

'Please.' Alison sounded as if she disapproved of Kate calling him Finn instead of Mr McBride. Perhaps you were supposed to be his PA for five years before you were allowed to use his Christian name.

'I'll put you through,' said Kate evenly.

Finn came out of his office a few minutes later. 'That was Alison,' he said unnecessarily.

'Oh,' said Kate, convinced that Alison's call would have

reminded him of how efficient and reliable she was. Unlike her temporary replacement.

'The doctor has said that she can come back to work next Monday.'

'Next Monday?' Kate was unable to keep the dismay from her voice. She had been expecting to stay at least another couple of weeks. Monday's too soon, she wanted to shout.

Finn cleared his throat. 'I told her there was no need to come back before she was ready, but she says she's keen to get back to things.'

'I see.' What else could she say?

'I thought...you might be staying a bit longer,' he said.

There was an awkward pause, as if neither of them knew what to say next.

'Well,' said Kate eventually with an attempt at heartiness, 'that's good news.'

'Yes,' said Finn, not sounding entirely convinced.

'You'll have a bit more organisation in the office again.' She glanced at Derek who had trotted in beside Finn and now flung himself panting at her feet. 'No stray dogs, anyway.'

'No.'

'I'd better tidy my desk,' said Kate after another agonising pause. She looked at the piles of papers and files without enthusiasm. Three days wasn't long to sort some order out of the chaos.

She forced a bright smile. 'Shall I get Personnel to ring the agency and let them know?'

'What agency?' asked Finn, who was standing by the window with his hands in his pockets, staring down at the street.

'The temp agency. They might be able to find me another job for Monday.'

'Oh.' He turned. 'Right. Yes.' He looked at Kate, and

then away, as if he wanted to say something but had thought better of it. 'Yes, you'd better do that.'

So that was it then. Just as well she hadn't got involved, thought Kate as she sat miserably on the bus that night. And she *wasn't* involved, whatever Bella might say. She had always known that there was no point in falling for Finn. She didn't want to spend her entire life being second-best to the beautiful, perfect, irreplaceable Isabel. That had been decided after intensive chocolate therapy on Sunday evening.

She wanted fun, fun, fun instead.

Somehow that had been easier to believe after the stiff vodka and tonic prescribed by Bella than it did now when she had to face up to the fact that after Friday she would never see Finn again.

The last three days were agony. Finn was taciturn and any conversation they did have was stilted in the extreme. By the time Friday came round, Kate almost began to be glad that she was leaving. At least she wouldn't have to endure this awful, constrained atmosphere any longer.

When Finn called her into his room, she braced herself for him to say something about her leaving. She had already decided how she was going to be: friendly but professional. He had to say something, surely, if only to sort out what to do about Derek, who had now become a familiar part of the office routine. Kate tripped over him at least six times a day.

She could hardly believe it when Finn merely asked her to tidy up a few matters before Alison came back. 'We want to try and leave things as clear for her as possible,' he said.

Right, they didn't want his precious Alison to have to do too much when she came back, did they? Kate was furious. OK, she might not be Alison, but she had been here six weeks, and she had worked really hard, not to mention walking his dog for him every lunchtime. It wouldn't kill him to say thank you.

'Is that it?' she asked him coldly as she got to her feet.

'There is just one thing,' said Finn almost reluctantly. His eyes rested on Kate, who was clutching her notebook to her chest and looking cross and ruffled. 'Sit down,' he added.

Kate sank resentfully back onto the edge of her chair and opened her notebook once more with martyred sigh. Pen poised, she looked at him. 'Yes?' she prompted him.

'You don't need to take notes,' he said with an edge of his old irritation. 'I was only going to ask if you'd got a job lined up for Monday.'

'Oh.' Kate lowered her pen. She had been trying not to think about Monday. 'No, not yet.'

'How would you feel about a change of career?' asked Finn carefully.

She stared at him. 'What?'

'You mentioned when we were at dinner with Gib and Phoebe that you were thinking about changing career. I wondered if you were serious or not.'

'I suppose that rather depends on what I'd be changing *to*,' said Kate. 'Did you have something in mind?'

'Housekeeper,' he said.

Kate laughed. 'You're not serious!'

'Why wouldn't I be?'

'You know how messy I am,' she said, still smiling. 'And you saw the state of our kitchen on Sunday. I'd have thought I'd be the last person you'd want as a housekeeper!'

'Tidiness isn't important. The fact that Alex likes you is.' Finn got up abruptly and began pacing around the office. 'She doesn't like many people. What I really need is someone who can meet her from school and keep an eye on her until I get home. You can cook, too, which is a bonus.'

Narrowly avoiding stepping on Derek who was stretched out in the middle of the floor, Finn muttered something under his breath and turned back to Kate. 'You could also look after that dog,' he pointed out crossly. 'I think we might as well forget the fiction that Alex is ever going to let you take him to your parents, so it looks as if I'm stuck with him, and I don't think Alison is going to be that keen on a dog in the office.'

'What about Rosa?' Kate asked. 'Isn't she coming back?'

'She rang last night. Her mother is going to need her full time for the foreseeable future. I told her I would make temporary arrangements, so that if she was in a position to come back in a couple of months, she could if she wanted to, but I don't think she will.'

'So you're not thinking about a permanent post?'

Finn shook his head. 'No. Alex isn't keen on anyone else living with us, so I might see if we can manage without a housekeeper—although it's going to be a lot more difficult now there's a dog to consider,' he added.

'Then why are you asking me?' Kate asked, ignoring that little sideswipe.

He stopped pacing and shoved his hands in his pockets. 'Because my sister's coming in a couple of weeks.'

Ah, yes, the scary Stella, Kate remembered.

'She'll just make a fuss if we haven't got anyone to help,' Finn went on, unaware of her mental interruption. 'It would just be for while she's here, so we're not talking about you staying for ever. That's why I thought if you didn't have anything else organised you might consider it. I'd pay you, of course,' he added. 'It would be more than you would make temping like this.'

Kate scribbled mindlessly on her notebook as she thought about Finn's offer. She had never been a big career girl, and had fallen into secretarial work simply because she couldn't think of anything else to do.

Phoebe and Bella were much more serious about their work, but deep down Kate was still nursing the childhood fantasy of living in a cottage in the country with a kitchen where she could make jam and bottle things, roses round the door and a big garden with room for lots of animals and children. Being a housekeeper might not be quite what she'd had in mind, but she was sure she'd be happy pottering around a house all day.

The more she thought about it, the more appealing the idea became. The money would be useful for a start, and a guaranteed job was better than hanging around waiting for the agency to get back to her.

Besides, she liked Alex and she liked Derek. The fact that she would be spending more time with Finn himself was just incidental, and had absolutely nothing to do with the flutter of anticipation that was stirring deep inside her.

She moistened her lips, striving to sound businesslike. 'Would it be a live-in post?'

'Preferably,' said Finn.

'I'd have to check with Bella,' said Kate, looking doubtful. 'It would mean she would be the only one in the house.'

'I'd cover the cost of your rent if you wanted to be sure of keeping your room,' he said unexpectedly, and she glanced at him in surprise.

'The rent's not such a problem since Phoebe married Gib,' she said frankly. 'There's nothing like a lovely, rich husband to stop you worrying about mortgages! Bella and I just pay a token rent now and look after the house for her. No, I was thinking about the cat.'

'The cat?' repeated Finn as if he didn't want to believe what he was hearing.

'I'd have to ask Bella to look after him, and he's bitten

her ankles so many times she might not be that keen! Unless I could bring him with me?' Kate looked at Finn hopefully but he wasn't having any of it.

'No,' he said firmly. 'The dog is enough trouble. I'm sure Bella would feed the cat for you. It's not as if it would be for ever. Stella usually spends a couple of weeks with us, then travels around the country visiting her old friends for ten days or so, before coming back for the last few days before she flies back to Canada, so I don't anticipate needing you for longer than a month or so.'

Well, that told her. Lucky she hadn't done anything silly like falling in love with him, wasn't it?

Kate chewed the end of her pen. There was no point in feeling hurt that Finn wanted a definite time limit to the time she would be spending with him. He was just being practical, and she should be the same.

Did she really want to be a housekeeper?

If nothing else, it would be a change, she told herself. It might be fun. It would be money. It wasn't for ever, as Finn had been so keen to point out.

It would mean that she didn't have to say goodbye to him at the end of today.

'All right,' she said, suddenly making up her mind.

'You'll do it?' Finn sounded almost as surprised as she felt.

'Yes.' She would have to clear the cat feeding with Bella, who would grumble like mad, but she would agree in the end. In the meantime, it was up to Kate to make it very clear that she was going to be as businesslike as Finn.

'When do you want me?' she asked briskly, only to hear the double meaning in her words too late. 'To start,' she added, colour creeping into her cheeks.

So much for sounding businesslike.

Fortunately, Finn didn't appear to have noticed. 'Perhaps

we can discuss the details over dinner?' he said stiltedly. 'Are you free tonight?'

'Yes,' said Kate, ruthlessly sacrificing the opportunity to meet lots of Will's single friends at a party. She would ring Bella and explain that she couldn't make it. Making chit-chat with a lot of corporate types at a noisy party couldn't compare to dinner with Finn, even if it was only to talk about her duties as housekeeper.

'Good.' Finn seemed rather at a loss. 'Could you book a restaurant?'

'Did you have somewhere in mind?' she asked, trying not to sound put out. It wasn't exactly a romantic date if you had to book your own restaurant, was it? Perhaps she should just order a pizza to be delivered and be done with it.

'You choose,' said Finn indifferently, turning away to the window.

Serve him right if she booked a table at the Dorchester, thought Kate, getting to her feet once more. Finn was still staring abstractedly at the rain, so it looked as if her interview was over.

'Book somewhere nice,' he said as she reached the door. 'There's something I want to ask you.'

'Something he wants to ask you?' Bella repeated when Kate recounted the conversation that evening. 'He didn't say what?'

'It'll be something to do with being housekeeper, I suppose.'

'Come on, Kate!' Bella rolled her eyes dismissively. 'You don't invite a girl like you out to dinner to talk about how many hours you're going to spend vacuuming!' She paused. 'Maybe he's going to make a pass?'

'I don't think that's very likely,' said Kate, unwilling to admit to Bella that she had already wondered about this possibility and been unable to imagine Finn doing anything of the kind. 'He's had plenty of opportunity to do that without wasting money on a meal.'

'Ah, but you've been working for him up to now,' Bella pointed out. 'He sounds the sort of strait-laced type who doesn't approve of office affairs, but he might have been nurturing a secret passion for you for weeks, and now that he's got a window of opportunity this weekend when you're technically unemployed he's decided to go for it!'

Kate pooh-poohed the idea, of course, but it didn't stop her stomach churning with nerves as she got ready that evening. She had booked the Italian restaurant round the corner, not that she thought that she would be able to eat anything. Bella told her she should have gone for somewhere more expensive, but Kate didn't want Finn to think that she was expecting anything special. Best just to treat it as a business meeting, she had decided.

Which made it difficult to decide what to wear. He had seen all her work clothes and, even though it clearly wasn't a proper date, Kate couldn't help wanting him to see that she could look nice when she tried. At length she settled on a short, flirty little dress with a beaded cardigan and her favourite shoes. They weren't very suitable for walking through a dank March night, but she didn't have anything else that would go.

'You look great,' said Bella when Kate went downstairs. 'Not at all like a housekeeper.'

Kate immediately lost her nerve. Perhaps it *was* a bit inappropriate. 'Do you think I should change?'

'Into what?' Bella was appalled at the very idea. 'A demure grey dress with a white collar and a load of keys hanging from your waist? Of course don't change! You look fabulous as you are. Finn won't be able to keep his hands off you!'

For once Bella was quite wrong. Finn didn't seem to be having any trouble at all keeping his hands to himself, Kate reflected dismally as they struggled to make stilted conversation on the way to the restaurant. He had certainly noted her change of image, and he had looked a bit taken aback, but all he had said was that she looked 'different'. As compliments went, it was hardly overwhelming.

Finn obviously wasn't over-impressed by the restaurant either. Tough, thought Kate. He should have organised somewhere himself. He ought to count himself lucky that she hadn't taken up Bella's suggestion of booking a table at Claridge's.

'Is this it?' he said, looking around him at the red and white checked tablecloths, the faded posters on the wall and the candles stuck into Chianti bottles. The last word in style in the Sixties.

'I'm a cheap date,' said Kate defiantly, and then, when he lifted an eyebrow, lost her nerve. 'Not that this is a date, of course,' she added hastily.

Unfortunately the waiters hadn't got that particular message and kept fussing around them, promising them a secluded table and showering Kate with embarrassing compliments while a muscle in Finn's gritted jaw began to twitch. She wished they would all shut up. Any minute now a posse of violinists would pop up to serenade them, and there would be some pseudo-gipsy insisting that Finn bought her a rose at an exorbitant price.

'She is very beautiful, no?' The head waiter demanded, determined to foster what he thought was a budding romance.

Finn looked across at Kate, who was cringing, sinking further and further down into her seat. She looked so uncomfortable that his own rigid expression relaxed into something that was almost, but not quite, a smile.

'Yes,' he said. 'Very. Now, could we have a menu, please?'

Kate's cheeks burned. 'I'm sorry,' she said when the

waiter had departed, still wreathed in smiles. 'They're not usually like this here.'

'Perhaps you don't usually look as beautiful as you do tonight,' said Finn, picking up the wine list.

Kate opened her mouth and closed it again, but before she could think of anything to say two waiters descended on them again and they were caught up in the kerfuffle of being offered menus and bread and having water poured, while her pulse boomed in her ears and her heart lurched around her chest.

Finn had said she was beautiful.

She risked a glance across at him. His head was bent over the wine list, and his expression was hard to read. From where she sat, he looked as if he was absorbed in the relative merits of Valpolicella and Lambrusco. The fierce, dark brows were drawn slightly together, and his eyes were shielded, so that all Kate could see was the strong nose and the line of his mouth.

Her entrails twisted at the sight, and she looked quickly away. She must have misheard. Nobody, not even Finn, could say something like that and then calmly turn his attention to what they were going to drink. He couldn't tell her that she was beautiful and then carry on as if nothing had happened, could he?

Could he?

Maybe he hadn't meant it. Maybe he had just said it to shut the waiter up. Kate's hands shook as she pretended to study her own menu, but the words danced in front of her eyes and she couldn't concentrate. *Did* he think that she was beautiful? Was Bella right after all?

At last they had ordered, the wine had been tasted and poured, and the last hovering waiter had backed off to leave them alone. Having longed for them to go away, Kate now wished they would come back. They might be annoying but at least they would break the uncomfortable silence that had fallen.

She fiddled with her fork. Finn seemed to have forgotten that he wanted to say something to her. Why had he bothered to ask her out if he didn't want to talk to her? 'When would you like me to start as housekeeper?' she asked eventually, unable to bear it any longer.

Finn had been tearing a piece of bread apart, but he looked up at that, as if relieved that she had started the conversational ball rolling. 'Whenever you can manage it,' he said. 'As soon as possible as far as Alex and I are concerned. It would give you a chance to get settled in before Stella arrives.'

'I could move this weekend if you wanted,' Kate offered.

'Good. In that case, we'll come and pick you up on Sunday,' said Finn, but he seemed abstracted, as if there was something else on his mind.

'When is your sister arriving?'

'Two weeks on Tuesday. We'll need to make a bit of a fuss of her when she arrives,' he added.

'That's all right, I'm good at fuss,' said Kate, feeling a bit more cheerful. 'I'll make everything special for her. Flowers in her room, fresh towels, luxury soap, a nice welcoming meal...we'll lay on the works for her!'

Finn raised his brows slightly. 'You sound like you've done this kind of thing before?'

'We always had lots of guests at home when I was growing up,' she told him. 'I love having people to stay too.'

'I'm afraid I'm a bit out of the way of it,' said Finn, turning his fork absently between his fingers. 'I haven't done any proper entertaining since Isabel died. Stella's the only person we've had to stay for any length of time.'

Their starters arrived just then. Kate waited until the plates had been deposited with a flourish in front of them.

'Is that what you wanted to talk to me about?'

Finn had picked up his knife and fork, but at that he laid them down again. 'Partly,' he said. 'At least...well, no, not really,' he finished abruptly.

'What is it?' asked Kate, puzzled.

'I don't quite know how you're going to take this...' Finn trailed off and she looked at him curiously. She had never seen him this nervous before.

'I won't know until you tell me,' she pointed out.

'No.' Finn drank some wine and set his glass down carefully. 'It's just that Stella rang the other day. You remember I told you that she was very keen to introduce me to women she thinks would make suitable stepmothers for Alex?'

'Yes,' Kate encouraged him when he seemed likely to stop again.

'Alex spoke to her first. Stella was telling her all about some friend of a friend of hers who she thought it would be nice for me to meet and why didn't she invite her to dinner one night, and I gather Alex didn't like the sound of her at all. So she told Stella that she didn't need to bother finding a stepmother for her any more because I'd met someone and was going to get married.'

'Oh, dear...'

'Exactly.' A mirthless smile twisted Finn's mouth. 'Of course, Stella then insisted on talking to me. I could have told her that Alex was joking, but they have quite an uneasy relationship as it is, and I didn't want Stella coming over and going on about how spoilt and difficult she was, which would just make Alex defensive. It was bad enough last time.'

Finn sighed. 'Anyway, the upshot was that I played along. I remembered what Alex had suggested that day we all went to Richmond Park, and I suppose I thought—well, why not? It would shut Stella up at least, although not initially. She demanded details of course, wanted to know the name of my fiancée, how we had met and so on.

There was an odd feeling in the pit of Kate's stomach. 'What did you tell her?'

Finn looked her straight in the eye. 'I told her it was you,' he said.

CHAPTER SEVEN

SHE should have been expecting it, but somehow she wasn't. Kate wrenched her eyes away from Finn's and looked down at her plate, appalled at the sudden realisation of how much she wished that he had meant what he said to his sister, that he loved her and wanted to marry her.

She felt very strange. It was as if all the oxygen had been sucked out of the air, leaving her light-headed and faintly dizzy, so that it took her a little while to realise what Finn was saying.

'I wanted to ask you if you would pretend that it was true.'

Pretend. Kate made herself focus on the one word that made all the difference. This wasn't her wishes coming miraculously true at all, it was Finn making it clear that he wasn't talking about anything real.

'I know it's not fair on you, and that it's a lot to ask, but it would mean a lot to Alex. And to me,' he added after a moment. 'Of course, it would just be a pretence,' he hastened to explain when Kate said nothing but just sat staring dumbly at him. 'I wouldn't expect you to...to think of it as anything other than a job.'

'A job?' Kate latched onto the word as if it was the only one she had understood. Her heart was thudding so loudly that it was hard to hear, and she was afraid she might miss something important.

'I wouldn't ask you to do something like that for free,' said Finn. 'I'd make it worth your while financially. We could agree your salary as housekeeper with a bonus on top of that at the end for...everything else.'

He spoke very formally, making it clear that as far as he was concerned it would be a purely business transaction, and somehow Kate managed to pull herself together.

'What exactly would you want me to do?' she asked, amazed at the calmness of her voice.

'To be around when Stella is with us. To make her believe that you and I...'

'Are in love?' Kate finished for him bravely when he hesitated.

Finn let out a breath. 'Yes.'

'I used to be good at drama,' she said after a moment. 'I always wanted a starring role but only ever got bit parts, so perhaps I could look on this as my chance to get back into acting.'

'You mean you will consider it?' he said as if he could hardly believe that she was serious.

'Why not?' Kate had herself under control now.

The one thing she mustn't do was let Finn guess that she had fallen in love with him. He would be appalled if he knew, and he certainly wouldn't ask her to pretend to be his fiancée. Convincing him that she was treating the whole thing lightly would at least let her be near him, Kate told herself. It might not be for long, but it could be her only chance.

'It will be much more fun than temping, anyway,' she told him brightly. 'It sounds like easy money to me!'

'You might not think so when you meet my sister,' said Finn with a wry look. 'She has very sharp eyes and she isn't a fool. She'll be watching us very carefully.' He paused delicately. 'If we're going to convince her that we really are engaged, we might have to give the impression that we're more intimate than we really are.'

Treat it lightly, Kate reminded herself. 'You mean we might have to kiss occasionally?'

'That kind of thing, yes.' Finn seemed a little nonplussed by her casual attitude. 'How would you feel about that?'

How would she feel? Kate let herself imagine being able to reach across the table and take his hand. She imagined putting her arms around him and leaning into his solidity, daring to touch her lips to his throat. She thought about being held by him and how that stern mouth would feel against hers, and desire knotted sharply inside her, driving the breath from her lungs.

'I think I could manage.' She meant to say it casually, but her voice came out treacherously husky and she had to clear her throat and start again. 'It would just be part of the job. It wouldn't mean anything.'

'Right,' said Finn, sounding oddly wary, and Kate was suddenly terrified in case he had glimpsed how badly she wanted him.

'I'll close my eyes and think of the bonus,' she tried to joke.

'Yes, I think I've got the point that you won't be taking it seriously.' There was a distinct edge to Finn's voice now, and Kate eyed him uncertainly.

What had she said? She'd have thought he would have been glad that she wasn't going to go all soppy on him! Kate sighed inwardly, torn between exasperation at the withdrawn look on his face and the longing to reach for him and tell him that all she wanted was to hold him and kiss him and be with him for ever, and you couldn't get more serious than that.

'How does Alex feel about all of this?' she asked instead.

Finn's rigid expression relaxed slightly. 'She's very pleased with herself, taking credit for the whole idea. I told her I was going to ask you if you'd play along tonight, so she'll be cock-a-hoop when she hears that you've agreed.' He glanced across the table at Kate. 'Alex doesn't take to many people, but she likes you.'

'I like her too.'

There was a pause while the obvious question—And what about you? Do *you* like me?—seemed to shimmer in the air between them.

Kate swallowed the words. She wasn't going to ask Finn that. Her eyes fell on her starter, forgotten and growing cold in front of her. She wasn't hungry—love seemed to have destroyed her appetite—but she picked up her fork and began to eat while the silence stretched uncomfortably.

'What have you told Stella about me?' she asked with a kind of desperation at last.

'Just your name and that we met when you came to work with me.' Finn didn't seem to be enjoying his meal any more than she was. 'I thought it would be easiest if I stuck to the truth as far as possible.'

'I bet she wanted to know more than that,' said Kate. 'If my brother told me that he was getting married, I would demand to know every last detail!'

A faint smile of acknowledgment lifted the corners of his mouth. 'She did ask what you were like,' he admitted.

'What did you tell her?'

Finn looked at Kate with an unreadable expression. 'That you were warm and funny and kind, and that Alex liked you. Which is true.'

What was true? That Alex liked her, or that he thought that she was warm and funny?

Kind. Warm. There was nothing wrong with being either, but it was hardly sweep-you-off-your-feet stuff, was it? Kate pushed her mushrooms glumly around her plate. She wanted him to have described her to Stella in rather more lover-like terms. Beautiful. Desirable. Irresistible. How come none of those words had popped into his head when he thought about her?

She knew why.

Because Finn didn't think she was beautiful or desirable, and he could resist her quite easily.

Because he didn't love her.

She was just going to have to live with that.

Kate laid down her fork, unable to face any more. 'Didn't Stella want to know what had made you change your mind about getting married?'

'I said that she would understand when she met you,' said Finn.

Their eyes met across the candle in the middle of the table, and something leapt in the air between them, something that jarred Kate's heart and was gone before she could tell what it was.

She moistened her lips. 'What would you have done if I'd said no?'

'I'm not sure,' he admitted. 'I was relying on your kindness. I suppose I could always have pretended that you'd left me for someone else just before she arrived.'

'I wouldn't do anything like that!' Kate protested involuntarily, and that keen grey glance flickered to her face and then away before she could read his expression again.

'No, maybe you wouldn't,' he agreed.

'You could always have invented some family crisis,' she offered helpfully.

'It would take more than a family crisis to stop Stella,' said Finn. 'She'd track you down somehow!'

'Anyway, I didn't say no,' Kate pointed out.

'No.' Finn abandoned his own plate. 'We'll have to think of some reason to end our supposed engagement after Stella leaves though, or she'll be booking her ticket back to the wedding. As it is, we'll be lucky if we get away with not getting married while she's here! Oh, don't worry,' he added, misinterpreting Kate's flinch. 'It won't go that far!'

'Good.' Kate managed a weak smile. 'We don't want that, do we?'

'No,' Finn agreed, his voice empty of expression. 'We don't want that.'

'Are you sure this is a good idea, Kate?' Bella and Phoebe, sitting across the table from her like an interviewing panel, looked at her in concern.

'Earning money is always a good idea, isn't it?' said Kate defiantly.

'There are easier ways to earn it than pretending to be in love with your boss!'

'Oh, I don't know...'

Kate didn't want to tell them that the problem was going to be a whole lot more complicated than that. She was going to have to pretend to be in love with Finn while pretending not to be. No point in explaining that to them, though. Bella would only say 'I told you so.'

'It'll be better than temping in some dreary office,' she told them instead, 'and Finn's going to give me a huge bonus for the engagement thing which will mean I can clear my credit card bill. I might even have some left to save up for a holiday. Besides, I like Alex and it solves the problem of what to do about Derek during the day.'

'Oh, well, that's all right then!' said Bella sarcastically. 'As long as the *dog* is sorted out...!'

'Look, it will be fine! I don't know why you're both making such a fuss. It's just a job.'

'Just a job where you have to sleep with your boss!'

'I'll have my own room.'

Phoebe looked dubious. 'His sister's not going to believe you're going to get married if you're not even sleeping together.'

'Well...we can say it doesn't seem appropriate with Alex in the house,' said Kate a little defensively.

Bella pretended to shake her head and look disorientated.

'Sorry, I seem to have stepped into a time warp! What year are we living in?'

Kate ignored her. 'OK, so we'll share a room when his sister is there. It's not a big deal.'

'We just don't want you to get hurt,' Phoebe tried to placate her, hearing the edge in Kate's voice.

'I'm not going to do anything silly,' said Kate grittily. It was too late now, anyway, although she had no intention of confessing *that*!

'Finn's still in love with Isabel, I know that. Even if he wasn't still obsessed by her, he's completely different from me. He's much older, his experience is different, his life is different.'

All true, and it didn't make the slightest difference to loving him.

Kate faced her friends squarely, marvelling that they couldn't see how different *she* felt now. Couldn't they tell that falling in love with Finn had turned her life upside down, consuming her to the point where she was prepared to risk the certainty of being hurt just to be with him?

'There's no point in me getting involved with him or his daughter or his dog,' she told them, knowing that was true too but unable to do anything about it. 'But it's not like I've got anything else lined up that I can do instead,' she pointed out. 'It's that or hang around waiting for the agency to get in touch. Frankly, I'd rather be paid generously for living in a comfortable house for a few weeks!'

Phoebe was unconvinced. 'It's very easy to get carried away in situations like that,' she said. 'And I should know!'

'Yes, you're the last person who should be advising Kate against a mock engagement,' said Bella with a grin. 'Look where it got you and Gib!'

Phoebe smiled, but her eyes were serious as she glanced across at Kate. 'Finn's not like Gib,' she said. 'I just think you should be careful, that's all.'

Too late, thought Kate. All she could do now was make the best of the time she had.

'This is your room.' Alex opened the door and showed Kate inside proudly. 'I made it look nice for you.'

Kate looked around her, touched. 'It all looks lovely,' she said. There was even a little vase of flowers on the chest of drawers. 'Did you do it all yourself?'

'Dad made your bed,' Alex admitted, 'but I did everything else.'

Kate looked at the bed and imagined Finn making it, smoothing his hand over the sheet where she would lie. Shaken by a gust of longing, she cleared her throat. 'That was nice of him, but I could have made it myself.'

'I don't think he minded,' said Alex casually. 'Do you want to see my room?'

Maybe that would be safer.

Kate admired Alex's room and was suitably appreciative of the fact that it had been specially tidied for the occasion. A pinboard by her bed was covered in photographs, of Alex and her mother and of Finn. Most of them showed him with Isabel, smiling and relaxed with the sun in his eyes, and Kate felt hollow inside to realise that she had never seen him look happy like that.

Might never see him looking happy.

'That's my mum,' said Alex, following Kate's gaze. 'She was beautiful, wasn't she?'

'Yes,' said Kate. 'She was. Do you remember her at all?'

'Not really, but Dad tells me about her and he kept some of her things for me. Look.' Alex dived under her bed for a box which she pulled out and opened reverently.

Kate sat on the bed and took the things Alex handed her. A lipstick, used. A bottle of perfume, half full. A soft silk scarf. A book of medieval poetry. A diary full of scribbled notes. A pair of earrings. A baby's footprint.

'That was mine,' said Alex.

There was a hard lump in Kate's throat as she thought about Finn carefully choosing the things that would give her the sense of what her mother had been like long after she had gone. It must have broken his heart all over again.

'This was her engagement ring,' Alex said, opening a little jewellery box and pointing at one of the rings. 'Dad says she left it to me, so I can wear it later if I want to. Those blue stones are called sapphires. Dad bought that ring because they reminded him of Mum's eyes.'

'It's a lovely ring,' said Kate, perilously close to tears. Her heart ached for Finn, but she didn't want to break down and weep in front of Alex.

She looked up from the box instead only to find Finn watching her gravely from the doorway. For a long, long moment, they looked at each other, Kate's brown eyes, shimmering with tears, before Alex noticed her father and jumped up.

'I'm showing Kate Mum's box,' she said.

'So I see.' Finn's smile looked strained, but all he said was that he had made some tea if they wanted to come downstairs.

Kate felt awful, as if she had been caught nosing around in his private memories but when she tried to apologise while Alex was carefully putting the box back under her bed, he brushed it aside.

'I'm glad she wanted to talk about Isabel,' he said, handing Kate a mug of tea. 'I don't think she's ever shown anyone that box before. She's always kept her feelings to herself, and it's difficult to get her to talk about what's worrying her sometimes. If you can get her to talk to you, I'd be very grateful. She's already much chattier than she used to be.'

As if to prove his point, Alex came clattering down the stairs with Derek and burst into the kitchen. 'Dad, I've just thought of something when I was putting Mum's ring away. Kate should have a ring too if she's going to be your fiancée, shouldn't she?'

'Oh, no...no, there's no need for that,' said Kate hastily. She held up her hand to show the rings she was wearing. 'I could use one of these.'

Finn took her hand as if it were a parcel, and he and Alex inspected her meagre display of rings. Neither of them was impressed.

'I don't think any of them are likely to convince Stella,' said Finn, looking down his nose. 'Let me have that one,' he said, pointing to the one on her third finger.

Kate's hand was burning where he had touched her as she tugged off the ring. 'What for?' she asked.

'It'll give me your size. I'll get you a proper ring.'

'Really, I don't think it's necessary—' she began, but he interrupted her.

'You don't know my sister. She'd smell a rat if you were wearing a cheap little ring like that. Why are you looking like that?' he demanded, his voice sharpening at the involuntary change in Kate's expression.

'Seb gave me that ring.' The fact that Finn had instantly recognised it as cheap made Kate realise at last just how little Seb had valued her. She had treasured the ring, so certain that the fact that he had given her one at all meant that he cared, but all along it had been worthless, just like Seb.

Finn frowned. 'I won't lose it.'

'It doesn't matter. I don't think I want to wear it again.' Kate summoned a bright smile and got to her feet. 'I'd better start thinking about supper.'

Finn was all for getting a take-away, but Kate was determined to show him that she hadn't forgotten why she was there. 'I may as well start earning my salary,' she said.

There wasn't a lot in the fridge, but she found enough

to make a sauce for some pasta. It seemed very ordinary fare to her but Finn and Alex carried on as if she had produced something worthy of a Michelin star.

'I think you've been having too many take-aways,' said Kate. 'That's all going to change!'

By half past eight, Alex was wilting. 'Time for bed, young lady,' said Finn. 'You've got school tomorrow.'

Ensuring that she had cleaned her teeth, kissing her goodnight and dealing firmly with her last-ditch attempts to delay the moment of lights out took some time, and then there was the washing up and tidying to do, but after that Finn and Kate had no excuse not to realise that they were alone with the dog.

By tacit agreement, they stayed in the bright, safe light of the kitchen rather than retreat to the comfort and intimate shadows of the sitting room. Kate sat on the other side of the kitchen table from Finn, where there was no danger of brushing against him by mistake.

Now all she had to do was chat brightly to break the yawning silence, but she couldn't think of a single thing to say. All she could think about was Finn sitting on the other side of the table, about his mouth and his hands and how nice it would be to be able to get up and go round to sit on his lap, to put her arms around his neck and kiss the tiredness from his face.

In the end it was Finn who spoke first. 'I hope you're all right with this,' he said, lifting his eyes to fix Kate with that disturbingly acute grey gaze. 'I mean...with the situation.'

'Of course,' said Kate brightly, as if she hadn't given the fact that they were alone together with only the dog as chaperon a moment's thought.

Finn looked around the kitchen as if trying to see it through her eyes. 'A job like this isn't much fun for a girl like you.'

'That rather depends on what kind of girl you think I am,' she said.

He considered the matter seriously. 'I suppose I think of you as someone who likes to have a good time,' he said eventually. 'You seem to have lots of friends, and you're always out. I can't help feeling that you might find it a bit dull stuck in the house all day.'

'It'll be a lot more fun that being stuck in an office,' said Kate. 'I've always liked pottering around the house. I'm not the tidiest person in the world—as you know!' she added seeing the sardonic lift of Finn's brows. 'But I love cooking and sewing and gardening and if I've got a dog to walk and Alex to chat to when she gets home from school...well, I think I'm going to have a lovely time. In fact, I don't know why I didn't think about being a housekeeper before,' she finished.

'You know, you're not a bad PA when you concentrate,' said Finn carefully. 'I'm sure you could have a more interesting career than housekeeping if you applied yourself.'

Kate turned her glass between her fingers on the table. 'I don't really want to,' she said frankly. 'The trouble is that I haven't got any ambition.'

'What, none?'

'Only for very ordinary things,' she said. 'It seems a bit shameful to admit it, but all I've ever really wanted was to find someone special. To have children and a house I could make a home. That's not asking too much, is it?'

Finn's expression was unreadable. 'No.'

'Phoebe and Bella think it would be boring, but I'd be so happy keeping chickens and making jam and helping out at the school fête.' Kate sighed a little. 'That's partly why I was so broken up about Seb. I'd made myself believe that he was the one, and that I could have that dream with him.

'I was stupid, of course,' she went on, keeping her eyes

on her glass, not looking at Finn. 'Seb wouldn't be seen dead at a school fête and he doesn't care where his eggs come from. It made it worse when I had to accept that. It's like giving up on a dream of what my life might be like as well as giving up on him.'

'Dreams are hard things to let go of,' said Finn quietly.

Kate knew he was thinking of his dead wife, and her throat tightened. 'Is that what you had with Isabel? The dream?'

He lifted his shoulders slightly. 'It feels like a dream now,' he told her. 'I'm sure it can't have been that perfect and that we must have argued sometimes, but I don't remember that. I just remember how special it was to be with her.'

'You're lucky to have had that.' Kate stopped, hearing her words too late. 'I'm sorry,' she said. 'That was tactless of me. You probably don't feel very lucky.'

'I know what you mean,' said Finn with a faint smile. 'And in a lot of ways I was lucky. A lot of people never find what Isabel and I had. Sometimes I can't believe I found love like that once, and the statistics are against me finding it a second time. It's just not going to happen.'

His mouth twisted. 'That's when I miss Isabel most,' he told Kate. 'When I remember how completely happy I was with her and know that I'm never going to have that again.'

That night Kate lay in bed and stared up at the dark ceiling, thinking about the expression in Finn's eyes. It was terrible to feel envious of someone who was dead, but she couldn't stop thinking about Isabel and how much Finn had loved her.

'It's not going to happen a second time,' he had said, and she would have to accept that, too. It was no use dreaming that she might become his second chance at happiness. The statistics were against it, weren't they?

Kate's heart cracked and she squeezed her eyes shut.

What was wrong with her? Why did she keep falling in love with men who couldn't, or wouldn't, ever love her back?

This job had offered her the chance to be with him and she had jumped at it, but now Kate wondered if it had been such a good idea. It wasn't as if she hadn't always known that falling in love with Finn was hopeless. It might have been better to have said goodbye and walked away while she still could.

But it was too late for that now. She was just going to have to get on with it, Kate told herself. If she couldn't make Finn happy, she could at least try to make him comfortable for a while, and if pretending to be his fiancée would make his life easier during his sister's visit, then she would do that too.

It felt odd not to be going into the office to be with Finn the next day, but having made her decision, Kate was quite as happy as she had said she would be pottering around the house. She took Alex to school and, by the time she had walked the dog, cleaned the house, inspected the cupboards and done the shopping, and walked the dog again, it was time to pick Alex up.

When Finn came home that evening, the two of them were in the kitchen. Kate was in the middle of making supper and Alex was sitting at the kitchen table doing her homework.

Finn bent to kiss his daughter, and then looked at Kate, who had the dizzy feeling that the obvious thing for him to do next was to walk across and kiss her too. She turned firmly back to her sauce.

'How was your day?' she asked, grimacing at the corniness of it. Any minute now she would be offering to bring him his pipe and slippers!

'Fine.' There was a faint frown between Finn's brows as

if he was remembering something that hadn't been fine at all. 'Busy.'

'How was Alison?' Kate made herself ask.

'She was...fine.'

Fine was obviously the key word for the day. Finn wrenched at his tie to loosen it.

'You didn't miss me then?' she said, making a joke out of it.

'Funnily enough, I did.'

Kate's heart stumbled, and without thinking she turned to face him. 'Really?' she said, still clutching her wooden spoon.

'Really,' said Finn.

His eyes seemed to reach right inside her and squeeze her heart until Kate's breathing got into a muddle and she forgot whether she was supposed to be breathing in or breathing out.

He had missed her. He wasn't just saying it, he had really missed her! OK, it wasn't a fraction of what he still felt for Isabel but, as Kate stared back at him, unable to tear her eyes away from that piercing grey gaze, she told herself that it was enough.

There was a long, long pause. Kate could feel the air shortening even as silence lengthened, and when the phone rang jarringly she actually jumped and dropped the wooden spoon.

Her hands were unsteady as she washed it under the tap.

Alex had pounced on phone. 'Oh, hello, Aunt Stella,' she said, and for the next few minutes dutifully answered questions about school. 'Yes, he's here,' she said after a while, and then, ultra-casual, 'He's just talking to Kate.'

She beamed at Finn as she held the phone out to him. He took it, visibly bracing himself. Stirring her sauce intently, Kate could hear only one side of the conversation, which seemed to consist of a lot of talking on Stella's part and brief replies on his.

'No, you can't talk to her,' she heard him say eventually. 'I don't want you interrogating her over the phone... You can meet her when you come... No, we're not planning on getting married while you're here. There's no rush. Kate's living here now and we're all perfectly happy as we are.'

Shaking his head, Finn put down the phone. 'My sister...!' He turned to Kate who was still concentrating fiercely on her sauce. 'Well, it looks as if we're committed now,' he said. 'I hope you don't want to change your mind?'

'No.' Kate took the saucepan off the heat and turned off the element. 'I won't change my mind.'

'Good.' Finn walked over to where she was standing by the cooker. 'Give me your hand. No, not that one,' he said as he pulled a box out of his jacket pocket. 'The other one.'

Kate had to steel herself against the shiver of response that shuddered through her as he took her left hand and turned it over, spreading it so that he could slide a ring onto her third finger.

'What do you think?'

If she hadn't known better, Kate could have sworn that he was nervous about her answer. She looked down at her hand. He seemed to have forgotten that he was still holding it and she was excruciatingly conscious of the warmth of his fingers.

She made herself focus on the ring. It was an antique, a cluster of pearls around a topaz on warm old gold. 'It's beautiful,' she said with difficulty.

Alex was less impressed. She peered round her father, studying the ring critically. 'It ought to be diamonds, Dad,' she said severely.

'Diamonds wouldn't be right for Kate.' Finn seemed to

remember that he was still holding Kate's hand and let it go abruptly. 'They're too cold.'

Kate bit her lip as she twisted the ring on her finger. 'It must have been terribly expensive,' she said worriedly.

'It will be worth it if it shuts Stella up,' said Finn, stepping back.

There was a pause. 'Do you really like it?' he asked as if the words had been forced out of him

'I love it,' she said honestly.

'I could get you a diamond ring if you'd rather.'

'I don't want diamonds,' said Kate. She risked a glance at him, and the light in her eyes turned them almost exactly the colour of the topaz. 'This is perfect.'

CHAPTER EIGHT

ALEX refused to be convinced. 'I still think it should be a diamond ring,' she said stubbornly. 'If Aunt Stella sees that old thing she might think you don't love Kate.'

Kate looked down at her beautiful ring. *That old thing?*

Finn was regarding his daughter with some exasperation. 'We'll just have to make her believe that I do anyway.'

'How?'

'Well...I'll tell her that I do.'

'I don't think that will be enough for Aunt Stella,' said Alex, making a face. 'You know what she's like.'

'I'm sure we'll think of something to convince her,' said Finn, and tried to change the subject by suggesting that she laid the table for supper.

Alex was not to be so easily diverted. 'I think you might have to kiss Kate,' she said as she set out the knives and forks.

'Possibly,' he said repressively.

Kate busied herself draining potatoes and avoided looking at either of them.

'Have you ever kissed her?' Alex asked her father with interest.

There was a frozen pause. 'I don't think that's any of your business, Alex,' he said in a curt voice.

It didn't seem to have much effect on Alex. 'I only thought you might need to practise if you haven't,' she said, all injured innocence.

'Well, we're not going to practise now,' Finn said with a something of a snap. 'We're going to have supper instead, and then *you* are going to bed!'

Only Alex seemed unaware of the air of constraint in the kitchen. She chattered on and Kate smiled mechanically and thought about kissing Finn. She wouldn't mind if it was just a practice. It would still be a kiss.

Please, please let him kiss me, she prayed.

She cleared up in the kitchen automatically while Finn was saying goodnight to Alex. She mustn't seem too keen. If he suggested taking Alex up on her idea, she would pretend to think about it and then agree casually.

Only Finn didn't suggest it. He made no reference to Stella's visit or Alex's conversation or anything at all that might give Kate an opening. He just helped her tidy up, moving efficiently and expressionlessly around the kitchen without once coming anywhere near her.

Frustrated, Kate wondered if she dared raise the subject herself. She didn't think she would have the nerve at first but, as the silence lengthened uncomfortably, she changed her mind. Dammit, they were both supposed to be grownups here! Why *shouldn't* she say something? It was exactly the kind of thing she ought to be able to discuss if she was treating this purely as a job.

Folding a tea towel and picking up some plates, Kate took the plunge. 'I've been thinking about what Alex said.'

'Which particular thing?' Finn asked. He was putting glasses back in the cupboard and sounding abstracted, as if he was thinking about something else entirely. 'I can't believe I used to worry that she was too quiet,' he added. 'She never shuts up now.'

Kate eyed his back with some resentment. He obviously wasn't going to make it easy for her!

'We were talking about your sister's visit,' she prompted him, and Finn turned, grey eyes suddenly alert.

'Ah.'

'Alex suggested that it might be an idea to practise a kiss

before Stella arrives,' said Kate, amazed at how calm she sounded.

'And what do you think?' asked Finn.

To her outrage, there was an undercurrent of something that might have been amusement, or possibly surprise. Whatever it was, it was enough to make Kate put up her chin and clutch the plates she was carrying defensively to her chest.

'I think we should,' she said coldly. 'There's no point in this elaborate charade if we're going to look as if we've never touched each other before. If your sister is as shrewd as you say she is, she'll see that we're uncomfortable together and it won't take her long to guess that we're not really engaged at all.'

'I suppose you're right,' Finn admitted grudgingly.

Kate's lips tightened. That's it, make it sound like kissing her would be a tiresome chore he'd really rather get out of!

'It's not going to be easy for either of us,' she said sharply, annoyed with him and even more annoyed with herself for wanting him even when he was making her cross. 'I just think it would be a lot less embarrassing if we don't have to kiss for the first time in front of an interested audience.'

Finn put the last glass away and closed the cupboard door. 'So you want me to kiss you?'

Yes.

'I don't *want* you to kiss me,' lied Kate with a frosty look. 'I'm merely suggesting that it might be sensible if we practised kissing each other in advance so it's not too awkward when we have to convince your sister.'

'OK,' said Finn. 'Shall we do it now?'

'Now?' faltered Kate. Having won her point, she was unprepared for him to follow it up quite so quickly.

'We might as well get it over with.'

Charming! But she was the one trying to convince him

that it was just a job as far as she was concerned, Kate acknowledged reluctantly. She could hardly turn round now and demand a romantic setting or a more intimate moment.

She swallowed. 'All right.'

Finn came over and took the plates from her nerveless hands. He put them on the table and turned back to where Kate stood, her pulse booming thunderously in her ears and her knees treacherously weak.

'Shall we do it then?' he asked, unsmiling.

Her throat was so dry that Kate couldn't speak. She nodded dumbly instead, and Finn took her by the waist to draw her slightly closer. Trying to anticipate and make it easier for him, Kate tilted up her face as he bent his head, but they ended up bumping noses and he released her awkwardly.

'It's just as well we're practising,' she said huskily, trying to laugh but not really succeeding.

'Just as well,' Finn agreed. 'Shall we try again?'

'OK.'

This time, he put his hands on her arms and slid them slowly to her shoulders as he looked down into her eyes almost thoughtfully. Locked into that cool, grey gaze, Kate stood mouse-still while he cupped her face between his warm hands. She was quivering with anticipation, and there was a fluttery feeling of excitement beneath her skin that jolted as Finn bent his head towards hers once more.

It was a better kiss this time. Much better. So much better, in fact, that Kate felt the floor drop away beneath her feet as his mouth touched hers. She put her hands out to steady herself against him, and he kissed her again and then things got a bit confused.

Afterwards, Kate wasn't sure how it had happened, but one moment she was standing there being controlled—relatively, anyway—and the next her arms were sliding round his waist, and she was melting into him, holding him, kissing him back.

Finn's fingers had drifted from her cheeks and were tangled in her hair. Kate had always thought of his mouth as being cool and stern, even hard, but it didn't feel like that now. It was warm and persuasive against hers, and it felt so right that she stopped thinking at all and gave herself up to the heady pleasure of kissing and being kissed while the tiny tremor of excitement inside her grew stronger and stronger, feeding on the touch of his lips and the taste of his mouth and the feel of his hard, solid body against hers, until it overwhelmed that gentle, reassuring rightness and spun Kate out of control.

She clung to Finn, half thrilled, half terrified by the intensity of it, not knowing how to break the kiss, not wanting to, but afraid that unless she did there would be no way she could keep him from knowing how she really felt.

Perhaps Finn sensed her confusion, or perhaps he too was alarmed by how quickly the brief practise kiss had taken on a life of its own, swamping their sensible intentions and sweeping them into uncharted territory, for he hesitated and then, with difficulty, lifted his head.

There was a long, long moment when they just stared shakily at each other, and then he seemed to realise that his fingers were still entwined in her soft, brown curls, and he pulled his hands abruptly away.

Kate was left reeling. It was all she could do to stay upright. She was dizzy and disorientated, and her heart was pumping with something close to terror at how badly she wanted to throw herself back into Finn's arms and beg him to kiss her again.

Finn was looking aghast, and he stepped back as if afraid that she would do just that.

'Well...' he said, and then hesitated, evidently not knowing what else to say.

'That...that was better,' Kate managed unsteadily. The appalled expression on Finn's face was enough to bring her crashing back to earth. So much for dreams when all it took was a single kiss to make the scales fall from his eyes and persuade him that he might be able to love her after all.

All she could do now, Kate decided, was try and treat it lightly and whatever she did, not let him guess how much kissing him had meant to her. She wasn't sure she could pretend to have hated it as much as he obviously had, but she could at least reassure him that she wasn't going to make a big deal out of it.

'Yes,' said Finn, sounding almost as dazed as she felt. 'I suppose it was.'

'And at least we know we can do it now.'

'Yes.'

An agonising pause. What should she do now? Kate wondered wildly. Reassure him that it wouldn't happen again? Ignore the whole thing? Or finish putting the plates away?

In the end it was Finn who broke the silence. 'I've got a few letters to write,' he said as if he had never kissed her, never had his fingers entwined in her hair. 'I'll be in my study if you need me.'

Kate watched him go, churning with frustration and still dizzy with desire. Perhaps she should go along in a few minutes and knock on his study door and tell him that she needed him to take her upstairs and make love to her all night and promise to let her stay with him for ever.

She wouldn't, of course. She wasn't supposed to need him for anything more intimate than the need to service the boiler, or to sort out a muddle with her housekeeping money.

Drearily, Kate picked up the plates once more. Thinking about that look on Finn's face after he had kissed her made her wince. The kiss had been a mistake.

It hadn't felt like a mistake, though. Not to her.

But Finn clearly wished it had never happened. She should never have suggested it, Kate realised. They had just got to the stage where they could talk to each other without too much constraint, and now the kiss had changed everything. Finn had retreated to his study, and there was no point in hoping that he would emerge ready to discuss what had happened. Kate was prepared to bet that he had never read any of those magazine articles which insisted on the importance of communication and talking things through in a successful relationship.

Not that they *had* a relationship, she reminded herself with a sigh. She had a job, and Finn had a potential embarrassment, but that wasn't much of a basis on which to build a life together, was it?

It didn't stop her waiting tensely for Finn to make at least some reference to the fact that they had kissed. It had been pretty shattering, after all, and judging from his expression when he let her go, for him as well as for her.

But Finn never so much as mentioned it. He carried on exactly as before, having apparently wiped the whole experience from his mind. Kate wished, not without some resentment, that she could do the same, but the memory of that devastating kiss was like a constant strumming just beneath her skin, leaving her edgy and unable to settle.

The days weren't too bad, and there were times when she was walking Derek or laughing with Alex that Kate even managed to persuade herself that she was well on the way to forgetting it quite as effectively as Finn. And then he would come back from work and walk into the kitchen looking solid and austere, and she would remember the kiss in such vivid detail that he might as well have bent her over the kitchen table and kissed her all over again.

Although *that* clearly wasn't going to happen. Finn was polite but guarded, and he was very careful to keep his distance. Even a brush of the fingers was clearly out. Swinging wildly between resentment and frustration, Kate grew increasingly tetchy with him until even Finn was driven to comment.

'What's the matter with you at the moment?'

'Nothing.'

'Please don't make me guess,' he said with an exasperated sigh. 'I've had a difficult day and I'm not in the mood for playing games. You might as well just tell me what's wrong.'

Oh, yes, she could just see herself doing that! Well, Finn, she could say, the thing is that I'm desperately in love with you and finding it all a bit frustrating. I know you'd rather pick up slugs, but do you think you could just take me to bed anyway and make me feel better?

Kate was half tempted to say it just to provoke Finn into a reaction other than his habitual range from expressionless to irritable but, as she strongly suspected that it would turn out to be one of unadulterated horror, she thought she would spare herself the humiliation. She took out her feelings on the potatoes instead, mashing them with a vengeance.

'There's nothing wrong,' she said. 'What could be wrong? I'm just doing my job.'

Finn wrenched off his tie and tossed it onto the back of a chair. 'Your job doesn't involve you carrying on like an aggrieved wife!'

'No,' Kate agreed, banging the potato masher onto the side of the saucepan with unnecessary force. 'It involves looking after you, your daughter, your house and your dog. I don't have time to behave like a wife, let alone an aggrieved one!'

He sighed irritably. 'If you want some time off, Kate, why don't you just tell me?'

'Look, I'm just in a bad mood, all right?' she snapped.

If he pushed her any further she jolly well *would* tell him what was bothering her, and then he'd be sorry! 'There doesn't have to be a reason, does there? Or is there a clause in my contract which says I have to be Mary Poppins the whole time?'

'If this is just a bad mood, perhaps you'd better have the night off anyway,' said Finn.

'It's a bit late for that now,' Kate pointed out crossly. 'Besides, I'm going out tomorrow night.'

'Oh? Who with?' he demanded, sounding oddly disgruntled for a man who only a moment ago had been practically pushing her out of the door.

'With you,' said Kate. 'We're having drinks with your neighbour.'

The dark brows drew together ominously. 'Which neighbour?' he asked with foreboding.

'Laura. She's been away for a few weeks and thought it would be nice to catch up on all your news.'

Laura had been a very glamorous divorcee, and Kate had identified a distinctly predatory gleam in her eyes when she had rung the bell earlier that evening and asked for Finn. She hadn't been at all pleased to see Kate instead of Rosa, and even less happy when Kate made sure she could see the engagement ring on her finger.

Finn was still scowling. 'I hope you said I was busy.'

'No, I said we'd love to come.'

'We?'

'Yes, *we*, you and me! I realise that you've wiped it from your mind, but we are supposed to be engaged!'

'Pretending to be engaged!'

Kate flushed. 'That's what I meant.'

'And it's only when Stella's here,' Finn went on crossly. 'There's no need to rope the neighbours into this particular fantasy!'

'I wasn't roping anyone in,' she protested. 'This woman

came to the door, clearly planning an intimate tête-à-tête with you while I had this whacking great ring on my finger. Of course she noticed it straight away, that's what women do.' No need to tell Finn that she had made quite sure that Laura had seen it and was forced to comment on it. 'What was I supposed to do? Pretend I didn't exist?'

'You could have said you were engaged to someone else.'

'Oh, well, excuse me while I just go and shoot myself,' said Kate sarcastically. 'I am just so useless at telepathy and knowing who I'm allowed to tell and who I'm not! What's the big problem with Laura knowing anyway?' she added as a sudden suspicion crossed her mind.

Finn was pouring himself a large whisky. 'The problem is that I've been avoiding that woman ever since she moved in next door and discovered that I was a widower. I've managed to fob her off so far by saying that I'm not ready for another relationship.'

'So? Tell her that you changed your mind when you met me.'

Dream on, Kate!

'Great! So when you go, I'll have to tell her that our "engagement" is off, and then she'll think there's no reason for me not to think about another relationship,' grumbled Finn.

'You'll just have to learn to say no rather than hiding behind the fact that you're a widower,' said Kate robustly. 'I wouldn't have thought *you* would find that too hard,' she added with a slight edge. 'Off-putting seems to be your speciality!'

He paused with his glass halfway to his lips. 'What do you mean by that?'

'Well, you're not exactly approachable, are you?' she said, putting on oven gloves. 'This Laura must be a brave woman or very thick-skinned if she's been after you all that time. The rest of us wouldn't dare—we're all terrified of you!'

'I can't say I've ever noticed you being very terrified,' said Finn with an acid look.

'I just put a good face on it,' said Kate. 'I told you I was good at acting'

'You must be even better than I thought,' he said dryly, and for some reason the kitchen flared suddenly with the memory of the kiss they had shared. It burned in the air between them, bright and dangerous and so vivid that Kate could practically see herself clinging to him, practically feel his lips, and his hands in her hair.

Jerking her eyes away, she bent to take the casserole out of the oven, glad of the excuse to hide her hot face. 'Maybe I am,' she said, not quite as steadily as she would have liked.

By the time she straightened and had taken off the lid to stir, Finn was sitting at the table, staring broodingly down into his whisky.

'You didn't really say we would go round for drinks tomorrow, did you?'

'Yes, I did.' Kate had herself back under control. 'I didn't see any reason not to,' she said, sniffing appreciatively at the casserole. 'Once Laura discovered that she couldn't have you to herself, she started talking about inviting other people as well. It might be fun.'

Finn grunted. 'Making polite chit-chat over a lukewarm drink doesn't sound like much fun to me!'

'Oh, come on, you might meet someone interesting.'

'And what about Alex?' he said as if she hadn't spoken.

Kate rolled her eyes as she turned from the cooker. 'We're only going next door for an hour or so. Alex could probably come with us, or I'll ask Bella or Phoebe to come over. I'm sure they wouldn't mind. Anyway, I've accepted for you, so you'll have to go now,' she said putting an end to the argument. She started to untie her apron. 'See if you can get home a bit earlier tomorrow evening—we're invited for half past six.'

'You look nice.' Bella was playing cards with Alex at the kitchen table when Kate came downstairs the next evening wearing a full skirt with a tight waist and a laced top. 'Very Nell Gwynn! All the men will be panting to buy oranges from you!'

Kate tugged fretfully at her neckline. 'You don't think this is a bit low?'

'No, if you've got it, flaunt it!' said Bella cheerfully.

'I wish I'd brought more clothes with me. Laura looked awfully sophisticated.'

'I think you look beautiful,' said Alex loyally. 'Don't you, Dad?'

Kate spun round. She hadn't heard Finn come into the kitchen behind her, and her heart jerked at the sight of him, tall and austere in a dark suit.

He looked at Kate. 'She looks fine,' he said.

'Oh, Mr McBride, please stop!' said Kate, hiding her disappointment behind a pretence at being overcome. 'You'll turn my head with all these compliments!'

Finn sighed. 'You look absolutely beautiful... stunning... glamorous... What else am I supposed to say?'

'Thin,' prompted Kate.

'Sexy,' Bella suggested.

His eyes rested on Kate's cleavage. 'And sexy,' he said.

There was a tiny pause. Finn checked his watch. 'If you've quite finished fishing for compliments, we'd better go,' he said brusquely. 'The sooner we get there, the sooner we can leave.'

'Quite the party animal, isn't he?' said Bella.

Kate took him by the arm to turn him towards the door.

'Stop grumbling, it'll be fine,' she said. 'Just think of it as a dry run for when Stella comes—and you might at least *try* to look as if you're happy to be with me!'

As she had suspected, Laura had abandoned the idea of intimate drinks alone with Finn since Kate had thrust a spoke in her wheel, and a number of other neighbours had been invited along as well. The women were all wearing discreetly elegant numbers and Kate knew from the moment Laura opened the door that the laced top had been a mistake. Next to the others, she looked garish and flamboyant and more than a little tarty.

Her outfit seemed to go down very well with their husbands, though. Since it was too late to go for a sophisticated image, Kate opted for being fun instead, and Finn grew more and more boot-faced at the gales of laughter coming from the group around her.

'You're back early,' said Bella when they returned. 'We weren't expecting you back for ages. How did it go?'

'Excellent,' Finn bit out. 'Kate managed to ruin my reputation and break up several of my neighbour's marriages in a few short minutes!'

'I don't know what you're talking about,' said Kate crossly, still flushed and more than a little annoyed at being dragged away from the party on the flimsiest of excuses. She had been quite enjoying herself.

'Oh, yes, you do!' snarled Finn. 'You made a complete exhibition of yourself! Laura won't be at all surprised to hear our "engagement" is off after the way you were carrying on,' he said furiously. 'You were practically in Tom Anderson's lap!'

'I was not! Not that you would have been able to notice even if I had been,' she retorted. 'You spent the entire time pinned in the corner by Laura and you weren't exactly struggling to get free and circulate. Your body language is very revealing you know.'

'Not as revealing as that top,' Finn snapped back.

'Now, now, children, play nicely,' said Bella. 'I think you'd better work on how to look as if you're engaged before Stella arrives,' she told them. 'You see, generally when people get engaged it's because they love each other and want to spend the rest of their lives together, and not because they fight at parties. That usually comes *after* they get married!' she explained kindly.

'We're certainly going to have to do something different when Stella gets here,' said Finn. 'She's never going to believe we're a couple if Kate carries on the way she did this evening!'

'That shouldn't be a problem,' Kate informed him loftily. 'I was just excited at being appreciated for a change, and I know that's not going to happen when I'm with you!'

'Perhaps you need to give Stella a bit more evidence,' Bella put in diplomatically. 'I was talking to Phoebe while you were out, and we thought it would be a good idea to have a sort of engagement party for you while Stella's here. It's the sort of thing we would do if you were really engaged, and as you're a friend of Gib's, Finn, and Kate's a friend of Phoebe's, it would be natural for them to have a dinner for you and close friends—that's me and Josh and partners.'

She turned her blue gaze on Finn. 'We'll invite your sister along, of course. I'm sure if she saw your friends treating you as an engaged couple she'd be quite convinced, no matter how much you and Kate seemed to argue.'

'It's possible,' said Finn grudgingly, still in a bad mood with Kate. 'But there's no need for you to go to any trouble. This whole business is getting out of control as it is, without you and Phoebe getting involved as well.'

'Don't worry about us,' said Bella. 'Any excuse for a party! What do you think, Kate?'

Kate suspected, like Finn, that things could easily get out

of control, but he had been so irritating this evening that she didn't feel like supporting him now. 'I think it's a wonderful idea,' she said firmly. 'I'll give Phoebe a ring tomorrow and we'll sort out a date.'

Stella was due to arrive the following Tuesday. Kate spent the day before spring-cleaning the house from top to bottom. She put flowers in the guest room and set out soap and towels before shutting the door so that Derek couldn't roll on the bed. This was a new trick of his that worked better, from a canine point of view at least, the wetter and muddier he was. It hadn't gone down at all well with Finn when Derek had tried it on his bed.

She had planned a special welcome dinner for Stella, too, and was making individual rich chocolate mousses when Finn came down from saying goodnight to Alex the night before she was due to arrive.

'Is everything under control?'

'I think so,' said Kate. After that disastrous evening at Laura's, they had both recovered their equilibrium and were being polite to each other with only the occasional sharp aside. 'I've just got to finish these now. Her room is ready for her, and I'll put some champagne in the fridge tomorrow.'

Finn raised his brows. 'Champagne?'

'It's a celebration,' she pointed out with an edge of exasperation. 'You haven't seen your sister for a while, and we're getting married—at least as far as she's concerned. Of course we've got to have champagne!'

'If you say so.' Finn dipped his finger into the chocolate mixture, just managing to whip it out of the bowl before Kate swiped it.

'There's no point in going through with the whole pretence unless we're going to do it properly,' she said.

'No, you're right.' He licked his finger, ignoring her frown. 'This chocolate stuff is good.'

Carefully, Kate poured the chocolate mixture into individual ramekins. She waited until she had divided the last of it before asking Finn the question that was most on her mind. 'Do you think we'll be able to carry it off?'

'If we don't lose our nerve. Stella's very astute, though, so we can't afford to relax while she's here. She'll pick up instantly on anything odd. In fact—'

'What?' asked Kate when he stopped abruptly.

Finn didn't answer immediately. He paced around the table, his hands in his pockets and his shoulders hunched, debating whether to continue or not.

'I'm not sure how to ask you this, Kate,' he said at last, 'but I wonder how you would feel about sleeping with me while Stella is here.' He saw Kate's head jerk up from the bowl she was scraping and corrected himself hurriedly. 'I don't mean *sleep* with me, of course,' he said. 'I just mean...share a room.'

Of course. He wouldn't want to sleep with her, would he? Kate put down the bowl.

'I think Stella would think it a bit strange if we didn't,' Finn went on.

It's not a big deal. Wasn't that what she had said to Bella? She was the girl who wasn't going to take the situation seriously. The actress who wasn't bothered by silly little things like kisses or jumping into bed with her boss. She couldn't change her image now.

Kate started gathering up whisks and spoons and bowls to wash. 'Sure,' she said.

Finn looked at her, taken aback by her ready agreement. 'You will?'

'I was just saying that we might as well do the thing properly,' she pointed out reasonably. 'I don't mind sharing with you while your sister is around. I know you wouldn't...' She trailed off, embarrassed when it came to the crunch. 'That we wouldn't...you know...'

'I know,' he said dryly.

'We might as well start tonight, don't you think?' Kate suggested, determined to recover her confidence and carry the situation off with style. 'Then we'll look more natural when she gets here tomorrow morning.'

Of course, it was all very well being brisk and practical in the kitchen, but it was a different matter when the moment came. At least she had a nightdress with her. Kate got undressed in her own room and put it on, smoothing the silky material over her hips. She couldn't believe that she was actually going to walk along to Finn's bedroom and get into bed beside him! Her whole body was pumping and twitching with nerves.

Not a big deal, right?

Right.

Wrapping a dressing gown tightly around her, Kate took a deep breath and opened her door.

Finn was waiting for her, looking ill at ease in a crumpled pair of pyjamas. Kate guessed that he didn't normally wear them and had dug them out of a drawer to preserve the decencies.

'I'll take a pillow and sleep on the floor,' he said when she hesitated in the doorway.

'That defeats the purpose of the exercise, doesn't it?' Kate was amazed at how cool she sounded. 'What if Stella came in and saw that you were sleeping down there? It looks like a big bed,' she went on, still without a tremor, and she even managed a sort of laugh. 'I trust you to keep your hands off me!'

A wary expression had descended on Finn's face. He was probably baffled by her transformation from messy, muddled sentimentality to brisk practicality.

'Which side do you normally sleep?' said Kate, taking matters into her own hands.

'Over here.' He pointed, and she walked round the bed

to the other side and pulled back the duvet. Taking off her dressing gown, she draped it over a chair and got into bed. If Finn was waiting for her to make a fuss about the situation, he would have a long wait. Bella would be proud of her. She was cool.

After another puzzled glance, Finn switched off the main light. Kate pretended to be making herself comfortable as the bed creaked and dipped when he got in the other side and clicked off the bedside lamp.

'Well...goodnight,' he said.

'Goodnight.'

There, that was easy, thought Kate, trying not to think about the fact that Finn was lying bare inches away, or about how easy it would be to roll against him in the night. He flexed his shoulders to make himself comfortable and she caught her breath, wondering if it might just be the prelude to him moving closer...but no. He settled and lay still, and after a while there was only the steady sound of him breathing quietly in the dark.

Very, very gradually, Kate let herself relax. When it was obvious that Finn had fallen asleep, she congratulated herself on her cool. Really, there was nothing to it. Everything would be fine.

CHAPTER NINE

IT WAS still dark when Kate drifted out of sleep to find herself lying on her side with an arm over her. A hard, male arm holding her against the hard, male body behind her.

Finn. He must have rolled over in his sleep, she realised, blinking dreamily. She could feel his breath, deep and slow, just stirring her hair and that was enough to wake every nerve in her body, and set each one tingling, alert with wicked anticipation. 'No going back to sleep now!' they seemed to scoff at Kate's attempts to close her mind to his closeness. 'It's too late for that.'

It was much too late. Even with her eyes squeezed shut, Kate was aware of every millimetre of her own body, burning where it touched his. It felt so good to be held by him. She wished she could turn and nuzzle in to him, to wake him with soft kisses, and her eyes snapped open as her entrails liquefied at the thought.

She *could* turn.

She could kiss him.

She could pretend that she was sleeping too.

Once the idea was in her head, she couldn't dislodge it. It would be silly, and it might be very embarrassing, the sensible part of Kate's mind pointed out. She was supposed to be keeping her distance and impressing him with her cool. Snuggling up against him and running her hands over his body while she kissed her way to his mouth wouldn't do that.

But it would feel so good.

She could always stop, Kate reasoned to herself. She

didn't have to go that far. She didn't even need to wake him. She just wanted a glimpse of what it would be like if she belonged here in his arms, if Finn knew exactly who he was holding against him and would smile at the feel of her lips on his skin.

That wasn't asking too much, was it?

Kate stirred experimentally, but Finn just kept breathing into her hair. He must be sound asleep, she thought with a spurt of resentment. How could he be sleeping when she was awake and churning with desire? Couldn't he feel how much she wanted him?

Well, she could lie here all night or she could see what would happen if she turned over. She might as well accept that she wasn't going to go back to sleep either way.

Taking a deep breath, she sighed as if she were dreaming and rolled towards Finn, who promptly rolled away in his turn to lie on his back, the arm that had been around her now outflung across the pillow.

Typical. Kate eyed his slumbering form with frustration. Even in sleep he seemed determined to resist her. Well, they would see about *that*!

She shifted across the sheet, warm from his body, until she could snuggle into the solid strength of him. Finn was much taller than her standing up, but lying down Kate just fitted him nicely. She was very comfortable pressed into his side. She could put an arm over his chest to keep him close and rest her face against his throat, breathing in the scent of his skin, and all without him waking.

Stop now, Kate told herself sternly. Comfort wasn't everything, but it was enough for now.

Only it wasn't. Of course it wasn't.

Without making a conscious decision, Kate touched her lips to Finn's throat, and then again, and again, until she was working her way up and along his jaw. Her hand seemed to have acquired a will of its own, too, sliding under the pyjama jacket and around his lean waist.

She was playing with fire, and she knew it, but she couldn't help herself and she didn't care. Her kisses drifted back down to his collar, and she was just unfastening the top button when all at once Finn's breathing stilled.

She had woken him. Slowly, Kate lifted her head until she could look down into his face and see the gleam of his eyes in the darkness. She couldn't pretend that she was asleep now. With one part of her mind she registered that she might regret this moment in the morning, but now...oh, now was not the time for regrets.

Finn lay motionless beneath her, blinking away sleep. Kate could see him trying to adjust to wakefulness, and she braced herself for the moment when he realised who she was and what she was doing and jackknifed away from her in horror. But he just stared up at her for a long, long time before the arm behind her head came round so that his fingers could slide into her hair, and pull her head down towards him with exquisite, dreamlike slowness.

When their lips met at last, the dreaminess shattered and Kate sank into Finn and they kissed hungrily, again and again, as if to make up for all the waiting. Finn's other hand was sliding insistently over her satin nightdress, searching for the hem, and when he found it, it slipped beneath, rucking up the slithery material as he explored her thigh, the back of her knee, the curve of her hip.

The feel of his hand on her bare skin made Kate gasp, and fumble for the buttons of his pyjama jacket, but her fingers were so clumsy that in the end Finn simply pulled it over his head before rolling her beneath him abruptly. With a sigh of release, Kate wound her arms around his neck, pulling him closer, luxuriating in the feel of his bare back under her hands.

She was terrified that Finn would wake properly and realise what he was doing. She didn't care about the morning, didn't think about what they would do and say to explain this away. For now all Kate wanted was to abandon herself completely, to the touch of his hands, to the feel of his mouth as it drifted tantalisingly over her, to the hard demand of his body.

To the clutching pleasure and the slow, irresistible burn of excitement that left them gasping and powerless while a timeless rhythm swept them both up, up, up, too high, beyond thought, beyond feeling, to the very edge until Kate fell abruptly, tumbling into a heart-stopping intensity of sensation.

When she came to, Finn was lying heavily on top of her, breathing raggedly. She was having trouble working her lungs herself. They seemed to have forgotten how to function by themselves, and it took a conscious effort to draw each tiny, shuddering breath.

After a while, Finn moved away from her, muttering something that Alex would have had no trouble in identifying as a rude word.

Oh, yes! Kate wanted to say. Yes, indeed! But she thought she had better not.

He lay on his back beside her, trying to bring his breathing under control. 'I'm sorry,' he said at last. 'I didn't mean that to happen.'

'It was my fault.' Kate made a half-hearted effort to force some contrition into her voice. She knew she ought to feel guilty, but it was as if all those nerve endings that had been twitching and fretting uncomfortably for the past few weeks were now stretching and smirking with satisfaction. Her body didn't feel guilty at all. It felt very, very good. Better than it ever had before, in fact.

'I forgot where I was.' Which wasn't strictly true, but she was feeling too pleased with herself to worry about little details. 'I suppose I got a bit carried away.'

'I think we both did,' said Finn dryly.

Kate shifted onto her side so that she could look at him properly. 'Are you really sorry?' she made herself ask.

He turned his head on the pillow. 'No,' he said honestly after a moment. 'No, and I can't say that I didn't know what I was doing either, but it was very irresponsible. I wasn't planning on this happening. What if you got pregnant?'

'I won't do that. I'm still on the Pill.'

She still felt amazing, relaxed and replete. Even her toes were tingling with remembered pleasure. It wasn't a feeling she wanted to give up, not yet anyway. Given half a chance, she knew that Finn would say that it should never happen again. Kate wasn't sure that she could bear that.

'Look,' she said persuasively, 'we haven't hurt anybody else tonight. I think we both needed a bit of comfort, and we took it. What's wrong with that?'

She would have to be careful not to alarm Finn by seeming too keen. 'It doesn't mean anything to either of us,' she told him, 'but that's no reason why we shouldn't have some fun. It's not as if we're talking about for ever. I'm only here for a few weeks, and since we're going to be sharing a room, don't you think we should make the most of it? Unless you'd rather not,' she finished lamely, unnerved by the way Finn was watching her in silence.

'I daresay I could resign myself to it,' he said.

It took a few moments for Kate to realise that he was teasing. Dizzy with relief, she smiled at him. 'It would only be a temporary thing,' she tried to reassure him. 'Just while your sister is here.'

'Of course,' said Finn expressionlessly.

'No big deal.'

'No.'

'Neither of us is going to get involved.'

'Right.'

Silence. Kate studied Finn a little uneasily, not sure what to make of his curt replies. Was he regretting his decision already? In the darkness, his face was even harder to read than usual.

The main thing was that he hadn't repulsed her, she reasoned. There would be more nights like this. She couldn't ask for more than that. It was greedy to want him to love her as well, to want her for ever.

For now, Kate decided, she would do what she had said she would do, and make the most of what she had. She looked at Finn through the darkness and thought about his lips against her skin and the feel of his body beneath her hands, and the breath dried in her throat. For now, that was enough.

'Anyway, I'm sorry if I woke you,' she said, and then shivered with pleasure as Finn reached out and pulled her unresisting towards him.

'How sorry?' he asked.

She smiled as he kissed her. 'I'll show you,' she said.

The crunch of tyres on the gravel drive sent Derek into a frenzy of barking, and Kate paused in front of the hall mirror, running her fingers through her hair in a vain attempt to smooth her wild curls. She was surprisingly nervous about meeting Stella. Finn and Alex had gone to pick her up from the airport, and now this would be the moment of truth.

In the cool light of morning, Finn had made no reference to the night before. He had behaved so exactly as normal, grumbling about the state of the kitchen and refusing to allow Alex to meet her aunt in combat trousers and scruffy trainers, that Kate might have wondered if it had just been a wonderful dream if her body wasn't still pulsing with remembered pleasure.

Reeling, replete and short of sleep, she could hardly

string two words together, and her conversation at breakfast had been completely incoherent, at least judging by the funny looks Alex had given her. It was just lucky that Finn had to do the driving and not her.

Now she had to face the terrifyingly astute and perceptive Stella. Still, thought Kate with one last glance at her reflection as she headed for the door, there shouldn't be any problem convincing Stella that *she* was in love. She had that dazed, dopey look down pat.

On first sight, Stella had little in common with her brother. Several years older than Finn, she was plump and elegant, with beautifully cut grey hair, but she had the same shrewd grey eyes.

Waiting to greet her on the doorstep, Kate found herself enveloped in a warm hug. 'I cannot *tell* you how glad I am that Finn has found someone at last!' said Stella. She held Kate at arms' length and examined her face. 'Finn didn't tell me how pretty you were.'

Didn't he think she was pretty? Kate wondered with a pang. What *had* he told Stella, exactly? That she was nice-enough looking, but could never compare to the exquisite Isabel?

Finn was lifting an enormous suitcase out of the car. 'She's not pretty,' he said to his sister, whose jaw dropped, and even Kate was taken aback. She wasn't that bad, was she?

She stuck on a smile. Luckily, some people hadn't forgotten that they were supposed to be engaged! 'Thanks!' she said, finding no trouble at all in acting the part of aggrieved fiancée right then. 'You know, there's such a thing as being *too* honest!'

He set the suitcase on the gravel. 'I don't think you are pretty,' he said. 'Pretty's not enough for you.' He glanced at his sister, who was looking indignant on Kate's behalf.

'She's beautiful, not pretty,' he said, 'and I didn't tell you because I thought you'd be able to see it for yourself.'

There was a moment of stunned silence. Kate's face was hot and she stood feeling foolish and unsure what to do with herself. Finn had sounded so convincing that for a second or two there she had even wondered if he meant it. He was a better actor than she had thought.

Stella recovered first. 'Isn't that typical of Finn?' she said, linking arms with Kate. 'He gets you really cross and then says something like that which makes it impossible to stay furious the way you want to, so he always gets the last word!'

Alex was desperate to introduce her aunt to Derek, who was scratching behind the door to be let out to join the excitement, but the meeting was not a huge success. Stella was unimpressed.

'What kind of dog is *that*?'

'A very badly behaved one,' said Finn.

Alex leapt to Derek's defence. 'He's not!' she said hotly. 'He's very intelligent and perfectly trained, isn't he, Kate?'

'Well, maybe not *perfectly*,' Kate amended, thinking of the hours she had spent chasing Derek to try and get him on the lead, not to mention the chewed shoes and the stolen meat and the bed-rolling game.

Stella eyed Derek askance. She didn't actually say that he was the ugliest dog that she had ever seen, but she might as well have done. 'Where on earth did you find him?'

'It's Kate's fault,' said Finn. 'She fell into a pile of rubbish and came up with the dog, who has single-pawedly managed to disrupt my home and my office and is now costing me a fortune in vet bills and dog food!'

'Oh, Dad...!' said Alex reproachfully, and he smiled as he put an arm around her and hugged her.

Stella's eyes narrowed speculatively as she studied first

her brother and her niece, and then Kate. 'It looks like things have changed around here,' she said.

Apparently it wasn't just her brother who had changed. She frowned in a way that reminded Kate of Finn as she looked around the kitchen. 'I can't quite put my finger on it, but the whole house seems different,' she said. 'It's much warmer and more inviting somehow.'

Kate tried to see the room through a stranger's eyes. Already the kitchen seemed utterly familiar to her, although it wasn't quite as pristine as when she had first seen it, it had to be admitted. 'I think Finn would tell you it's much messier,' she said ruefully.

'I certainly would,' he said, getting mugs out of the cupboard. 'We can blame Kate for the difference in the house too.'

'Well, I think it's a great improvement,' said Stella as Kate plunged the cafetière.

Finn put the mugs on the table. 'So do I,' he said.

Kate's breath clogged in her throat. 'I'll remember that the next time you complain about my mess,' she managed, not knowing what to do except make a joke out of it, as the alternative was to throw her arms around him and beg him to say that he meant it. 'Alex, you're my witness!'

Stella was obviously dying for a chance to get Kate on her own, so she waved aside Finn's offer to show her to her room. 'You come with me, Kate,' she said.

Upstairs, she looked around the guest bedroom with pleasure. 'It all looks perfectly lovely,' she said, sniffing one of the scented soaps that Kate had put out for her. 'You're spoiling me—thank you!'

Kate shifted uncomfortably. 'I know Finn appreciates you coming all this way,' she said. 'He's told me how much you've done for him since Isabel died.'

'Oh, that was a terrible time,' sighed Stella, sinking down onto the bed. 'I did what I could, but Finn isn't easy to help. He keeps things to himself too much. Well, you must know how stubborn he is! It broke my heart to see him struggle on his own all these years. Sometimes it seemed as if he wouldn't ever let himself be happy again.'

'He loved Isabel very much.' Kate made herself say Isabel's name. It was as well to remember that last night didn't change anything, and that whatever Finn might say in front of his sister, her place in his life was only ever going to be temporary.

'I know he did,' said Stella, 'but he had Alex to think of as well as himself. I've been telling him for years that she needed a mother figure, and look at the difference in her now! I've never seen her so animated. She's come out of herself completely, and Finn says it's all thanks to you.'

She smiled at Kate. 'What he doesn't realise, of course, being a man, is that the real difference is in *him*. For years it's been like he was holed up behind a brick wall, refusing to let anyone close, but you've got under his guard. You must have done if you got him to give a home to that funny little dog! Finn doesn't even like dogs.'

'I think he likes Derek more than he admits,' said Kate loyally.

'That just proves my point!' said Stella getting to her feet. 'I haven't seen him look this happy and relaxed for years, and it's all because of you.' There were tears in her eyes as she embraced Kate. 'Finn won't say it, of course— you know what he's like!—but I can tell by the way he looks at you how much he loves you.'

So much for Stella and her famously astute perception!

Kate knew that Finn's sister was wrong. He didn't love her, but he *was* more relaxed, she could see that. Whether he was happy or not, she didn't ask. After Stella's arrival they were rarely alone together except for when they closed the bedroom door at night and they didn't talk then. They had said everything there was to be said that first night.

For both of them, the days that followed were a time out of time. Kate had to keep reminding herself that this was just a brief fling. It was about now and not for ever. They were being grown-up about the whole thing, and not taking it seriously at all. She was in thrall to the long, sweet nights they spent together, and refused to spoil them by thinking about the future or reminding Finn of reality. There would be time enough for that when Stella went home to Canada.

That was what Kate told herself, but it didn't stop her falling deeper and deeper in love with him. Sometimes she would look at him being perfectly ordinary like driving or putting on his glasses to read the paper, or just sitting and listening to his sister and daughter, and the air would evaporate from her lungs, while her heart clutched with the need to go over and touch him, to press her lips to his skin, and wind her arms around his neck and whisper a plea for him to take her upstairs, *now*.

Stella was a demanding guest, but Kate liked her much more than she had expected to. She was forthright and brisk at times, and she could be very tactless with Alex, but she clearly adored Finn, and she entered into whatever was going on with boundless enthusiasm. When Kate broached the idea of going to an engagement party at Phoebe's, Stella was thrilled.

'That sounds like a wonderful idea!' she said. 'If you hadn't been so obviously in love, I might be wondering if you two were actually going to get married,' she said that night over supper. 'You don't seem to be making any plans. Have you even picked a date for the wedding?'

Finn glanced at Kate. 'There isn't any rush.'

'There isn't any reason to wait, either,' Stella pointed out tartly. 'You're both old enough to know your own minds, neither of you has any other commitments and you're even living together. What's wrong with going ahead and getting married?'

'That's between Kate and I,' said Finn, gritting his teeth at his sister's interference.

'Of course, but you might think about other people, too.' Stella wasn't ready to give up yet. 'If you give us enough warning, Geoff and the kids can come over with me. I'm sure Kate's parents will want to know when the wedding is going to be too.'

'They're away at the moment,' said Kate, seizing on the excuse. 'That's one of the reasons we're waiting. I haven't told them about Finn yet.'

'Well, I don't see the need for all this secrecy,' grumbled Stella. 'Thank goodness these friends of yours are prepared to get into the right spirit and have a bit of a celebration! If it was left to you two it might never happen.'

'Stella, will you please stop trying to organise our lives? Kate and I are perfectly happy.'

'If you're not going to think about yourselves, you might at least think about Alex.'

'Alex is perfectly happy with the way things are, too,' said Finn tensely. 'Aren't you, Alex?'

'Ye-es,' Alex agreed cautiously. 'But it would be better if you and Kate did get married,' she added, taking Finn and Kate aback. 'Then I'd know Kate would stay for ever and look after Derek.'

Stella shot her brother a triumphant look. 'Your daughter's got more sense than you,' she told him. 'I might not make that dog my priority, but in every other way she's got it right. You'll lose Kate if you're not careful, and you don't want that, do you?'

Finn looked across the table at Kate, who was looking acutely uncomfortable. She was wearing one of those vibrantly coloured tops of hers and her hair tumbled as messily as ever to her shoulders. Her cheeks were flushed, and the brown eyes which met his for a fleeting moment were bright and clear.

'No,' he agreed softly, 'I don't want that.'

'Hey!' Kate thought it was time to lighten the atmosphere. 'I'm not going anywhere. This is a very nice house and Derek is a very nice dog, and I suppose you two aren't bad either,' she added, winking at Alex. 'Why wouldn't I stay for ever?'

To her surprise, Alex came to stand by her side 'Do you promise?' she said intensely.

What could she say? Kate put an arm around her to hug her close. 'I promise,' she said, and wished that it could be true.

'It's going to be a posh-frock affair,' Phoebe told Kate on the phone the next day. 'Make sure you all come dressed up to the nines.'

'Bella said it was just supper.'

'No, we've decided to have a proper dinner party since you and Finn met at dinner here.'

Kate held the phone away from her ear and stared at it in a puzzled manner. 'We met at work, Phoebe!'

'You met here for the first time socially,' said Phoebe firmly. 'And we want to make it a proper celebration for you.'

'Phoebe,' said Kate carefully, lowering her voice in case Stella came into the kitchen. 'You do know that Finn and I aren't really engaged, don't you? The party is just a bit of icing on the cake to convince his sister.'

'Of course I remember,' said Phoebe with such dignity that Kate was pretty sure that she and Bella had got carried away with their planning and forgotten little details like the fact that she and Finn weren't actually going to get married at all. 'But that's no reason not to do things in style,' she added, making a swift recovery.

'Well, don't get carried away!'

Phoebe pretended to sound hurt. 'Would I?'

'Bella would,' said Kate. 'Keep her under control, Phoebs. Stella seems to have accepted our supposed engagement so far, but she's not an idiot and she's bound to get suspicious if you go over-the-top with this dinner.'

'Relax,' said Phoebe soothingly. 'It'll be fun!'

Kate wasn't so sure. She loved her friends dearly, but she was ridiculously nervous about the night ahead as she and Finn got ready to go out that evening. It was hard enough keeping up the pretence in front of Stella without the interested gaze of all her closest friends on her. They would be watching her and Finn together and, knowing Phoebe and Bella, it wouldn't take them any time to see how she really felt about him. Kate just hoped they wouldn't give her away.

'I wish we weren't going out,' she sighed as she searched for her favourite earrings on top of the chest of drawers.

In the mirror above, she could see Finn shrugging himself into a shirt. The casual intimacy of getting dressed in the same room still gave Kate a tiny thrill each time.

'I know,' he said as he began fastening buttons. 'I'd rather stay in myself, but Stella is raring to meet everyone else.' He sighed. 'She's probably hoping to recruit some allies in her campaign for an early wedding.'

'It's all getting a bit complicated, isn't it?' said Kate, thinking of the promise she had made to Alex. She shouldn't have made a promise she couldn't keep, she thought guiltily.

'It's my fault,' said Finn. He tucked his shirt into his trousers. 'I should have known that my sister wouldn't stop at satisfying herself that you really existed. She won't be happy until she has the details of table settings and flowers and which hymns we have chosen!' He reached for a tie and looped it round his neck. 'I tell you, sometimes I wish we had never started this pretence!'

'Do you?' asked Kate.

Finn's hand stilled at his tie and his eyes met hers in the mirror. 'No,' he said.

His cool grey gaze locked with her warm brown one in the mirror, and for Kate it was as if the world stopped turning. Without taking his eyes from hers, Finn finished his tie and walked over slowly to put his hands on her shoulders.

'I can't imagine what we did without you,' he said as if coming into the middle of a conversation. 'Whenever Stella has been over before the visits have been a bit tense, but it's gone really well this time, and it's all due to you. Stella thinks you're wonderful.'

He paused, his hands warm and strong on her shoulders, and Kate let herself lean back against him just because she could and it felt so good.

'I've never thanked you properly for everything you've done,' Finn said soberly. 'And I don't just mean the pretence. The house looks great, you produce endless good meals, and then there's Alex...she's happy.'

'And you?' Kate nerved herself to ask.

Finn turned her slowly between his hands until she was facing him and he could look down into her face. 'I'm happy, too,' he said, and bent his head to kiss her.

Kate put her arms around his waist and leant blissfully into him. It wasn't a long kiss, but it was very sweet, and it was the first time he had kissed her when it wasn't dark and there wasn't anyone to convince. This kiss was just between the two of them. Neither of them could pretend now that it was only for show.

'Hey, you guys!' Stella was banging on the door, startling them apart. 'Hurry up, the taxi's here!'

When Finn released her, Kate could barely stand. Adrift in a wash of sensation, she felt oddly insubstantial, as if it was another person entirely who shimmered as she walked down the stairs, got into a taxi, and gave the driver directions to Phoebe's house dropping off Alex with Finn's neighbour first.

'Kate, you look absolutely fabulous!' said Gib, jaw dropping in surprise as he opened the door, and the others were just as complimentary.

'Look at her, she's glowing!'

'It must be love!'

Kate hardly heard any of it. She was finding it hard to concentrate on anything except the thought of going home with Finn, saying goodnight to Stella, and closing the bedroom door, when Finn would kiss her again and peel the dress from her shoulders and pull her down onto the wide bed...

'Kate, Kate, wake up!' Bella was waving a hand in front of her face, startling Kate out of her dreams.

'What?'

'We're about to open a bottle of champagne for you. You might at least make an effort to look as if you're on the same planet as the rest of us!'

Blinking, Kate looked around her. Stella was nose to nose with Phoebe and Josh, and the others were encouraging Gib as he eased the cork out of the champagne bottle. Finn was there, too, but slightly apart, smiling austerely, and Kate felt herself melting inside as someone put a glass of champagne into her hand.

'OK,' said Gib, when the champagne had been poured and everyone had a glass. 'I'd like to propose a toast to Finn and Kate. Unlikely as it seemed at first, they seem to go together perfectly, and I think we all want to wish them every happiness, because they both deserve it more than anyone else I can think of.'

'To Finn and Kate!' the others chorused. 'Hear, hear!'

Kate looked at Finn, wondering what they were supposed to do now. He didn't seem particularly perturbed, it had to be said. His grey eyes were alight, and he was smiling, and she couldn't help smiling back.

Oblivious to everyone else, he came over to put his arm around her, and pulled her into his side. 'Thank you,' he said simply. 'We're very grateful to all of you,' he said, glancing around, and then he looked down into Kate's face. Her brown eyes were shining. 'Aren't we, Kate?'

'Yes,' she breathed, not knowing what he said, but understanding that he wanted her to agree with him. 'Oh, yes.' But she wasn't thinking about being grateful, she was just thinking about how much she loved him and how she couldn't wait for his arm to tighten around her and his mouth to come down on hers.

When it did, she gave herself up to the sweetness without a thought for their audience, and when Finn finally released her, it was bizarre to hear a splatter of applause.

'I think that answers all our questions,' said Gib dryly.

'Except when is the wedding?' Stella put in, spotting her chance.

'Yes, good point.' Phoebe and Bella chimed in as Finn released Kate reluctantly. 'When is it?'

Finn didn't take his eyes from Kate's. 'Soon,' he said.

CHAPTER TEN

PHOEBE and Bella had obviously spent days planning and preparing dinner, and had put so much effort into decorating the table and bullying everyone into dressing up that Kate felt desperately guilty that it wasn't for real. They couldn't have made more fuss if she and Finn really had been engaged—in fact, Kate was beginning to suspect that her friends didn't quite believe that the whole thing was a pretence.

Bella's boyfriend, Will, was there, and Josh had brought along a new girlfriend, and together with Phoebe and Gib and Stella, who was on fine form, they made a lively party. Finn and Kate weren't required to contribute much, which was just as well.

Part of Kate wished that she could enjoy it all more, but she was having trouble concentrating on the conversation. All she could think about was going home with Finn and closing the bedroom door and shutting out the rest of the world. She made an effort to laugh and smile at the right points, but with Finn sitting beside her it was hard to focus. She wanted to put her hand on his thigh, to kiss his throat, to make him stand up and drag her away from the chatter and the laughter and the pretending.

'So, that's it then,' said Phoebe, when Kate pulled herself together sufficiently to help carry the plates through to the kitchen after the main course.

'What do you mean?'

'You're in love with Finn, aren't you?'

Kate set the plates carefully on the draining board. 'Why do you say that?'

'It's obvious. I don't think you've even registered that there's anyone else in the room!'

'Sorry,' Kate muttered. 'I really do appreciate all the trouble you and Bella have gone to but...'

'But Finn is the only person in there who seems real?' Phoebe smiled. 'I know.'

'OK, so I am a bit in love with him,' said Kate with a shade of defiance.

'A bit?'

Kate gave in. 'A lot.'

'What about Finn? I mean, I can see he's making an effort to join in, but there's something about the way he's making a point of not looking at you that's a dead giveaway. I reckon he's pretty smitten too.'

'I don't think so,' she said sadly. 'He's just a good actor. I haven't told him how I feel, and I'm not going to. We're having a nice time at the moment, but I know it's not going to last. As soon as Stella leaves, I'll get a new job and that will be that. It's just a temporary thing.'

Phoebe looked at Kate in concern. 'Is that going to be enough for you?'

Kate looked bleakly back at her friend. 'It's going to have to be,' she said.

But the conversation with Phoebe had had its effect. It was true that Phoebe knew her better than most, but if her feelings for Finn were that obvious, she would have to be careful.

It would be awful if Finn guessed that she was in love with him. Kate cringed inwardly at the thought. It would make the situation unbearably awkward for them both. The last thing she wanted was to put him in the position of having to explain to her that he wouldn't—couldn't—ever love anyone the same way as he had loved Isabel. It wasn't as if she hadn't known all along that she could never compare to his dead wife.

Kate decided that it would be easier for Finn if she tried to keep more of a distance, but it was hard not to respond when he reached for her in the dark, or to pretend that she wasn't pleased to see him when he walked through the door. She just couldn't do cool and reserved, no matter how hard she tried.

It was even harder when Stella went off to visit various friends. She was away nearly a week, and Kate was alarmed to discover how easy and comfortable it felt with just the three of them—plus the dog, of course—in the house. It was like being a proper family. Sometimes Kate had to make herself remember that she was only a temporary member of it, and that she wouldn't always be able to chatter with Alex or hum as she pottered around the kitchen or climb into bed next to Finn.

Stella's departure should have meant that they could drop the fiction that Kate was more than a housekeeper, but Alex continued to treat her in exactly the same way, and when Finn and Kate discussed the matter in bed the night before she left, they decided that it was hardly worth reverting to the previous sleeping arrangements while she was away.

'You know what Stella's like,' said Finn. 'I wouldn't put it past her to turn up again without warning just to have another nag about fixing a wedding date.'

'We might as well stay as we are, then,' said Kate, trying to sound offhand, as if she didn't really care one way or the other.

'Might as well,' Finn agreed in an equally indifferent voice, but then he rolled Kate beneath him and she felt him smiling as he kissed her throat, and her heart swelled with relief and happiness.

Better to make the most of the time she had left, she decided. Plenty of time to be cool when Stella had gone back to Canada and there was no more reason to share Finn's life, no excuse to turn to him in the night and wind her arms around his neck and kiss him back. She would store up memories instead, and squirrel them away to comfort her in the bleak future that stretched ahead when her job here was over.

Stella's absence meant that Finn took the opportunity to go back to work, and with Alex at school, and the days brightening, Kate decided to spring-clean the house again. She was being paid to be a housekeeper, she reminded herself, so she might as well keep house.

She started at the top, blitzing the bathroom and all the bedrooms. Inspired, she pulled out the beds, vacuumed into the corners, dusted and polished and tidied away the clutter that irritated Finn so much.

When it came to his room, Kate was quite embarrassed at the state she had reduced it to. Each side of the bed reflected their different personalities. On her side, the table could hardly be seen beneath a mass of moisturisers, tissues, pens, nail polishes, emery-boards, books, magazines, bits of jewellery and cotton wool, buttons, torn price tags, receipts...ah, there was that comb! She had been looking for it for ages.

Good God, where had all this stuff *come* from? It was as if her things were breeding and taking over Finn's room. They had yet to make a break for his side of the bed, but it could only be a matter of time.

Kate swept everything away and gave the table a good dust before heading round to Finn's side. Tidying *his* table wasn't going to take long. Apart from the businesslike lamp and electronic alarm clock, all that marred its pristine state was a small pile of coins that he had emptied out of his pocket last night.

Hardly a mess, then, but Kate was determined to tidy them away as a point of principle. Unsure what to do with them, she opened the little drawer under the table and was about to tip the coins in when she stopped. A framed photograph was lying face down in the drawer.

Slowly, Kate lifted it out, knowing what she would see when she turned it over. Isabel.

Of course Finn would have had a photograph of her by his bed, where she would be the first thing he saw when he woke, and the last before he slept. Kate's heart cracked at the thought of how much he still loved and missed his wife.

Holding the photograph in her hands, she sank down onto the edge of the bed. He must have put it away when they had first discussed sharing a room, unable to bear the thought of seeing Isabel's face when another woman was where she ought to be. The contrast would have been too much to take.

Kate looked down at Finn's wife. She had been so beautiful with those great, dark eyes and that sweet smile. How could Finn ever think about putting anyone in her place?

Biting her lip, she leant forward to slip the frame back into the drawer and saw a letter on the floor. She must have pulled it out inadvertently when she took out the photograph. She picked it up, not wanting to read it, but unable to avoid a glimpse of the words 'love always and for ever' written in Finn's black, decisive scrawl.

Always and for ever.

Kate stood up, put the letter back underneath the picture and closed the drawer.

Time to get real. Finn was never going to love her the way she loved him. It was no use hoping and pretending and burying her head in the sand. Oh, of course she had told herself that she knew that Finn still loved Isabel, but she hadn't really *believed* it until now. Finn didn't say things he didn't mean. He *would* always love Isabel. He would love her for ever.

Kate was quiet that evening, but when Finn asked her

what the matter was she smiled and shook her head. 'Nothing. I'm a bit tired that's all.'

And when they went to bed, she clung to him, unable to imagine how she was going to be able to bear saying goodbye, but knowing that she was going to have to find a way.

Stella came back from what she called her 'tour of England' three days later, and immediately noticed the change in Kate. 'What's wrong?' she demanded bluntly the moment the two of them were alone. 'Have you two had a fight?'

'Of course not,' said Kate.

'I know Finn can be difficult,' said Stella, clearly not believing a word, 'but you're so good for him, and Alex is so happy now, too,' she went on. 'I couldn't bear it if it didn't work out between you and Finn.'

Stella was just going to have to bear it, the way she was, Kate thought sadly.

'Really, Stella, everything's fine,' she lied.

They all went to the airport to see Stella off. Kate was sorry to see her go, and not just because her departure meant that there was no excuse to stay with Finn and Alex any longer. Finn's sister could be abrasive at times, but her heart was in the right place, and Kate liked her warmth and her enthusiasm and her no-nonsense approach.

Even so, she was surprised at how emotional Stella got when it came to say goodbye. She hugged Kate tightly and thanked her for everything she had done, and then she turned to her brother.

'You keep hold of Kate,' she told him as she kissed him. 'She's just what you need.'

Alex was the last to be hugged. 'Make sure your father doesn't do anything stupid,' said Stella.

'Promise you'll let me know as soon as you've decided a date for the wedding,' were her parting words before she went through passport control.

'I don't know how I'm going to tell her that there's not going to be any wedding,' sighed Finn as they headed back to the car with that sinking sense of anticlimax that comes with a goodbye. 'She's never going to forgive me.'

'Maybe you won't have to tell her,' said Alex, scuffing along beside him.

'What do you mean?'

'You could go ahead and get married.'

Finn stopped in mid-stride. 'Alex, the only reason Kate and I have gone through all this is because you said you didn't want a stepmother.'

'I wouldn't mind Kate,' said Alex.

There was a moment of appalled silence while the three of them stood as if marooned in the middle of the busy terminal. Kate didn't dare look at Finn, but she could feel the tension in him. She was going to have to do something to defuse the situation before he exploded.

'I think you'd soon get bored of me,' she told Alex in an effort to pass it off lightly. She even managed a feeble smile.

Alex's mouth set in a stubborn line. 'No, I wouldn't.'

'I'd be very strict. It would be bed at eight o'clock every night, and no television during the week. You wouldn't like that, would you?'

'No,' Alex admitted, 'but it would be better than you going.'

'All right, Alex, that's enough,' said Finn in a curt voice. 'Kate's done us a favour, but she's got her own life to live now.'

'But—'

'I don't want to hear any more about it,' he said with an air of finality and strode out through the doors towards the car park leaving Alex and Kate to trail silently behind him.

It was a tense drive home. Finn shut himself in his study as soon as they got back, telling Kate that he was going to do some work and didn't want to be disturbed. Alex sulked in her bedroom with Derek.

Kate wasn't sure what to do. Carry on as normal, she supposed. Whatever normal was now.

At least she could spare Finn an awkward conversation, she decided, and quietly moved all her things out of his room and back into her own before he had to ask her to do it. She made up her old bed and changed Finn's sheets. Now they could pretend that nothing had ever happened.

Finn didn't notice until later that night when he had said goodnight to a still sullen Alex. He came downstairs to find Kate wiping down the cooker and trying not to think about what she was going to do next.

'You've moved your things,' he said abruptly.

'Yes, I...I thought it would be easier that way.'

'Easier?' Finn repeated as if he didn't understand the word.

'We agreed that we would only sleep together until Stella left,' Kate made herself say.

'I know we did, but—' Finn stopped, thinking better of what he had been about to say. 'Yes, you're right of course,' he said stiffly instead. 'There's no reason to carry on now that she's gone.'

'No,' she said bleakly.

There was an uncomfortable silence while the air between them churned with things left unsaid.

'It was just a temporary thing,' said Kate to reassure him that she understood and wasn't going to make a fuss.

'Yes.'

Another agonising pause.

Kate wrung out the cloth she had been using to wipe the hob and fixed on a bright smile. 'I'd better think about what I'm going to do next,' she said, setting about the draining board. Anything other than look at Finn and having to resist the impulse to throw herself into his arms and beg him to let her stay.

'Do you know what you want to do?'

Stay with you and Alex. 'No,' said Kate instead, 'but I'm sure I'll find something. I can always go back to temping.'

Finn took a turn about the kitchen. 'I don't suppose you would consider staying on, would you?' he asked suddenly, as if the words had been forced out of him against his will.

Kate's heart lurched into her throat and she had to swallow hard before she could speak. 'I thought you were going to try and manage without a housekeeper?'

'That was the idea—it was what Alex wanted—but it's going to be difficult. Rosa's definitely not coming back and...well, the truth is that I've been thinking about what Stella said,' he went on in a rush. 'Alex does need a woman here and she likes you. She's just been begging me to ask you to stay.'

He stopped. 'Would you think about it?'

Kate twisted the cloth between her hands. She wanted to stay, but would she be able to bear just being a housekeeper now?

'I don't know,' she said hesitantly. 'I don't think I could be a housekeeper for ever.'

'I was thinking more about you being a wife,' said Finn.

Kate's head jerked up to stare at him incredulously. 'A *wife*?'

'I don't seem to be putting this very well.' Finn raked a hand through his hair with a sigh. 'I'm trying to ask if you'll marry me.'

Kate opened her mouth and then closed it again. 'But... *Why*?' she managed at last.

'It seems sensible,' he said. 'It would solve the problem of finding someone to look after that dog for a start!'

'Oh, well, that seems like a good enough reason!'

'Seriously,' he said, 'Alex likes you. She's never been prepared to even consider the idea of having a stepmother before, but you...you're different. I think she'd be happy if you were here as a housekeeper, but she'd feel much more secure knowing that you would always be there for her.'

Kate looked at him, her brown eyes very clear. 'How would *you* feel?'

'I'd be happy, too,' said Finn, meeting her gaze. 'We've got on well these last few weeks, haven't we?'

Kate thought about the long, sweet nights, about waking to his lips on her shoulder, about being able to turn in the dark and run her hands over his lean, hard body. 'Yes,' she agreed huskily. 'Yes, we have.'

'It would mean you wouldn't have to go back to temping. Of course you could get a job if that's what you wanted to do, but you've always said that you're not that interested in a career, and you're much better at making a home than at being a secretary.'

Finn seemed determined to outline all the advantages for her, as if she couldn't work them out for herself. 'It might not be very romantic,' he told Kate, 'but there are worse reasons for getting married than comfort and security.'

True, thought Kate, but she had always imagined getting married for the best reasons. She had managed to crumple the dishcloth into a tight ball, and she bit her lip as she went back to wiping around the sink.

'What about Isabel?' she asked.

Finn hesitated. 'I think she would understand. She would want what was best for Alex, and that's what I want too.'

So he wasn't even going to pretend that he was marrying her for love, thought Kate, mindlessly wiping. Perhaps it was better that way. She wouldn't have believed him if he'd tried to convince her that he wanted her for more than practical reasons.

It was funny, she thought wistfully. You could dream and dream about something but somehow when it came true it was never quite as you had imagined it.

Be careful what you wish for, she reminded herself with a wry inward smile, or you just might get it. Only a few minutes ago, she had longed for Finn to ask her to marry him, and now he had. What was the point now in wishing that she could have his heart as well? She had known all along that it would always belong to Isabel.

Folding the cloth, she laid it carefully on the draining board. 'Can I think about it?' she asked Finn, amazed at her own calm.

'Of course.' Finn was a bit disconcerted by her self-possession as well. Not surprising, given how eagerly she had always responded to him. He must have thought that she would jump at the chance, Kate thought. 'I don't want to push you into something you don't feel comfortable with,' he said.

Kate looked at him. The only thing that would make her comfortable right then would be for him to put his arms around her, and tell her that he wanted her to stay, not for his daughter, not for his dog, but for him.

But you could only have so many dreams come true in a day, couldn't you?

She smiled at him a little remotely. 'I think I'll go to bed,' she said. 'It's been a long day.'

Finn watched her as she went to the door. 'Kate,' he said abruptly, and she turned.

'Yes?'

'I...' Whatever it was, he changed his mind. 'Nothing,' he said.

'*Marry* him?' Bella stared across the table at Kate. The three of them were sitting in their favourite bar where Kate had called them to an urgent case conference the following evening. 'You're not seriously considering it, are you, Kate? *Are* you?' she added suspiciously before slumping back in her chair and shaking her head. 'You are!'

'Well, I've been thinking about it,' said Kate with a shade of defiance. All night and all day, in fact. She hadn't been able to think about anything else since Finn's proposal.

'I know it's not the kind of marriage we all dream about, but we can't all have the perfect romance like Phoebe. I bet I wouldn't be the first woman to compromise on the starry-eyed stuff,' she said defensively. 'There might be other things that would make up for all that.'

'Like what?'

'Respect…liking…giving a little girl love and security…'

'You wouldn't be marrying Alex—or the dog, before you drag him into it,' Phoebe pointed out astringently. 'Of course marriage is about compromise, but not about something so important and especially not for a born romantic like you. I think you'd need to know that Finn loved you to be happy.'

'You've changed your tune, haven't you?' said Kate, cross with her friends for filling her mind with doubts again just when she thought she had made up her mind. 'You were the one trying to set me up with Finn in the first place.'

'We thought you'd be good together, and you would, but not unless Finn really is over Isabel. Of course he won't forget her, but he needs to move on. He needs to want you for yourself, not just as a glorified housekeeper.' Phoebe leant forward seriously. 'You can't go through life believing that you'll always be second-best as far as he's concerned.'

It would be better than going through life without him, thought Kate. She had lain awake long into the night, missing Finn beside her and envisaging the days and weeks and months and *years* ahead when he wouldn't be there. If she married him, she would at least have him physically. They might have children, and that would bring them closer. She might never have what Isabel had, but she would have *something*. That would be better than nothing, surely?

'You deserve the best, Kate,' said Phoebe. 'Second-best isn't good enough for you.'

'I think it might be,' said Kate.

Phoebe and Bella did their best to caution her against making a terrible mistake, but the more Kate thought about it, the more marrying Finn seemed the right decision. Their marriage might not be perfect, but at least this way she would be able to see him and touch him. Alex would be there, too. They could be a family.

And what, after all, was her alternative? Bella might say that she would meet someone else, but Kate didn't want anyone else. She only wanted Finn. The thought of life without him, with nothing to do except miss him, was too awful to contemplate.

Finn was waiting up for her when she got home. 'I've been thinking about what you said last night,' Kate said baldly as she watched him fill the kettle and set it to boil for tea.

He turned, grey eyes suddenly alert. 'About marrying me?'

'Yes.'

'And?'

'And...' Kate opened her mouth to tell him that she would marry him when she suddenly realised that she couldn't do it, and she stopped. She couldn't live with him and not tell him that she loved him. It had been hard enough up to now. Could she really spend years not being completely honest about how she felt?

'I was going to say yes,' she told him honestly, 'but I've

just realised that it wouldn't be fair on either of us.' Slowly she drew the ring he had bought her off her finger and laid it on the table.

'I thought I could go with all the sensible reasons,' she said. 'I told myself that they were good enough reasons to get married without love, but I think now that they won't be. We nearly made a terrible mistake, Finn,' she said, meeting his eyes squarely. 'I think it's better if I go.'

Finn looked bleaker than Kate had ever seen him, but he didn't try to persuade her. 'Alex will be disappointed,' was all he said.

Alex was more than disappointed. Devastated would have been a better description of her reaction when Kate told her that she was leaving. 'But you said you would stay for ever!' she wailed. 'You promised!'

Finn's face was drawn. 'She had to say that while Stella was here, but you knew the situation all along. You knew Kate was just pretending.'

'She shouldn't have said it if she didn't mean it!' Alex burst into tears, and rushed out of the room.

Kate was close to tears herself by that stage. 'Shall I go after her and try and explain?'

'No, leave her,' said Finn wearily. 'She'll come round.' He pinched the bridge of his nose between his finger and thumb. 'I just hope she doesn't make the new housekeeper's life hell. She's more than capable of it.'

In fact, when the agency sent along a new girl a couple of days later, Alex went out of her way to be nice to her, and punished Kate by ignoring her completely. Megan was an Australian on a working holiday. She was friendly and competent, with a very pretty, open face. Kate tried to be pleased that she was going to fit in so well, but her heart cracked with misery and jealousy as she packed her case.

Finn had said that he would drive her back to Tooting. He asked Alex if she wanted to come, but she shook her head in an offhand way and said that she would rather stay with Megan. At the last minute, though, she rushed out to the car as Kate was about to get in and threw her arms around Kate's waist to hug her tightly.

'Goodbye,' she said in a cracked little voice, and then, without looking at Kate directly, she ran inside again.

Kate's throat was so tight that she could hardly speak, and the tears rolled down her cheeks as she got into the car. She wiped them away with the back of her hand.

'She will miss you, you know,' said Finn apologetically. 'She's just upset.'

'I know. I'll miss her too.'

'Perhaps you could come and see us sometime,' he suggested. 'You could check that we're looking after that dog properly.'

At the moment the prospect felt as if it would be too much to bear. 'Perhaps,' she said.

It was all Kate could do not to howl as they drove away from the house. She felt as if a great weight was crushing her. Why, why, why had she chosen to leave? She should have stayed and then there would be no nice, pretty, friendly Megan for Finn to go home to, to get to know, to make part of his life.

Heartsick, Kate let Finn drive her back to her old life. He carried her case into the house from the car, and upstairs to her bedroom, while Kate lingered reluctantly in the hall. She had always liked this house, but with Bella out it felt cold and lonely. Like her life was going to be from now on.

She was dreading the moment when she would have to say goodbye to Finn, but trying to keep her composure was such agony that she almost wished he would go. 'Thank you,' she said as he came down the stairs. Her voice was hard and tight, the only way she could speak without crying.

Finn seemed very close to her in the narrow hallway. Kate edged towards the front door.

'I should go,' he said, but he didn't move. For once he seemed at a loss to know what to do next.

'Yes,' said Kate. 'Alex will be waiting for you.'

He squeezed past her to turn to her on the doorstep. Kate gazed at him hungrily, as if storing up the memory of his stern face, and that mouth...she might never see him again, she thought in panic.

'Thank you for everything, Kate,' Finn said stiffly, and as if on an impulse leant forward to kiss her on the cheek.

It was only the briefest of touches, the mere grazing of cheeks, but Kate closed her eyes with longing. Instinctively, her hands lifted to his chest to cling to his shirt. 'Goodbye,' she whispered as she kissed his cheek in return.

They looked at each other for a long, desperate moment, and then her hands fell. Finn turned without another word and walked along the pavement to his car. He opened the door and, with one last look back at Kate, he got in and drove away, leaving her desolate and alone in the doorway.

One thing about misery, it made for a great diet. The weight fell off Kate as she struggled through the next few days, but she was too unhappy to appreciate the way her clothes had started to hang off her. She had signed on with an agency, but there were no jobs as yet, which was a pity. Money wasn't a problem after the generous cheque Finn had given her, but not working left her with too much time to think.

Too much time to remember.

Too much time to ache with longing for Finn and the life she had thrown away.

'You've done the right thing,' Bella tried to reassure her. 'I know it's hard, but it's better for Finn to deal with his feelings for Isabel first. He needs closure on that.'

'Closure? What does that mean?'

'It means he has to decide himself that it's time to accept her death and move on. Once he's done that, he can think about his feelings for you.'

'I don't think he has any,' said Kate drearily.

'In that case, it's just as well you didn't marry him, isn't it?'

Kate knew that Bella was right. All the reasons why marrying Finn would have been a bad idea circled endlessly in her brain, but none of them stopped her wishing that she was back in the house in Wimbledon, with Finn coming back from work, wrenching at his tie as he came into the kitchen. Alex would be sitting at the table doing her homework, and Derek would have picked the most inconvenient spot to lie as usual, so that she tripped over him whenever she moved.

The image of them all was so vivid, and her need to be there so acute that Kate pillowed her head in her arms and wept all over again. At the other end of the table, the cat stared contemptuously at her. It had already learnt to distrust the sound of crying which usually meant that the humans would be too preoccupied to think about feeding him.

Kate hadn't thought that it was possible to cry this much. She kept waiting to run out of tears, but after five days there was still no sign of them drying up. Her eyes were permanently red and puffy, and whenever she caught sight of her reflection she recoiled at how awful she looked. No wonder no one would give her a job! What was the point of being thin like this if the rest of you looked so frightful?

Bella put an arm around Kate's shoulders. 'Oh, Kate...' she sighed. 'What are we going to do with you?'

'I don't know,' wept Kate. 'I don't know what to do with myself either!'

'I've asked Phoebe to come round,' said Bella. 'You know how good she is in a crisis. Ah! That'll be her now,' she added as the doorbell went. 'I'll go and let her in. She's bound to be able to sort you out.'

Kate didn't even bother to lift her head. She loved Phoebe dearly, but there was nothing her friend could do about her raw, sore heart. Only Finn could make that better.

'Kate?'

That wasn't Phoebe. Kate stilled, her head still buried in her arms and her hair spilling out over the table where the cat toyed with a few strands in a bored way. It had sounded like Finn's voice. She must be imagining things.

'Kate!' A definite note of exasperation had crept into the voice, the faintly irritable edge that could only belong to Finn.

Very, very slowly Kate lifted her head. Finn was standing there, watching her with hard, anxious grey eyes. She stared at him, hardly able to believe that he was real, that he was *there*.

It was definitely him. Nobody else had that austere face or that mouth that made her melt just thinking about what it could do to her. But he didn't look quite the way he had done whenever she had fantasised about seeing him again. In her imagination, the sight of her had started a smile in his eyes which would slowly illuminate his face as he held out his arms to her.

This was real life, not a fantasy. She could tell by the fact that he wasn't smiling and his expression was one of puzzled irritation.

'Didn't you hear me?' Not *my darling*, or *I can't live without you*.

'Yes, but I didn't think it could be you,' said Kate obscurely.

The faint frown between his brows deepened. 'Are you all right?'

Kate knuckled the tears away from under her eyes. Why did he have to turn up now, when she was looking at her worst? The spurt of resentment was invigorating. After all her dreaming and longing to see him again, he was finally here refusing to follow the script!

'Do I look all right?' she asked tartly.

'You look terrible.'

'Sorry, but I've never mastered the art of blubbing gracefully.' Kate sniffed and blew her nose on a tissue.

It was strange. Part of her was really quite cross with Finn for catching her unawares and being so obtuse about the state she was in, but the rest of her was unashamedly joyful just to see him again. It was as if all her senses had suddenly woken up from a leaden sleep and started carrying on like cheerleaders, high-kicking and shaking pompoms about with sheer exhilaration.

Finn pulled out the chair beside her and sat down. 'What are you crying about?'

'What do you think?' asked Kate almost rudely.

'Is it Seb?'

'*Seb*?' It was so long since she'd given Seb a second thought that it took Kate a moment to work out who he was talking about. 'No, of course not.' She scrubbed a tissue under her eyes. 'Why would I be crying about Seb?'

'You told me that you loved him once,' said Finn. 'I thought that maybe when you said that you couldn't marry me without love you were thinking about him. I was afraid you might be hoping to get back together with him, and that it hadn't worked out.'

It was so far from the truth that Kate made a hiccuping sound between a sob and a laugh. She shook her head. 'No, I wasn't crying about Seb.'

'Then why?'

Kate didn't answer. 'What are you doing here, Finn?' she asked instead.

'I wanted to see you,' he said simply.

Blowing her nose again, she drew a jagged breath. 'Don't tell me Megan hasn't worked out. She seemed so suitable.'

'She's fine, but she's a bit bored with us,' said Finn. 'I think she would like to move on to somewhere more exciting.'

'She's bored with you?' echoed Kate, finding it hard to imagine.

'None of us is much company at the moment,' he told her. 'We're all miserable.' He paused. 'We all miss you.'

Kate stopped in the middle of wiping the tell-tale evidence of tears from her cheeks. 'You do?'

'Alex cries herself to sleep at night, the dog is pining, and as for me...' Finn shook his head. 'I miss you more than either of them,' he said.

Kate's heart began to thud. 'Really?' she asked huskily.

'Really.' He turned in his chair to face her. 'Do you remember when Stella left, she told Alex to make sure that I didn't do anything stupid? Well, I did something stupid. I didn't tell you how I really felt about you.'

'Why not?' said Kate, hardly daring to breathe.

'I was afraid you would think that I was too old and intense for you. You always seemed like so much fun. I couldn't believe that you would really be interested in someone like me. I kept remembering what you'd told me about Seb, and even if you hadn't wanted him again, it was obvious that a younger man like that—or that financial analyst of yours!—was going to be much more your type.

'I couldn't bear the thought of you leaving, though, so I tried to persuade you to stay by making it seem more like a job. And that really was stupid, as my dear sister explained to me at length,' he finished acidly.

'Stella knows about us not really being engaged?'

'She does now. Alex rang her and told her that I had been stupid just as she had warned. The next thing I knew I had my sister on the phone, demanding the full story and wanting to know why I had thrown away my best chance of happiness in years. I said that I had asked you to marry me and that you had refused, but it didn't take her long to prise the whole truth out of me. She couldn't believe what a mess I'd made of it. "For an intelligent man," she said, "you sure are stupid!"'

Kate gave a watery smile. She could practically hear Stella saying it.

'She told me that I should come back and tell you everything I'd left out before,' Finn said. 'So here I am.'

He looked down at his hands, and then straight into Kate's eyes, which were still red and swollen with tears, but shining now with hope. 'Can I tell you now, or would it make you uncomfortable?'

Kate swallowed the lump in her throat. 'No, I'd like to hear it.'

'I didn't tell you how much I love you,' he said. 'I didn't tell you how empty the house would feel without you. How empty my *life* would be without you.'

Taking her hands in both of his own, he held them tightly. 'I can manage the school run. I can walk the dog, and sort out the cooking and the cleaning. I can manage all of that, but I can't manage without you. And I want to do more than just manage. I want to be able to wake up and find you beside me. I want to come home and find you there.' He paused. 'I didn't tell you how much I need you, Kate,' he said in a low voice.

The cat chose this moment to yawn widely and stand up, presenting its bottom to their faces, and then sitting with a glare of affront when it failed to provoke the usual reaction.

There was a glow starting deep inside Kate, spreading out to every pore. Her fingers were curling around his. 'What about Isabel?' she asked as she had asked before.

'I loved Isabel,' he said quietly. 'Nothing can change that, but I don't feel as if part of my life is missing any more. I never expected to fall in love again,' he told Kate. 'I thought I'd had my chance at love, and that I'd never get another chance at that kind of happiness, and then you came along and turned my life upside down. You made me happy again.'

His fingers tightened around hers. 'You're not a replacement for Isabel,' he said. 'I never wanted anyone to be that. You're *you*, and it's you I need.'

The grey eyes were warm and serious as they looked into Kate's. 'If I had said all that to you when I asked you to marry me, would your answer have been different?'

'Yes,' said Kate.

'So if I asked you again now...?'

Her eyes shimmered with tears. 'I'll say yes,' she promised.

Then there was no more talking and Finn had pulled her into his lap and was kissing her so hungrily that Kate thought that she would pass out with happiness.

They might have stayed like that for hours if not interrupted by the cat, who was tired of being ignored and took a swipe at Finn's arm.

Jerking it back, Finn inspected the scratch. 'What did he do that for?'

'He's just looking for attention,' said Kate consolingly. 'He didn't mean to hurt you.'

'Well, he'll have to learn that I've got more important things to attend to at the moment,' said Finn, gathering Kate back into his arms, only to pause as a thought occurred to him. 'I hope he's not coming with you?' he asked in a voice of foreboding.

'I'm afraid so,' said Kate. 'I can't ask Bella to look after him. He won't be any trouble.'

Finn looked down at the scratch on his arm. 'I suppose the house is going to be taken over entirely by waifs and strays now,' he pretended to grumble, but he was smiling as he kissed his way along her jaw.

'Will you mind?' she asked, winding her arms around his neck.

'Not if you're there.'

Kate turned her head to meet his lips for a long sweet kiss. 'At least Stella will be happy now,' she sighed happily when they broke apart at last and she rested her head on his shoulder.

'Oh, no, she won't! You wait,' said Finn. 'We'll just get the wedding over, and she'll be nagging us about Alex needing a brother or sister.'

Kate laughed and kissed him again. 'I don't mind seeing what we can do about that,' she said.

'Anything to shut my sister up?'

'Anything,' said Kate.

A WHIRLWIND ENGAGEMENT

For Sally

CHAPTER ONE

'THERE'S Bella.' Aisling nudged Josh, and he turned in the pew to see Bella and Phoebe hurrying down the aisle.

As befitted best friends of the bride, they had pulled out all the stops. Phoebe was dark and striking in an acid-yellow suit, while Bella had gone for a more romantic look in what Josh inexpertly assessed as a floaty pink number, with a spectacular hat that was clearly intended to knock all the others in the congregation into the shade.

Josh didn't pretend to know about such things, but even he could see that she had probably succeeded. Even Aisling's hat, which had made him raise his brows when he first saw it that morning, seemed tame in comparison. Typical Bella, he thought affectionately. She had always had the ability to turn heads, with or without a hat.

Phoebe waved as she spotted Josh and Aisling, and pointed Bella in their direction before heading up to have a word with her husband, Gib, who was best man and waiting with a very nervous Finn in the front pew.

Josh saw Bella register his presence, and an odd expression flitted over her face. It even seemed to him that she hesitated before sliding into the pew beside them, and his brows drew together slightly. Bella was his best friend, but she had been oddly distant recently.

'Sorry I can't kiss you,' she said, indicating the enormous brim of her hat. 'This isn't designed for close contact.'

'Yes, it is a bit awkward, isn't it?' Josh ducked underneath to kiss her cheek, anyway, and was sure he felt her tense at the touch of his lips.

He frowned as he drew back. 'Is everything OK?'

'Yes, of course,' said Bella, but he noticed that she didn't meet his eyes as she leant round him to greet Aisling. 'You know what weddings are like,' she went on, sitting back. 'There's always some last-minute panic when things get a bit tense.'

Just a fraught morning, then, thought Josh, telling himself that explained the unusual brittleness of her smile. 'How is Kate?'

'A bit jittery, but she'll be fine. She should be here any minute.'

On his other side, Aisling leant forward to talk across him. 'I'm surprised you're not Kate's bridesmaid, Bella,' she said. 'You are her best friend, after all.'

'So is Phoebe.' Bella's tone was cool. 'And Kate's not very tall. She'd look ridiculous with both of us towering over her.'

'Yes, but Phoebe's married.'

'So?'

'So as the only unmarried friend left, it would have been quite natural if Kate had chosen you as her bridesmaid,' Aisling tried to explain.

'Oh, I think I'm a bit old for that, don't you?' said Bella pleasantly enough, but sitting between the two women Josh could feel a distinct undercurrent of tension.

'I wouldn't have thought so,' said Aisling. 'You can't be much more than thirty-five, surely?'

Josh cleared his throat and shifted in the pew. Aisling was treading on dangerous ground. Bella was very sensitive about her age for some unfathomable reason.

Glancing sideways, he saw Bella's blue eyes narrow beneath the brim of her hat. 'Not quite,' she said thinly. 'As it happens, I'm only thirty-two.'

And she shot a glance at Josh which said more clearly than words ever could that he wasn't even to *think* about adding 'nearly thirty-three'.

'Really?' Aisling was tactlessly surprised. 'I always thought you'd be more Josh's age since you were students together.'

'No, Josh was a bit older than the rest of us when he started,' said Bella grittily, and Josh decided it was time to change the subject.

'Is Kate not having any bridesmaids then?' he asked hurriedly.

'Alex is going to have the starring role all to herself. Alex is Finn's daughter,' Bella added for Aisling's benefit. 'She's absolutely thrilled—more excited than Kate, I think! She couldn't stand still while we were helping Kate get ready.'

She smiled at the memory. 'It's much more appropriate for Kate to have her stepdaughter, and anyway, if I'd been bridesmaid I wouldn't have been able to wear this hat!'

'And that would have been a crime,' said Josh solemnly.

Bella adjusted the hat on her head, and sent him a speculative glance from beneath the brim. 'What do you think of it?' she asked him.

'It's...very...big,' was the most diplomatic thing he could come up with.

She laughed and for a moment it was the old Bella beside him, her face vivid and the bright blue eyes alight with laughter. It made Josh realise how much he had missed her recently.

Not that he hadn't seen her, but somehow she just hadn't been herself. Their friendship had always been such an easy one, but recently Bella had been strangely constrained. Something was wrong, and Josh didn't like it. She had lost her sparkle, and he missed it.

Of course, she might be having problems with Will but he had seen Bella through more romantic crises than he cared to remember, and it had never affected her relationship with *him* before.

Maybe it was different this time. Maybe Will was more important to her than all the others.

For some reason, Josh didn't like that thought very much. Will wasn't nearly good enough for Bella in his opinion.

'Where's Will?' he asked trying not to betray his dislike of the other man. 'I was expecting him to be keeping a pew for you.'

Bella had picked up the order of service and was studying the front, which was embossed simply with the names Kate and Finn, and the date, 6th September. 'Will?' she said a little too casually. 'He's in Hong Kong.'

'Hong Kong!' Josh scowled. 'What's he doing there?'

'He's got a meeting,' said Bella, opening the order of service to look at the hymns.

Josh snorted contemptuously. 'When did he arrange that?'

'It came up at the last minute.'

'Couldn't he have arranged to go next week? He must have known about Kate's wedding for ages.'

Bella kept her eyes on the order of service. 'Yes, but this was important,' she said, sounding reticent. 'There was some kind of crisis and he had to drop everything and go.'

'You're important, too,' said Josh angrily.

That was typical of Will! Swanking off to the other side of the world instead of supporting Bella. Josh had always thought him a prat of the first order, and this just confirmed it.

He couldn't understand why Bella always went for men like Will. They were too smooth by half, in Josh's opinion. Will was suave and handsome and drove a Porsche, but he didn't impress Josh. When the chips were down, Will wasn't a man you could rely on, and his attitude to Bella just proved it.

'It's not as if he's a brain surgeon,' he went on pugnaciously. 'He doesn't *do* anything. He just sits in some plush office in the City and plays around with money. What's important about that?'

'It's his career,' said Bella, tight-lipped. 'And he doesn't just "play around" with money. He deals with millions and millions of pounds, and when something goes wrong with that kind of money, it can affect the international money markets which affect economies around the world, which affect our jobs and our income and our quality of life. I think that's important,' she finished defiantly.

Josh wasn't ready to be convinced that Will had any useful contribution to make to society. 'If I thought the economic stability of the world rested on Will's ability to rush off to Hong Kong at the drop of a hat, I'd be really scared,' he said. 'As it is, I suspect that the global economy wouldn't so much as totter if he'd left it until Monday instead so that he could be with you today.'

Bella glared at him. 'Look, what's your problem? If I understand why Will can't be here, and Kate understands, and Finn understands, I don't see why *you* can't!'

'I just think he should be here to support you,' said Josh stubbornly.

'I don't need support! I'm at the wedding of one of my dearest friends, surrounded by people who know me. Why would I need supporting?'

'I think Josh is concerned that you might be feeling a bit left out,' Aisling put in unwisely. 'He's told me how close you were to Phoebe and Kate when you all shared that house, and now they've both married and are moving on. I can see it might be quite a vulnerable time for you,' she finished with a sympathetic look.

Bella shot her a glance of dislike. 'If you're trying to suggest that I'm jealous, you're quite wrong,' she said clearly. 'I couldn't be happier for Kate, and for Phoebe. They've both found the perfect man for them, but I don't feel at all *left out*, as you put it, because I happen to have found the perfect man for me too. Will and I are very happy together, so I don't feel the slightest bit vulnerable or in need of support, thank you very much!'

'You don't seem very happy, Bella,' said Josh.

'That might have something to do with fact that my best friend and his girlfriend are busy slagging off my boyfriend and making me feel that I need to be pitied in some way!' she snapped back. 'Would that make *you* happy?'

Josh opened his mouth, but before he could reply Phoebe was scrambling into the pew beside Bella. 'Here she comes!' she said, blowing a kiss in Josh's direction and moving Bella along with a shove of her hip as the organ struck up the 'Bridal March'.

Bella found herself pressed against Josh, and expressed her feelings with a vigorous shove of her own which sent him shuffling into Aisling, who ended up squeezed against a pillar.

Not very dignified behaviour for a wedding, perhaps, but it made Bella feel a whole lot better.

Turning, Bella watched Kate coming slowly up the aisle on her beaming father's arm, and her throat tightened. It was such a cliché to describe a bride as radiant, but it really was the perfect word for Kate that day. Everything about her seemed to shine, and the brown eyes fixed on the man waiting for her at the altar were luminous with love.

Bella followed Kate's gaze and looked at Finn, who had turned and was watching his bride walk towards him. The expression on his face made her want to cry.

Would anyone ever look at *her* with that kind of desire? Bella wondered. She tried to imagine herself in Kate's place, but somehow she couldn't picture the man who would be waiting for her.

It wasn't going to be Will, anyway, in spite of what she had told Josh and Aisling. Aisling! What a stupid name, thought Bella. Apparently it was supposed to be pronounced Ashling, but she always made a point of saying it just as it was spelt, just to annoy. There was just something about Aisling that rubbed her up the wrong way.

Guiltily aware that she should be thinking about the fact that Kate and Finn were getting married at last, Bella hurriedly fixed her eyes on the bride and groom.

Kate had turned and was giving her bouquet to Alex, who was bursting with pride at her important role. Her tongue stuck out with concentration as she stepped back with the precious flowers, but when Finn winked at his daughter, her face lit up with a dazzling smile that brought tears to Bella's eyes.

It was a traditional country wedding in the village church, and Bella found herself absurdly moved by the familiar ceremony. She and Phoebe were not the only ones who spent most of the service wiping their eyes, and when the earlier clouds dissolved letting Kate and Finn emerge from the rose-edged porch into brilliant sunshine, they looked so right together that Bella started to cry all over again.

'This is awful,' she wept to Phoebe. 'I haven't cried this much since *Terms of Endearment*!'

'I know,' Phoebe sniffed. 'They just look so *happy*!'

'What's wrong with you two?' demanded Josh. 'Weddings are supposed to be joyful occasions!'

'It's a woman thing,' Gib told him knowledgeably. 'Apparently snivelling like this means they're having a good time. They'll be all right when they get some champagne inside them!'

Aisling wasn't crying, Bella couldn't help noticing. No fear of *her* mascara running! Instead she clung to Josh's arm looking cool and pretty in a simple aquamarine shift with an annoyingly stylish hat. Bella had been so pleased with her own hat, but next to Aisling's she was suddenly convinced that it seemed over-the-top and ridiculous.

Everything about Aisling made her feel that way. Where Aisling was quietly confident, she was loud. Aisling was elegant, she was blowsy. Aisling knew how to put up a tent and abseil down a cliff, she was city girl incarnate.

Aisling was perfect for Josh, in fact, and she was just his friend.

Bella turned quickly away and pinned on a bright smile to watch the photographs being taken. Gib had organised it well, and after the inevitable family groups, they moved rapidly onto photos of friends with the bride and groom. There was one of them with Kate's original housemates, Caro and Phoebe and Bella, with Caro and Phoebe's husbands, of course.

And then there was Kate and Finn with their close friends and partners, which meant Phoebe and Gib, Josh and Aisling, and Bella.

Bella was very conscious of being on her own in both photos. It was a new experience for her. She had always been the one with a boyfriend, while Phoebe and Kate moaned about the lack of men, so it was ironic that she should be the odd one out now.

Not that Bella had any intention of giving Aisling the

satisfaction of thinking that it bothered her. She kept a smile fixed to her face, and laughed and chatted animatedly as the last photographs were taken and the entire party walked back through the village to where a marquee had been erected in the garden of Kate's parents.

She thought she was putting on a pretty good show of not having a care in the world, but it didn't seem to fool Josh. Sometimes he knew her too well, thought Bella with an inward sigh, wishing he would stop asking if something was wrong. She didn't want to tell him that she was feeling edgy and unsettled, because then he would ask why, and she didn't know why.

Only that wasn't *quite* true, was it? She did know.

It was something to do with the way Aisling's arrival on the scene had brought her up short. Something to do with looking across the table at that engagement dinner for Kate and realising that Josh was no longer the familiar, slightly geeky student she had known for so long.

For Bella, it had been like finding herself suddenly face to face with a stranger. There was nothing obvious about Josh. He had a quiet, ordinary face, ordinary blue-grey eyes, ordinary brown hair, she had always known that.

But she had never before noticed how he had thickened out and grown into his looks, or how the fourteen years they had known each other had given him a solid, reassuring presence and an air of calm competence that was impressive without being intimidating.

She had never noticed his mouth before or his hands or throat or that line of his jaw. Never noticed that he had a great body. He wasn't exceptionally tall but he was lean and compactly muscled, and he moved with an easy, loose-limbed stride.

And now that she *had* noticed, Bella couldn't stop noticing.

It made her uneasy. This was *Josh*. Her best friend, the one who had seen her through endless romantic ups and downs. She had cried on his shoulder and laughed and talked and hugged him without a thought for more than ten years now. He had seen her without her make-up, seen her tired and cross and sick and hungover, and she had taken him for granted. Being with Josh had been like being with Kate or Phoebe, as comfortable as an old pair of slippers.

But now, suddenly, she didn't feel comfortable with him any more and she didn't understand why. She just wanted to go back to the way things had been before.

Here he was now. Bella felt her nerves crisp as Josh came up to her in the marquee, and she took a steadying slug of champagne. He was the same old Josh he had always been. It was nonsense to think that anything had changed between them.

'Are you OK?' he said, eyeing her with concern.

'Of course. Why?'

'You seem a bit tense, that's all. I wondered if you and Will might be having problems.'

'I don't know why you're so determined that my relationship with Will is a disaster,' said Bella, annoyed with him for hitting the nail so unerringly on the head. 'What could be wrong? Will's fantastic. He's incredibly attractive, generous, clever, successful…'

And he *was*, she reminded herself with a kind of desperation. She had been mad about Will when she first met him. Why couldn't she feel like that again?

'I'm just missing him while he's away,' she offered, hoping that the explanation would stop Josh probing any further. 'And the house feels very empty without Kate now.'

'It must do.' To her relief, Josh allowed himself to be diverted. 'Are you going to stay there on your own?'

'I think so. I only pay a token rent as it is. Phoebe doesn't need the money—one of the many advantages of having a rich husband!—so I can afford to have the house to myself.'

'I'm surprised you don't move in with Will if he's as perfect as you say he is,' sniffed Josh. 'Doesn't he want to "commit"?' he added, hooking sarcastic inverted commas around the word.

'That's good coming from you!' said Bella, provoked out of her awkwardness. 'You've never committed to anyone!'

'I'm just waiting for the right woman,' he said loftily.

'No, you're not,' she said. 'You're scared to take a risk.'

Josh's jaw dropped. 'How can you *say* that, Bella?'

'Yes, yes, I know that you've taken convoys through war zones and rescued people off mountains in blizzards and all that stuff,' she said with a dismissive wave of her hand.

Before he set up his own company to provide executive training a couple of years ago Josh had provided logistical support for expeditions. Most of them were providing disaster relief but sometimes he would organise fund-raising expeditions for the aid agencies he dealt with. Bella had never been able to understand why someone would want to pay good money to be tired and cold and terrified for a month, but they had always proved very popular.

'I know you've been in loads of dangerous situations,' she went on, 'but those are physical risks. Have you ever taken any other kind of risk?'

'It was risky setting up my own company,' said Josh, sounding a bit huffy.

Bella was unimpressed. 'That was a financial risk. I'm talking about emotional risks.'

Josh hunched a shoulder. 'You have to approach all risks the same way. Look at the situation logically, not emotionally, and balance the likelihood of possible outcomes.'

When he went all logical on her like that, Bella always wondered how on earth they had come to be friends. Mentally, she raised her eyes to heaven.

'It just so happens that as far as relationships are concerned I've never been convinced that the risk was worth taking,' he was saying, 'but it's not a question of being *scared*.'

The scared thing had obviously rankled.

'We're not all like you,' he accused her, 'investing everything in a relationship five minutes after you've met a man. You'd think experience would have taught you to keep something back, but no! You're barely over one disastrous affair before you plunge into another one!'

'Better that than dithering around on the edge for ever, wondering if you might just have missed the chance of a perfect relationship,' Bella retorted.

'And that's what you've got with Will, is it?' Josh asked sceptically.

She lifted her chin defiantly. 'I think so, yes.'

'So why not live together?'

'Because we're both happy as we are. We've each got our own place to live and that means we can give each other some space. We all need that.'

Josh didn't bother to hide his disbelief. 'You? You're the most sociable person I know! I can't see you hankering after your own space.'

'Perhaps you don't know me as well as you think you do,' said Bella crossly. 'As a matter of fact, I'm looking forward to living on my own. I've been getting gradually used to it since Kate has been spending so much time with Finn and Alex, so it won't be that different now. I might go back to sharing eventually,' she conceded, 'but it wouldn't be the same. Where would I find someone I'd get on with as well as Phoebe and Kate?'

'What about Aisling?' said Josh casually.

Bella looked wary. What *about* Aisling?

'She's looking for somewhere to live at the moment,' he explained. 'And you'd be bound to get on. I'd have thought she'd be perfect for you.'

What planet was he living on? Bella stared at him in disbelief. He didn't really see her and Aisling as bosom buddies, did he? Didn't he know her at all?

'I'm not sure we've got that much in common,' she said carefully.

Josh looked surprised. 'Don't you? I think you're very alike. Aisling's in marketing and you're in PR—they're not that different as careers go, are they? And she's a bit of a social butterfly, too.'

'I thought she spent her whole time climbing mountains or knocking up rafts out of a couple of tin cans and a piece of string?' said Bella a little sourly.

'She's got a lot of expedition experience,' Josh agreed, 'but she's a good-time girl like you on the side as well.'

Oh, right. So Aisling swung both ways. She could hack her way through a rainforest *and* wear lipstick. Bully for her. Bella took another slurp of champagne.

'She's not quite such a princess as you, though,' Josh was adding with something less than his usual tact. 'She doesn't actually require somewhere to plug in her hairdryer when she's camping!'

Bella eyed him with some hostility. Josh had once insisted on taking her camping in the Yorkshire Dales, and had been appalled when he discovered that not only had she taken a hair-dryer with her but she had actually used it. He had never let her forget it. Bella was quite sure that Aisling had heard that story and laughed prettily at the idea that anyone could be quite that much of a city girl.

'I'm not sure Tooting would be very convenient for Aisling,' she said. 'It's not exactly handy for your office, is it?'

'Aisling's been trekking across the Sahara,' Josh pointed out. 'I don't think she would find changing tubes a problem!'

Well, that put *her* in her place, thought Bella grumpily.

'Yes, well, I'll talk to Phoebe,' she said without enthusiasm. 'It's her house, so it's her decision really.'

'Great,' said Josh. 'I'm sure Phoebe won't mind.'

'Where is Aisling, anyway?' said Bella. She had to get to Phoebe before Josh did. There was no way she was going to share a house with Aisling.

Josh looked around the marquee, and pointed. 'Over there, talking to Finn's sister.'

As if she had heard him, Aisling looked over, and beckoned imperatively. In spite of being anxious to get rid of him so she could go and find Phoebe, Bella couldn't believe it when Josh just *went*. He ought to have more pride, she thought crossly.

Still, now was her chance to grab Phoebe.

'So you will say no, won't you?' she begged when she had dragged Phoebe away from Gib and poured the whole story into her ears.

'If you want,' said Phoebe, 'but I don't know what I'm going to say to Josh. I can't think of any reason to object to Aisling. She seems very nice.'

'I don't like her,' said Bella.

'Why not?'

'I just don't,' she said a little sulkily. 'There's a little too much of that bubbly Irish charm if you ask me. And I don't think she's right for Josh.'

Phoebe looked at her narrowly. 'Are you sure you're not just jealous?'

'Jealous? *Jealous?*' spluttered Bella, spilling most of the champagne in her outrage. 'Don't be ridiculous! I have *never* been jealous of Josh, you know that. I've always got on really well with all his girlfriends.'

'Mmnn, but then none of them were at all like you.'

'Nor is Aisling!'

'Yes, she is. I'm sure that's why you don't like her. You've only got to look at her!'

Bella turned to stare across the marquee to where Aisling was snuggling up to Josh. She obviously couldn't keep her hands off him. Josh would hate that, Bella thought disapprovingly. He was definitely a behind-closed-doors sort of man.

On the other hand, he wasn't exactly fighting Aisling off, was he?

She looked away. 'I'm nothing like Aisling,' she told Phoebe. 'She's got red hair, for a start!'

'OK, but change the colour of her hair and eyes, and what have you got? She's ridiculously pretty, has legs up to her armpits, and that glamorous look that is just *so* different from Josh's previous girlfriends. Admit it, Bella, she's practically a clone!'

Bella wasn't prepared to admit anything of the kind. 'What, apart from looking completely different and having completely different personalities? I'd say all Aisling and I had in common was our gender! Josh is always telling me how practical she is and how she likes doing hearty things like climbing and camping.'

Phoebe shrugged. 'Have it your own way.'

'Anyway,' Bella went on, a defensive edge to her voice, 'Josh and I agreed a long time ago that we would just be friends. There's no question of jealousy.'

'Didn't you *ever* find him attractive?' asked Phoebe curiously, and try as she might, Bella couldn't quite make herself meet her friend's eyes.

'He wasn't my type,' she said.

'Do you think you were ever his?'

Had she been? For the first time Bella found herself wondering.

'He never said, and anyway, he always seemed to have some outdoorsy girl who didn't fuss about her hair or wear make-up or mind getting up at six to go potholing or whatever it was they used to do at weekends. Josh and I used to make each other laugh, and we had a great time doing that. We didn't want to spoil it by sleeping together.

'Besides,' she added honestly, 'he wasn't at all attractive then. He was a bit thin and nerdy.'

Phoebe glanced across the marquee. 'He's changed,' she said.

'Yes,' said Bella, following her gaze. Through the crowds, she could just glimpse Josh. The lean, compact figure was at once alien and utterly familiar.

He was talking to someone out of sight, but as she watched he threw back his head and laughed, and her stomach abruptly disappeared, as if she had stumbled unawares off the edge of an abyss. The sensation of falling was so intense that Bella had to close her eyes against a sickening wave of vertigo, and when she opened them again she felt dizzy and hollow inside.

'Yes,' she said again. 'He has.'

There was a silence. Frightened by the strength of her physical response, Bella drank her champagne shakily, and it was some time before she realised that Phoebe was watching her expectantly.

'What?' she demanded, and Phoebe held up her hands, one still clutching her champagne glass.

'I didn't say anything!'

That was the worst thing about friends who knew you really well. They didn't need to say anything for you to know exactly what they were thinking!

'I'm not jealous, all right?'

'All right,' said Phoebe equably. 'So what is the problem?'

'Who says there's a problem?'

Phoebe sighed. 'Come on, Bella, it's obvious! Is it Will?'

'No.... Yes...sort of,' Bella admitted with a sigh.

'What happened?'

'Nothing, that's just it.' Bella stared miserably down into her glass. 'It's just that I've been feeling...I don't know...*restless*, I suppose, for a while. We haven't had an argument or anything. It was Will who suggested that we give each other some space, and I think that's all I need. I mean, Will's fantastic, isn't he?' She hated the doubtful note in her voice.

'He certainly seems very nice,' said Phoebe noncommittally.

'And drop-dead gorgeous and intelligent and solvent and not screwed up... What more could I ask for? He would have come today if I'd asked him,' she went on with a sigh. 'I need my head examined to let him go off to Hong Kong! What's *wrong* with me?'

'There's nothing wrong with you. Will just isn't the right man for you, that's all.'

'But if someone like Will isn't the right man, who is?'

'I don't know,' said Phoebe, 'but *you* will when you find him.'

CHAPTER TWO

BELLA wished she had Phoebe's confidence. She was beginning to wonder if there was something wrong with her. It wasn't that she was particularly vain, but she knew she was pretty, and there was never any shortage of men wanting to go out with her. Somehow, though, it never came to anything. She fell headlong into love and just as quickly out of it.

She might never find that special man, Bella thought glumly as she helped herself to a canapé, and now she might not even have Josh to fall back on. They had once agreed that if they both reached forty without finding anyone they would marry each other.

Bella actually remembered laughing at the time. The truth was that it had never occurred to her then that Josh might marry someone else. He was so self-contained that it was hard to imagine him sharing his life with anyone. None of his girlfriends had ever moved in with him.

Looking for him now, her eyes found him instinctively in the crowded marquee. There he was, Aisling clinging as usual to his arm, and no matter how much she wanted to think that he looked irritated by her possessiveness, she just couldn't do it.

Bella drifted around the edge of the marquee to get a better view. That was better. Now she could see Josh quite clearly, talking to Gib. He was wearing a morning suit, and the crisp white shirt made his skin, weathered from so much time spent in the tropics, look even browner than usual.

He looked surprisingly good in formal clothes, she thought. Even now, dressed identically to most of the other men in the marquee, he had the tough, competent air of a man who should be hacking his way through a jungle or bumping along a dusty track in faded khakis, not sipping champagne and eating canapés in an English garden.

Bella's gaze rested on him. Really, it was amazing that it had taken her so many years to realise what a great body he had, lean and hard and tautly muscled in an intriguingly restrained way. If she had walked into the marquee as a stranger, she would definitely have clocked him.

His face wasn't that bad either. Not jaw-droppingly handsome like Will, of course, but still, there was nothing actually wrong with it. He had nice eyes, creased around the edges from too much squinting at the sun, and they held a lurking smile sometimes that might be really quite disturbing if you weren't used to it, the way she was.

Nice mouth too, Bella thought judiciously. Not the kind of mouth you noticed at first, maybe—it was too quiet and cool for that—but if you looked at it for too long, something about it made you squirm suddenly.

Like that. A strange feeling shuddered down Bella's spine, and she jerked her eyes away.

It felt all wrong to be thinking about Josh like this. He was her friend, the one person she could talk to about anything at all.

Except this.

Bella imagined herself strolling over and saying, 'Hey, Josh, I was just thinking what a great body you have and wondering what it would be like to kiss you,' and she winced, picturing already his appalled expression. She couldn't do that to Josh.

More to the point, she couldn't do it to herself! Honesty was one thing, humiliation quite another.

Gib's attention had been claimed by another guest and, as Bella watched, Josh tightened his arm around Aisling and gave her a quick private kiss. The pain that sliced through her at the sight was so unexpected that it took Bella's breath away, and the champagne spilt from her glass as she flinched instinctively.

Bella turned abruptly away. This wouldn't do! She was the life and soul of a party, not someone who mooned around on the edges feeling left out. It was time to circulate and exert some of that charm she was so famous for.

She succeeded so well that one of Kate's young brothers informed her owlishly at the end of the reception that he had been in love with her since he was fourteen, and asked her to marry him. Touched and amused, Bella let him down kindly but secretly she couldn't help feeling a bit better. She might be tottering on the verge of thirty-three and she wasn't a camping queen like Aisling, but *some* men wanted her, even if they were only twenty-one and had been imbibing freely of their father's champagne.

She seemed to have developed a sudden attraction for very young men. At the ceilidh in the marquee that evening Bella found herself the centre of a group of besotted boys. Their undisguised admiration was very flattering of course, but she wasn't entirely sure that it was a good sign. Did she really look old enough to be in the market for a toy boy? Bella wondered.

Still, it was nice to feel wanted for a change, and she glanced across the marquee to where Josh had Aisling entwined around him as usual.

Determined to show Josh, should he happen to look in her direction, that she was having a wonderful time, Bella let one of her admirers after another swing her eagerly on the dance floor. Her partners appeared deaf to the bellowed instructions of the member of the band who was desperately trying to tell everyone the moves to the Scottish dances, but what they lacked in skill, they more than made up for in enthusiasm. More than once Bella found herself being spun out of control so that she ended up cannoning breathlessly into other couples. Fortunately few of them seemed to have a clue what they were doing either.

Bella told herself she was having a fantastic time, and laughed as she shook back her hair over her shoulders.

From another set, Josh watched her dazzle the boy she was dancing with. He couldn't be more than sixteen and obviously could hardly believe his luck, Josh thought indulgently. He had seen how effortlessly Bella had cast her spell over every man she came across. Even Kate's famously grumpy great-uncle had not been immune to the old Stevenson charm.

It had been the same ever since he had met her. Josh remembered the first time he had seen her. She had walked into the seminar room, blonde, beautiful and impossibly glamorous amongst all the other scruffy students, and when she smiled and sat down next to him, he had gulped like the schoolboy she was dancing with now.

There had been a starry quality about Bella, even then, he thought. For the first few weeks, he had gawked at her from a distance. She was so clearly out of his league, that it never occurred to him that they could ever be friends, but when he did get to know her properly, he was bowled over by the charm that made him feel as if she had been waiting all this time just to meet him, plain Josh Kingston. He had been amazed to discover how friendly and natural she was, and how funny. She might look like a princess, but she had an infectiously dirty laugh.

Not that Josh ever tried to take advantage of the closeness that grew up between them. His role was as a friend, the one constant male in the dizzying ups and downs of her romantic life.

And Josh didn't mind, or he told himself he didn't, anyway. At least that way he saw Bella, and he kept on seeing her in a way the men she fell in and out of love with didn't. None of them ever lasted very long. Bella might look sophisticated, but beneath her glossy veneer beat the heart of a true romantic, determined not to settle for anyone less than Mr Perfect.

Maybe she had found him in Will. He seemed an unlikely Mr Perfect to Josh, but he had never understood Bella's taste in men. He had wondered if things had run their course with Will earlier, when she had seemed tense and unhappy, but there was no sign of that now.

Josh's mouth curled affectionately as he watched Bella dancing up and down the line in the other set, laughing that laugh of hers. She was being swung around and around between each couple, her hair shimmering as it flew around her vivid face and her skirt swirling around those spectacular legs.

'Josh!' Aisling hissed at him, and he started as he realised that he was supposed to be joining hands and going down the set with her, not watching what was going on elsewhere.

He didn't get a chance to dance with Bella herself until much later in the evening.

'I'm tired,' she said when he held out his hand to pull her onto the dance floor.

'Tired? You? Never!'

'I am,' she protested. 'I've been dancing all night.'

She fanned her hot face, unwilling to let him know reluctant she was to take his hand. 'Ask Aisling.'

'She's dancing with Gib.'

'Honestly, Josh, I'm exhausted,' Bella tried, but Josh was determined.

'This isn't going to require any energy,' he said as the band struck up a slow tune to give everyone a chance to cool down. 'We just need to stand there and sway a bit, I'm no good at doing anything else anyway.'

He put out his hand again. 'Come on, Bella, you can manage that, and it's only me!'

That's right, it was only Josh. Bella clung to the thought as she relented and took his hand. Following him onto the floor, she told herself that she could hardly refuse to dance with him. He really would think something was wrong then, and there wasn't. It was only Josh.

Only Josh's arms around her. Only Josh's broad chest tantalisingly close. Only Josh's cheek resting comfortably against her hair. They had danced like this countless times before, so why was it different now? Why this sudden longing to tighten her arms around his back, to lean against him and press her face into his throat?

Bella swallowed. 'Great wedding.'

'You certainly seem to have been having a good time.' Josh sounded amused rather than jealous. 'What's with this new interest in toy boys, Bella? I've lost count of the callow youths I've seen you reduce to stammering incoherence tonight! You realise you've spoilt them for life,' he went on cheerfully. 'They're going to be dreaming about finding a woman like you for years to come, and most of them are going to end up disappointed. You ought to come with a health warning for young men!'

'It never bothered you,' said Bella, more sharply than she had intended, and Josh pulled away slightly to look at her with puzzled frown.

'It was different for me.'

'I know,' she said.

Why? she wondered. Why didn't he desire her like other men? He had never so much as hinted that he wanted her as anything more than a friend. And she would have been appalled if he had, Bella reminded herself honestly.

So why was it suddenly so hard to dance with him like this? It was if something was unravelling uncontrollably inside her, and she didn't know what it was or how to stop it. She was agonisingly conscious of him as he held her against him, not too close, but close enough to be aware of the solid strength of his body, of the warmth of his hand on her back, and the feel of his fingers curled around hers.

Terrified that she was pressing herself against him, Bella held herself stiffly. Her tongue seemed to be stuck to roof of mouth, and she felt absurdly shy of him. As the silence lengthened, she was even reduced to asking how work was going.

'Very well,' said Josh, almost as if he too was relieved at her attempt to break the increasingly tense silence. 'Things have really taken off since Aisling joined us. With her background at C.B.C.—they're our major client—she's been incredibly useful, as she knows how both organisations work.'

'Really?' said Bella, trying to force some interest into her voice.

'There's a possibility of a big contract coming up. It could be the one that changes everything for us.'

'Why is it so important?'

'It would mean expanding internationally,' Josh told her. 'C.B.C. are based in Paris, but they've got subsidiary offices around the world. We did some work for head office recently, and now they want us to implement the same training system globally.'

Bella perked up a bit, impressed in spite of herself. 'That sounds cool.'

'It might be "cool", but every national office has a lot of independence, and most are very resistant to the idea of trainers being parachuted in from head office. In some countries it's vital to establish a personal relationship with the senior executives before you start doing business.'

'You can hardly go around the world introducing yourself to every office!'

'Quite,' he agreed in a dry voice, 'but once a year C.B.C. invite the most successful executives and partners on an all-expenses-paid holiday. It's mainly intended as a social occasion and a reward for high-achievers, but it also ensures they all share in the same company ethic.'

'I'd share the ethics of any company that sent me on an all-expenses-paid holiday,' said Bella, glad that the conversation seemed to be distracting her somewhat from the pulse that beat in Josh's throat, right where she would most like to rest her face.

'That's my Bella, ever the moralist!'

Bella tore her eyes from his pulse. 'So where do they do all this bonding?'

'It's in the Seychelles this year. They're taking over a hotel on one of the small islands, and C.B.C. suggested that I go along. They think it would be a good opportunity to meet a lot of those people I may have to deal with on a social basis.'

Only Josh could sound glum about being offered a free trip to the Seychelles!

'Are you going to go?'

He lifted his shoulders as well as he could given that he had one arm round her waist and the other was holding her hand. 'Those kinds of corporate jaunts aren't really my thing,' he said, 'but Aisling thinks I should go.'

Surprise, surprise, was Bella's first jaundiced thought. 'I suppose she'll be going as well?'

'Yes.' If Josh noticed the acid tinge to her voice, he gave no sign of it. 'She's the one with all the contacts and she says it's important for me to meet people and talk about what we can do for them.'

'Really?' said Bella again, this time with a distinct layer of frost. For years now, she had been telling him that he needed to network if he wanted his company to take off, but he had never listened to *her* when she suggested that he needed to go out and meet people.

At least that unsettling urge to turn her face into his and press her lips against his jaw was receding, which was something of a relief. Getting cross seemed to be an excellent cure for *that*, anyway.

'I'm sure Aisling's right,' she said coolly, 'but I'm not sure I can see you on a beach holiday.'

'God, no.' Josh shuddered at the thought. 'I'd go mad if I had nothing to do but sit in the sun all day, but Aisling says these events are always activity-based.'

'Oh?' Bella was getting a bit sick of hearing what Aisling said.

'It's not dissimilar from the way we work with people on expeditions to build up teamwork and trust,' he said. 'Activities like diving or climbing or bush-walking are an excellent way for staff from different offices to get to know each other and bond at a more than superficial level. When you're all being challenged, you've got to be able to communicate.'

'So you're always saying,' said Bella, who had never had any trouble communicating from a sofa with a phone in her hand.

Josh grinned. 'I know your idea of the great outdoors doesn't extend beyond a veranda, but other people get a lot out of being pushed to do things they've never done before.'

'That'll be schmoozing a room for you,' said Bella tartly. 'What else is on offer?'

'I'm not sure. Aisling's keen to go scuba-diving, and there'll probably be sailing as well, so I might not be too bored.'

She sighed. It all sounded a bit too hearty for her. 'What's wrong with lying on warm white sand?' she asked. 'You can network just as effectively at a beach bar, you know.'

'We don't all have your ability to forge intimate bonds over a pina colada,' said Josh.

'It's a lot more useful than being able to dive. How much networking can you do underwater? It's just a lot of pointing and blowing bubbles.'

'You being such an expert on diving!'

'I've seen it on telly,' said Bella a little sulkily.

Josh laughed. 'You just don't like the idea of getting your hair wet. Luckily, Aisling isn't quite such a princess in these matters!'

Of course not. Aisling would tie her hair up sensibly, wear practical clothes and leave her high heels behind.

Good luck to her, thought Bella sourly. If she wanted to spend a week underwater in a rubber suit with a tank on her back when she could have a soft tropical beach and a warm lagoon and a long, cool drink brought to her lounger on a tray, that was her problem!

'By the way,' said Josh, swinging Bella round in what was for him a nifty bit of footwork, 'did you get a chance to talk to Phoebe?'

He had tightened his arm around her so that she didn't lose her balance as she swung, and it was enough to make every nerve in Bella's body jump to attention. Her heart did an odd sort of flip-flop and then settled with a thud that left her momentarily breathless.

'Talk to Phoebe?' she echoed, struggling to sound normal.

'About Aisling moving in to the house.'

'Oh, yes. Yes, I did.' Bella took a steadying breath.

She wished the music would stop and that Josh would let her go. It might be easier to concentrate then.

'What did she say?'

For a treacherous moment Bella wondered if she could throw the blame onto Phoebe, but she knew that wouldn't be fair. 'She left it up to me,' she told Josh the truth instead. 'But to be honest I think I'd like to keep the house to myself for a while.'

There, that sounded reasonable enough, didn't it? More tactful anyway than 'I'd rather stick pins in my eyes than share a house with Aisling,' which was the alternative.

'Fair enough,' said Josh. 'Aisling will be disappointed, though. She thought you would get on really well together.'

'Did she?'

'Yes, she likes you a lot.'

Bella didn't believe *that* for a minute. Aisling might smile sweetly, but her green eyes had always held a distinctly cool look. Bella had a fair idea it was a pretty accurate reflection of her own expression when the two of them met.

'Really?' she said in what she hoped was a suitably neutral tone.

'Oh, yes.' Josh nodded. 'She's told me so several times.'

Oh, well, if he was going to believe everything Aisling *said*…!

How naïve could you get? Bella wondered. She would have expected Josh to be more perceptive. He must be really besotted with Aisling if he believed every word she said. The thought was profoundly depressing somehow.

To Bella's intense relief, the music ended just then, and Josh let her go. 'I hope she'll find somewhere else soon,' she said, feeling more in control of herself and thinking she had better make the effort to be pleasant. 'I'm sure there are more convenient places than Tooting, in any case.'

'Perhaps you're right.' Josh didn't seem unduly perturbed. 'She can move in with me in the meantime anyway. You couldn't get more convenient than that!'

'What?' Bella stopped dead in dismay.

'Well, she's got to live somewhere,' he pointed out reasonably. 'She has to move out of her current flat at the end of next week, and she won't have anywhere else to go.'

'But you never wanted anyone living with you before!' Josh was famously solitary.

He shrugged. 'Aisling's different. She's a very special lady. We get on really well, and we've got a lot in common.'

Bella felt sick. Now look what she had done! 'You don't think it'll be a bit much, living and working together?'

'We won't know until we try, will we? It hasn't been a problem keeping our professional and private relationships separate so far. I think it'll work out fine.'

So that was that.

Bella couldn't believe how disastrously her refusal to share the house with Aisling had backfired. She had never dreamt that Josh was serious enough to ask Aisling to move in with him! He had always guarded his privacy so carefully. Previous girlfriends might spend the weekend with him, but he had never asked them if they wanted to leave so much as a toothbrush.

And now here he was, sharing his flat and his life with Aisling, of all people!

Bella didn't like it. Before, she had always known when she could find Josh on his own, but now he was with Aisling all the time. As the weeks after Kate's wedding passed, she saw him less and less often. When she did, she looked for signs that he was feeling crowded, or to hear that Aisling was moving into her own place, but she had to admit that they both seemed perfectly happy.

And she had no one to blame but herself. Bella could see that quite clearly. She had pushed them into living together, and now she was just going to have to accept the situation.

She didn't have to like it, though. And she missed Josh. She missed him terribly. Just his friendship, of course, she reassured herself, but still, it was a big gap in her life.

For a while she pinned her hopes on Will. She convinced herself that everything would be different when he came back from Hong Kong. Absence would work its usual miracle and the moment she saw him again she would realise just how much he meant to her.

Only it wasn't like that. She was pleased to see him, and they got on well, but something had changed. Will could see it as clearly as she did.

'I'm sorry,' she said miserably. 'It's not you. I don't know what's wrong with me.'

'Hey, don't worry about it,' said Will, who was turning out to be a real sweetie. Bella had never appreciated him properly before. 'We can still be friends.'

In some ways, Will took over Josh's role, although he could never know her as well as Josh did. Bella knew it wouldn't be long before he found someone else—he was too good-looking to stay single for long—but in the meantime they got on much better than when they had been a couple.

Her life was much quieter than it had been before...before *what*? All Bella knew was that she didn't feel like going to parties any more for some reason, and that now she preferred meeting friends for a quiet drink or going to see a film.

The theatre had never held any interest for her before either, but when Will said that he had managed to get a couple of tickets for the newest and most spectacular show in town, she actually found herself looking forward to it instead of rolling her eyes and wishing they were going to the hottest new club.

She met Will in the foyer of the theatre and together they climbed the sweeping staircases to the main bar. The room was crowded with theatre-goers anxious to get a drink before the curtain went up. Together they pushed their way through to the bar, only to come face to face with Josh and Aisling, who had managed to get their drinks and were heading out of the throng.

Bella's heart jerked horribly when she saw Josh, and she plucked frantically at Will's sleeve to catch his attention.

Josh, on the other hand, was unaffectedly pleased to see her. 'Bella! Where have you been hiding yourself?'

Clearly *his* heart wasn't somersaulting sickeningly around in his chest at the sight of her, and it cost him nothing to lean forward, still grasping both drinks, to kiss her cheek.

'I haven't seen you for ages!' he said, and then his eyes fell on Will and his face hardened. 'Oh,' he said flatly. 'You're back, are you?'

Will was rather taken aback by his tone. 'Back?'

'According to Bella, you were single-handedly saving the global economy in Hong Kong while the rest of us mere mortals were at Kate's wedding.'

'I wouldn't say that,' said Will modestly, 'but we did manage to brush through that particular crisis.'

'When did you get back?' Josh's tone was unfriendly, and he was eyeing Will like a dog with its hackles up.

'Some time ago—'

'I'm sorry we haven't been in touch—' Bella interrupted, putting her arm around Will's waist and leaning winsomely into him '—but you know what it's like when one of you has been away.' She gave him a meaningful squeeze. 'We haven't seen anybody really, have we, darling?'

Will's expression flickered, but he rose to the occasion wonderfully and put his arm around her and agreed that they hadn't felt like being very social.

'I'm glad everything's going well for you,' said Josh, not looking in the slightest bit glad, and not sounding it either.

'Oh, yes, everything's perfect,' cooed Bella. 'Isn't it, Will?'

'Perfect,' he echoed, somewhat woodenly.

'Anyway, enough about us! How are things with you two?' Bella asked brightly.

Josh handed Aisling her drink so that he could put his free arm around her in imitation of the way Will and Bella were standing. 'We're great,' he said.

Did Bella imagine it, or was that a defensive edge to his voice?

'It's not like you to come to the theatre, Bella,' Aisling put in. 'Josh was just saying that you've always been too much of a drama queen yourself to ever want to watch anyone else getting all the attention on stage!'

Bella could imagine Josh saying that, but not in the way Aisling made it sound. 'No, well, I'm rather surprised to see you two here as well,' she countered sweetly. 'I thought you preferred being outdoors, competing as to who has the muddiest boots or the dirtiest towel.'

'We like being active,' Aisling agreed, her smile every bit as fixed as Bella's. 'But we enjoy culture too.'

Josh didn't look as if he was enjoying himself. Bella raised her brows, but before she could retort, Will had tugged at her. 'If you want that drink, Bella, we'd better get going.'

'Of course.' Bella smiled sweetly at Josh and Aisling. 'See you later!'

'*Culture!*' she exploded the moment they were out of earshot. 'It's only a musical! And Josh will hate it!'

'So, do you want to tell me what that was all about?' said Will when he had caught the barmaid's attention and could hand Bella a gin and tonic.

Bella didn't pretend not to know what he was talking about. 'I didn't want Josh to know that we've split up.'

'I gathered that,' he said dryly.

'Thanks for playing along,' she told him.

Will looked at her curiously. 'I thought Josh was your big buddy?' he said. 'I assumed he'd be the first person you would tell if you split up.'

'Normally he would be,' admitted Bella, 'but he was so unpleasant about you at Kate's wedding that it made me cross, and besides—'

'Besides what?' asked Will when she stopped.

'Nothing.' She couldn't explain why it had seemed such a good idea at the time to let Josh believe that she was still madly in love with Will.

Will raised his brows. 'It must be six weeks since Kate got married. Do you mean to say that he still doesn't know?'

'I just haven't had an opportunity to tell him,' said Bella, swirling her gin defensively.

'You did more than not tell him just now,' he pointed out. 'You went out of your way to make him think that we were still very much together!'

'I know,' she said guiltily. 'I just can't stand the thought of Aisling feeling sorry for me. You saw what she was like. She'd be all warm and sympathetic and oh-so-slightly smug because she and Josh are so cosy together.' Bella grimaced at the thought and took a slug of gin. 'You know they're living together now?'

'Ah,' said Will.

Bella lowered her glass suspiciously. 'What's that supposed to mean?'

'It explains why you're so upset.'

'I'm not upset,' she said with something of a snap. 'I just don't like Aisling. Josh and I were fine until she came along.'

'But it's not Aisling who's the problem, is it? It's you.'

'Me?'

'You're in love with Josh.'

Bella opened her mouth to deny it vehemently. She was fully intending to tell Will that he didn't know what he was talking about, and that there was no *question* of being in love with Josh, who was just her dear friend and absolutely nothing else.

But somehow the words wouldn't come out. Instead she felt a peculiar sinking sensation, as if she were teetering at edge of a cliff, not daring to look down at what lay in the abyss below. Closing her mouth, she swallowed hard.

'I'm right, aren't I?' said Will, as the bell warning the audience to take their seats sounded.

Smiling ruefully, he took Bella's glass from her nerveless hand and set it on a nearby table. Then he took her arm and propelled her towards the stairs. 'Poor Bella. You look like you've been hit by a truck!'

That was exactly how Bella felt. Numbly, she let Will guide her up the stairs and into her seat. Having resisted it for so long, now the truth was staring her in the face, she couldn't avoid it and she felt suddenly, horribly afraid.

How could it have happened? She had never loved Josh before, or at least not in this new, scary way, and there was no reason for her to start falling in love with him now.

Bella didn't want to be in love with him. She wanted to go back to the way they had been before, but the certainty that she could never do that now was cold around her heart. As long as she had refused to acknowledge it, things were OK, but Will's careless words had been all that were needed to let the genie out of the bottle, and now she could never get it back.

The truth was out there now, implacable, undeniable. After all these years, she was in love with Josh.

CHAPTER THREE

BELLA stared unseeingly at the dancers on the stage and remembered what Phoebe had said to her at Kate's wedding. 'You'll know when you find him,' she had said.

But she hadn't known. It had taken Will, not normally the most perceptive of men, to point out the obvious, and now her life had changed for ever.

What was she going to do? Always before when she hadn't known what to do she had talked to Josh, but he was the one person now she couldn't, *mustn't*, tell.

If sleeping together all those years ago would have spoilt their friendship, it was nothing to what confessing how she felt now would do. Josh was with Aisling, Bella reminded herself bleakly. She was just going to have to accept that friends was all they were, and make an effort to like Aisling for his sake.

That wasn't going to be easy, but she would try.

She might not be able to tell Josh how her life had changed so completely, but she could tell him the truth about Will. It was stupid to carry on pretending, Bella decided. She had never lied to Josh before, and it didn't feel right. If they were friends, and they had always been that, she should just admit that Will was not her ideal man after all.

But there never seemed to be an opportunity over the next couple of weeks. In spite of her determination to try harder with Aisling, Bella balked at trying to explain why she had pretended the way she had in front of her. She wasn't sure she could stand Aisling's sympathy or—worse—her understanding.

So when she got an email from Josh one day saying that Aisling was going out with some old colleagues and suggesting that the two of them meet up for a drink the following evening, Bella thought it would be her best chance to straighten things out. Some of them, anyway.

'Absolutely,' she emailed back. 'Don't seem to have had a good chat for ages and have lots to tell you. Usual time, usual place?'

'News for you too,' Josh replied immediately. 'See you tomorrow.'

Bella was ridiculously nervous next day, and so tense and snappy at work that others in the office took to edging round her. Really, it was worse than going on a first date!

She couldn't believe that she felt this twitchy about meeting Josh. She was pinning her hopes on a miraculous cure, whereby one look at him would be enough for her to realise that she had blown everything out of proportion—and, let's face it, it wouldn't be the first time she had done *that*!—and to discover that she wasn't in love with him at all.

But part of her knew that this was just wishful thinking. She was stuck with this now.

Her hands shook as she brushed her hair and put on fresh lipstick in the ladies' loo at the end of the day.

'You look nice,' said her boss's PA, who was also titivating in front of the mirror prior to going out. 'Heavy date tonight?'

'No,' said Bella, moistening her lips. 'Just meeting a friend.'

A *friend*. That was all he was. She must remember that. Never mind that she couldn't even say his name without her insides twisting themselves into a knot.

She arrived at the bar ten minutes early, unheard of for her. It was a standing joke that her watch ran twenty-five minutes slower than Josh's. She got herself a drink and sat down at a table, twisting the glass nervously between her hands.

This was awful! She didn't know whether she longed for Josh to arrive or dreaded it.

When he did, bang on time as usual, he didn't even bother to look for her, but glanced at his watch, assumed she would be late and went straight to the bar.

Bella's heart jerked painfully at the sight of him and stuck, hammering frantically, in her throat. It was lucky that he hadn't seen her and come straight over, as she couldn't have spoken if she had tried. So much for her hope that she would turn out not to be in love with him after all.

Her eyes rested on him hungrily as he stood at the bar, wearing chinos and a battered old jacket. She had spent years rolling her eyes at his complete absence of any sense of style at all, and the boring way he insisted on having his hair cut. Now just looking at the back of his neck was like a hand squeezing hard inside her.

Josh might not be the sharpest of dressers but he exuded a kind of tough competence, and he wasn't a man who got ignored by bar staff. He was served far more quickly than Bella had been, and turned with a beer in his hand to look for a table.

Swallowing hard, Bella waved to attract his attention, and his searching expression changed ludicrously to one of surprise.

'Bella!' He put his beer down on the table and bent to kiss her cheek. 'You're on time! Did I slip into a parallel universe without noticing? What's come over you?'

I'm in love with you.

Her face tingled where his lips had brushed against her skin. She felt absurdly shy.

'Things were quiet at work so I left early,' she said.

'Things quiet in the PR world?' said Josh as he sat down opposite her. 'This *is* a parallel universe!'

He picked up his beer. 'Cheers,' he said and they chinked glasses. Taking a sip he set the glass down again and smiled at Bella. 'So,' he said. 'You're looking good.'

'So are you.'

He looked more than good. He looked wonderful. Bella couldn't take her eyes off him. She wanted to crawl over to him, sit in his lap and run her hand up his arm and along his shoulder, to kiss his throat and then work her way along his jaw to his mouth...

Appalled at the sheer grip of lust, she gulped her wine shakily. All those years she had taken Josh for granted, and now she could hardly keep her hands off him! Thank God he was sitting opposite and hadn't chosen the seat beside her. Even so, she tightened both hands around the stem of the glass where she could see them on top of the table and keep them under control.

'How are things with you?' she managed.

'Great. And you?'

'Yes, fine.'

This was ghastly. Bella felt close to tears. It had always been so easy with Josh before. They would get their drinks and spend the rest of the evening talking and laughing and teasing each other, and now they were sitting here being *polite* to each other.

'Are you still going off to the Seychelles?'

Josh nodded. He was obviously picking up on the awkward atmosphere. 'In a couple of weeks,' he said.

'Lucky you. I wish I could go away in November. It's always so dark and miserable then.'

God, now they were reduced to the weather!

Josh didn't even try and pick up on that particular conversational gambit. He drank his beer instead and an uncomfortable silence fell.

Bella concentrated on making patterns with the condensation on the bottom of her glass. She was supposed to be telling him about Will but she wasn't sure how to do it without explaining how her feelings had changed, and if Josh probed too far in that direction it wouldn't take him long to realise that she had changed, and then he would want to know why and...oh, God, perhaps it would be better not to say anything?

'So,' said Josh again, sounding rather strained. 'What's new with you? You said you had a lot to tell me.'

'You go first,' she said quickly. 'You said you had news too.'

'Yes...yes, I do.'

He sounded almost as hesitant as she felt. He obviously didn't know where to begin either. A tiny chill crept into Bella's stomach.

'Is it good or bad?' she asked, trying to make light of it.

'Good,' said Josh after another tiny hesitation.

'You don't sound very sure!'

He didn't. Josh could hear it himself. 'No, it is good. Definitely good,' he said.

The best, in fact. So why didn't it feel fantastic? Josh wondered. It had seemed such a good idea when Aisling suggested it. More than that, it had made perfect sense. He should be standing on the table, shouting his luck to the world.

He just hadn't expected it to be so difficult to tell Bella, that was all.

She was looking at him curiously across the table. 'Is it something to do with work?'

'No, no, nothing like that.' Josh took another desperate drink of his beer.

Bella pursed her lips, rolled her eyes and shook back her long, blonde hair in an achingly familiar gesture of exasperation. 'Well?' she demanded, sounding like the old Bella, and not the strange new, shy, prompt Bella who had been sitting opposite him a moment ago. 'Do I have to guess, or are you going to tell me?'

'Aisling and I are getting married.'

Josh winced as he heard how he blurted out the words as if he felt guilty or something. He had meant to lead up to it more gently.

He looked at Bella, unsure of how she would react. She seemed to have frozen, and for a second or two her expression was completely blank. Then the blue eyes dropped to her wine and she stared at it for a few moments, until Josh began to wonder if she had heard him.

'Bella?' he asked, but she had already lifted her gaze and there was a bright smile on her face.

'Well...congratulations!' she said in a voice that matched her smile, and she half stood to lean across the table and kiss him on the cheek.

Her hair swung against Josh's face, and he could smell her perfume. She always wore exactly the same one. 'Allure,' she had told him when he asked once what it was, and she had grinned at him. 'Feel free to buy me a huge bottle whenever you want!' Sometimes when she had been in his flat, he could sniff the fragrance still lingering in the air. It always made him think of her.

What perfume did Aisling wear? Wasn't that the kind of thing a fiancé should know?

'When did all this happen?' she asked, sitting back

down with the same bright smile that for some reason intensified Josh's feeling of unease. But she looked just the same, the same blue eyes, the same tilting lashes, the same swing of spun gold around her face as she shook her hair out of the way.

It was just the smile that was wrong, but Josh couldn't put his finger on why.

'Last week,' he said.

They had just won a big contract, and the whole company had been out celebrating that evening. When they got home, Josh had tried to tell Aisling how much he appreciated what she had done. There was no doubt that she had made a huge difference. She had finely honed marketing skills, and with her background knowledge of clients like C.B.C. she had been able to steer the company in a new direction which was paying dividends already. This had been an important contract to win, and if they could get the C.B.C. deal as well, the future would be assured.

'We couldn't have done it without you,' he had told her, still high on the relief and euphoria of the staff. They had all worked hard but Aisling's input had been key and they all knew it. 'We make a fantastic team.'

'I think you and I make a fantastic team whatever we're doing,' Aisling had said, smiling. 'Why don't we make it permanent?'

And Josh hadn't been able to think of a reason not to. Aisling was beautiful and intelligent and she shared his interests. He knew they could live together. She didn't have any annoying habits.

Bella, for instance, would drive him mad. She would never close drawers or put the tops back on bottles and she would leave her clothes strewn all over his flat. She would clutter his streamlined bathroom with cosmetics and monopolise his phone and embark on cooking overelaborate meals, half of which would end up in the bin.

There was nothing like that with Aisling. Josh couldn't imagine ever finding anyone who fitted into his world with so little fuss.

Everyone else was settling down. What was the point of holding out for…what? Bella was wrapped up in that pillock, Will, and if it wasn't Will it would be some other chinless wonder who worked in the City.

Bella had been telling him for years that he had no sense of romance, and Josh didn't have a problem with that. Romantics—like Bella herself—had this rosy and, in his view, completely unrealistic view about relationships. They wanted everything to be perfect, and life was never like that.

Josh was trained in survival, and that was all about adapting to different situations, about keeping your options open as long as you could and compromising when you couldn't. And when you had to make a decision, you had to make it fast and stick with it.

Aisling was right, he had told himself. They did make a good team, and if he had learnt anything from his years on expedition, being part of a good team was everything. Why not commit himself and make it permanent?

'Last week?' Bella was staring at him, the blue eyes hurt. 'Why didn't you tell me?'

'I wanted to wait and tell you on your own,' said Josh awkwardly. 'I haven't told anybody else yet.'

'Why not?'

'I wanted you to be the first to know.' He looked at her anxiously. 'I know it's a bit sudden, but what do you think?'

Bella's smile wavered a little but she took a deep breath.

'I think it's fantastic news, Josh,' she said. 'I'm so happy for you.'

'Really?'

'Of course. I'm a bit stunned, I suppose but...yes, of course I'm happy for you. I can see Aisling's perfect for you.'

'She is, isn't she?' Josh was conscious of trying to force enthusiasm into his voice. That couldn't be right, surely?

'Absolutely,' said Bella, who could feel her smile growing fixed.

'You do like her, don't you?'

'Of course,' she lied.

She could feel another silence threatening. 'So when's the wedding?' she hurried on.

'We haven't decided on a date yet.'

'Are you going to go traditional, or do something different?'

'That'll be up to Aisling,' said Josh. 'I don't think she's made any plans yet.'

Bella's jaw was beginning to feel rigid with the effort of keeping her smile in place. 'Can I be your best man? It's supposed to be your best friend, isn't it?'

Josh looked at her. 'You'll always be that, Bella,' he said.

'Well, this calls for another drink.' Bella drained her glass with an edge of desperation. 'I'll have a glass of champagne this time!'

'I'll get them.' Josh leapt to his feet. 'You stay there.'

It was such a relief to stop smiling. Bella found that she was breathing very shallowly. She was shaking, too, she realised dully. It had taken everything she had to appear pleased for Josh while inside she felt so sick and utterly desolate that she could hardly think straight.

She had known it was coming. The moment he hesitated

about telling her his news, she had sensed what it would be, but even so the savage twist of pain had caught her unawares and she had almost cried out. Instead she had had to smile, and she would have to go on smiling, whatever it cost.

Josh must never know how she felt now. He mustn't even guess. It wouldn't be fair now that he had made his choice. He would be appalled and embarrassed, and even though it wouldn't change the way he felt about Aisling, it might make him feel awkward about celebrating his engagement, and Bella wasn't prepared to do that to him.

So she put her bright smile back on when Josh came back with a bottle of champagne in an ice bucket. 'This is more like it,' she said as he eased out the cork with a typical lack of any kind of flourish and poured the champagne.

'Congratulations, Josh,' she said, picking up her glass and touching it to his.

'Thanks, Bella.' Josh's face relaxed. 'It's stupid, but I was worried about telling you.'

'You shouldn't have been. You know I just want you to be happy.'

'We'll still be friends, won't we?'

'Of course we will—but who's going to marry me now when I get to forty and no one else wants me?' Bella kept smiling to show that she was joking. 'I thought I could rely on you!'

'I can't imagine that happening,' said Josh. 'As long as I've known you there's always been a long queue of men just desperate for the chance to show you how much they want you! What about Will?'

Bella studied her champagne. 'Ah, well, there's a vacant place at the front of the queue at the moment.'

Josh's face changed and he put down his glass. 'Bella?'

'Yes, I'm afraid my news isn't quite as exciting as yours,' she said. 'Will and I split up.'

'But you seemed so happy with him. You thought he was perfect!' Josh seemed at a loss. 'What happened?'

'Oh, you know...' Bella shrugged.

'No,' said Josh. 'Tell me.'

'It was just one of those things,' she said, avoiding his eye.

She had decided to tell Josh the truth about Will, but that was before she had known that he was going to marry Aisling. Everything had changed now. If Josh thought that the decision had been a mutual one, he would start to wonder why she was so unhappy, and Bella didn't want him going *there*. He knew her much too well.

No, far better for him to think that it was Will she loved. It would explain why she wasn't herself at the moment, and it would give her a good excuse to stop smiling, which would be a huge relief.

'Will isn't ready to settle down,' she told Josh. That at least was true. There had never been any question of making things permanent. Will was no more keen to marry than Bella had been. 'He's having much too good a time being an eligible bachelor.'

Which was also true. Will had found her attractive, and she had blended nicely with his décor, but he had never really loved her. That was one reason they were able to get on so well now.

'It was all getting a bit intense for him,' she explained.

'Isn't that usually your line?' said Josh, lifting an eyebrow.

'I know. Ironic, isn't it? All those years I've spent dumping men the moment they start to crowd me, and now I'm getting a taste of my own medicine.' Bella forced a smile. 'I'm sure you're going to tell me it serves me right!'

'No, I'm going to tell you I never thought Will was good enough for you. I know you thought he was perfect, but clearly the man has no taste. You'll find someone much better,' he told her confidently.

'The trouble is that I don't want anyone better,' she said in a low voice. 'There's only one man I want.'

'Bella...' Josh frowned. 'That sounds serious.'

'I think it is.' Bella twisted her glass between her fingers, unable to look at him properly. 'Oh, I know I've fallen in and out of love before, but this is different. It's more than liking a man with a smart car who can show you a good time. This is needing someone with every tiny bit of you and wanting to be with him and be able to touch him and knowing that you've lost your chance.

'It's too late,' she finished dully.

'*Is* it too late?'

Bella lifted her eyes from her glass and looked at him, so dear and so familiar and so suddenly, unexpectedly gorgeous.

And so engaged to Aisling.

She swallowed, and nodded, all at once unable to speak.

Josh got up without a word and sat down next to her so that he could put his arm around her. 'Poor Bella,' he said gently. 'Does it hurt?'

To her horror, Bella felt a tear trickle out of the edge of her eyes, and then another. Frantically, she tried to brush them away with the back of her hand, but it only seemed to make them come faster.

'I'll get over it,' she said unsteadily.

'You have got it bad, Bel,' said Josh, tightening his arm around her, which made things even worse.

Bella longed to be able to turn her face into his throat and cling to him but she couldn't let herself relax or she would lose control completely. She would fling her arms around him, and blizzard kisses all over his face and beg him not to marry Aisling. She would tell him that he was the one she loved and needed and wanted, and implore him to kiss her back, to pull her down onto the floor and make love to her and promise that he would never let her go.

The thought of how the quiet, restrained Josh would react to such a melodramatic scene was enough to make Bella give a hiccup of laughter through her tears. Poor Josh, she could never to do that to him.

'Honestly, I'll be fine,' she said, straightening out of the comfort of his arm before she really did do something she regretted. It was one of the hardest things she had ever had to do.

She dug in her bag for a tissue and blew her nose fiercely.

'Do you want me to kill Will for you?' asked Josh. 'I will if you want.'

Bella managed a shaky smile. 'Thanks, but I don't think that would help. And it's not Will's fault,' she added, in case Josh decided to track down the unsuspecting Will and give him a piece of his mind. 'He can't help how I feel.'

'He could give you a chance.'

Bella shook her head. 'I've had my chance, and I blew it,' she said.

Absently rubbing her cheeks with the crumpled tissue, she put her smile back into place. 'I'm sorry about that,' she said, sitting up straight and squaring her shoulders. 'I didn't mean to go all tearful on you. We're supposed to be celebrating your engagement here!' She held out her glass. 'Come on, let's have some more champagne!'

Josh topped up their glasses obediently, but he was worried about Bella. At least he now knew the reason for the strain behind her bright smile.

He hadn't been entirely joking when he asked Bella if she would like him to kill Will. OK, he might not go quite as far as murder, but when he saw the pain in her blue eyes, he was gripped by such a cold rage that he almost wished that Will would walk into the bar so that he could have the satisfaction of hurting him in return. He wanted to see Will on his knees, grovelling to Bella, and preferably with a bloody nose.

What was wrong with the man anyway? Josh thought about how warm and soft she had felt as she leant against him, the silkiness of her hair under his cheek. Will needed his head examining. How could a man turn his back on Bella, with those legs and that figure and those mischievous blue eyes? Or her warmth and her humour and that dirty chuckle?

It wasn't even as if she was just an airhead. There was a lot more to Bella than that. She could be infuriatingly frivolous sometimes, but when she chose to use it she had a perfectly good brain behind that ditzy blonde façade, as Josh had frequently pointed out. Not that Bella ever took any notice of him.

Look at her now. Her face was a little flushed, and her eyes held a suspiciously manic glitter, but she was putting on a brave show to hide her broken heart. Josh wanted to reach out and hug her again, but he had sensed a certain resistance before, as if she was only holding herself in with an effort.

And it wasn't his arms she wanted around her, was it?

'We must have a party to celebrate your engagement,' Bella was saying, and his mouth turned down at the corners.

'You know I'm not a big party person.'

'All right,' she conceded. 'What about a dinner, like we did for Phoebe and for Kate when they got engaged? It'll make quite a change to celebrate a real engagement rather than a pretend one! Do you think Aisling would like that?'

Aisling! Josh was startled to realise that he had forgotten about Aisling there for a few minutes.

'Yes...yes, I'm sure she would,' he said awkwardly.

'Good, that's settled then. Shall we go for next weekend? I'll talk to Phoebe and to Kate and I'll email you with a date.' Bella lifted her glass to him. 'Cheers,' she said.

It was her own fault for not recognising how important Josh was to her sooner. Bella could hardly bear to think now about all the years when she had peacocked around, always with some gorgeous man in tow, taking it for granted that Josh would be there when she got bored or wanted comfort or a laugh.

Well, now he was there for someone else, and she would just have to endure it. Aisling had seen in Josh everything that she had been standing too close to see. Had been too silly and self-absorbed to see.

That Josh was a man, not the boy she remembered. That he was quiet and competent and self-contained. That his eyes gleamed with humour. That his hands were square and strong, and his body hard and his cool mouth could tie you up in knots just by thinking about it.

He had been the best of friends to her for so long, and now she would be the same to him, Bella vowed. She would keep her feelings to herself, and be happy for him, and pull out all the stops to celebrate his engagement.

She planned a spectacular meal that no one would ever forget, and then had to ring up Kate and beg her to come and help her before everyone else arrived.

'Does it have to be quite so over-the-top?' Kate asked,

raising her brows as she studied the menu Bella had drawn up after poring over recipe books for days.

'I want it to be memorable.'

'It'll certainly be that if you can pull it off! A croquembouche! What's that?'

'A big pile of profiteroles filled with cream. It's supposed to be held together with spun sugar, but I thought I'd pour over chocolate instead,' said Bella. 'Only it doesn't seem to have worked very well.'

Glumly she contemplated her profiteroles which she had spent hours making the night before. The light-as-air little choux buns shown in the recipe book had ended up like pancakes. Stuffing them with cream was going to be a nightmare. They lay turgidly on a plate, not so much a pile as a mess.

'Hmmnn.' Kate studied them, unimpressed, and then went back to the menu without further comment. 'What else? Canapés, individual soufflés, beef Wellington…! You couldn't have picked at least one uncomplicated dish?'

Bella sighed. 'It seemed like a good idea at the time.'

'Josh would be just as happy with a tin of baked beans.'

'I know,' she said, restacking recipe books to try and clear the decks a bit. 'But he needs to know that I've made a special effort for Aisling.'

Kate pulled an apron over her head and tied the strings behind her back. 'Because you hate the fact that he's marrying her.'

'Yes—no!' Bella corrected herself hastily, hearing what she had said, and then she stopped, realising there was no point in trying to fool Kate. 'I suppose it's obvious?'

'It is to us, lovey. We've known you a long time.'

Bella bit her lip. 'Josh has known me a long time too.'

'Yes, but it'll be different for him. I know he can be

incredibly perceptive sometimes, but he's still a man,' said Kate kindly. 'He probably hasn't got a clue that you don't like Aisling.'

'No,' said Bella, remembering how sure he had been at Kate's wedding that she and Aisling would get on. 'I don't want him to know that, though. He'd be really hurt.'

'Don't you think Aisling is right for him?'

'Do you?'

Kate considered, her head tilted to one side. 'I can't quite believe he's going to marry her at all,' she admitted at last. 'I suppose Phoebe and I always assumed that you and Josh would end up together.'

Bella was glad of the fact that she had her back to Kate as she opened the fridge in search of mushrooms. She had her expression under control by the time she turned back and pulled out a chopping board.

'It's too late for that now,' she said, and was proud of the careless note in her voice.

Kate took the board and the mushrooms and began chopping pensively. 'Maybe Josh won't marry her after all.'

'I don't see that happening,' said Bella. 'You know what Josh is like. His word is his bond and all that. If he's decided to marry Aisling, then he will.'

'Aisling might change *her* mind,' Kate suggested hopefully.

But there was no sign of Aisling changing her mind when she and Josh arrived for the celebration dinner. She was looking stunning in a sheath dress, and was full of wedding plans as she flashed her diamond ring around.

'It's lovely,' said Bella, admiring it dutifully.

'Josh took me to the jeweller's at the weekend. It took me hours to decide which one I wanted, didn't it, Josh?'

'Hours,' he agreed somewhat thinly.

Aisling gave a silvery peal of laughter and hugged his arm. 'Poor Josh! He was getting a bit bored at the end. You know what he's like, Bella!'

Bella handed her a glass of champagne without looking at Josh. 'Yes,' she said. 'I know what he's like.'

CHAPTER FOUR

'I'M AFRAID it was terribly expensive,' Aisling was burbling on, 'but he *did* say I could have whichever one I liked best.'

'I'm sure he thinks you're worth it,' said Bella evenly.

Pouring another glass, she gave it to Josh, forcing herself to meet his eyes. 'I know you'd rather have a beer, but I'm afraid champagne is obligatory on these occasions!'

'Thanks.' Josh took the glass from her, but Bella was so on edge that as their fingers brushed, she jerked her hand away as if from an electric shock, and half the champagne spilt onto the floor.

'Sorry,' she muttered, scarlet-cheeked, and when she topped up his glass, her hand holding the bottle was not quite steady.

'Are you OK?' he asked in concern.

'I'm fine. Just a bit nervous about the meal,' she offered as an explanation. 'I've been a bit too ambitious, I think.'

Josh's face relaxed into a grin. 'You always do this, Bella. You plan these incredibly elaborate menus and then get into a state when they don't work out. I wish you'd throw all those recipe books away and stick to offering your guests cheese on toast!'

'I might do after tonight,' she said, a reluctant smile tugging at her mouth and as their eyes met it was as if the two of them were alone for a tiny moment in a private world.

Josh was the first to look away. 'It's good of you to

have gone to so much effort,' he said looking around the kitchen.

'Yes, it all looks lovely,' said Aisling, who had observed the way their eyes had locked with a narrowed gaze.

Bella had found an antique damask cloth for the old pine table where she and Kate and Phoebe had spent so many hours drinking wine and putting the world to rights, and she was pleased with the effect now that it was laid with gleaming glasses and flowers and lit candles.

It all looked just as romantic as she had intended—if you looked one way, at least. The effect was rather spoiled if you looked the other by all the dirty dishes piled up beside the sink. She had used just about every implement in the kitchen already and there was still so much to do. She had always loved the big cosy kitchen, but sometimes you could see the point of a separate dining room where you could pretend everything was under control.

'I do like this kitchen,' Aisling was saying. 'It's the main reason I was hoping to move in at one time.'

'I'm sorry,' said Bella, remembering how she had turned down the idea when Josh had suggested it.

She swallowed. That brief, intense exchange of looks had left her feeling peculiar, almost jarred, as if she had stumbled in the dark. You weren't supposed to gaze into a man's eyes when you were just friends, and especially not when you were celebrating his engagement to someone else.

'I must have seemed very unfriendly when I insisted on keeping the house to myself,' she said by way of an apology.

'Don't worry about it,' said Aisling, waving a careless hand so that the diamond on her finger glinted in the candlelight. 'I'm sure I'd have felt exactly the same. And anyway, as things turned out it was best thing that could have happened, wasn't it, darling?'

She took Josh's arm in a proprietorial manner. 'If you'd agreed to let me come here, I wouldn't have moved in with Josh, and we would never have discovered just how compatible we were,' she said. 'We probably wouldn't even have thought of getting married, would we, Josh?'

'It's hard to know,' he said.

'So it's all thanks to you, Bella.' Aisling lifted her glass with the hand that wasn't clutching Josh and sent her a glittering smile. 'Thank you!'

Bella's own smile was feeling more than a little fixed, and she turned away to pick up a plate. 'Have a canapé,' she said.

'Ooh, I shouldn't really...' Aisling inspected the plate. Bella was proud of her way with nibbles, and she had spent hours making these look spectacular with exquisite garnishes.

'These are the only part of the meal that have worked, so I should make the most of them if I were you,' she told Aisling.

'Well, maybe just one.' Aisling let go of Josh and her hand hovered over the plate until she had selected the one she evidently judged the least fattening. 'Delicious,' she said.

'Have another.'

'Oh, no, thanks.' She patted her perfectly flat stomach complacently. 'I've seen the perfect dress already but I can't afford to put on so much as a milligram if I want to get into it for the wedding.'

'Have you decided when it's going to be?'

Bella was hugely grateful to Phoebe for coming up and joining in the conversation just then. Possibly she had seen that Bella herself was close to taking her canapés and shoving them down Aisling's ample cleavage.

'Next May,' said Aisling. 'I think a spring wedding is lovely, don't you?'

There was a feverish glitter in Aisling's green eyes and she seemed on a high. Bella supposed she couldn't blame her. She would be euphoric if she were wearing Josh's ring and had Josh to go home with at the end of the evening, but she hadn't anticipated that every word Aisling spoke would be like a knife twisting inside her.

'Excuse me,' she said, suddenly desperate to get out of the kitchen so no one could see her face. 'I must just go and see about the starter.'

Phoebe was listening to Aisling's increasingly manic wedding plans, and Josh looked down into his champagne with a slight frown.

'Don't worry,' Gib said in his ear. 'I brought some beer with me.' He peered into his own glass with a grimace. 'I don't know why women insist on drinking this stuff! Down that, and I'll get you a proper drink.'

Josh grinned and drained his glass obediently. Gib could always make things seem better.

The meal couldn't be described as a culinary triumph—Bella's never were—but there was plenty of wine and good company. While Aisling was on extra sparkling form, Bella was much quieter than usual, but once she stopped jumping up and down to see to the food she did relax, and it was a great evening.

When she got up much later to make some more coffee, Josh followed her to the working end of the kitchen to give her a hand while the others carried on a spirited argument at the table.

'In case I don't get a chance to say it later, thank you,' he said.

'Sorry about the beef,' she sighed. 'And the pudding. It was all a bit of a disaster, wasn't it?'

'It was delicious,' Josh lied manfully. 'And anyway, it doesn't matter what the food was like. What matters is all the trouble you went to. It's been a very special evening, and I really appreciate it. So does Aisling,' he added as he put his arms around Bella and gave her a hug.

For a second or so she leant into him, but then pulled away and made a big deal of filling the kettle.

'Still no word from Will?' Josh asked.

'I see him occasionally,' she said, carefully spooning coffee into the cafetière, 'but it's not the same.'

'Isn't it getting any easier?'

Bella stopped and looked straight at him. 'No,' she said.

Right, she was going to have to get on with her life, Bella told herself the next morning as she tackled the monumental pile of washing up. Oh, for a dishwasher!

Miracles were not going to happen. Aisling was hell-bent on marrying Josh, and judging by the conversation at dinner last night had turned overnight into an obsessive who could talk about nothing else. They had heard all about Aisling's plans for the wedding, some of which were clearly news to Josh, and had even been treated to a summary of every possible honeymoon location.

'We're off to the Seychelles in a couple of weeks anyway,' Aisling rattled on, 'so we can check it out and see if it's a place we'd want to go back to. It looks beautiful, but there might not be enough to do there apart from diving.'

'Most honeymoon couples don't have any problem finding something to do!' said Gib, amused, but Aisling took him seriously.

'Josh and I aren't like that. We need to be able to climb

or sail or go white-water rafting. We'd both be bored to death lying on a beach all day.'

Bella had been unable to resist exchanging a speaking glance with Kate and Phoebe.

'Not one of us!' Kate had mouthed back.

'She's protesting too much if you ask me,' Phoebe had murmured in Bella's ear a bit later. 'Bet she hates all that tough stuff really.'

Bella didn't think Phoebe was right. Aisling might have rattled on obsessively about weddings all night, but she was equally at home out in the wild like Josh, and once the wedding of the century—as theirs was clearly intended to be—was over, she would settle down and be good for Josh.

Which meant that *she* had to get a grip. No more misery, no more longing for Josh or dreaming that things could be different. It was time to restart her life.

Easier said than done. Bella did try. She made herself go to parties again, and she tried to keep herself busy the rest of the time so that she didn't have too much time to think, but the thought of Josh was like a constant ache inside her. It was the first thing Bella was aware of when she woke, and the last thing before she went to sleep, and in between it throbbed dully and insistently and made it impossible to think of anything else.

She lost weight, which didn't suit her, and she knew that her skin looked tired and there were dark shadows under her eyes. Kate and Phoebe tutted in concern when they saw her.

'You look awful!'

'Thanks!'

'Seriously, Bella, you're not sickening for something, are you?'

Only with love, thought Bella drearily.

'I'm just tired,' she said. 'I need a holiday, but I can't afford to go anywhere. My last credit card bill was so enormous I thought I was going to pass out when I opened it. I wish someone would offer *me* a free week in the Seychelles,' she sighed.

The thought of a week with nothing to do but lie on a tropical beach was incredibly inviting. No diving, no sailing, just lying there with your eyes closed...yes, she could handle that!

'It would be nice, wouldn't it?' said Kate. 'It's all right for Josh and Aisling!'

'When are they off?' Phoebe asked, getting up to freshen their glasses.

'Soon, I think.'

'I haven't seen them since your dinner. How is Josh?'

Bella's throat tightened at the mere sound of his name. 'I don't know,' she said as casually as she could. 'I haven't seen him either.'

Phoebe frowned. 'I hope nothing's wrong. It doesn't sound like Josh to drop out of sight like that. Hasn't he been in touch at all?'

'He rang and left a message thanking me for the dinner,' Bella admitted, 'but it wasn't the kind of message that needed a reply, so I didn't.'

'But Bella, he'd expect you to call him back anyway, wouldn't he?'

She hunched a shoulder, unable to explain how hard she found the idea of talking to Josh now. 'I didn't want to intrude,' she said defensively. 'They probably just want to be alone at the moment.'

'They probably think you're ignoring them,' said Kate, sounding unusually astringent. 'I thought you wanted to make Josh think that you liked Aisling?'

'I do...I just need a little time to get used to the idea of him getting married,' she confessed.

'You've had nearly three weeks, Bella,' said Phoebe gently as she handed her back her glass. 'You're going to have to come to terms with it some time.'

Bella sighed and sipped her drink. 'I know.'

The trouble was that she couldn't imagine having a normal conversation with Josh now when all she could think of to say was I love you, I love you, I love you. She *could* ring and wish them a good trip, she supposed bleakly. At least it would give them something to talk about.

'I'll call him,' she promised.

To her relief, her friends let the matter drop then. 'I'm not sure we can run to a week in the Seychelles, but what else can we do to cheer you up?' asked Kate. 'It's Friday tomorrow. Why don't you come round and have supper with us? You look as if you could do with a decent meal.'

'I'd like to, but I'm supposed to be going to some party in Battersea,' Bella said without enthusiasm.

By the time she got home from work the next day she felt even less enthusiastic about the prospect. It was a vile November evening, and her umbrella had been useless in the gusty wind. The walk from the tube was enough to leave her wet and bedraggled, and she wasn't sure she could face tarting herself up, going out into the rain again and spending the evening smiling and looking as if she was having fun.

But the alternative was to sit at home missing Josh and trying not to cry.

Maybe a drink would perk her up? Bella made herself a vodka and tonic and slumped on the kitchen sofa, not noticeably perked but appreciating the drink anyway. She was still trying to summon up the energy to have a shower when the doorbell rang.

Drink in hand, she went out to peer through the peephole, and her heart did an alarming somersault when she saw Josh standing on the other side of the door, huddled into his coat, with the collar turned up. His hair was plastered to his head, and the rain was running down his face.

'Josh!' Hastily Bella opened the door and stared at him. 'What are you doing here?'

'I needed to see you.'

Josh hadn't thought about what he was going to say. He had just followed his instinct which was to get to Bella. He couldn't explain on the phone, he had wanted her presence, and he went straight out into the rain. It was only when he got to her doorstep that it had occurred to him that she might not be there.

But there she was, as he had somehow known she would be, looking very Bella in a short skirt and spectacular shoes, the golden hair falling around her face, and a glass in her hand.

'Come in,' she said in concern, stepping back and holding the door wide open. 'You're sodden!'

She helped him peel off his coat and hung it over the back of a chair in the kitchen. 'Sit down,' she said. 'I'll get you a drink. You look like you need it.'

He must look as shell-shocked as he felt, thought Josh as he dropped onto the old kitchen sofa, but he was feeling better already. There was something amazingly comforting about coming into this house, and especially this big, shabby kitchen with its mess and its clutter and its complete absence of steel or granite or anything remotely trendy.

'Here.' Bella put a glass of whisky into his hand and

sat cross-legged on the sofa, turning so that she could face him. 'Now, tell me what's happened.'

'Aisling's left me,' said Josh, a little surprised at how easy it was to say.

'Left you?' Bella stared at him blankly. 'What do you mean, *left* you?'

'She's gone. She doesn't want to marry me any more.'

It was almost a relief to see that the news was as unexpected to Bella as it had been to him. Josh would have felt a fool if he had been the last one to suspect anything, but looking at Bella he could see that she was as stunned as he had been.

'But...but...*why*?' She stammered. 'She was so excited the other day when we were all here. She couldn't talk about anything but marrying you.'

'She was trying to convince herself that was what she wanted,' he said evenly, 'but it wasn't. She's been in love with someone else all along.'

Bella shook her head trying to take it all in. 'Who is he? Do you know him?'

'His name's Bryn. I haven't had much to do with him but he's a senior executive at C.B.C. Aisling worked there before she joined us, and that's where she met him. She told me this evening that they'd had a passionate affair for nearly a year and that she was mad about him. But he's married, of course, and although he'd talked about leaving his wife, he kept coming up with excuses about how it wasn't the right time, and in the end Aisling decided to call the whole thing off.

'She was desperate to leave C.B.C. so that she wouldn't have to see him every day. I knew her because of previous work we had done for the company, so when I offered her a chance to move, she jumped at it. She told me tonight that it seemed as if it was meant.'

'No wonder she was so keen to come and work for you!' said Bella tartly. 'So all that stuff about wanting a more fulfilling job and working with a smaller organisation was her being just the teensiest bit economical with the truth, was it?'

'Not exactly. She enjoys working with us, but it wasn't quite the complete break she had hoped for,' said Josh. 'You know we're hoping to win this big contract from C.B.C.? If we get it, it'll be largely because of Aisling's contacts, and part of her job now is to deal with this Bryn on a regular basis, which hasn't been easy for her.'

Bella wasn't in the mood to feel sympathetic for Aisling's problems. 'God, Josh, you're starting to sound sorry for her!'

'I am a bit,' he said. 'Aisling tried everything she could to put him behind her, but she just couldn't. He's all she wants, and she had to try and cut herself off from that. That takes guts,' he added fairly.

'I might feel a bit more respect for her if she'd done it without using you,' said Bella. The blue eyes were stormy as she put her glass down on the table with a sharp click.

'That makes her sound too cynical.' It was ironic that he should be the one who ended up defending Aisling, Josh thought. 'It wasn't as if she didn't like me. She said she did, she liked me a lot, and she thought she could make a fresh start with me, but when it came down to it, it wasn't the same. She tried to talk herself into wanting to be with me, but it wasn't what she felt for Bryn. That was something much stronger and in the end she couldn't resist it.'

'And did she give *you* any thought in all of this?'

'I think she tried,' he said. 'She really wanted to make a go of it with me, and for a while it seemed as if it would work. She said she found me attractive, and we had lots of interests in common. There was no reason why it shouldn't really. Successful marriages have been built on less, and Aisling was hoping that if she threw herself into wedding preparations, she would forget all about Bryn.'

'So what made her change her mind?' Bella was still tight-lipped with anger on his behalf.

'Bryn rang her yesterday. He told her that he was getting a divorce and that he wanted to be with her. Aisling said that she knew then that it wouldn't be fair to get married to me feeling the way she still did about Bryn. She said she was sorry,' Josh added.

'Big of her!' said Bella tightly.

'Come on, Bella. At least she was honest,' he said. 'It was a classic relationship on the rebound. I'd much rather she told me now than after we were married. The longer she left telling me, the harder it would be.'

'I suppose so.'

Belatedly Bella realised that she wasn't being very supportive. 'I'm sorry,' she said, putting a hand on his arm. 'I just can't believe how calm you are. I can't believe any of it really. Aisling seemed so happy with you. And...and you were good together,' she added.

'Were we?' Josh drank his whisky. He was warmer and dryer, and sitting here on the sofa with Bella, it didn't seem so difficult to take in. 'It's hard to tell now.'

'I'm sorry, Josh,' she said again quietly and he shrugged and smiled crookedly.

'I'm sorry for dumping it all on you like this.'

'I seem to remember crying on your shoulder a few times,' said Bella, taking the empty glass from his hand and refilling it. She sat back down beside him straight-backed and crossed her legs once more.

'How do you feel?' she asked. 'I mean, really? No stiff upper lip!'

Josh sipped gratefully at his whisky. 'A bit stunned, I suppose.'

He couldn't tell Bella that his first reaction had shockingly been one of secret relief. He hadn't realised that he had had reservations at all until Aisling had announced that she didn't want to marry him after all, when he felt as if a burden he had hardly been aware of before had been lifted from his shoulders.

'It was the last thing I expected to hear when I got home this evening,' he told Bella. 'Aisling's been full of wedding plans all week, and we were working together all day. She seemed absolutely normal then. She's very good at keeping her professional and personal life separate.'

Bella didn't know about that. As far as she could see, Aisling had managed to sleep with her boss wherever she worked, and you couldn't mix up your personal and professional life more completely than that!

But she would have to be careful what she said. Josh was putting on a good front—stiff upper lip to the end—but Bella thought that he was more hurt than he was letting on. It was typical of him to take it on the chin like a gentleman and say that it was better for Aisling to break it all off now than later. No ranting and raving for Josh!

'What did you say?' she asked quietly instead.

'What could I say? If Aisling feels this away about Bryn, there's no point in her being with me.'

Bella ached for him. She had dreamt of hearing that Aisling wasn't going to marry Josh after all, but now that the moment had come, all she could think of was that he was hurting. Now was not the time to throw herself into his arms and tell him that she would love him for ever. He was raw and vulnerable, and still in love with Aisling, she reminded herself. He wasn't ready to think about anyone or anything else.

'Perhaps she'll come back,' Bella tried to comfort him. 'She might find that she doesn't feel quite the same when she's actually living with this Bryn. The romance wears off pretty quickly when you're picking up dirty socks and squabbling about who leaves the top off the toothpaste.'

'Perhaps,' said Josh, but he didn't sound convinced.

'Aisling's a fool if she doesn't,' Bella told him stoutly. 'She doesn't have any idea how lucky she is. She couldn't ask for more than you!'

'Except that she does,' he pointed out. 'I'm not the one she wants.'

Bella thought that her expression didn't change but Josh put his drink down abruptly and pulled her over to hug her. 'I'm sorry, Bella, I'm a fool. You know what that feels like.'

Agonisingly aware of his arms around her, she nodded into his shoulder. 'Yes,' she said quietly. 'I know what it's like.'

Everything should be perfect. He was free, she was free, and his arms were around her, holding her tight. What more could she want? Her face was pressed into his throat, and she could smell his skin. If she opened her eyes, she could see the pulse beating below his ear. It would be so easy to put her lips to it.

Except that it *wasn't* that easy, Bella realised. If she hadn't been able to tell him how she felt before because he was happy with Aisling, it was going to be even more difficult now. He might be putting a good face on it but Josh must be feeling raw with rejection. He needed her support, not the emotional equivalent of kicking a man when he was down.

It would be important for Josh that she at least was constant. He would need her to be the way she had always been. The last thing he wanted right now would be her confusing the issue and throwing the basis of their friendship into question when the rest of his life was in flux.

What would be the point of telling him now, anyway? Bella thought. Did she really want him turning to her on the rebound, the way Aisling had done to him? No, she would have to be very careful. Let him carry on believing that it was Will she was breaking her heart for, at least for the time being.

Josh's arms tightened around her. 'We're a pair, aren't we?' he said, and his effort to sound jocular tightened Bella's throat. 'Both in the reject bin! What's wrong with us?'

'What's wrong with *them*?' Bella countered and Josh kissed her hair.

'I'm glad you're here, Bella,' he said.

'I'm always here for you, Josh,' she said in a low voice, knowing that he couldn't possibly understand how much she meant it.

'I know,' he said quietly as he let her go.

Bella was trembling slightly as she sat back and picked up her drink, and it was a real effort to keep her voice steady. 'What are you going to do now?'

'There's nothing to do,' said Josh, reaching for his own glass. 'Aisling and I are going to be working together, so we'll just have to be civilised and carry on.'

'You mean she gets to keep her job after the way she's treated you?' Bella was outraged.

'I can hardly sack her because she's not in love with me,' Josh pointed out dryly. 'I don't think that would go down very well at an industrial tribunal if she decided to contest it! Anyway,' he said, 'she's very good at her job. We need her if we want to clinch this big contract with C.B.C.'

Bella couldn't believe that Aisling was *that* important.

'But it's going to be incredibly awkward, isn't it?' she objected. 'Everyone else at the office must know that you've been living together and were planning to get married.'

Josh shrugged. 'We'll just have to get on with it. I'll have a word with the others and ask them not to make things difficult for Aisling by asking too many questions. In any case, we'll be in the Seychelles next week, so they can get all the gossip out of the way then and with any luck they'll have something else to talk about when we get back.'

Bella eyed him with frustration. He could be infuriatingly reasonable at times! By rights, he should be swearing and tearing his hair out, and if not actually plotting revenge then at least vowing to make Aisling sorry.

But no! He was going to be the perfect gentleman and make everything nice and easy for her.

'Why don't you let Bryn take your place in the Seychelles while you're at it?' she said crossly. 'Pack their cases for them and take them to the airport!'

'I don't need to give up my place,' said Josh. 'Bryn's going anyway. He's one of C.B.C.'s most successful sales managers, and he's taking Aisling with him instead of his wife. He's changed the ticket into her name and has told whoever's doing all the organisation that Aisling will be taking his wife's place.'

Bella's jaw dropped. 'But...what about *you*?' she demanded.

'I'd be lying if I said I was looking forward to it,' he said with a sigh. 'Frankly, the last thing I feel like doing at the moment is spending a week stuck on an island having to suck up to potential clients. I'm no good at that kind of thing at the best of times. That's why it was important that Aisling came with me. She can do all the chit-chat.'

'If she's still working for you, she can manage that, can't she?' said Bella tightly.

Josh sighed and drank his whisky. 'I expect she will, but it won't be the same if she's not associated with me. If I'd been able to introduce my fiancée and keep everything on a very light social level, it would have made everything much easier. As it is, I'll stick out like a sore thumb being there on my own, and it's going to be very obvious that I'm there for work—the very impression C.B.C. didn't want me to give!'

'In that case, do you really need to go at all?'

'I think I'm going to have to,' said Josh, running a hand over his head in a gesture of weariness. 'C.B.C. have been insistent that they want me to be there to make personal contact with the executives I'd be working with, and the contract is too important to the company not to make that effort. It's not just about me. There are other people who work for me and who are depending on that contract for some security over the next three or four years. I'd be letting them down if I didn't go.'

He drained his glass and put it down on the table. 'I'll just have to do what I can. I'd better contact C.B.C. first thing tomorrow and let the know I won't be taking my fiancée with me after all. It'll be very short notice, but they might be able to cancel the flight and change my room.'

'Unless you just change the name of your fiancée,' said Bella.

Josh looked puzzled. 'What do you mean?'

'Well, Bryn seems to have been able to put his poor wife's ticket into Aisling's name. Why can't you do the same?'

'What would be the point of that? Aisling's got a ticket already.'

'I wasn't thinking of Aisling,' said Bella a little tartly. 'I was thinking of me.'

CHAPTER FIVE

HE STARED at her. 'You?' he said carefully.

'It sounds to me as if there's a spare ticket to the Seychelles going begging,' said Bella. 'You might not like the idea of a week on a tropical beach, but I haven't had a holiday for ages.'

She was groping her way cautiously, not wanting to spook Josh, but desperate to convince him to let her go with him. She couldn't bear the thought of him facing that week on his own. He would be fine, of course—Josh could cope with anything—but it would still be very hard for him to be there, having to face Aisling and Bryn every day. He might be tough, but even the tough needed some support occasionally.

'I could come with you,' she went on casually. 'I've been so miserable recently but I can't afford to go away by myself. I just thought that if there's a chance of spending a week on a beach at someone else's expense...' she trailed off suggestively, and Josh's mouth quirked.

'You could bear it?'

'I'd be helping you out at the same time,' Bella reassured him in a mock virtuous tone so that he wouldn't guess that was what she really wanted to do. 'You said yourself that it would be easier if you had a partner with you—who's to know that I'm not actually the fiancée you said you were taking with you?'

'Aisling and Bryn, for a start,' said Josh.

'I think after the way they've treated you, the least they could do is keep quiet,' said Bella stringently. 'None of the people you have to impress are going to know, are they? I might not have Aisling's contacts, but I can do chit-chat, as you call it, just as well as she can. Probably better,' she added, thinking about it.

'Oh, I know you can chit-chat for England!' said Josh.

'Well, then.'

He looked at her with a puzzled expression. 'I'm trying to think why it's not a good idea,' he said slowly. 'It feels like it shouldn't be, but I can't actually think of a reason why it wouldn't work.'

'It feels wrong because you'd be going with me instead of Aisling,' said Bella evenly. 'I know it's not what you wanted, Josh, but it *would* be a way to save face. It's not as if you'd have to be careful the way you would with a total stranger. We're so comfortable with each other I think we'd be quite convincing as a couple. You know how often we've been out and people have thought that we were together because of our body language.'

'I can see body language wouldn't be a problem,' Josh agreed, 'but other things might be. How comfortable would you be about sharing a room, which is what we'd have to do?'

'I could cope with that,' said Bella. 'It's not as if we've never done it before.'

'A long time ago,' he pointed out. 'That was when we were students. It's not the same any more, and it's no use pretending that it is.'

No, it wasn't the same, thought Bella, looking at him and remembering those carefree days when Josh had just been a mate, before he had started to seem as necessary to her as breathing.

'You're right,' she said slowly, 'it's not the same, but I just think it's going to be really hard for you to see Aisling with Bryn—which by the way is a totally stupid name. I bet you anything he's called Bryan and he's just dropped the ''a''!'

She stopped, realising that she'd gone off at a tangent. 'Where was I?'

Josh grinned. 'You were trying to be deeply sympathetic about how hard it was going to be in the Seychelles and then you spoiled everything by making me laugh. I'm never going to be able to look at Bryn in the same way again!'

'Oh, yes,' said Bella, delighted to see the glint back in Josh's eyes but refusing to let herself be sidetracked onto the issue of Bryn's name again. 'Well, I do think it will be incredibly difficult and I can't help feeling that it would be easier if you had a friend with you. Don't you think so?' she asked anxiously, suddenly afraid that she was pushing him into something that he didn't want to do.

'I suppose that depends on the friend,' said Josh, straight-faced, and then relented. 'But yes, if you mean you, it would be nice—very nice!—to have some support.'

'That's what I'd be there for,' Bella told him. 'And if supporting you means pretending to be your fiancée to keep up appearances, fine, and if *that* means sharing a room, I'm not exactly going to make a fuss. We know each other too well for that.'

'What if it means sharing a bed?'

Bella hesitated, picking her words with care. 'We both know how things are, Josh,' she said. 'I know you're in love with Aisling, you know about Will. There's not much room for misunderstanding in our case, is there?'

She reached for his empty glass. 'Have a think about it while I get you another drink.'

Josh had already had two stiff whiskies. Perhaps that was why Bella's idea was seeming to make perfect sense, he thought hazily. But she was right, wasn't she? How could it be awkward for two such old friends to share a bed? Especially when it was absolutely clear that she was still in love with Will? There would be no room for any misunderstanding *there*, just as she had said.

And as for him, thought Josh, he was naturally devastated about Aisling. No man with any sense of decency would be sitting there, barely hours after his engagement had been broken off, wondering what it would be like to share a bed with another woman.

He wouldn't be thinking about her softness as she hugged him—purely sympathetically, of course—or the fragrance of her hair. About the indignation in her blue eyes or the curve of her mouth as she smiled.

He certainly wouldn't be thinking that sleeping with her might not be that easy after all.

Discovering that you weren't the decent man you thought you were was all he needed after the day he had had, thought Josh with an inward sigh.

Really, he didn't deserve Bella's sympathy, Josh thought guiltily. He knew she was offering to go out to the Seychelles because she felt sorry for him, but she probably *could* do with a break. She had had a hard time over Will, and if her finances were as chaotic as usual, he could well believe that she couldn't afford a holiday by herself.

Giving Bella a week in the sun would at least be one good thing to come out of this whole sorry mess with Aisling. Josh didn't mind letting her believe that he needed her support more than in fact he did. And it would be good to have her there, he had to admit. She would charm everyone, with the possible exception of Aisling and Bryn, and her presence would make things less awkward all round.

Oh, yes, there were lots of reasons why it would be good to take Bella up on her offer, but when it came down to it, the only one that mattered was that he wanted her with him. Josh had had enough intensity and conversations about weddings over the last few weeks. It would be fun with Bella.

Here she was, putting another enormous whisky into his hand. 'Well?' she asked, 'Have you had a think?'

'I have.'

'And?'

'And I think we should go for it,' he said, and smiled at Bella's whoop of delight before reminding himself that he would need to be careful. If he slipped too quickly out of the role of rejected fiancé, she might start to wonder why he needed her there at all. 'I think it would make things easier for Aisling too,' he said.

The blue eyes narrowed. 'That was naturally my main concern!'

'Sarcasm, Bella?'

'Just another service we offer!' she retorted even more sarcastically. 'Honestly, Josh, the woman only dumped you a couple of hours ago! I know how important she is to you, but I think it's a bit early for you to be bending over backwards to *make things easier* for her! What about a bit of anger or bitterness? I'm sure it would be much more healthy!'

'The thing is, I can't feel that way about Aisling,' said Josh, knowing that it was a lack in himself. If he had really loved Aisling, he would have been just as bitter and angry as Bella wanted him to be. As it was, he had been much angrier with Will for hurting Bella. 'You weren't angry or bitter about Will,' he pointed out, 'but I can tell that you're heartbroken all the same.'

Bella opened her mouth, only to change her mind about what she was going to say and close it again. 'I hope you aren't expecting me to be nice to Aisling too?' she said after a moment, and Josh wondered what she had meant to say instead. 'I'm not as tolerant as you.'

'I'd rather you were,' he told her. 'It's not going to be an easy time for any of us, but we need to focus on getting the C.B.C. contract. Given that we're supposed to be teaching these guys how to communicate effectively and work as a team, it's not going to impress them if we're all squabbling amongst ourselves.'

'Oh, all right,' sighed Bella with a martyred air. 'I'll be good.'

Josh smiled and sipped at his whisky as he settled back into the sofa, stretching his legs out in front of him. For a man who was supposed to have had his heart broken earlier that evening he was feeling surprisingly mellow. It was good to be back on his own with Bella again. It hadn't been same when Aisling had been around.

'So that's settled then.' Bella took up her familiar position on the sofa beside him, with crossed legs and a straight back. 'When do we leave?'

'Check-in is noon on Monday,' he told her. 'I'll come and pick you up in the morning and we can go out to Heathrow together.'

Bella flashed him a look underneath her lashes. 'You mean you don't trust me not to be late!'

'I know that if it was up to you you'd stroll up five minutes before the plane's due to leave,' said Josh, 'but I don't think my nerves will stand it! Since we're pretending to be engaged, why don't you go the whole hog and pretend to be a normal person who turns up on time for a change?'

Bella poked her tongue at him. She had never actually missed a plane, had she? True, there had been a couple of close calls, and she had given up booking train tickets in advance, but really, it wasn't as if planes ever left on time anyway.

'I suppose you'll be wanting to leave at the crack of dawn on Monday and get there four hours early just to be on the safe side,' she grumbled. 'It doesn't leave long to get ready. Still, I suppose I don't need much.'

Mentally, Bella ran an eye over her wardrobe. It had been so long since she had had a decent holiday all her hot-weather clothes were hopelessly out of date. She might just have to have a little shop tomorrow. Josh wouldn't understand, but facing Aisling required a major style offensive. Nothing too obvious, of course, but certainly enough to make Aisling feel that she was never *quite* wearing the right thing...

Josh was evidently thinking along more practical lines.

'What about your job, Bella? Will they let you take time off at such short notice?'

Why was Josh worrying about her job? There were far more essential things to think about. Reluctantly, Bella dragged her attention away from the important question of a wardrobe designed with the daily discomfiture of Aisling in mind.

'I might try ringing my boss at home later,' she said. 'She won't like it, but we're not that busy at the moment and I've done lots of overtime recently so I'm entitled to time off in lieu. Luckily, Louise is a real romantic,' she confided. 'If she gets too sticky about the whole thing I'll just tell her we've decided to get married on the spur of the moment and that you're whisking me off to the Seychelles to celebrate.'

Josh looked unconvinced. 'Don't tell her that we've known each other for fourteen years,' he said. 'It would take more than a confirmed romantic to interpret that as a whirlwind affair!'

'Oh, I don't know,' said Bella, considering the matter. 'Louise knows we've been friends a long time, but I'll just tell her that everything has suddenly changed and that realising that we were meant to be more than friends has caught us both unawares.'

There was a tiny pause. 'Do you think she's likely to fall for that?' said Josh in a dry voice.

'It happens,' she said without looking at him. 'Sometimes you fall in love when you least expect it.'

'It sounds quite convincing when you put it like that,' he said.

Another silence. For some reason Bella's heart was slamming against her ribs. Don't look at him, she told herself frantically. You'll only make a fool of yourself.

Her eyes skittered around the room but it was as if an invisible, irresistible force was dragging them back to Josh's face, where their gazes locked for a long moment before Bella managed to wrench hers away.

'As long as it convinces Louise,' she said shakily. 'That's the main thing.'

'Of course,' echoed Josh. 'That's the main thing.'

In spite of her best efforts, Bella found her eyes flickering back to his once more before they both looked away.

The pause was even longer this time, and it reverberated unnervingly up and down Bella's spine. She longed to be able to say something to break the silence but her mind had gone blank and all she could think of was how close Josh was and how easy it would be to lean over and touch him.

She swirled her glass, staring down into it as if fascinated, but she was so acutely aware of Josh by that stage that she might as well have been staring straight at him. It was as if those fleeting eye contacts had imprinted an unnervingly vivid image of him on her brain, not of the old familiar Josh, but of a stranger, a man, with a cool mouth and a firm jaw and intriguing creases around his eyes.

In the end it was Josh who spoke first. He cleared his throat. 'Are you sure you're happy to do this, Bella?' he asked awkwardly, as if he too was unsettled by the strange tightening of the atmosphere.

Flippancy was the only response Bella was capable of right then. 'Well, a free week in the Seychelles *will* be a bit of bore, of course, but for you...anything!'

'It's just that you didn't sound too keen on the idea when Aisling was talking about it.'

'That's because she kept going on about all the activities you would be doing together. I presume all the hearty stuff isn't compulsory.' Belatedly a wary look crept into the blue eyes. 'I don't have to go diving, do I?'

Josh shook his head. 'You would if you loved me,' he said solemnly. 'If you want to convince people that you're my fiancée, you probably should make an effort to get involved in some the activities.'

His face was completely straight, but she caught the gleam of humour in his eyes. He was teasing...phew!

'I'll just tell everybody that our relationship is based on the attraction of opposites,' she said firmly. 'Bet you anything I won't be the only person heading straight for the beach, so if it's all the same to you, I'll concentrate my charm offensive there. After a few days on a lounger, with nothing to do but listen to the coconuts drop or cool off with a paddle in the Indian Ocean I should be able to be nice to anybody—even Aisling!'

'You're going *where*?' said Kate when Bella rang her the next morning. 'With *who*?'

Impatiently, Bella explained the situation all over again. She had already been through all this with Phoebe. Now that she was used to the idea herself, it seemed such an obvious solution that she couldn't understand why the others didn't seem to grasp it at once.

'So let me get this right,' said Kate at last. 'You and Josh have got engaged without even *consulting* me or Phoebe?'

'It's just for a week,' said Bella. 'And it's just pretending. I don't know why you're making such a big deal of it,' she huffed. 'You and Finn did exactly the same thing.'

'Yes, and look what happened!' said Kate. 'I'm all for it, but you want to be careful, Bella. Pretending isn't nearly as easy as you think in that situation.'

'I know,' said Bella, whose main problem wasn't going to be pretending that she was in love with Josh but pretending that she wasn't.

Kate hesitated. 'It will be difficult for Josh, too. He must be feeling pretty raw about Aisling and it's going to be awful for him having to see her with this other guy so soon. You can't expect even someone as level-headed as Josh to be thinking clearly under those circumstances.'

'What are you trying to say, Kate?'

'Just...be careful,' she said slowly. 'I know you and Josh are old friends, but you're going to be thrown into a very intimate situation and things won't be the same. It's easy to imagine how you might end up turning to each other.'

'I thought you and Phoebe wanted us to end up together?' said Bella, trying to make a joke of it, but Kate took her seriously.

'Only if it's for the right reasons. Josh deserves better than getting together because you feel restless and unsettled, and you deserve more than being second-best to Aisling.'

Bella was still thinking of this conversation when she

met Josh for lunch later that day so that he could report that he had been able to change Aisling's ticket into Bella's name, and Bella that after much grumbling her boss had agreed to her having the whole week off.

Kate was right, she knew that, and she *would* be careful, Bella vowed, but her spirits had risen in spite of herself at the prospect of the week ahead.

She felt better today, less edgy and aware. It was like old times, meeting Josh for lunch on a Saturday, and they were both more relaxed, talking and laughing as if the tension of the night before had never happened.

So much so, in fact, that Bella had to keep reminding herself about Aisling. Josh seemed to be fine, but then, he would. The phrase 'keeping a stiff upper lip' might have been coined especially for him.

Josh hadn't forgotten about Aisling though. 'I rang her this morning,' he told Bella.

'What was that like?' she asked with a grimace, imagining what a tense conversation it must have been. 'Was it awful?'

'No, it was fine.' Josh had been surprised himself at how normal it had all seemed. 'I told her that you were going in her place and she and Bryn have promised not to let on to anyone else that you and I aren't really a couple.'

Big of her, thought Bella with a mental sniff.

'If they don't say anything, it shouldn't be a problem to convince the others,' Josh went on. 'All you need is a ring to flash around and no one will think to question whether you're a real fiancée or not.'

Bella looked down at her fingers. She had a silver ring on her right hand but it wasn't the kind of thing you could really pass off as an engagement ring. What she needed was a rock. Glass would do, she thought. She could never tell the difference between real gems and glass, and she bet none of the others would be able to either.

Mentally she reviewed her jewellery. She had plenty of fun earrings and necklaces but very few rings. 'I'm not sure I've got anything suitable,' she said doubtfully.

'I'll buy you one,' said Josh. Glancing at his watch, he drained his glass and pushed back his chair. 'Come on, let's go and do it now.'

'You can't buy me a ring!'

'Why not?'

'Well...it doesn't seem right,' said Bella, getting to her feet more slowly and shrugging on her coat. 'Anyway, there's no need surely,' she added, thinking about the knuckleduster Aisling had been flaunting at the engagement dinner. 'What about the ring you bought Aisling?'

'I said she could keep it.'

'And she did?' asked Bella indignantly.

Josh was in one of his infuriatingly reasonable moods. 'What was I going to do with it?' he pointed out.

'You could have taken it back to the shop!'

He held open the door of the bar for her. 'I think that would have been a bit petty, don't you?'

'No, I don't!' Bella shivered as they emerged into the raw November afternoon. Suddenly the Seychelles seemed very, very appealing. 'I can't believe Aisling could coolly walk off with that ring after the way she treated you! It must have cost you a fortune. Really, you're too much of a gentleman for your own good sometimes, Josh!' she told him, turning up her collar against the wind.

'I think having the ring flung back in my face would have been worse,' said Josh. 'Besides, Aisling loved that ring. If she wanted to keep something from me, I didn't mind.'

She must shut up about Aisling, Bella caught herself up

guiltily, remembering what Kate had said. Just because Josh was putting on a good face didn't mean he wasn't hurting inside, and the ring would be a sensitive issue. He could be hoping that Aisling would decide to come back when she realised that generous men who let you kick them in the teeth and walk away with a ring worth thousands of pounds were few and far between.

'It just seems a waste of money to buy another ring for me,' she said in an attempt to steer the subject away from Aisling.

'We're not paying for anything else during this week,' Josh pointed out. 'C.B.C. are even covering the bar bills, so I can look on it as a justifiable expense. If it makes a difference to winning that contract, it might even be tax deductible! Look, that's where we bought Aisling's ring,' he said suddenly, dragging a still reluctant Bella over the road.

'We can't go in there,' she protested, eying the discreet display of jewellery in the window. There were no prices on view, always a bad sign. The whole place looked very classy.

And very expensive.

Josh didn't appear to be at all intimidated. 'Why not?'

'They might remember you buying that ring for Aisling, for a start.'

'Nonsense,' he said briskly, propelling her towards the door. 'Come on, Bella. They must have loads of customers and it's over a month since Aisling and I were here. There's no way they're going to remember me.'

'Good afternoon, sir,' said the urbane man behind the counter. 'How nice to see you again. What can we do for you today?'

'See!' hissed Bella, turning back towards the door, but Josh had her arm in a firm grip and was forcing her on.

He didn't even have the grace to look embarrassed, (a) at being recognised, and (b) at being proved so comprehensively wrong!

'We'd like to look at your engagement rings, please,' he said coolly.

The jeweller took his request without a blink. 'Certainly, sir. Did you have anything in particular in mind? Diamonds, perhaps? Or emeralds?'

'Not emeralds,' said Josh, appreciating the sly reference to the ring he had bought Aisling. 'We had emeralds last time.' He smiled blandly, not at all discomfited by any other subtle digs the jeweller might have up his sleeve.

'This lady is very different,' he said, drawing forward a fierily blushing Bella. 'Have you got any nice sapphires?'

'He must be wondering what on earth you're up to,' she whispered as the jeweller went in search of sapphires and kept his inevitable reflections to himself.

'Let him wonder,' said Josh. 'It's not his business how many rings I buy or who I buy them for. If he thinks I'll be coming back on a regular basis, he might even offer me a discount for regular custom!'

When the tray was laid reverently before her, Bella was dazzled by the array of beautiful rings. She wished there were prices on so that she could at least choose the cheapest.

'Don't pick out the smallest,' said Josh, reading her mind. 'It'll just make me look mean. Choose one you really like.'

'I don't know...' Bella dithered over the tray until he selected an exquisite sapphire with diamonds clustered around it.

'Here, try this one,' he said and held out his hand in a way that made it impossible for Bella to do anything other than put hers into it.

Excruciatingly aware of the warmth and strength of his fingers, and paralysed by a new and sudden shyness, Bella stared fixedly at the ring.

'Do you like it?' asked Josh, who seemed to have forgotten that he was still holding her hand.

'It's lovely.' She swallowed and drew her hand free. 'I'm sure all these are far too expensive, though,' she whispered.

'Look, Bella, will you stop worrying about the expense,' said Josh, exasperated. If he had noticed her not-so-subtle attempt to free her hand, he gave no sign of it. 'You can give it back at the end of week and I'll sell it back if that makes you feel any better.'

It wouldn't, but she could hardly say so. 'I suppose so,' said Bella instead.

'Right. Now, relax and enjoy it.' He picked out another ring. 'What about this one?'

Eventually they chose a very simple band of square-cut sapphires and diamonds which fitted her finger perfectly. Bella admired it glinting on her hand. She had never worn anything like it before. It was going to make the rest of her jewellery look cheap and tatty, but now that she had it on her finger she wasn't sure how she was ever going to be able to bear taking it off.

She would worry about that later, Bella decided, her earlier doubts and hesitations dissolved in the pleasure of the sparkling stones. Nothing had changed. It was still too early to let Josh know how she felt, and much too soon to assume that he was over Aisling, no matter how together he seemed, but at least he was free now. At least she could hope. For now she had Josh beside her and a whole week with him to look forward to.

And his ring on her finger.

Bella's spirits soared and she smiled as Josh came back

from a discreet exchange with the jeweller. 'It's beautiful,' she told him. She had no idea how much he had paid, but it certainly hadn't been cheap, 'I'll look after it,' she promised before he had a chance to tell her not to lose it.

'Please do,' he said with a crooked smile.

Ah, definitely *not* cheap then.

Over his shoulder, Bella could see the jeweller watching them with a speculative expression. What was he thinking? Had he guessed that Aisling had dumped Josh, and that she was a mere substitute?

They couldn't have that, thought Bella. If he had to think anything, it was that Josh was the kind of man who had women queuing up to marry him, and preferably the sort of cad who could string two, and possibly more, along at the same time.

Bella glanced at Josh, so obviously decent and straightforward and reliable. Still, the jeweller wasn't to know that his restrained appearance didn't disguise a bounder of the first order, was he? It would be fun to make him believe that here was a case of still waters running deep!

'Thank you, darling,' she said and to Josh's evident surprise, fortunately concealed from the jeweller, she put her arms around his neck and smiled seductively at him. 'I'll thank you properly when we get home,' she said throatily, 'so this is just to be going on with...'

To the extent that Bella had a "plan", it was to kiss Josh on the corner of his mouth, but now that she actually had her arms around his neck and an excuse, however frivolous, that *did* seem a waste of an opportunity. If she wanted the jeweller to secretly admire and envy Josh, a peck on the cheek simply wasn't enough.

In any case, it seemed as if her lips had a plan of their own. They skimmed the crease of his cheek, drawn by some irresistible force to his mouth where they settled as if they had found the one place they were meant to be, and the next thing Bella knew she was kissing Josh in a way she had never kissed him before and it didn't feel particularly daring or strange at all. It felt utterly and completely right.

She felt Josh's arm encircle her waist and draw her closer. After the first stunned moment, he had evidently decided to go with the flow and ask questions later. The trouble was that having started the kiss, Bella didn't know how to end it.

Worse, she didn't want to.

With a superhuman effort, she managed to withdraw her lips for a fraction of a second before succumbing to the desire for just one kiss more, and the next time she tried, it was Josh who followed her mouth with his and refused to let her break contact.

It was as if their kisses had taken on a will of their own, as the initial sweetness and rightness gathered and hardened into something much more dangerous, something almost scary that clutched at the base of Bella's spine. Josh must have felt the same frisson, for he was the one who succeeded at last in lifting his head.

They stared at each other for a long, shaken moment before Josh swallowed hard and collected himself with an effort. 'I think we'd better go,' he said.

He turned to thank the jeweller who was studiously rearranging the rings on the tray, a suspicion of a smile hovering about his mouth, while Bella struggled to get herself under control. She had always thought the phrase 'weak at the knees' a complete cliché, but suddenly she knew exactly what it meant. It wasn't just her knees, either. Her whole body felt disjointed and she wondered how she was going to get out of the door without support.

She had visions of herself groping her way around the counters, but in the end Josh simply took her arm and propelled her through the door. Once safely outside though, he let her go abruptly.

CHAPTER SIX

'Do YOU want to tell me what that was all about?' he asked, and Bella noted with some resentment that he had his breathing well under control once more.

Which was more than could be said for her.

'I was just trying to bolster your image,' she said, but her voice came out all thin and funny and breathy at all the wrong points.

She told Josh her plan to impress the jeweller, but it sounded even stupider when punctuated by odd gasps for breath, and when she finally stumbled to the end she wasn't surprised to see Josh shake his head in exasperated disbelief.

'I don't want you to think I don't appreciate the thought,' he said dryly, 'but I'd already told him the truth.'

Nothing could have been guaranteed to cure Bella's breathing problems more quickly. 'You did *what*?' she demanded. 'Why?'

'I could tell he was wondering what was going on, and I didn't want him thinking that I was taking advantage of you.'

It was Bella's turn to be exasperated. 'That's absolutely typical of you, Josh! I go to all that effort to improve your image with people and you just throw the opportunity away!' She scowled, remembering the jeweller's smile as he opened the door for her. 'He must have thought I was a complete idiot kissing you like that!'

Josh started to grin. 'I must be his favourite customer

now. Not only do I buy extremely expensive rings from him, but he gets free entertainment thrown in!'

How humiliating! Bella tried to be offended, but after a moment she gave in and laughed too. Perhaps it was just as well to treat the whole incident as a joke. It felt so good to be laughing with Josh again, relaxing the tension between them after that shattering kiss.

She would have to be careful, Bella decided as Josh spotted the bus they wanted, and they ran for the stop. She had probably revealed far more of herself in that kiss than she had intended.

The last thing she wanted was for Josh to think that she was trying to worm her way into Aisling's place. That would make her seem like an emotional ambulance-chaser, one of those girls who cruised around looking for relationships in trouble before homing in on the newly single man.

Bella had known several girls who complained that the lack of men meant that unless they moved quickly, they would never get a man at all, but she didn't want Josh thinking that she was like them. She didn't want him turning to her for comfort, or falling into bed with her just because she was there and available and it would be easy.

No, thought Bella, that wouldn't be enough. She wanted to be the beat of his heart. She wanted him to love her and want her and need her, to feel that she was the only one who could make his life complete. To recognise, as she had done, that what he had been looking for had been right in front of him all along.

But Josh needed to realise that for himself. In the meantime, she would have to be very patient.

And, yes, careful, just as Kate had warned.

'You do realise that we're only going for a week?' said Josh when he saw the size of Bella's suitcase on Monday morning.

Bella looked at the neat cabin bag at his feet. 'Do *you* realise that we're going for more than five minutes?'

'Now, now, children, don't quarrel,' said Phoebe, banging the door of the boot closed. She had offered to drop them off at the airport on her way down to Devon to interview a woman who claimed that cats had a language which she could understand.

'Which should be fun,' Phoebe had said, 'but not as much fun as a week in the Seychelles!'

She kissed Josh and gave Bella an extra tight hug. 'Have a lovely time, both of you,' she said. 'We're all hoping that you two are going to follow tradition and that your mock engagement will turn into a real one as well. Then we can give you a party when you come home!'

'No fear of that,' said Josh lightly. He nodded at his neat little bag sitting next to Bella's huge case. 'You only need to look at how much we think is essential for a week away to see that we're totally incompatible!'

'There's more to love than luggage, Josh,' said Phoebe with a wink at Bella, who was looking daggers at her over her heavy hints.

Ignoring her friend's pointed glare, Phoebe blew them a kiss, got into the car and drove off smartly, leaving Josh and Bella with their mismatching baggage standing in front of the terminal.

'I suppose we're going to get a lot of that,' said Josh carefully.

'I'm afraid so,' Bella sighed. 'I should never have told Kate and Phoebe that I was going with you instead of Aisling. Now they're determined that we're going to end up married the way they did.'

A raw November wind was blowing her hair about her face, and she held it back with her hand as she glanced at him. 'It's ridiculous, of course, and I've told them there's no question of it, but you know what they're like. That's why I'm glad you said what you did about being incompatible,' she added casually.

'It didn't seem to have much effect on Phoebe,' Josh pointed out with a wry look.

'No, well, they'll realise what a stupid idea it is when we come home in a week's time and go right back to the way we were before.'

'Right,' said Josh.

The only trouble was, he couldn't remember how things had been before Bella had kissed him on Saturday. How was he going to remember what they were like after a week sleeping next to her?

The thought of it made something twist deep inside Josh. He wished Bella hadn't kissed him.

He hadn't been prepared for that jolt of response when her lips touched his, and although he knew he should be taking it lightly, still he had found himself holding her against him, tightening his arm, refusing to let her break the kiss. Josh could still feel how warm and pliant she had been. He couldn't get her softness or the sweetness of her lips or the deep, dark thrill that had uncoiled so unexpectedly out of his mind.

He would have to try, Josh told himself sternly. Bella had laughed afterwards, and it had been clear that she didn't intend to take the kiss seriously at all, so he should do the same. After all, this was Bella, not some mysteriously sexy and seductive stranger.

He glanced at her now, hugging her arms against the cold while the long, golden hair was whipped about her face. Yes, that was Bella all right. She was as stylish as ever, but quite unsuitably dressed for travel in a short figure-hugging dress that looked as if would crease the moment she sat down. All she had to keep her warm was an insubstantial little cardigan, and her feet with their immaculately painted toes were encased in fragile sandals with—Josh did a double take—yes, *jewelled* straps of all things. Over the years, Bella's ridiculously impractical shoes had become something of a running joke, but these ones really took the biscuit!

Aisling would never get on a plane wearing shoes like that, even without all those absurd fake jewels. Once her feet had swollen during the long flight, there wasn't a hope in hell that Bella would be able to get those tiny straps on again, so she would be hobbling off the plane at best.

No doubt Bella would carry it off with style, though. She might be unsuitably dressed but she was undeniably gorgeous with her long legs, that warm curving mouth and those blue eyes with their tilting lashes.

Josh made himself look away. She had always been gorgeous, of course. He just wished that he could stop noticing just how gorgeous now. There was no point in noticing. Bella was his friend, and any relationship they had was based on personality and not on looks.

'*We both know how things are,*' she had said. '*I know you're in love with Aisling, and you know about Will.*' There would be no room for misunderstanding, she had said.

And there wouldn't be, Josh told himself firmly.

'Come on,' he said, seeing her shiver, 'let's go and check in.' He reached for her case only to grunt as he heaved it off the ground. 'For God's sake, Bella! What have you got in here?'

'Just a few essentials,' she said airily.

'But you're only going to lie on a beach! How many clothes can you wear every day?'

'It's not just clothes,' Bella said, teetering along beside him in her absurd shoes. 'You've got to be very careful about the sun nowadays. UV rays can do terrible things to your skin and hair, so I've brought all sorts of special moisturisers and sun screen and after-sun lotions. And then you've got to worry about your hair,' she told Josh, who had never given his hair a moment's thought. 'I've got a protective lotion to put on when I go into the sea, and a conditioner for when I come out, and there's shampoo, of course, and another conditioner for the evening...'

She chattered on as they waited in the queue for the check-in desk. Josh was desperately aware of her beside him as she combed out the tangles in her wind-blown hair and threw the golden mass back from her face. She was like a cat with her constant grooming, he tried to think disapprovingly, but he kept losing track of what she was saying and why he was supposed to be exasperated as his mind drifted back to the warmth and softness of her lips against his.

'Anyway, enough of that.' Bella shook back her hair and laid a hand on his arm, her eyes deep and very blue. 'How are you feeling, Josh?'

How *was* he feeling?

Alarmed by the frisson that went through him at the touch of her hand.

Disturbed by the memories of her kiss.

Guilty about the treacherous way his mind kept wandering.

'Fine,' said Josh a little hoarsely.

'Yes, I know you're going to *say* fine,' she said as the queue shuffled forwards, 'but you don't need to be stiff-upper-lipped with me. How do you really feel? Are you dreading seeing Aisling with Bryan or Bryn or whatever he calls himself?'

Aisling. Josh clutched at the thought of her. She was the perfect excuse for his distraction this morning.

'I can't say I'm looking forward to it,' he said.

She tucked a hand into his, and when he looked at her, the blue eyes were warm with sympathy. 'I know it will be hard,' she said, 'but don't forget that I'm here for you.'

Josh's throat was absurdly tight. 'Thanks, Bella,' he managed and his fingers curled and tightened around hers in spite of himself. 'You're a good friend.'

'I always will be,' said Bella, her own smile wavering a little.

All in all, it was a relief when they reached the check-in desk at last, and Josh was forced to let go of her hand. He had a nasty feeling that he wouldn't have been able to do it otherwise.

He must pull himself together, he told himself with an edge of desperation. Wasn't he supposed to be the expert on dealing with difficult situations? The trouble was that it was easy to know what to do when you had to rescue a colleague who had fallen down a crevasse in the ice, or get someone dangerously ill out of the jungle and into hospital when your radio wasn't working and it was three days' trek to the nearest settlement.

Even winning the contract with C.B.C. was a doddle compared to coping with this sudden, disturbing awareness of his best friend. Josh didn't like feeling out of control. He could train executives how to analyse a situation, assess the risks involved and communicate effectively to resolve problems, but he didn't know how to deal with this.

He handed Bella her boarding pass. 'We'd better go and find the others,' he said, clearing his throat. 'They're probably in the bar.'

It was Bella who spotted Aisling first, warning Josh with a nudge as she put her arm through his and tilted her chin at a combative angle. There was a look in her eyes that Josh recognised, and it usually meant trouble. When Bella wore that expression it made you very glad that she was on your side.

'You promised you would be nice,' he reminded her. 'Remember we've got a contract to win here.'

'Of course,' said Bella, but Josh didn't entirely trust the smile she flashed at him.

He was so preoccupied with whether she would behave that he came face to face with Aisling before he had a chance to think about how it was going to feel to confront the woman he had been planning to marry until three days ago. In the event, Josh was puzzled to find that he didn't feel anything at all.

'Hello,' he said, as he kissed her on the cheek. 'You're looking very well.'

It was true. He had never seen her look so beautiful before. She was glowing with happiness. If Josh had needed anything to convince him that Aisling had made the right decision, one look at her now would have been enough. He had never made her happy the way being with Bryn clearly did.

As he had guessed, she was dressed much more sensibly than Bella in loose khaki trousers, a soft cream shirt and sandals that managed to look elegant and practical at the same time.

'Hi, Josh,' she greeted him, and then lowered her voice so that none of the others waiting in the bar with them would hear. 'How *are* you?'

Josh was beginning to get a little tired of being asked that. 'I'm fine,' he said again, although he doubted whether Aisling would believe him any more than Bella had. He *was* fine, though. Why couldn't they just accept that?

Beside him he could feel Bella bristling but she seemed

to have herself under control. 'You remember Bella, don't you?'

'Hello, Aisling,' she said in a frosty voice.

There was scarcely more warmth in the way Aisling returned her greeting, and the green eyes were distinctly cool.

'Congratulations,' she said for the benefit of their audience. 'I gather you and Josh have just got engaged,' she added. 'Quite a whirlwind romance!'

'No,' said Bella, meeting her eyes squarely. 'It's just taken us fourteen years to realise how much we love each other.'

'Convenient that you realised in time for a trip to the Seychelles,' Aisling commented slyly.

Josh tensed, but Bella managed an insincere smile. 'Wasn't it?' she said sweetly. 'I can't tell you how thrilled I am.'

She turned to the man beside Aisling. He was tall and classically good-looking and seemed exceptionally pleased with himself, Josh noted sourly. Just Bella's type, in fact. He found himself watching her anxiously, but she just shook Bryn's hand with a cool smile.

'I bet you anything I'm right about him being called Bryan,' she whispered under her breath to Josh as he steered her quickly away to meet some of the others. 'See if you can get a look at his passport!'

'You're supposed to be being good,' said Josh repressively, but he couldn't help grinning.

As if by common consent the party had all forgathered in the bar. There were sixteen of them altogether, and although those who worked for C.B.C. naturally knew each other, their partners were strangers and conversation had evidently been stilted to begin with.

Things picked up noticeably when Bella joined the

group. She had always had an ability to get the party going, and before long she was making everyone laugh and relax. Josh watched her animated face as she leant forward to draw out the shy wife of one of the junior C.B.C. executives. She might not have the necessary skills to survive out in the wild, but there was nothing he or anyone else could tell her about how to get on in a social setting!

He had found them seats on the other side of the group from Aisling and Bryn, who were talking to the senior C.B.C. manager and her partner, and he began to relax himself until he noticed that Bella had sat back next to him and was sending searching glances at Bryn from beneath her lashes.

Josh's immediate thought was that she had found Bryn attractive after all, and he glowered. 'Why do you keep staring at Bryn?' he demanded crossly.

Bella leant closer. 'I'm trying to imagine him with a personality,' she confided in his ear and Josh was startled at the rush of relief he felt.

'He's completely bland,' she went on, going back to her study of Bryn with a puzzled frown. 'I can't understand it. How could Aisling leave you for someone like that?'

'She's in love with him,' said Josh, trying to be fair.

'Yes, that's obvious,' Bella agreed. 'She's all lit up, and anyone can see that it's because of him. I just can't see *why*, that's all.'

Josh followed her gaze. Now that he knew that Bella wasn't interested, he could study the other man dispassionately. 'He's very good-looking,' he offered as an explanation.

'I suppose so.' Bella sounded unconvinced, and Josh glanced at her in some surprise.

'I'd have said that he was just your type.'

She looked taken aback. 'Really?'

'He's got that smug, self-satisfied look you seem to go for,' said Josh, unable to resist it. 'You've got to admit that he looks a bit like Will, who looked just like all your other boyfriends.'

Bella stared openly at Bryn. 'I don't think he looks *anything* like Will,' she told him. 'There's nothing to him at all.'

Josh didn't think there had been anything to Will, either, but he remembered just in time that Bella was in love with the man. He would have to be more tactful. *She* hadn't stooped to making personal comments about Aisling, although knowing the sharpness of her tongue on occasion and judging by the frostiness of the atmosphere between the two women she was more than capable of it.

'Bryn's not your type, then?' he asked lightly instead, and she turned from Bryn to look directly at him, blue eyes unusually serious.

'No,' she said. 'He's not my type at all.'

Josh was conscious of an odd hollow feeling inside as he stared back into her eyes, and he swallowed. 'Good,' he said, but his voice sounded very strange.

He felt a bit odd too. If he wasn't someone who was never ill, he would be wondering if he was coming down with something. At least it would explain this peculiar fuzzy feeling and inability to focus. He shook his head slightly, hoping to clear it. He must be more tired than he had thought.

Bella had turned and introduced herself to the woman sitting on her other side.

'I've been admiring your ring,' Bella's new friend was saying. When Josh looked at her more closely he realised that he had met her before. What was her name again? Sue? Sarah? No, Sally, he remembered.

'It's beautiful,' Sally said enviously. 'Have you two been engaged long?'

'Not long, no,' said Bella. 'Actually, only since last Friday.'

'Oh, how romantic!'

'Well, it is and it isn't,' Bella said. 'We've known each other for a long time, so it's not as if we're rushing into anything.'

'So what made you decide to get married now?'

Bella glanced at Josh and then away. 'It's a funny thing,' she said slowly. 'I just looked at him one day and knew that I wanted to spend the rest of my life with him, and that being friends wasn't enough any more.'

Sally smiled. 'And Josh felt the same?'

Bella's own smile was a little strained. 'You'd have to ask him that.'

She was very convincing, Josh thought bitterly, and he was almost relieved when Aisling moved to a chair slightly behind him and drew him out of the circle.

'I just wanted to thank you for taking it all so well, Josh,' she said under cover of the general conversation. 'You could have made it very difficult for me to come on this trip with Bryn if you'd wanted to.'

'There's no point in that,' said Josh, feeling curiously detached. It was hard to believe that this was a woman he had slept with, a woman he had planned to spend the rest of his life with. 'We're still working together after all,' he pointed out, 'and I want us both to be able to concentrate on winning this contract. It's not just your job that depends on it.'

Aisling looked a little daunted by his matter-of-fact attitude. He was obviously supposed to be broken-hearted by her rejection. 'I hope you know I never meant to hurt you,' she said.

'Don't worry about it,' said Josh briskly. 'I'm glad you seem so happy.'

'I am. I hope you will be, too.'

Involuntarily, Josh glanced at Bella, deep in conversation with Sally and completely oblivious of him.

Aisling followed his gaze. 'You know, Josh, it would have been a terrible mistake if I had married you,' she said. 'Bella would always have been there between us.'

'Bella's not like that at all,' he objected furiously.

'Maybe she isn't, but she would have come between us all the same,' said Aisling. 'I wasn't at all surprised when you said that you were bringing her in my place. I always thought you had always been much more in love with her than you wanted to admit.'

Josh felt as if he had walked smack into a wall in the dark, leaving him jarred and disorientated. 'That's rubbish,' he said unevenly. 'Bella and I are just good friends. We always have been and we always will be. You've seen us together, Aisling. You know there's no question of anything else.'

Aisling smiled faintly as she got up. 'Isn't there?' she said.

Josh stared after her. In *love* with Bella? No, he couldn't be! Aisling didn't know what she was talking about. He loved Bella, of course, the same way he loved his sister.

Except that he never knew whether his sister had been in the room just by the fragrance in the air, did he? He couldn't close his eyes and conjure up his sister's image down to the last tilt of her lashes. And, fond as he was of her, he never felt better just knowing that his sister was there.

The way he did with Bella.

Oh, God, he *was* in love with her!

It was as if the world had suddenly tilted, leaving Josh

sliding and slipping towards a precipitous drop, and struggling frantically to claw his way back to safe ground where Bella was just the same as she had always been.

When had it happened? Had she changed, or had he?

'What did Aisling want?' Bella broke into his reeling thoughts and Josh stared at her stupidly.

'She just...'

Just wanted to blow his life apart. To rock the foundations of his world. To throw everything he thought he felt about his best friend into doubt.

'... she just wanted to thank me,' he said, astounded that his voice came out sounding almost normal.

'What for?'

'For understanding how she felt about Bryn. She said she was grateful.'

'As well she might be,' Bella sniffed, remembering the emerald ring Aisling was still flaunting. At least she had had the decency to wear it on her right hand.

That had been a very intimate chat the two of them had been having, though, and Josh had looked shell-shocked when Aisling had walked away. 'Did she say anything else?'

Josh hesitated. 'Only that she thought it would have been a terrible mistake if we had got married.'

'She would say that, wouldn't she? Mind you, she's not the only one that thinks so,' Bella told him. 'I've just been talking to Sally there. She says she's worked with you a couple of times and that she likes you a lot but she was never mad about Aisling when she was at C.B.C. She told me that she'd heard rumours that the two of you had got together, and she said she was glad when she met me to find out that it wasn't true.'

'What did you say?'

It was Bella's turn to hesitate. 'Well, I thought I'd better let her believe that she'd misunderstood, so I said that you were mine and always had been.'

She laughed to show that she hadn't really meant it, and then she made the mistake of looking into Josh's eyes again, and the desperate expression she saw there made her heart stop for a second. She had never seen Josh look like that before.

'Are you OK?'

'Yes...' He shook his head as if to clear it. 'It was just something Aisling said...' He stopped, unable to continue.

A tide of shame and guilt surged through Bella. What had she been thinking of, joking about their pretend relationship and making snippy comments about Aisling when it was all still so raw for Josh? She had forgotten how he might feel about seeing Aisling again. He was so cool and self-contained that it was easy to forget that he might not be nearly as fine as he claimed to be, but she of all people should have known better.

'I'm sorry, Josh,' she said, contrite.

That strange expression flickered in his eyes again. 'It's not your fault,' he said.

What had Aisling said to him? Even she wouldn't be tactless enough to ask, thought Bella, but it must have been something that had made the whole situation come home to him.

She hated the bleakness in his face, couldn't bear the thought of him hurting like that. 'It'll be all right, Josh,' she tried to reassure him, putting a hand on his knee.

Josh just looked at her oddly. 'Will it?' he said.

The hotel was wedged between a steep mountainside covered in luxuriant vegetation and a curve of dazzling white sand edging the Indian Ocean. The shallows sighing onto the shore were the palest minty green, deepening to an impossible blue further out into the bay. Bella couldn't help gasping when she saw it. After London in November, it was hard to believe that it was real.

The bus from the airport emptied them out into a cool, dim bar furnished in dark tropical wood and open on two sides to catch any breeze from the sea. There they were greeted by a representative from C.B.C. who introduced herself as Cassandra and bustled around the party, ticking them officiously off her list.

'Josh Kingston...?' she echoed when it was Josh and Bella's turn. She ran her pen down the clipboard. 'Kingston, Kingston, Kingston...ah! Here you are. You're down as plus one!' She laughed merrily and looked at Bella. 'This is your wife, is it?'

'My fiancée,' said Josh curtly. 'Bella Stevenson.'

Cassandra swooped on Bella's ring. 'How gorgeous!' she gushed, brandishing a diamond of her own under Bella's nose. 'I'm getting married myself next year. We must get together and compare notes.'

Bella couldn't think of anything she would want to do less, but she smiled politely. 'We haven't started thinking about the wedding yet,' she said. 'We've only just got engaged.'

'Oh, I'll be able to give you lots of ideas,' Cassandra promised. 'I've got a few magazines with me too. You can read them on the beach.'

What could she say? I won't be needing any bridal magazines? 'That would be lovely,' said Bella dutifully.

Delighted at the prospect of long, girly chats on the subject closest to her heart, Cassandra beamed at them both. 'You're going to love your room. It is *so* romantic!'

It *was* romantic—or it would have been under different circumstances. Like Josh not pining for Aisling, for instance, thought Bella with an inward sigh. It was all clean wood and crisp linen, and sliding doors opened onto a little veranda with steps down to the beach.

The first thing Bella saw, though, was the big double bed, with frangipani blossoms laid invitingly on the pillows.

'Very romantic,' she said to Josh as she looked at everything except the bed. She was trying to sound light-hearted and amused at the situation, but wasn't quite sure that she was carrying it off. 'Cassandra was right.'

Picking up one of the frangipani flowers, she held it to her nose and breathed in the exotic perfume. 'It's a pity they didn't throw in a free bottle of champagne while they were at it. If we're going to pretend to be engaged we might as well enjoy some of the perks!'

There was no response from Josh, and when she glanced at him under her lashes she saw that he was looking pre-occupied and seemed hardly to have heard her. Clearly her attempts to lighten the atmosphere weren't working.

She should just shut up, thought Bella dully. All Cassandra's talk of weddings and romantic rooms must have been all too bitter a reminder of what things might have been like if Aisling had been with him.

She had been hoping that things would be easier once the long flight was over. Sitting so close to Josh but unable to touch him had been a nightmare. Bella hadn't been able to keep her eyes off him. She tried to concentrate on her book but it was hopeless when her gaze kept sliding sideways, skittering over his severe profile, between the creases at the edge of his eye and down the hard, exciting line of his cheek to his jaw and then to the pulse that beat in his throat.

Bella would wrench her eyes away, only to find them wandering hungrily back to his shoulder, down his sleeve to his forearm and his wrist and those strong, square hands, and her stomach would disappear in a sickening lurch of desire. She wanted to snuggle closer, to kiss her way along his jaw and nuzzle his neck. To put her arms around him and cling to the solid strength of him until he kissed her back.

Gulping, Bella forced herself to start reading the same page of her book all over again.

At one point she must have nodded off in spite of herself, because when she stirred and blinked, it was to find that her head was resting against his shoulder. Josh had obviously had no trouble resisting the urge to put his arm around her and shift her into a more comfortable position.

Fighting the temptation to press closer to him anyway, Bella willed herself not to move. At least this way she was touching him. But when she lifted her eyes cautiously, she could see that Josh's jaw was clenched, and that he was staring blindly at the seat back in front of him, his mouth clamped shut in a rigid line, and she straightened abruptly to move away from him.

Whatever Aisling had said had touched him on the raw. This was no time to be snuggling up to him, Bella told herself. She would have to give Josh time to come to terms with losing Aisling, and it would probably be easier for him if she kept her distance rather than constantly reminding him that he was with the wrong woman.

Bella cast a doubtful look at the bed. She wasn't sure how she was going to keep her distance tonight. It wasn't *that* big.

She sighed. She would just have to worry about that when the time came. There was no point in wishing that he wanted to be with her, or imagining what it would be like if they were lovers, if they had been able to fall laughing onto the bed as soon as the door was closed, kissing as they undressed to make love with the sound of the ocean shushing onto the beach beyond the veranda.

In the meantime, she should just leave Josh alone.

CHAPTER SEVEN

JOSH had barely glanced at the bed. He had opened the sliding doors and was standing watching the sea through the coconut palms, and something in the set of his shoulders made Bella's throat ache. She couldn't bear him being this unhappy.

Quietly she went out to join him and for a while they watched the sunlight rippling over the shallows in silence. 'It looks beautiful, doesn't it?' said Bella at last. 'Do you fancy a swim?'

'Not right now,' said Josh. 'I think I'll have a shower instead.'

'OK,' she said brightly. 'Well...I think I'll go.'

It was almost as if he was deliberately trying to avoid her. Bella told herself that it was stupid to feel hurt as she changed into her bikini and slathered on sun cream. It was so long since she had seen the sun that she would burn to a crisp if she wasn't careful.

For the first time ever she felt self-conscious about her body. Josh had seen her in a bikini loads of times, and in the past she wouldn't have given a moment's thought to sashaying past him down to the beach just as she was.

But that was then and this was now, and everything seemed different. Bella dug around in her case until she found a sarong, and wrapped it tightly around her, knotting it under her arms before she went back out onto the veranda.

'See you later then,' she said as casually as she could.

'OK.' Josh's voice was tight. He watched her disappear

past the coconut palms onto the soft, white sand, and reappear a few moments later through another gap in the trees. She had unwound her sarong and was wading into the shallows in her bikini, while the light bounced off the water and over her skin.

He looked down at his hands. They were shaking. God, how was he going to get through this week?

It was all Aisling's fault. If she had kept her mouth shut, he could have carried on as he had before, confused and unsettled by this new and intense physical awareness of Bella, but able to tell himself that he was just upset about Aisling's rejection and not thinking clearly.

He couldn't do that now. Everything was too clear. Until Aisling had pointed it out, he hadn't let himself question the depth of his feeling for Bella, but of course she was right. Of course he was in love with Bella, and probably always had been. As long as he could tell himself that he loved her as friend, everything had been fine, but now that the truth was out there he couldn't deny it any longer: he didn't just love Bella, he needed her and wanted her and his hands itched to explore her, unlock her, and make her properly his.

Only he couldn't even let himself *think* about that. Bella had been very clear that she had come to support him as a friend. He couldn't turn round and take advantage of her now, especially not when he knew how she still felt about Will.

And even if he could tell her he loved her, why would she believe him? He had to be pretty fickle to be engaged to one woman on Friday morning and in love with another on Monday, Josh reminded himself ruefully. If Aisling hadn't decided that her love for Bryn was too strong to resist, he would have married her.

Or would he? Their engagement had always had an air

of unreality about it for Josh. Aisling's suggestion that they marry had seemed to make sense at the time. Now he could see that Aisling had merely been desperate to put Bryn behind her, but at the time the way the whole thing had ballooned out of control had been alarming. Josh didn't resent her. He was just glad the truth had come out before it was too late.

And now he couldn't think about anything but Bella, about the way she smiled and the way she moved, about the soft warmth of her body and the tantalising sheen of her skin and the silky, spun-gold hair. About the allure of her eyes and that wonderfully dirty laugh and the scent that drifted in the air long after she had gone.

It had taken an heroic effort of will not to put his arm around her when she was sleeping against his shoulder in the plane, and even worse torture to have to stand out here and let her walk past him in that damned sarong that was just asking to be untied so that he could spin her free of it and pull her back into the room and down onto the cool, inviting bed.

And tonight he had to get in there beside her and pretend that she was just a friend. How was he supposed to do that?

The contract. Josh told himself to focus on that. He was here to work and that was what he would do. If he concentrated hard enough on winning the contract then maybe he would get his thoughts back under control. He would stop thinking about lying next to Bella at night and what it would be like to reach for her, and he would start remembering that she was just a dear friend who was only here because she felt sorry for him.

Maybe.

When Bella found him later, he was sitting in the bar with Aisling, papers spread out on the table in front of them. After realising that he was hanging around like a besotted fool waiting for Bella to come back, Josh had made himself go out, where he bumped into Aisling. Since she was on her own, too, they taken the opportunity to go through their strategy for the week and decide the key points to be made and which executives needed to be targeted particularly.

Josh was feeling better. Having a shower and getting back to work had been just what he needed. Luckily Aisling was keen to get on with things too and it had taken no time at all to re-establish a good working relationship. In fact, it was already hard to remember that they had ever had any other kind of relationship.

Josh was just congratulating himself on getting a grip when Bella walked barefoot into the bar. The sarong was tied around her waist now, and her hair hung damp and tangled from the sea down her bare back. Inevitably, she had collected a group of friends on the beach, and they were laughing as they headed to the bar without noticing Josh and Aisling in the corner.

Josh didn't recognise any of the people she was with, but he recognised the lustful expression on the men's faces when they looked at Bella all right, and he scowled. She ought to go and put some more clothes on.

'Sorry,' he said to Aisling, 'what were you saying?'

They tried to carry on working, but it was hard to concentrate when the others were obviously having such a good time. When they all had a drink, they headed over to a table in the shade looking out over the beach, and it was only then that Bella saw Josh and Aisling.

She stopped, murmured something to her new friends and then padded over in her bare feet. 'Where's Bryn?' she asked coolly.

'Sleeping,' said Aisling. 'He's used to travelling business class, so he couldn't get comfortable in those economy seats.'

'How terrible for him,' said Bella, who had never been in business class and had still found the seats incredibly uncomfortable. 'I'm surprised you didn't upgrade if things were that bad.'

'One of the purposes of this week is to build team spirit,' Aisling pointed out with equally insincere sweetness. 'Obviously Bryn could see that as one of the senior executives here it wouldn't look very supportive if he didn't travel with the rest of the group.'

Bella was unimpressed by Bryn's sacrifice. She glanced at Josh. 'It looks as if you're working, so I won't disturb you,' she said as she turned to go. 'See you later.'

Josh followed her with his eyes as she carried her glass over to join the others on long rattan sofas arranged around a low table. Two of the men shifted along to make space on the sofa between them when they saw Bella approaching.

They probably couldn't believe their luck, thought Josh sourly. One of them was short and balding, the other had a distinct paunch. Weren't these guys all supposed to have wives with them?

Beside him, Aisling sighed. 'Why don't you just tell her how you feel?' she asked in a resigned voice.

'What do you mean?'

'Look at you, you can't take your eyes off her!' said Aisling with an edge of exasperation. 'Just tell her that you love her.'

'I can't,' said Josh as if the words were wrenched out of him. 'She's in love with someone else, and even if she wasn't, I don't want to risk our friendship.'

Aisling looked at him curiously. 'Odd,' she commented, 'you've spent most of your career putting yourself into dangerous situations and taking risks when you had to. I wouldn't have said you were an emotional coward either. You were prepared to take a risk on me, weren't you?'

'It's not the same.'

'Isn't Bella worth a risk?'

Josh stared out at the pool where an energetic game of water polo was in progress. 'She's too important to me to risk anything,' he said, and knew that it was true. 'I don't want to lose her.'

'Maybe she feels the way you do,' said Aisling. 'Have you thought of that? She certainly doesn't like *me* one little bit. I think she's jealous.'

'That's just Bella being protective. She thinks you've hurt me,' he told her. 'No, she's told me how she feels about Will. She has to get over him first, and I have to help her do that, not throw our whole friendship into question just when she needs it most.'

It was time to change the subject. Josh picked up one of the papers in front of him. 'Let's run over that last point again...'

But it was impossible to concentrate with all the hilarity at Bella's table, and eventually Josh had to give in. Aisling was distracted and every time he heard Bella's laugh he lost track of what he was supposed to be saying.

'Come on,' he said, stacking the papers neatly together with a sigh. 'We might as well join the others.'

He bought Aisling a drink at the bar, and they made their way over to the table, where he glared at one of the men whose thigh was a little too close to Bella's for comfort until he shifted over and asked if Josh would like to sit next to Bella. Clearly Josh was expected to say no, he was fine where he was.

'Thanks,' said Josh, squashing himself determinedly in beside her. Then he wished that he hadn't. Her body was tantalisingly close and warm. She had a glow from the sun already and he could see where the sea salt had dried on her back.

The sarong covered her legs, which was something, Josh supposed, but her midriff and arms and shoulders were bare. Next to him in his conventional trousers and short-sleeved shirt she seemed lush and exotic and practically naked. *Not* a thought which Josh needed to have right then.

She was leaning forward, her face animated and her smile burning at the edge of his vision. Josh found his hands clenching. He wanted everyone to disappear, to leave him alone with her so that he could ease her down onto batik cushions and make love to her...

'Hi, everybody! Sorry, Josh, did I make you jump?' Cassandra patted him on the shoulder from behind, amused by the way she had broken into his thoughts. 'Are you all having a lovely time?

'I'm glad I've got a few of you together,' she went on without waiting for an answer, and waved her clipboard vaguely. 'I need to let the diving instructors know who wants to sign up for their course. That starts first thing tomorrow for those of you who are interested. I can arrange deep-sea fishing as well if anyone wants that, and later in the week we'll be organising some boat trips out to other islands.'

Pausing for breath, she looked expectantly around the group. 'So, who's for diving?'

'Not me,' said Bella firmly. 'I'm happy on the beach with a book.'

Cassandra winked. 'I'll bring you some more mags tomorrow,' she promised. 'What about the rest of you?'

'I know Bryn's keen to go deep-sea fishing,' said Aisling, 'but I'd like to learn how to dive.'

'Great!' said Cassandra enthusiastically, scribbling down Aisling's name. 'Anyone else?'

Josh hesitated, but at that moment Bella shifted to reach for her drink and her bare arm pressed against his for a moment, which made him make up his mind abruptly. The further away he was from Bella at the moment the better.

'I'll go diving, too,' he told Cassandra.

Bella swung round to stare at him. 'But you know how to dive!' she objected. 'You don't have to go on a course.'

'I haven't done it for a while,' he said. 'There's no harm in a refresher course.'

'OK, so I've got Josh and Aisling,' said Cassandra. 'Any more takers?'

Most of the others opted to relax on the beach like Bella rather than sign up for any strenuous activity.

'I get enough of that at home looking after the kids,' sighed one weary mother.

'So that's just Josh and Aisling for diving,' Cassandra concluded, having been round them all. 'We'll see if we can find some others as chaperones so you and Bryn don't need to worry, Bella!' she added with an extremely irritating laugh.

'I'm not worried,' lied Bella, who in fact was furious with Josh. Why didn't he make things easier on himself by keeping out of temptation's way? If he wanted to make a fool of himself by following Aisling around with his tongue hanging out when anyone could see she was mad about Bryn, that was his problem, but he might at least think about how he was making *her* look.

'I must say I admire you for being independent,' said one of her new friends from the beach. 'When I was engaged I spent my whole time trailing after my husband and doing the things he liked rather than what I liked, just because I was terrified of what he might get up to if I wasn't there to keep an eye on him!'

'Oh, I never think about that.' Bella put a possessive hand on Josh's knee, which seemed like a suitably adoring thing to do until she felt his instinctive flinch. Mortified, she snatched her hand back. Why not stand up and shout that he didn't like her touching him?

Tough, she thought. She was trying to act a role here, even if he didn't have a clue about how a fiancé behaved. Defiantly, she put her hand back again. 'I know Josh would never be unfaithful,' she told the others. 'Would you, sweetie?'

Josh would hate being called 'sweetie'. It served him right, thought Bella. If he would just relax and behave naturally with her instead of recoiling at her slightest touch she might not have to resort to cute names.

'No,' he said in a voice that sounded oddly hoarse. He cleared his throat and started again. 'Never.'

Well, that was a *bit* better, Bella allowed grudgingly.

Cassandra had put away her clipboard and had squeezed onto the sofa opposite. 'Did you get a chance to look at that magazine I gave you on the beach, Bella?' she asked, leaning across.

'I did. It was very interesting.' Bella was rather embarrassed by the fact that she had been riveted by a copy of *Bride* that Cassandra had insisted on thrusting into her hands. She had always felt that it was vaguely unlucky to look at a magazine like that unless you were actually planning a wedding, but now that she had the perfect excuse to read it, it seemed a pity not to…

'It had some great ideas, I thought,' she told Cassandra, and glanced speculatively at Josh under her lashes. Her hand was still on his thigh, and it was obviously making him tense.

'I've been wondering whether we should go for a themed wedding,' she said. 'You know, the Arabian Nights or something. We could decorate the marquee as a desert tent with rugs and brass lamps, and I could have lots of veils. Josh could be dressed as a sheikh. What do you think, Josh?'

'Over my dead body,' he said.

Bella pretended to pout. 'Oh, I thought it would be fun to bring out your unconventional side,' she said. 'And it would be appropriate, too. You have spent a lot of time in deserts.'

'I've also spent lot of time in England,' Josh pointed out, and Bella was secretly relieved to hear the crispness return to his voice. 'I'm quite happy staying in touch with my conventional side, thank you very much. A morning suit is as wacky as I'm prepared to go.'

The very idea of Josh in a morning suit gave Bella a pang and she forced her mind away from imagining him in the local church where her parents lived, waiting for her to arrive—and there was no use pretending she hadn't picked out exactly the dress she wanted from Cassandra's magazine—and tuned back into the conversation.

Cassandra was explaining how she was planning a traditional wedding, 'But there's going to be an overall sea theme. The bridesmaids and pageboys are going to be in little sailor suits, there'll be shells on the table and even the place cards are going to be decorated with starfish.'

'Wow,' said Bella. Clearly behind Cassandra's fluffy exterior lurked the organisational abilities of a brigadier. 'When is the wedding?'

'Not till next year. What about you?'

Never, the way things were going. Still, she had better stay in her role, thought Bella, snuggling perversely into

Josh and risking a kiss on his jaw. 'The sooner the better as far as we're concerned. That's right, isn't it, Josh?'

'Yes,' he said abruptly, and then ruined what little credibility he had as a fiancé by literally shaking her off as he stood up. 'It's getting late,' he said. 'We should go and get ready for the reception this evening.'

Aisling got to her feet as well. 'Yes, I'd better go too and wake Bryn.'

Right. Why not announce to the world that they wanted an excuse to snatch a few more minutes alone?

Already humiliated by Josh's brusque rejection, Bella's eyes flashed dangerously. He had pointedly not held out his hand to help her up and include her in his unilateral decision to go and get ready, but he needn't think that she was going to sit here tamely while he went mooning after Aisling. They had already had quite enough of a tête-à-tête "working", as they called it, in the bar.

Bella's lips tightened and she drained her glass. She was here as Josh's fiancée, and that's how he should treat her. 'I'll come with you,' she said. 'I want a shower before dinner.'

She took a childish delight in making him take her hand as they left the bar with Aisling, but the moment they were out of sight of the others, he dropped it abruptly. Bella hugged her arms miserably around her to give her hands something to do.

They left Aisling at the door to her room, then walked across the grounds in tense silence. The sun was dropping down to the horizon, staining the sky pink and orange and there was a hushed, expectant feel to the air. Even the ocean seemed to have gone quiet as it waited for the night to fall.

It was such a waste to be miserable in such a romantic place, thought Bella. Even if she and Josh went back to being friends, it would be better than this. They needed to relax and to talk, she decided.

'Shall we walk along the beach?' she suggested, thinking that even Josh couldn't resist the appeal of a tropical beach at sunset.

Apparently he could. 'I thought you wanted a shower?' he said.

'I do, but there's no hurry.'

'You should have stayed in the bar with the others,' he said, an edge to his voice. 'You seemed to be having a good time.'

Bella was rapidly losing patience. 'I would have done,' she said tartly, 'but I haven't forgotten that I'm supposed to be here as your fiancée, and no self-respecting fiancée would be happy about letting her man stroll off into the sunset with another woman.'

Josh made an exasperated noise. 'We weren't strolling anywhere. Aisling was on her way back to her room. You know that.'

'I might do, but it doesn't look that way to everyone else. People are already commenting on how much time the two of you spend together, and we've only been here a few hours!'

They had reached their room and Josh fished the key out of his shirt pocket. 'You just need to tell them that Aisling and I work together,' he said impatiently as he unlocked the door.

'It would take more than that to stop them speculating,' said Bella, stalking into the room. 'I think they're beginning to wonder who exactly it is that you're engaged to. You certainly don't seem to want to spend any time with me!'

'For God's sake, Bella, you're the one who said we've only been here a few hours!'

'Look,' she said, unfastening her sarong, too cross by this stage to feel self-conscious about her body in front of him. 'I'm just saying that you don't seem to be a very convincing fiancé.' In spite of herself, Bella was unable to keep the hurt from her voice. 'You flinch if I touch you, jump at the chance to spend your days with another woman, and generally don't want anything to do with me. There's not much point in my being here if you're going to carry on like that!'

They glared at each other until Josh suddenly blew out a breath and ran a hand through his short hair in a gesture of weariness. 'I'm sorry, Bella,' he sighed. 'You're right. I'm no good at pretending, that's all.'

Bella's exasperation evaporated at the defeated expression on his face. Josh's inability to keep away from Aisling might hurt her, but she knew just how he felt, didn't she?

'No, it's my fault,' she said gently. 'I know it's a difficult situation for you, Josh. It's easy to say that you should get on with your life, and that there's no point torturing yourself by being with the person you love when you know they don't love you and that you can't have them, but if you really love someone, you can't just give up like that.'

She hesitated, wanting to put her arms round him, but not trusting herself if she did. 'I do understand, you know.'

'It sounds as if you do,' he said heavily.

'I hope this week isn't going to be too hard for you,' said Bella. She had thrown her sarong over a chair and dressed only in her bikini was looking through her case for a brush.

Josh looked at her, warm and vivid and practically naked in the room with the double bed between them.

'I think it will be,' he said. 'I think it'll be a lot harder than I ever expected.'

Bella sat on the edge of the bed and threw her hair down over her face to brush it vigorously. In spite of all the lotions and potions she had spent a fortune on and which promised that her hair would be a silken, shining gold curtain at all times it had dried into a salty tangle.

'You know, I don't think you should give up,' she said, proud of how steady her voice sounded. 'I mean, it's obvious that Aisling still likes you a lot. She might be wrapped up in Bryn now, but he's such a prat, isn't he? I only talked to him for a few minutes, but that was enough to find him deeply irritating. And did you see how he was swanking around at Heathrow? I wouldn't be surprised if a week in his company is enough for Aisling to come to her senses and send him back to his wife—who is probably extremely glad to be rid of him!'

Confident that she had her face back under control, Bella straightened and tossed her hair back over her shoulders. 'When that happens, she's bound to turn back to you,' she told Josh, who was standing looking out at the rapidly gathering darkness, his hands in his pockets and his shoulders slightly hunched.

'So I just have to be patient?' he said.

'If that's what you want.'

He turned abruptly. 'What about you, Bella? I haven't been great company for you so far. I'm sorry.'

'Don't worry, I understand, and it's fine.' She smiled brightly as she got up and began unpacking her case. 'I'm having a great time. Most of the people seem really nice, I'm staying in this fabulous hotel for free, and I've got a whole week to lie in the sun and read. What more could I want?'

'Will?' suggested Josh.

Bella froze for a second, then busied herself hanging clothes in the wardrobe. It made a good reason to turn her face away so that Josh couldn't read her expression too clearly.

'We can't always have everything we want,' she said. 'Sometimes we just have to make the most of what we've got.'

Josh thought about what she had said as he lay sleepless beside her that night. Moonlight slipped into the room through a crack in the curtains and laid a stripe across Bella, who lay on her front, her face turned towards the window and her hair spilling over the pillow. The light was a bright band, highlighting the curve of her shoulder, and grazing the edge of her mouth. It lit the soft line of her cheek and turned her hair silver before striping on across the pillow and up the wall.

Was this the only way he could look at her properly now? Josh wondered in despair. When she was asleep?

She had looked wonderful earlier at the reception laid on by C.B.C. to welcome everyone, but Josh hadn't been able to gaze at her the way he had wanted to do. There were too many other people around, too many others vying for her attention, too many of them standing between him and Bella.

She had been wearing some kind of sleeveless red dress and yet another pair of absurdly fragile shoes. Josh didn't know very much about women's clothes, but he could see that the outfit made Bella the sparkling centre of the room. Amongst the muted colours everyone else seemed to be wearing, she stood out like a bright flame.

Torn between pride and jealousy, Josh watched her flirting and charming her way around the room. Apparently it was all right for *her* to ignore *him*, he had thought sourly, remembering her earlier complaints.

But it was hard not to admire her. She had been with these people less than twenty-four hours, and already she seemed to know everybody, and whether by design or not, had contrived to make firm friends with a number of the key people who would make the final decision about whether to award Josh the global contract or not. They kept coming up to Josh and telling him how nice Bella was, how pretty she was, what fun.

As if he didn't know.

He should have been pleased. He should have been grateful. He should have encouraged Bella. Josh knew all that. But all he really wanted to do was to push his way through the men thronging around her, grab her by the wrist and drag her back to the room. Instead he had to smile and agree that, yes, Bella was a very special person.

The dinner after the reception was nearly as bad, and then there was sitting around in the bar to be got through. Josh found himself longing for the moment when he would have Bella to himself, but when they finally left to go back to their room, it was even worse.

Once they would have laughed and compared notes about who they had met, and Bella would have conducted an extensive critique of what the other women had been wearing, the intricacies of which Josh had never really appreciated but which had always amused him. But now any attempt at conversation shrivelled in the air and the only sound to break the silence between them as they walked back to their room was the rasp of insects in the tropical darkness.

They were both determinedly matter-of-fact about going to bed. Josh had looked out some old pyjama bottoms and Bella was wearing a nightdress she had obviously chosen for its lack of seductive frills but whose uncharacteristic plainness only emphasised the glow of her skin and hinted at the lushness of her body beneath.

Josh waited on the veranda, listening to the insects and

the murmur of sea, and trying not to think about peeling that nightdress off Bella, while she spent what seemed like hours in the bathroom. His turn took a couple of minutes and, by the time he came out, she was in bed, the sheet pulled up to her chin.

'Are you cold?' he asked stiltedly. 'I can turn the air-conditioning down if you like.'

'No, I'm fine.'

Tightening his jaw, Josh threw back the sheets on his side and got in. He could lie without touching Bella at all, but he was desperately aware of how close she was.

'Are you ready for me to switch off the light?' he asked in a voice that didn't sound like his at all.

'Yes, thanks.'

One click, and the room was plunged into darkness, with just the sound of the air-conditioning rattling into the silence.

Josh cleared his throat. 'Well, this is odd,' he said.

'I know.' Bella sounded grateful to him for breaking the silence. 'It's lucky we're such good friends, isn't it? Imagine what it was like for Phoebe and Gib. They ended up sharing a bed with someone they didn't really know at all. It must have been really awkward.'

Josh wondered how it could possibly have felt more awkward than it felt now, lying next to Bella and knowing that whatever he did he mustn't reach for her.

'Lucky for us,' he agreed dryly.

CHAPTER EIGHT

JOSH hoped that things would get easier as the week went by, but they didn't really. The days weren't too bad. He spent most of his time diving, and in the evenings he was careful not to be alone with Bella if he could avoid it. She was always the centre of a big group anyway, so that wasn't a problem.

That meant that there were only the nights to get through. Josh told himself to treat them as an endurance test, like sitting out a blizzard halfway up a mountain, or carrying a heavy pack through the jungle when there were leeches insinuating themselves into your socks and you hadn't slept for three nights. If he could survive those, he could survive this.

Of course he could.

Aisling provided the most effective cover for his feelings for Bella, and Josh stuck as close to her as he could. It wasn't difficult. Bryn had turned out to be obsessive about deep-sea angling, and while Josh and Aisling were diving, he was out on a boat, strapped into a chair, and wrestling with, according to him at least, monster fish. In the evenings, he would relive his exploits in second by second accounts of his machismo to anyone who would listen.

Josh noticed that Aisling looked a little tight-lipped at times, and often manoeuvred to a join the table where he and Bella were sitting rather than sit alone with Bryn, and he began to wonder if Bella's theory was right and that Aisling's passionate romance was wearing thin already.

'I told you so.' Bella was almost snappy when he mentioned it to her. 'It must make you feel better.'

Better? Josh was puzzled for moment before remembering that he was supposed to be still in love with Aisling.

'Oh...yes, yes, it does,' he lied.

'Obviously all those hours you and Aisling spend diving are paying off,' said Bella with a brittle smile. 'I'm very happy for you.'

'You don't sound very happy.'

'No, well, it's hard to feel very happy about being dumped on the beach every day while you and Aisling go off together,' she snapped.

Josh looked at her in surprise. 'You said didn't want to go diving,' he reminded her. 'You said were having a good time.'

'It's not much fun being an object of pity for everyone else on the beach!'

He frowned. 'What do you mean?'

'You know what I mean, Josh!' said Bella angrily. 'I know you want to be with Aisling, and that's fine, but you might give some thought to what it's like for me stuck here all day. Everyone thinks we're about to split up.'

'*What?*'

'Of course they do! They see you with Aisling, never with me. We never do anything together.'

Bella was appalled at how close she was to tears. She had been trying so hard not to mind when Josh went off with Aisling every day. Nor had Aisling's growing impatience with Bryn been lost on her.

Any day now, Aisling was going to realise what she had lost when she left Josh for Bryn. With Josh so clearly still available and keen to get back together, she wouldn't hesitate to say something to him, and then what was going to happen to *her*? Bella wondered. She would have to try and be happy for Josh but she wasn't sure that she would be able to bear it.

She was in a crowd all day, and at night she lay stiffly next to Josh, yearning to be able to touch him. She was never alone and she had never felt lonelier. Josh was scrupulously polite but it was clear how he felt. Once she had rolled over and brushed against him by mistake, and he had flinched.

'Sorry,' she had muttered, horribly embarrassed, and huddled back to her own side of the bed.

What was it Josh had said about the week turning out to be even harder than he had expected? Now Bella knew exactly what he meant. She didn't know whether she longed for the week to be over, or dreaded it as the last chance she might have to be this close to Josh.

He was looking apologetic now. 'The diving course finishes tomorrow,' he said. 'Maybe we could do something together on Friday?'

Some of the others had hired jeeps and found secluded beaches or great little fish restaurants. 'OK,' said Bella, trying desperately not to sound too eager, but unable to stop her heart quickening in anticipation of some time alone with him. At least she could make the most of it before Aisling realised just what a mistake she had made in letting him go.

'Aisling says there's a boat trip out to some of the uninhabited outer islands then,' Josh said. 'There'll be a chance to go snorkelling, too. We could go on that together if you like.'

Sick disappointment twisted in Bella's stomach. It sounded as if he couldn't bear the thought of a day without Aisling. She was furious with herself for that brief moment of excitement, but if she objected, she would sound like a spoilt, sulky child.

'Sure,' she said dully.

In spite of her disappointment, her spirits rose on Friday morning. Josh had breakfast with her and there was no sign of Aisling. Maybe she had changed her mind, thought Bella hopefully. Meanwhile, the day stretched ahead of them, a whole day with Josh. They might not be alone, but at least he would be there. The way Bella felt at that moment, it would be enough.

And it was a beautiful day. The sky was a deep, cloudless blue, the sea still and translucent, and the early morning sun behind the palm trees threw ragged shadows on the white sand. It was a picture of paradise, thought Bella. Impossible to feel depressed in a place like this on a day like this.

To hell with Aisling, she decided defiantly. I'm going to enjoy today whether she's there or not.

Unfortunately, Aisling *was* there. When the rest of them arrived, she was waiting down by the jetty with Bryn, who had obviously been persuaded to take a day off from killing fish and looked as if he was regretting it already.

There were eleven of them altogether, including Cassandra. Having spent the week organising trips for everyone else, she felt she was entitled to go on one herself, she explained.

'Now, is everyone here?'

She began counting heads, while Josh frowned at the boat tied up by the jetty. 'Are we going in that?' he interrupted her.

'What's wrong with it?'

'It's very open and very low—and it's going to get even lower when we all get in it,' he pointed out.

Bryn strolled over to join in the discussion. 'What's the problem?'

'I'm just a bit concerned about the lack of protection,'

said Josh, not looking as if he welcomed Bryn's input at all.

'Good God, man, there's a perfectly adequate sunshade!'

'I wasn't thinking of the sun,' Josh said evenly. 'I'm thinking about what would happen if we ran into rough seas.'

'What rough seas?' Bryn was openly dismissive. 'The sea's like a millpond.'

Josh's slate-coloured eyes narrowed as he looked at the horizon where you could just make out a faint smudge. 'I've got a bad feeling about the weather,' he admitted.

Bryn followed his glance. 'Just a heat haze,' he pronounced. 'Come on, let's go.'

'Just a minute,' said Josh quietly, but something in his tone stopped Bryn in his tracks. 'Who's in charge of this boat?' he asked Cassandra, who was beginning to look flustered.

'It's Ron's boat. He's terribly reliable and he's done lots of trips for us before, but he can't come himself today so he's sent Elvis instead,' she said, and pointed at the boy sitting patiently at the tiller. 'He's only thirteen, but he's been helping his father on this boat since he could walk.'

'I'm sure Elvis knows what he's doing,' said Josh dryly. 'I'd just feel better if there was any sign of a life-jacket on board.'

'Oh, stop being such an old woman!' said Bryn. 'We're not going to need life-jackets on a day like today.'

'Yes, do stop fussing, Josh,' said Aisling. 'If we hang around looking for life-jackets it'll be too late to go at all.'

There was an immediate uproar from the others, and Josh found himself overruled as they piled into the boat, which promptly sank perilously low in the water. Josh didn't like it at all, but Bella, who had been chatting and hadn't heard any of the discussion, was already in. Short of dragging her out bodily, there wasn't much he could do about it, and he certainly wasn't letting her go off in a boat like this without him.

Reluctantly, Josh untied the rope for Elvis and got in as well with a last glance at the horizon. Maybe he was wrong about the weather.

For most of the day, it seemed that he was. The tarpaulin rigged over the boat gave some shade, but it was still very hot and the sea was oily and still as they puttered out to the furthermost islands. The mood was cheerful, as if everyone realised that they would be going home to winter in a couple of days and were determined to make the most of it. Only Josh kept a watchful eye on the horizon, but the smudge didn't move.

They anchored at last on a tiny exposed atoll where the coral wall fell away into deep, clear, turquoise water. Leaning over the edge of the boat, they oohed and aahed at the iridescent fish that darted in and out of the coral.

'See?' said Bryn with a sneer. 'If we'd listened to Josh, we'd still be looking for life-jackets and we wouldn't have seen this.'

Bella stood up abruptly. 'Where are the masks and flippers?' she asked, changing the subject before anyone else could jump on the jeering bandwagon Bryn was clearly intent on setting rolling. 'I don't know about the rest of you, but I want to go snorkelling before lunch.'

Josh wished that he could shake the uncanny sense of impending disaster. He was torn between watching that ominous smudge on the horizon and following Bella into the limpid water. Surely she'd be safe here? But tides could be treacherous, and sharks weren't unknown...

Suddenly afraid to let her out of his sight, Josh put on a mask and snorkel and tipped neatly into the water after the others. She had only been snorkelling once before and he caught up with her easily and shadowed her unobtrusively as she drifted happily along the reef, unaware of his presence until he touched her arm and pointed.

Bella looked to see a huge turtle swimming gracefully past, so unlike lumbering progress on land. Rapt, she watched it go then lifted her head out of the water to remove her snorkel as Josh surfaced beside her.

'Wasn't it *beautiful*? Oh, that's one of the best things I've ever seen!' She was so thrilled that Josh's unease began to recede. Bella was happy, he told himself. Everything was fine.

Not wanting to crowd her, he made his way back to the boat after a while, and sat and talked to Elvis until the others started to trickle back. Bella was one of the last. Josh saw her head pop up out of the water by the ladder and, in spite of his decision not to worry, he was conscious of a sharp sense of relief.

Throwing her flippers ahead of her into the boat, she climbed up the ladder and pulled off her mask. It left a red mark on her face and her hair was all wet and tangled, but she looked gorgeous, thought Josh. She was lit up with excitement, and bubbling with enthusiasm.

'Wasn't it fabulous? I can't believe the colours! What are those blue and yellow stripy fish called? And did you *see* the turtle?'

They were all happy and laughing, comparing notes on what they had seen and talking about lunch which the hotel had provided.

'I'm starving,' said Bella. 'Let's eat now and then we can have another snorkel later.'

She clambered over the muddle of snorkels and flippers towards Josh to retrieve her shorts and top but, just as she got there, someone else climbed onto the boat, making it rock suddenly. Losing her balance, she fell against him.

Josh caught her instinctively, and for a breathless moment he held her against him. She was still dripping, and she was warm and wet against his bare chest where their skin touched. Unable to stop his arm from tightening around her, Josh found himself looking straight into the blue eyes, and his heart missed a beat.

'OK?' he asked, dry-mouthed and shaken by how much he wanted her.

Bella nodded dumbly and jerked herself out of his arm before she did anything silly like running her hands up over his shoulders or down the broad, muscled back. She was shocked by the impact of their bare flesh, by the jolt of electric excitement that came from the briefest and most impersonal of touches.

The feel of his skin against hers was all that it took for her to forget all the careful resolutions she had made, all that deciding to make the most of what she had got, all those noble, self-sacrificing thoughts telling herself that she only wanted Josh to be happy.

Who was she trying to kid? She wanted a lot more than that. She wanted to cover him with kisses and taste the salt on his skin. She wanted to feel his hands hard against her body. She wanted him to pull her down into the mess of rubber and shoes in the bottom of the boat and make love to her there and then, and to hell with everyone else.

That would rock the boat, in more ways than one.

Swallowing hard, Bella concentrated fiercely on pulling on her clothes.

Meanwhile, Josh was trying not to think about how quickly she had pulled away from him. Had she noticed the instinctive tightening of his arm, or read the naked desire in his eyes? Was that why she had recoiled like that?

To take his mind off her, Josh turned to look at the horizon again, and stiffened. The smudge had resolved itself into an ugly black line advancing across the blue sky.

He got to his feet. 'I think we should go,' he announced.

Immediately there was a chorus of protests about lunch and wanting to stay where they were and other chances to see the turtle.

Josh cut across them. 'Look!' he said, and pointed to the blackness on the horizon.

'Oh, but it's miles away!'

'It's lovely here.'

'We need to go,' said Josh. 'Now.' The authority in his voice shut them up at last. 'Who's not here?' he asked.

'Bryn,' said Aisling. 'He said he wanted to look around the other side.'

'We'd better go and find him. Did you see which way he went?'

Elvis started the motor while Josh pulled up the anchor, and they made their way slowly around the atoll looking out for Bryn's snorkel. Everyone had picked up on Josh's sense of urgency by this stage and uneasy glances were cast at the advancing black line.

'There he is!' They had wasted precious minutes before Bella spotted the snorkel poking out of the water ahead.

Elvis brought the boat up alongside Bryn, who registered their presence enough to wave but blithely carried on snorkelling.

Josh sighed. 'I'll go and get him.'

Flipping neatly over the side, he swam to intercept Bryn. They were too far away for Bella to hear what they were saying, but it was obvious that Josh was having difficulty convincing him to get back in the boat, in spite of being able to point at the menacing black sky in the distance.

Aisling was watching them anxiously. 'Can't you do anything?' said Bella. 'He'll listen to you, won't he?'

'Not if he thinks I am trying to get him to do what Josh wants him to do.' Aisling glanced at Bella. 'Bryn's jealous of Josh because...well, you know...'

Yes, Bella knew, but this didn't seem the time for petty jealousies.

Fortunately, someone shouted just then that the two men were on their way back to the boat. It was never clear exactly what Josh had said to Bryn, but judging by the expression on Bryn's face as he climbed grudgingly into the boat it was nothing very pleasant.

'I don't know what all the fuss is about,' he grumbled to Aisling. 'Those clouds are nowhere near, and anyway, I'm not afraid of a bit of tropical rain!' He jerked his head to where Josh was consulting with Elvis. 'The Kommandant over there seems to be insisting that we head back, but I don't see what's wrong with staying here.'

'There's no shelter here,' said Bella clearly.

Bryn tapped his hand against the tarpaulin. 'This'll keep off the worst of the rain. We might get a bit wet, but it'll soon pass over. These tropical downpours always do.'

'This is going to be more than a passing shower,' said Josh, overhearing him. 'It's too exposed out here. We need to get back to one of those islands we passed on the way out and try and find some shelter if we can. At least we could get off the boat. It's not designed for rough weather.'

'Well, I say we should sit out here,' said Bryn loudly, looking around the boat. 'Who agrees with me?'

Josh stepped up until he was nose to nose with him. 'We're not putting this to the vote,' he said very quietly, but in a voice that sent a little frisson down Bella's spine. She had never heard Josh talk like that before and she was very glad that his anger wasn't directed at her.

'There's a storm coming,' he went on in the same cold, clear tone. 'This boat is unsafe and as Bella pointed out, there's no shelter out here. I am not prepared to risk Bella's life, or anyone else's come to that, on the chance that this will just be a "downpour". We're not voting on anything. We are going back to that last island as fast as we can so I suggest that you just *sit* down and *shut* up.'

Bryn sat.

Josh went to sit beside Elvis, who was looking very young and very nervous by now. 'OK, Elvis,' he said, clapping him on the shoulder. 'Full steam ahead!'

'Where does he get off ordering everyone around?' Bryn muttered. 'He'll have us all goose-stepping next! If I'd known I was signing up for the army, I'd never have come on this holiday.'

'Pity you didn't,' muttered Cassandra, who was sitting next to Bella.

Bella glanced at the nervous faces around her. 'Josh knows what he's doing,' she said, more for their benefit than for Bryn's.

'Yes, shut up, Bryn,' said Aisling, looking strained.

It was very hot still. The sun beat down, bouncing and glittering on the water, and they were all glad of the awning over the boat which at least gave some shade. The sea was flat calm and so clear that you could see shoals of fish beneath the boat, flashing silver as they turned suddenly and caught the light.

There was something eerie about the idyllic scene, thought Bella. Ahead, all was calm and perfect, but if you glanced behind, as they were all doing with increasing nervousness, the blackness was creeping menacingly closer, gobbling up the blue sky, as it advanced inexorably towards them.

The boat was pegging bravely onwards. Josh looked

over his shoulder. 'Is this the fastest she can do?' he asked Elvis casually.

'Yes, sir. This is top speed already.'

'Well, don't worry, we'll just keep going as we are. It's not much further now.'

Everyone began to look more hopeful, although Bella suspected that it was more because Josh sounded positive than from any evidence that the situation was improving. She had been scanning the horizon desperately for land, and she hadn't seen any sign of an island anywhere near by. It was as if they were all, with the exception of Bryn, instinctively looking to Josh for reassurance.

'It does seem to be getting closer,' said Cassandra in a quavering voice. 'Is it going to overtake us?'

'We might get a bit wet,' Josh told her cheerfully, 'but once we get to that island we can sit it out.' He nodded at the iceboxes which contained their lunch. 'We've got food and drink, so we won't starve. We'll be fine.'

There was something incredibly reassuring about him, thought Bella. He wasn't the best-looking man on the boat, he certainly wasn't the best dresser, and he didn't have smart cars or the latest technology to flash around. But he was the one person you wanted with you in a situation like this. He was so calm, so solid, so safe. It was impossible to believe that he would let anything bad happen.

'You're doing a great job, Elvis,' he was encouraging the boy, who smiled nervously and tried to stop biting his lip and darting glances over his shoulder.

'Oh, yes, great!' said Bryn sarcastically. 'Personally, I'd save my compliments for someone who bothered to listen to the weather forecast! I'm going to have something to say to the hotel when we get back,' he huffed. 'The whole situation is outrageous. I shall demand my money back, and suggest that they use more professional people in future for any boat trips they organise.'

Elvis was looking stricken. As if he didn't have enough problems right now with a boatload of westerners and the mother of all storms rushing up behind him, he could obviously see his family's livelihood disappearing as well.

Bella glared at Bryn. 'If we get back, it'll be thanks to Elvis, not you,' she said clearly. Under cover of a smatter of hear-hears, she leant across to Bryn, who was sitting almost exactly opposite her. 'Now shut up about it,' she said through her teeth. 'He's just a boy, and he's scared.'

'He's not the only one!' said Cassandra.

They were all sitting tensely, leaning forward slightly as if to will the boat faster through the water. It was hard to believe that only a few minutes ago they had been talking and laughing and thinking about lunch. Now they waited in increasingly ominous silence for the storm to catch them.

When someone spotted an island in the distance, their spirits rose dramatically, but just as they were congratulating themselves on the narrowness of their escape, a tiny puff of wind lifted the oppressive heat.

Josh leapt for awning, as the puff was followed by another, and then another. 'Let's get this down!'

'But it's going to pour,' Bryn objected as the blackness loomed. 'We won't have any shelter.'

'If the wind catches this, it'll tip us over, and keeping dry will be the last of our problems,' said Josh.

Three of the other men had got up to help him untie the awning while Bryn sulked, but already those first delicate puffs of breeze had grown into a wind that was making the task more difficult. The canvas was flapping horribly, while the boat tilted in the choppy water and the men staggered on their feet as they wrestled with the knots.

There were a few murmurs of distress, and Cassandra was not the only one looking suddenly white-faced.

Bella couldn't believe how suddenly the conditions had changed. One minute they had been puttering along in the flat calm and the next they were in the middle of a screaming gale. And the wind was just a foretaste of what was to come. Another second and the sun had been swallowed up by the boiling black clouds, and the rain hit them with the force of a ten-ton truck.

'Bella!' Josh had to bellow over the screaming wind and crashing rain. He had taken over the tiller from Elvis, who was frantically throwing water overboard with a ludicrously small plastic baler. 'Get everyone baling!'

Blinking through the water that streamed down her face, Bella gave Josh the thumbs up sign to show that she had understood.

How she was going to go about it was another matter. She looked around desperately before grabbing a mask from the muddle of snorkels and flippers and abandoned shoes which were already floating in the rainwater accumulating in the bottom of the boat and began baling. Not very effective, it had to be said, but it was better than nothing.

'I feel sick,' moaned Cassandra.

'Here.' Bella shoved the mask at her and groped around for another one. 'Help get rid of some of this water. You'll feel better if you've got something to do.'

Although what would *she* know? Bella asked herself wryly. Still, she had obviously convinced Cassandra who began scooping up water obediently with her mask.

Aisling had seen what they were doing and was handing out masks on the other side. Even Bryn took one. Bella wasn't sure that was a good sign. Things must look really bad for him to come out of his sulk and follow Josh's advice.

Buffeted by waves on all sides and submerging under the deluge of water, the little boat seemed to be standing still in the water. It seemed a lifetime since they had stood on the sunny jetty that morning and pooh-poohed Josh's caution about life-jackets, a lifetime of bending and scooping and chucking the water from the bottom of the boat that filled up as quickly as they could try and empty it. The rain was relentless, hammering down on them while the wind shrieked and the sea surged, slopping waves over the side and tearing at her hair.

Bella's shoulders ached with baling, but she managed to get into a rhythm eventually which made it easier. What am I doing here? she wondered. I'm a city girl. I should be at my computer or in some bar, not stuck on a sinking boat in the middle of the Indian Ocean. I do text messages and buying shoes, not survival.

Someone near her was crying, but Bella couldn't see who it was and anyway, if she had to do survival, she was going to survive, and that meant keeping on baling rather than stopping to offer comfort. She felt oddly detached. The whole thing had happened so suddenly and was so overwhelming that it seemed vaguely surreal, but beneath her surface calm she was absolutely terrified.

Whenever fear threatened to become too much, she would fix her mind on Josh. She could hardly make him out through the lashing rain, but even an indistinct glimpse of his solid figure, holding onto the tiller with one hand and baling like everyone else with the other, was enough to reassure her. Josh was there and in control, and he wouldn't let anything happen to her.

It was like being trapped in a nightmare. Bella baled and baled and baled, and forgot what it was like to feel warm and dry and safe. She was in such a zombiefied state that a shout from Elvis barely penetrated her consciousness and it wasn't until Cassandra prodded her that she looked up to see the island.

After longing for the sight of land, it loomed terrifyingly close through the driving rain, The little boat was already perilously close to the rocks that fringed the island, but still they all cheered at the sight and redoubled their efforts to stop it sinking before they could reach the shore.

After some consultation with Elvis, Josh put on his shoes and made his way cautiously to the front of the boat.

'What are you doing?' Bella shouted over the sound of the wind and rain as he passed her.

'We can't risk running the boat onto the rocks or we might never get off again,' he shouted back. 'Elvis is going to get as close as he dares, and by then it should be shallow enough for me to get in and anchor it. I can pull the boat the rest of the way.'

'You're going to jump into the sea?' Bella was horrified. 'Josh, you can't! It's too dangerous.'

His hand rested briefly on her cheek. 'Don't worry, it'll be fine.'

Bella could hardly bear to watch as he disappeared overboard. The water was wild and the wind furious, tossing the boat around spitefully. How could he even stand, let alone manoeuvre them into the shore?

It was hard to see what was going on, but those at the front of the boat passed the message back down the line that Josh's feet had touched the bottom and that he was slowly but surely, dragging them through the rocks into the shore. The waves slapped him in the face and made him stagger, but when he was knee-deep he signalled to Elvis to cut the engine and drop the anchor.

They would all have to wade the rest of the way but

they were so wet by that stage and so relieved to have reached land that no one objected, not even Bryn. Forming a chain, they passed the iceboxes, awning and various bags over their heads and then huddled together on the tiny beach.

If anything the storm seemed worse here, as if maddened by their attempt to escape its clutches. The palm trees bent almost to the ground before the force of the wind, which whipped their leaves savagely and tossed debris into the air, while the rain slashed down in a deafening torrent.

'Welcome to paradise!' Bella shouted above the tumult, and they all laughed rather hysterically.

Under the conditions, it was difficult to tell much about the island, but eventually it was decided to explore inland to see if they could rig up a rudimentary shelter with the awning.

Josh stayed behind with Elvis to see if they could make the boat more secure, but he watched Bella struggle up the beach with Cassandra, carrying an icebox between them. She was smiling encouragingly and apparently even managing to make jokes, judging by the way her companions laughed as if despite themselves.

It didn't take long to explore the island, which was rocky and covered in sparse vegetation. On the lee side Josh found another beach which was relatively sheltered, and they managed to tie the awning between some trees, where a rocky wall behind gave them the illusion of protection from the rain, although the benefit was largely psychological. By the time they had carried everything over there, they were all exhausted, and they collapsed together under the canvas with groans of relief.

CHAPTER NINE

ONLY Josh resisted the temptation to slump with the others. 'I think it would be a good idea to bring the boat round here,' he said, eyeing the beach critically. 'It's more protected here and we can keep an eye on it.'

Bryn heaved an exaggerated sigh. 'Oh, God, he thinks he's Robinson Crusoe now! Can't it wait? We've only just sat down.'

'It would be safer to do it now,' said Josh. 'I know we're all tired, but if the boat breaks loose we're going to be stuck here and it might be some time before anyone finds us and we really will get a chance to play Robinson Crusoe. It's just a question of walking it round the shoreline. I could do with a hand, though.'

'Take Elvis,' said Bryn dismissively. 'The boat is his responsibility.'

'Elvis is barely more than a child.' Josh glanced at where the boy sat slightly apart, not listening to what was going on but with his head slumped onto his knees. 'He's exhausted.'

'We're all exhausted! For God's sake—'

'Why don't we rest for a bit?' suggested Aisling quickly as it became obvious that Bryn was working himself up for a rant. 'Then we can deal with the boat.'

Josh hesitated. Bella could see that he was really concerned about the boat, and somehow she managed to haul herself to her feet.

'I'll go with you,' she said, although her limbs felt like lead and she wasn't sure she could even get back to the other side of the island, let alone struggle through the water with a boat.

The wind whipped her wet hair around her face as she stood there, utterly bedraggled and swaying with exhaustion. Josh had an incongruous vision of her as she had looked at Kate's wedding, glossy in her hat and her high heels. He had always given her a hard time for being a bit of a princess, but there was no doubt about it: she was a princess with guts!

Her offer shamed a couple of the other men into going with them and, although Bryn resolutely maintained that the expedition could wait until they had all recovered, the four of them set off straight away. They were only just in time, too, as the boat was straining at its makeshift mooring and it wouldn't have been long before it dragged itself free and smashed into the rocks.

Bella had expected it to be hard work to move it round to the other side of the island, and in the event it was much more difficult than even she had imagined. There were times during that terrible trip when she was sure they would never make it.

For most of the way, the water wasn't too deep, but the boat was difficult to manoeuvre in the choppy sea. The rain blinded them, and the waves pounded relentlessly at them, knocking them off their feet and pushing them back towards the rocks.

At a couple of points they had to edge their way carefully around rocky promontories, where the footholds were slippery and uneven, and the water deeper. Bella slipped and was submerged several times, and once she disappeared completely under the boat before Josh thrashed frantically through the water to drag her back, gasping and choking, to the surface.

He kept them all going by sheer will-power, shouting

encouragement and refusing to let them give up. Bella's hands were numb, but just when she was sure that she couldn't hold onto the boat a moment longer, the beach came in sight. The others were there to help pull it up to safety, but by then Bella couldn't even make it to the cover. She collapsed onto the sand, heedless of the thrashing rain, unable to move a second more.

The next moment she found herself lifted in strong arms as Josh carried her the last few yards. 'I'm all right,' she roused herself to protest, knowing that he must be as exhausted as everyone else. 'Put me down before you fall down!'

'Stop wriggling and shut up,' said Josh, raising his voice above the sound of the wind.

'Well, that's not very lover-like!' Bella pretended to be offended. 'We *are* supposed to be engaged, you know.'

She had wanted to make Josh smile, but although the corner of his mouth quirked upwards, his eyes were deadly serious as he laid her down under the awning.

'I hadn't forgotten,' he said.

Bella was embarrassed to find herself greeted as a heroine by the women who had stayed behind. In the way women do, they had contrived to make the makeshift shelter as much of a home as they could, ranging the bags around the edge, laying out towels and sarongs as sleeping mats, and setting out the iceboxes as a table. Bella half expected to see that someone had hacked their way into the undergrowth to find some flowers.

It was Cassandra who noticed that Bella's foot was bleeding and promptly whipped the towel out from beneath her leg. 'That's a really bad cut,' she said with a grimace.

'I must have done it when I slipped on the rocks. Those sandals were designed for walking to and from the pool, not clambering over rocks.' Bella contemplated her ruined shoes sadly. They had been her favourites, delicate, strappy affairs with appliquéd flowers and sequins. 'They're never going to be the same again!'

'You should be worrying about your foot, not your shoes,' said Josh sternly, lifting her left foot to inspect the unpleasantly jagged tear along one side. 'Cassandra is right. That's really nasty. Why didn't you say something?'

'I didn't know I'd done it. I still can't feel it, to tell you the truth.'

She could feel his fingers gently probing around the cut, though. He must be as cold and as wet and as numb as she was, but his hands were wonderfully warm against her skin.

Bella studied her foot with an odd air of detachment. She was usually a terrible baby about anything like that, and if she'd cut herself in London would have been squealing and yelping and demanding emergency treatment, preferably from a tall, dark, good-looking doctor in a white coat who might or might not have an uncanny resemblance to George Clooney. *E.R.* just hadn't been the same since he had left.

It was strange to be thinking about *E.R.* when she was stuck on an uninhabited island in the middle of the Indian Ocean with the wind howling and screaming and shaking the awning, and the rain thundering down onto their pitiful shelter, and Josh and Cassandra peering at her foot in concern.

'Must it be amputation, doctor?' she asked solemnly, and Josh's smile did more to warm her than a lorry load of duvets and hot-water bottles.

Although Bella wouldn't have said no to a nice, warm, dry bed right then. With Josh in it.

'I think you'll survive,' he said, breaking into her fantasy. 'You're going to need some stitches, I think, but we'll just have to tie it up for now.'

After a fruitless search for something that could be used as a bandage, Josh tore a wide strip off the bottom of his short-sleeved shirt. Like Bella's foot, it had been thoroughly soaked in sea water so at least had the advantage of being cleaner than any of the alternatives.

He bound up her foot with a brisk professionalism. 'There, how does that feel?' he asked as he secured it with a knot.

'Better than a pedicure,' said Bella.

Wet and weary as she was, she felt bizarrely happy. The storm was no longer terrifying, but merely background noise to the fact that she was with Josh and that horrible tension between them had been blown away along with their plans for a peaceful afternoon snorkelling.

Later, they shared out the food from one of the iceboxes. Bella was almost too tired to bother by then, but Josh told her roughly that she had to eat, so she chewed obediently on a sandwich. Packed into plastic boxes and sealed in the icebox, the food had stayed miraculously dry, and once they had started eating they all discovered that they were ravenously hungry. Eyes began turning to the other two iceboxes.

'Do you think we should keep the rest for later?' Cassandra asked, turning instinctively to Josh as their unelected leader.

'I think it would be a good idea,' he said. 'We should put out the empty icebox, too, and collect some rainwater.'

Bryn rolled his eyes to the awning above their heads where the rain was already gathering in another great pool. They had to keep knocking the canvas to send it cascading down the sides to stop the awning collapsing beneath the weight of the water.

'I wouldn't have said shortage of water was our problem here!' he said sarcastically.

'It might be when the storm passes,' said Josh evenly. 'I didn't see any fresh water on the island and it's best to be prepared. The boat got pretty bashed around on those rocks. If we can't get the engine going tomorrow we might be here some time and in that case the one thing we're going to need is water.'

'I'm sure you'd love that,' sneered Bryn. 'It would give you a chance to show off all those survival skills of yours. I can just see you rubbing sticks together to make a fire and impressing the girls by spearing a fish!'

'It wouldn't just impress the girls,' said one of the men who had helped bring the boat round. 'It would impress me too!'

'Yes, shut up, Bryn!' said Aisling sharply, getting up to put the empty icebox outside to catch the rain. 'You're behaving like a spoilt child!'

'Oh, right, just because I don't jump whenever your precious Josh says jump! Who put him in charge anyway?'

'He's in charge because he knows what he's talking about, which is more than I can say for you!' Aisling snapped back.

'If he's so perfect, why didn't you stick with him?' snarled Bryn.

'I'm beginning to wish I had!'

'Oh, well, fine!' he said petulantly. 'Just because I'm not macho man like Mr SAS over there!'

'You can say that again,' murmured Cassandra in Bella's ear. 'Did you know that his name is really Bryan? I had to collect in all the passports, so I queried it when the names didn't match. Apparently he dropped "a" because he thinks Bryn is sexier and suits him better. Talk about self-deluded!'

Bella was delighted to have her theory confirmed, but hoped that Cassandra hadn't picked up on Bryn's jibe about Aisling leaving Josh.

She had, of course. Bella knew that she would have pricked up her ears at that too, and she was beginning to feel that Cassandra might be a kindred spirit.

'What was that about Aisling and Josh?' she asked curiously. 'Did they use to go out?'

'They were engaged briefly,' admitted Bella reluctantly, and Cassandra shot her a perceptive glance.

'No wonder you didn't like it when they went off diving together all the time! You don't need to worry, though,' she went on comfortably. 'It's obvious that he absolutely adores you.'

Bella knew that Josh adored her, but not in the way Cassandra meant. Until she realised how much she loved him, she would have said the same. 'Oh, yes, I adore Josh,' she would say if anyone commented on how nice he was, or how close they seemed, but she had meant as a friend, not as a lover.

Not the way she wanted him to adore her now.

Josh had ignored Bryn's taunts, and had gone out to check on the boat, leaving Bryn and Aisling to argue in snappy whispers. When he came back, he lay down beside Bella and, without a word, lifted an arm so that she could nestle into him, too tired to worry about looking clingy or needy or revealing too much and needing only the warmth and comfort of his body.

'How long do you think those sandwiches will last?' she asked sleepily. Lying close like this, they could talk without being heard by the others above the sound of the rain and in the darkness it was like being in their own private world.

'They'll stretch to breakfast,' said Josh. 'I wouldn't bank on any lunch if we can't get the boat going.'

'I hope we don't have to revert to cannibalism,' she murmured. 'We might end up like that parlour game where you have to argue that you're so essential that you shouldn't be eaten, and I'd be bound to be the first one in the pot. It's true,' she said as she felt Josh shake with quiet laughter. 'I must be the most useless person here. PR isn't exactly a survival skill!'

'Making people laugh is,' said Josh. 'You're a lot more useful than most people here, but if it comes to it, I'll make sure you don't get the short straw.'

'Thank you.' Bella snuggled into a more comfortable position with her arm across his chest. 'Anyway, I get the feeling that awarding the honour of first in the pot to Bryn would be a popular move!'

Josh laughed softly. 'He's just scared like rest of us.'

'*You* weren't scared,' said Bella.

'Yes, I was.'

Josh thought about how terrified he had been when she had slipped out of his sight under the waves and wished he could tell her how essential she was to him. Unable to resist the temptation, he put his other arm around her and held her close into him. They might not be very dry or very warm or very comfortable, but at least she was here and she was safe.

The storm passed as suddenly as it had hit them. One minute the darkness was filled with the sound of the savage wind and lashing rain and the next there was a silence so deafening that for a moment none of those awake could actually believe that the awesome noise had stopped. There was just the slow drip, drip of the palm leaves and the trickle of left-over water running off the awning.

Bella heard it stop too, and felt guilty for being the only one to experience a pang of regret. The storm had at least given her a chance to lie in Josh's arms. Now that it was over, there was no excuse not to go back to reality, to being careful, to remembering that they were friends, not lovers.

It was too dark to do anything about the fact that the storm had passed, so one by one they all drifted off to sleep again. Bella was horribly stiff when she woke the next morning, and her foot throbbed painfully. She told herself that it must be a good sign that she could feel it now, but couldn't help wishing that it would go back to being numb. She felt awful, damp and dirty in a way she had been too tired to feel the night before.

Limping outside, she found most of the party grouped anxiously around the boat. Josh and Elvis were peering into the depths of the engine and there seemed to be a lot of tinkering going on.

'They can't start the engine,' Cassandra whispered to Bella. 'Just as well we didn't eat all those sandwiches. Do you think Josh really knows how to spear a fish?' she asked hopefully.

'I'm not sure about that. He's usually quite good on engines, though.'

The words were barely out of Bella's mouth before a cheer went up as the engine spluttered into life and Josh looked up with a grin that told Bella just how worried he had been.

'OK!' he said, clapping Elvis on the back. 'Let's finish off those sandwiches and then let's go!'

Although the centre of the storm had moved on, it had left behind a sullen sea and dreary blanket of grey clouds that eked a constant drizzle that was almost more depressing than the rain had been. It wasn't cold, but everyone was tired and sick of being wet, and very nervous in case the boat broke down again, so after the first euphoria of leaving the island, it was a silent journey.

Aisling and Bryn were pointedly not talking to each other, and the atmosphere was so oppressive that the sight of the rescue boat at last came as even more of a relief than anyone had anticipated. They were still a couple of hours from the jetty, and transferred eagerly onto the faster boat, except Josh, who volunteered to stay on the boat with Elvis to talk to the authorities and make sure he didn't get blamed.

'We'll follow you in,' he said.

As the rescue boat sped away, Bella looked back at him, sitting calmly beside the boy in the tattered remains of his shirt and her heart turned over with love for him.

With its powerful engine, it was no time at all before the rescue boat had them back at the hotel, receiving the exclamations and commiserations of the others. The hotel looked as if it had received a fair battering from the storm itself, but a single night sleeping on the wet sand had been enough to make the rooms seem so luxurious as to feel faintly surreal.

A doctor, not looking remotely like George Clooney and not even wearing a white coat, was summoned to stitch up Bella's foot and give her a jab. The foot was swollen and very painful by then, and Bella couldn't help wishing like a baby that Josh was with her to hold her hand. Really, she had to stop being so pathetic!

At least she had had a shower, and not just any shower. Indisputably the best shower of her life. Bella washed her hair three times to get rid of the salt and the sand and, when at last she felt clean and dry, she lay on the bed to wait for Josh.

It had started to rain heavily again by the time Josh

finally appeared. There was no wind this time, and Bella could see the rain falling in a steady downpour beyond the veranda and hear it drumming loudly on the roof above her head. She had been dozing, and the room was so dark that she switched on the bedside lamp to squint at her watch, amazed to see that it was late afternoon still and there was a good hour until dusk.

The sound of Josh's key in the door, made her struggle up onto the pillows and stretch luxuriously. 'You've been ages,' she said. 'Is everything OK?'

'They wanted to give Elvis a hard time for taking the boat out at all, poor kid,' said Josh, sitting down on the edge of her bed. 'I think I persuaded them that it wasn't his fault.'

She had been waiting and waiting for him to come, and now he was there, sitting solid and safe beside her, and she felt suddenly shy again. 'What happened to your shirt?' she asked, to stop herself flinging her arms around him and burrowing into his strong, sure body.

'I think they felt it was rather indecent, so someone gave me this one when they let us have a shower.' He plucked at the shirt, a luridly coloured affair with a florid pattern. 'Do you like it?'

'To be honest, I wouldn't have said that it was quite *you*.'

Josh's smile gleamed in the dim light and their eyes met and held for a moment before they both looked away.

It couldn't be said that there was a silence with the rain crashing down on the roof, but there was a funny, breathless little pause that set Bella's heart slamming slowly and painfully against her ribs. At least Josh wouldn't be able to hear it with the racket the rain was making.

'How's the foot?' he asked after a moment.

'Sore.' Bella lifted her foot slightly to show him. 'They

stitched me up and gave me a new bandage. I don't think they thought much of your other shirt either.'

Josh took her foot and held it gently in his hand. 'I shouldn't have let you help move the boat around,' he said. 'I should have insisted one of the other men came with me and to hell with what Bryn thought. It was too dangerous for you to be out there.'

'If it was too dangerous for me, it was too dangerous for you,' she pointed out. 'Anyway, I only cut my foot. It's not as if I was bitten by a shark or got swept out to sea.'

'You could have drowned,' said Josh, refusing to be comforted. 'Last night you said that I wasn't scared, but I was. When I saw you slip and disappear under that boat, I was absolutely terrified.'

His hand had moved almost absently up to Bella's ankle. She swallowed. 'I knew you'd save me.'

She hesitated, torn between giving in to the sheer tantalising pleasure of his hand smoothing up her leg and the need to tell him how she felt. 'You saved all of us,' she said. 'I don't know if we would have survived without you. I was so proud of you, Josh. The rest of us went to pieces at the first hint of danger, but you knew exactly what to do.'

She smiled waveringly. 'I understand why people go off on expeditions with you now.'

Josh's hand had reached her knee. 'I'd have you as my second-in-command any day,' he said.

'But I was useless! I didn't know what to do.'

'Yes, you did. You knew instinctively that when things get difficult you need someone who can defuse the tension, someone who can make people laugh in spite of everything, someone who can get on with everybody. Someone like you, in fact.' His hand was warm against her flesh. 'I was thinking that I should really take you on expedition one day. Do you think you'd like that?'

'That depends on whether I could take my hair-dryer or not,' said Bella a little breathlessly. She was excruciatingly aware of the touch of his hand on her skin, but it was hard to tell whether Josh even realised what he was doing.

'You could take it,' he allowed. 'Whether you would find anywhere to plug it in is another matter.'

Any further and his hand would be under her skirt. 'I think I'd have to take it as a matter of principle.' Bella was striving desperately to keep the conversation light, but she was having a lot of trouble breathing. 'And my best shoes, of course.'

'I'm afraid as expedition leader I'd have to draw the line at your shoes,' said Josh with mock solemnity. 'All high heels would have to be left behind. I'd need to maintain some kind of authority over my team.'

'Does that mean I'd have to call you "sir"?'

'Only in private.'

Unable to keep a straight face any longer, they both started to laugh, but the moment they made the mistake of looking at each other, their laughter died abruptly.

'I couldn't bear it when I thought I might lose you,' said Josh in a low voice. 'You're my best friend.'

'And you're mine.'

'Bella—' He stopped, his hand tightening against her leg as the air shortened between them.

'Yes?' Bella's heart was beating so hard that she could hardly breathe.

Josh couldn't put what he wanted to say into words. He just knew what he wanted to do. Very slowly, he leant towards her, giving her the chance to push him away, to make a joke, and break the moment which had them both in its spell.

But she didn't. She just sat there, her eyes dark with a desire that drew him irresistibly closer

He stopped a fraction of a breath away from her mouth, conscious that this was the moment of no return. They looked deep into each other's eyes, and in the end it was Bella who closed the gap, touching her lips with his.

It wasn't too late. One part of Josh's mind was very clear about that. He could draw back and leave it at a brief kiss that they could both pretend had only ever been friendly. He even knew that was what he should do.

But he didn't want to. Her response had been so piercingly sweet that he couldn't bring himself to stop, not now.

So he kissed her, the way he had been wanting to kiss her for so long, and it was as if their lips belonged together. Bella's hands slid up his shoulders to wind around his neck, and she was kissing him back, giving kiss for kiss as they sank down together on the bed.

Lost in the heady scent of her, Josh tangled his fingers luxuriously in her silky hair. He raised himself slightly to smooth the hair from her face, and his heart turned over as she smiled up at him.

'Best friends don't do this,' he said softly.

'Don't they?'

'Not normally.'

'This isn't a normal time,' said Bella, running her hands lovingly over his back. 'We survived a storm at sea, and now nothing seems normal. We can worry about what friends do when we know what normal is again.'

'It might be too late then,' warned Josh, but his touch belied the caution in his words, and Bella pulled him back down towards her.

'I know,' she murmured against his mouth, 'but let's not think about it now. Let's not think at all.'

*　　*　　*

Much later, as they lay softly together, Josh rubbed his hand tenderly up and down Bella's arm. He felt extraordinary. It had never been like that before, but mixed with the heart-swelling feeling of peace and absolute rightness was a tinge of regret.

They had been right to decide all those years ago that they would stick with being friends, because now it would never be the same again. From now on he would never be able to look at Bella and not remember this tropical afternoon, with the rain crashing on the roof and the rattle of the air-conditioner, and her warmth and her sweetness and the fire that had consumed them both.

How were they going to go back to being friends now? *This isn't a normal time*, she had said, and she was right. He mustn't assume that this meant more to Bella than the classic response to surviving a crisis. However much he might want it to happen, she wasn't going to have suddenly forgotten how she felt about Will. Josh told himself that he had to accept that and find some way of staying friends without her feeling awkward or embarrassed or having to pretend something she didn't feel.

Outside, the tropical night had fallen without either him or Bella noticing. The downpour had stopped abruptly at some point, too, and now the insects were resuming their chorus of rasping and whirring and clicking, punctuated only by the steady drip of rainwater from the veranda roof.

'It's just as well we don't get out of dangerous situations very often,' he said.

Pressed into his side, with her leg entangled with his and her arm over his chest, Bella was feeling utterly content, replete down to her fingertips and toes, and half-surprised to find that her body wasn't glowing with satisfaction in the dark.

She didn't want this moment to end, but Josh's wry

comment was bringing reality seeping back. It might feel as if everything had changed, but nothing had really. In theory, they were both free agents, but it might not feel that way to Josh. There was Aisling to think about, and although Bella knew there was nothing between her and Will, that wasn't what she had told Josh.

Now was not the time to tell Josh that she loved him, not Will. He would think that she was just saying it because that was the kind of thing women said when they slept with you.

But perhaps she would be able to tell him when they got home, Bella told herself hopefully. Surely he couldn't have made love to her like that if he was still bound up in Aisling? Bella could think of plenty of ex-boyfriends who were more than capable of separating sex from emotion, but she didn't think that Josh was like that.

On the other hand, he *was* a man, she remembered, confidence fading rapidly. She was so used to thinking of him as a friend that it was easy to forget that.

No, she wasn't going to spoil this moment by going all intense and emotional on him, Bella decided. Much better to show him that she wasn't going to put any pressure on him. Let him go home and return to normal. He needed to decide for himself that Aisling wasn't what he wanted and *then* perhaps she could tell him how she felt.

In the meantime, she would treat things lightly. 'Is this how you always react after a crisis on expedition?' she asked.

'I wouldn't say that,' said Josh dryly, 'but sex is a common human reaction to a disaster.'

'We weren't part of a disaster, though.'

'We were lucky,' he said soberly. 'Things were pretty touch-and-go for a while yesterday.' His arm tightened around her as he remembered how close he had come to losing her. 'If we hadn't made the island when we did, I'm not sure how long we could have kept that boat afloat.'

He hesitated. 'Is this going to change things for us, Bella?'

'You mean being friends?'

'Yes. I don't want it to affect our friendship.'

'Nor do I,' said Bella, unable to resist the temptation of smoothing her hand over his chest in a way that a mere friend would never do. 'I don't think it has to, not if we don't let it. Like you say,' she went on, proud of her casual tone, 'we were both reacting to a crisis. It might be different for you, but that was the closest brush to danger I've ever had. It's been a strange experience, and it still doesn't feel quite real. And if it feels like that here, it's going to seem even more like a dream when we get home. Perhaps we should think about it like that.'

It *would* seem like a dream, Josh thought. 'You think we should pretend it never happened?'

Bella wasn't sure that she would be able to do that. 'I meant more that this is like time out of time,' she said, struggling to find the words to explain. 'The usual rules don't apply.'

From her comfortable position nestled against his shoulder, Bella couldn't see Josh's face, but she could practically feel him lifting an eyebrow. 'The usual rules?' he echoed. 'What are they?'

'That we're friends, good friends, and being friends is important for both of us, and it's not something we confuse with…with this.'

'With sex?'

'Exactly,' said Bella, who had begun to flounder. 'We're going home tomorrow anyway. Then it'll be back to reality, and we'll go back to being just friends, and tonight will just be something that happened, and was wonderful, but doesn't have any connection with the way we are at home.'

She lifted her head slightly to look at him anxiously. 'Does that make sense?'

'I think so,' said Josh. 'Everything will be different tomorrow.'

'It's not tomorrow yet,' said Bella, letting her fingers drift suggestively.

'That's true.' Josh shifted so that she lay beneath him, and kissed the curve of her shoulder. 'Are you thinking we should make the most of tonight while it still seems quite real?'

His hand traced her contours, lingering lovingly on the curve of her hip, and Bella arched with a shiver of pleasure as she felt him smile against her skin.

'I think perhaps we should,' she agreed breathlessly and wrapped her arms around him to pull him closer.

CHAPTER TEN

'Are you hungry?'

'Starving,' said Bella, and as if to underline the point her stomach let out an embarrassingly loud gurgle.

Josh laughed and patted her tummy. 'It sounds like it. Shall I go and see if I can find something to eat?'

Bella stretched across him to peer at the illuminated alarm clock by the bed. 'We've missed dinner. Pity there's no room service here.'

'The kitchens will still be open,' said Josh, getting out of bed and searching on the floor for his trousers. 'Having survived a near shipwreck, I can't let you succumb to starvation.'

He was gone for what seemed like ages, but Bella knew that he wouldn't come back empty-handed. Josh was nothing if not resourceful. When he did finally appear, he was carrying a tray laden with freshly cooked fish and steaming vegetables, all steaming hot, as well as two ice-cold beers.

'How on earth did you organise all this?' asked Bella, impressed, as he laid the tray on the bed with a flourish.

'It turns out that Elvis is the nephew of the barman and one of the cooks,' Josh told her, wondering if she knew how desirable she looked with her hair all tousled and her skin glowing.

'He told them how I went with him to the police to tell his story, and now they're insisting on treating me like some kind of hero, although I didn't really do anything. It was quite embarrassing,' he said, remembering his reception in the kitchen with a grimace. 'And when I asked if there were any leftovers from dinner, I was made to have a drink at the bar while Elvis's uncle cooked all this from scratch.'

Bella sniffed appreciatively. 'It smells wonderful,' she said, settling herself more comfortably against the pillows. She smiled at Josh. 'You *are* a hero,' she said. 'Anyone who can arrange a meal like this at this time of night definitely gets to be a hero in my book!'

They ate everything, sitting up in bed and then lolling across it to pick at the last few bits, and chatting easily. It felt extraordinarily relaxed, Bella thought at one point. There should have been *some* constraint, surely, given what they had been doing earlier?

But no. It seemed quite natural to be lying here with Josh, aglow with remembered delight, her foot sliding up and down his calf, while they talked and laughed exactly the way they had always done before.

Afterwards they walked—or in Bella's case, hobbled—down to the beach, where they sat in the dark shadows underneath the leaning palms and listened to the soft shush of the waves against the sand. The rain clouds had mostly dispersed by now, and the moonlight cast a shimmering silver stripe across the water. Above their heads, the faintest of warm breezes rustled the palm leaves.

'It's so peaceful,' sighed Bella contentedly, leaning back against Josh.

'Hard to believe what it was like last night, isn't it?' said Josh.

He was trying not to think about how soon tomorrow would come. He couldn't stop touching her now, couldn't control the way his hands moved lovingly over her, couldn't bear to think that this might be the last time he could hold her like this.

'I feel as if I could sit here for ever and look at the sea

like this,' she was saying, but he could feel her quiver of response.

Make the most of it, wasn't that what they had agreed?

'Forget the view,' he murmured, and drew her down into the soft sand for a long, sweet kiss that was followed by another, and then another, until the sand began to get in the way.

'You'll never get the sand out of your hair,' he said contritely, twisting it between his fingers and feeling how gritty it was.

'Perhaps I should cut it off before I go on that expedition of yours,' said Bella lazily.

Josh hated the thought. 'You must never cut it,' he said, appalled. 'It's beautiful hair.'

'I thought you would approve of the idea. It would be so much more practical.'

'Maybe,' said Josh. 'But it wouldn't be you. I—' He caught himself just in time. 'I *like* you as you are,' he finished.

When they went back to the room, he made her sit on the veranda while he brushed all the sand out of her hair with long, loving strokes, and then they went back to bed and made love again with a kind of urgency, as if they both sensed that the night was short and that seconds were ticking away.

The airport the next morning was crowded and chaotic. It was only a small terminal and, judging by the cacophony of languages, there were several flights leaving for various parts of Europe all at the same time.

Josh dealt with the luggage while Bella waited to one side. She felt cut off from the bustle around her, as if she were still wrapped in the bubble of enchantment from the night before. They had moved quietly around the room as they got ready to leave, saying little. There was nothing they *could* say, thought Bella.

'How's your foot?'.

Wrenched out of her bubble of enchantment, Bella turned to see Aisling looking tired and strained.

'It's fine, thanks,' she said. Aisling was the last person she wanted to talk to this morning, but she would have to be pleasant for Josh's sake. 'It looks worse than it is really,' she said, nodding down at the professional bandage. 'How are you?'

'Feeling as if I've made the most monumental mistake,' said Aisling frankly. 'Bryn and I had the most terrible row when we got back. That awful time on the boat and then on the island made me realise that he's not half the man Josh is. I've been so stupid,' she sighed. 'I thought I loved Bryn, but I can see now that it was just infatuation. He's got quite a powerful position with C.B.C., and I think I was carried away by his good looks and all those status symbols he has.'

She bit her lip. 'I'm not even sure that he loves me,' she confessed. 'He said that he did, and that he was going to divorce his wife, but I wonder if he'll ever do it. I'd have been better off sticking with Josh.'

'Josh deserves better than being a safe option for you,' said Bella coldly. 'He's not just there for you to fall back on when things go wrong.'

'I know,' said Aisling. 'And I know it's too late. I just want to tell Josh that I realise what a fool I've been—and you how lucky you are,' she added.

The last enchantment from the night before trickled away, leaving Bella cold and exposed to hard reality. Aisling wanted Josh back. And she, Bella, was going to have to let him make that choice.

Every fibre of her being strained against standing back

and letting Aisling have another chance. Bella wanted to push her away, to tell her to leave Josh alone, that he was hers and always had been. But if she did that, she would never know if Josh had lingering regrets.

More than anything else, she wanted to spend her life with him, but not if she would always be wondering if she was his second choice, a fall-back position for him, easy and comfortable but not *really* what he wanted. She had told Aisling that Josh deserved better than that, and she did too. Josh would have to decide if he wanted Aisling or if he wanted her, and the only way he could do that was if she gave Aisling the opportunity to let him know she had changed her mind.

So she gave Aisling a brittle smile. 'Josh and I are just friends,' she said in a cool voice. 'You know that. He told you himself that we were just pretending to be engaged for this trip.'

'Well, yes,' said Aisling hesitantly. 'But I wondered whether the two of you had...?' She trailed off delicately.

'No,' said Bella. 'We're friends, and we want to stay that way.'

'Oh.' Aisling began to look more hopeful. 'In that case, maybe I'll have a word with Josh later.'

'Whatever.' Bella even managed a careless shrug. 'It's nothing to do with me.'

In some ways the journey back seemed longer and more unendurable than being caught by the storm. At least then she hadn't had time to think. Bella almost wished herself back there, frantically baling to keep the boat afloat, when all she had had to worry about was whether they would sink or not, rather than wondering if she had just thrown away her own chance to be happy with Josh.

She was very tired. Neither of them had wanted to waste the night before sleeping, and she was afraid that if she fell asleep against Josh now, she would lose what little resolution she had.

The only way Bella could cope was by withdrawing completely, and Josh seemed happy to keep her at a distance. She longed to ask him whether he had spoken to Aisling and what he had said, but she knew that she mustn't. They were both being very careful not to talk about anything that might remind them of those long hours of sweetness.

Bella yearned to be back there in that moonlit room where time had been suspended for a while. Whenever she thought about the way they had kissed, the way they had touched, she couldn't believe that Josh didn't see as clearly as she did that they were meant to be together. But then she remembered what he had said about Aisling, and how they both agreed that their friendship meant more to them than anything. Being Josh's friend meant wanting him to be happy, and if he wanted Aisling, she would have to accept that being friends was enough.

It was late by the time they landed at Heathrow after a delayed connection in Paris, and Bella was so tired and her foot was so sore that she felt terrifyingly close to tears.

'Let's just get a taxi,' said Josh, retrieving her huge suitcase from the carousel and loading it onto the trolley with his own small bag.

'Sure. I can drop you off on the way,' she said, so that he knew that she wasn't banking on him coming home with her.

'Great,' he said flatly.

They nearly ran into Aisling as they turned to go through Customs. She was glaring after Bryn's departing back.

'He's just walked off and left me!' she said furiously. 'He's gone back to his wife in Dorking. Apparently she "understands" him in a way I'll never do—I bet she does!' she added venomously, and then her face crumpled. 'What am I going to do? I was staying with him in his London flat, but he hasn't even left me a key to go there tonight.'

'You'd better come with us,' said Bella. 'You can always stay with Josh—can't she, Josh? Most of your stuff must still be there anyway, isn't it?'

'That's true.' Aisling looked hopefully at Josh. 'Would you mind, Josh?'

What could he say? Bella seemed intent on pushing Aisling towards him. Presumably she was worried in case he forgot their agreement that everything would go back to normal now—as if it could! Josh thought bitterly. There was no normal any more as far as he was concerned.

He wanted to shout at her that he hadn't forgotten what they had agreed. How could he forget when she had spent the entire day making it very clear that last night was last night, and now was reality, and there was to be no muddling up the two? But she was obviously determined to make sure that he didn't misinterpret how sweet and loving she had been last night.

There was no need for her to make it quite so obvious that she was afraid that he would make a nuisance of himself. Josh felt raw, hurt by her mistrust but more by the realisation that Bella had meant what she said, and that the night they had shared wasn't going to be repeated.

Fine, he thought. He would leave her alone if that was what she wanted. 'Of course you can stay,' he said to Aisling, who was watching him anxiously. 'I didn't even get round to putting your stuff away. Let's go and find a taxi.'

'I'm sorry, Josh,' said Aisling as the taxi headed out of the airport through the tunnel. 'I think I might have blown our contract. Bryn was well on his way to convincing himself that the storm was all your fault, and he certainly won't forgive me for the things I said last night. I should have been more careful, but he made me so angry! And now I'm afraid that he'll veto any move to award us the contract now. He's got a lot of clout at C.B.C.'

'Don't worry about it yet,' said Josh. 'We'll just have to wait and see what they say.'

'I'll understand if you want me to leave the company now,' Aisling said miserably.

'Of course I don't want you to leave,' he said. 'You've been doing a great job. And you were right about going on this trip. I made a lot of other useful contacts this week, which I wouldn't have done if you hadn't encouraged me to go. Even if the major contract doesn't come through, I think it will have been worth it.'

Of course he didn't want Aisling to leave, thought Bella dully. Aisling could obviously do what she liked—dump him, humiliate him, jeopardise an important contract—and Josh would still want her to stay.

The taxi waited with its meter ticking outside Josh's flat while he and Aisling got out and unloaded their bags.

'Well...see you,' said Bella brightly.

'Yes.' Josh hesitated, as if he would have said more, but in the end he stepped back and closed the door. 'See you.'

As the taxi turned round, Bella watched him unlock the door to his flat and stand back to let Aisling go in first. He followed her in without even glancing back to where she sat all alone in the back of the taxi.

So that was that. The end of the holiday and back to reality with a vengeance.

The house was cold and empty when Bella let herself in. The taxi driver had taken pity on her and carried her case to the door, but with her bad foot it was a struggle even to get it inside on her own. She would have to unpack it at the bottom of the stairs as there was no way she would ever be able to carry it up to her bedroom.

Bella limped into the kitchen and put on as many lights as she could. She had always loved this house, but all at once it seemed sad and lonely, and much too big for one person. She wished Josh were with her. It wouldn't feel lonely then.

But Josh wasn't there. He was with Aisling. Bella slumped down at the table and put her head in her hands, torturing herself by imagining them together. Were they sitting on his battered blue sofa, happy just to be back together again? Perhaps Aisling was telling Josh how much she regretted going off with Bryn, and then Josh could pull her joyfully into his arms, telling her not to worry about it just as she wasn't to worry about losing them the contract. 'You've come back to me and that's all that matters,' he might be saying right now.

Bella buried her head in her arms and wept.

In spite of her tears, she was so tired that she fell straight into a deep sleep as soon as she dragged herself to bed. She woke late the next morning, feeling terrible. Her eyes were all puffy and piggy, and a nagging ache seemed to have taken up residence in the pit of her stomach. Bella identified it eventually as a feeling of sick despair.

And as if that wasn't bad enough, it was Monday morning and she had to go to work. Somehow she was going to have to get herself out of bed and pull herself together!

One look in the bathroom mirror was enough to convince her that she was going to have her work cut out. She looked almost as bad as she felt. Bella sighed.

She had to face Phoebe and Kate, too. They had insisted on coming round to hear about the trip that evening. 'And don't think you can get away with just telling us it was fine,' Phoebe's message had warned. 'We want to know *all* about it!'

At least her eyes had gone down a bit by then, and she still had some colour from her days on the beach which helped disguise what would otherwise be a horribly white and strained face. Considering the oppressive cloud of misery that had been clinging to her all day and the rawness in her heart, Bella thought she looked pretty good.

Not that she fooled Kate and Phoebe for a minute. 'Bella, lovey, what on earth's happened?' asked Kate after one look at her face. 'You look absolutely terrible!'

'I don't look that bad, do I?' Bella asked Phoebe as she hugged her.

'Yes,' said Phoebe uncompromisingly. She held Bella at arm's length. 'What's wrong?'

Bella forced a bright smile. 'Nothing, unless you count my injury.' She showed them her bandaged foot. 'I'm not going to be able to wear any of my favourite shoes for ages.'

'That is bad,' agreed Kate.

'Exactly. Is it any wonder I'm not looking myself?'

'Well, come on, then.' They sat around the table where they had sat so many times when all three of them had shared the house and looked at Bella expectantly. 'Tell us all about it.'

'I don't really know where to start,' she said feebly.

'Start with the important thing,' advised Phoebe. 'How's Josh?'

'He's... He's...' Bella's throat closed so tight that she couldn't get any further. To her horror, her mouth began to wobble, and although she put up a hand to cover it, she couldn't hide the tears that scalded her eyes.

Phoebe looked at Kate. 'V&Ts all round, I think.'

'Yes please,' Bella managed to gasp. Now that she had started to cry she couldn't stop.

'I'll go,' said Kate, pushing back her chair.

There was a corner shop at the end of the road, and she was back a few minutes later, clutching several bottles of tonic. 'I brought chocolate too,' she said. 'I thought we might need it.'

Phoebe made the drinks and put a glass in front of Bella, who had given in completely by this stage and was sobbing with her head on the table. 'Come on, Bella,' she said, patting her on the back. 'This isn't like you. Here, have a drink.'

Bella lifted a blotched and tear-stained face and gulped immediately. It was so strong that she nearly choked, but when she had recovered, she took another, smaller, sip.

Silently, Kate handed her a box of tissues. Bella took one and blew her nose hard. 'Sorry,' she muttered, scrubbing at her cheeks with the crumpled tissue.

'We've all done it,' said Kate. 'Right here at this table too, in my case.'

Bella managed a watery smile. 'I remember.'

'And I seem to remember snivelling a bit over Gib,' said Phoebe, 'so we know what it's like.' She pulled out a chair and sat down next to Bella. 'Now,' she said firmly. 'You'd better tell us all about it.'

'Well!' exclaimed Kate when Bella had stumbled to the end of the story. 'I don't know why you're worrying, Bella. Even if we didn't know him, it's obvious that you're the one Josh loves.'

'Then why has he gone off with Aisling?' Bella demanded tearfully. 'He hasn't even rung to see if I got back OK.'

'You know, you could ring him,' Phoebe suggested gently.

'I can't,' she wailed. 'He's probably still in bed with Aisling, and even if he isn't, I can't start hassling him for attention. I said we would go back to being friends, but I'm not even sure I can do that now.' She groped miserably for another tissue.

'Of course you'll still be friends,' said Kate. 'You can't just stop being friends when you've been as close as you and Josh for all those years.'

'But that's the thing,' wept Bella. 'I don't think I can be friends if he's with Aisling. I couldn't bear seeing him with anyone now. But if we're not friends, I won't see him at all, and I couldn't bear that either. I don't know what to do,' she sobbed. 'I just know that I miss him, I miss him, I *miss* him…' Her voice rose to a wail.

Phoebe put an arm round her shoulder and exchanged a glance with Kate, who immediately launched into positive mode.

'I don't see Josh getting back together with Aisling,' she said. 'They never seemed that convincing as a couple. I never got the feeling they belonged together the way you and Josh do.'

'Kate's right,' said Phoebe, picking up the baton of encouragement. 'You and Josh are meant to be together and I'll bet you anything Josh knows that as well as you do.'

'Then why hasn't he rung?'

'Perhaps he's having problems getting rid of Aisling. You were the one who told us you thought he needed to be clear that relationship was over, so he probably feels that he has to sort that out and then he'll be round here like a shot!'

But Josh didn't come round. He didn't come round, and he didn't ring. He didn't email. He didn't even send a text.

Bella spent four days checking the phone to see if she had missed a call, although that wasn't likely as she took her mobile everywhere. Of course, his phone might not be working, she reasoned desperately, but then he could use the phone at work, couldn't he? Ditto computers. What were the chances that his laptop *and* his entire company network would crash at the same time? There had even been time for him to write her a letter and put it in the post!

'Do you think he might be ill?' she asked Phoebe on Friday morning.

'No,' said Phoebe patiently. 'I think he's waiting to hear from you. From what you told me about the way you were on the flight home, I think he's probably sitting there thinking that you don't even want to be friends any more.'

'Or he's too happy with Aisling to even think about me,' said Bella glumly.

'Well, you won't know until you talk to him, will you? Don't be silly, Bella,' said Phoebe sternly. 'Just ring him!'

In the end, Bella sent an email which took her ages to compose. She didn't want him to think that she had been pining, but she had to see him. So she pretended that she had been terribly busy and apologised for not being in touch sooner. Since she knew perfectly well that Josh hadn't even tried to be in touch with her, he wasn't to know that her inbox hadn't been jammed with messages and her phone permanently engaged, was he?

'What about a drink sometime?' she finished in what she hoped was a suitably casual way that would give him no indication of the degree of her desperation. Surely that sounded just like someone whose only concern was to pick up their friendship exactly where it had been before they had spoilt everything by sleeping together?

As soon as she had sent it Bella agonised about whether she had put it the right way. Every five minutes she checked her inbox to see if Josh had replied yet, and when his name finally popped up in bold, her heart lurched hammering into her throat.

God, she was in a bad way, she thought. It ought to take more than the sight of his name to reduce her to this state, but her hand shook on the mouse as she clicked to open the message.

'Doing anything this evening?' it read.

'Nothing special,' Bella typed quickly in reply. Apart from loving you and needing you and wanting you. 'Why don't you come round? We can have a bottle of wine and a chat. It'll be like old times!'

There, that didn't sound too intense, did it?

Josh's reply came back a few minutes later. Bella clicked eagerly. Perhaps he would say how much he was looking forward to seeing her, how much he had missed her even? Anything to give her some indication of what he felt.

She should have known better.

'OK,' said the message.

Bella was a terrible rambler when she got going, but Josh had succinct emails down to a fine art. They were always restrained, polite and to the point. Like him, really.

She was absurdly nervous before he arrived that evening, and dithered about the house wondering what to wear, how to look, how to *be*. It had never been a problem when she wanted to impress a man before. Kate had always said that she should have a Ph.D. in flirting, but she couldn't imagine flirting with *Josh*. She couldn't make play with her eyelashes or cross her legs or smile seductively at him. He would just ask her why she was fidgeting.

The peal of the doorbell broke into her thoughts, and Bella's heart jerked wildly. She had to take several deep breaths before she could even open the door, and when she did all the air evaporated from her lungs all over again at the sight of him standing there.

'Hi.' Her voice came out as a squeak, and Josh looked faintly surprised. *Not* a good start. Bella coughed. 'Sorry, frog in my throat,' she mumbled. She stood back. 'Come in.'

He was looking exactly the same as ever, she thought with a mixture of joy and despair. Joy because the mere sight of him now was enough to make her senses tingle and send happiness rushing along her veins. Despair because she could see no sign that she had the same effect on him. There was no outward indication that Josh had missed her at all, or that this evening was any different from all the other evenings when he had dropped round to see her as a friend.

He *did* look a little tired, though, Bella thought, studying him covertly as she got out a bottle of wine, but there could be lots of reasons for that. He wasn't drawn and puffy-eyed from crying himself to sleep every night like her, that was for sure.

'Have you been busy?' she asked as she rummaged for a corkscrew.

'Chaotic.' Josh sat down on one of the shabby sofas at the end of the kitchen. 'C.B.C. contacted us the day after we got back. They gave us that contract.'

'Really?' Bella looked up from the corkscrew in surprise. 'In spite of Bryn?'

'It turns out that the man who really makes the decisions at C.B.C. was on that boat trip as well,' said Josh. 'He was the short guy who helped us move the boat round the island. Anyway, he seemed to think that we were what their organisation needed.'

'Josh, that's fantastic news!' Bella was genuinely pleased for him. He had only set up his company a couple of years ago and she knew how much he needed a big contract like the one they had just won from C.B.C. to make it secure.

'He was very taken with you,' said Josh. 'He went on and on about how charming you were. I suspect you might have done more than the rest of us to get us the contract.'

'I'm sure that's not true.'

Bella poured the wine and carried the glasses over to the sofa. Handing one to Josh, she sat cross-legged at the other end of the sofa, where there was no danger of touching him, and leant forward to chink glasses.

'Thank you anyway,' he said.

There was a pause. For a man who had just secured his company's future, Josh seemed ill at ease. 'So, how have you been?' he asked after a moment.

'Fine. And you?'

'Yes, fine.'

Talk about stilted conversation, thought Bella despairingly. Anyone would think they were on a blind date.

'I wasn't sure if you would be coming on your own or not,' she tried again brightly. 'Where's Aisling tonight?'

'Aisling?' echoed Josh, as if puzzled by the question. 'I've no idea.'

The icy claws that had been clamped around Bella's heart since that awful taxi ride back from Heathrow eased their grip for the first time. Cautiously, it was true, but definitely eased it. 'So you're not...?'

'Not what?'

'Not together again?'

'No.' Josh sounded almost cross.

'I'm sorry,' she said, afraid that she had touched on a sore point.

'Why?'

Bella was flustered by the direct question. 'Of course I'm sorry if you're unhappy.'

'I'm not unhappy,' snapped Josh, and drank his wine morosely. 'Not about Aisling, anyway,' he added as an afterthought.

It was so unlike him to snap that Bella wasn't quite sure how to react. She eyed him a little uncertainly. 'Well, if it's not Aisling,' she said cautiously, 'what is it that's making you unhappy?'

Josh hesitated.

'You can tell me, can't you?' Bella persevered. 'A problem shared is a problem halved and all that. That's what friends are for, isn't it?

'That's the trouble,' said Josh, putting down his glass with a sharp click. 'I don't think I can be friends with you any more.'

He said it so seriously that for a moment Bella could only stare at him. Surely he didn't mean it? 'You can't just stop being friends, Josh,' she said in a voice that wavered in spite of herself.

Josh looked bleakly back at her. 'I just think it would be easiest if I didn't see you any more.'

'But...*why*?'

'Because being friends isn't enough for me any more.' He dropped his head into his hands as if unable to look at her stricken face. 'I'm sorry, Bella,' he said. 'I just can't do it. The last thing I want to do is to hurt you but I don't think I can stand it any longer. We should never have slept together that night,' he went on, not stopping to see her reaction. 'It's ruined everything. I knew it would. I *knew* we wouldn't be able to go back to the way we were before, and we can't, or at least, I can't. It was OK when I could just think of you as a dear friend, and I'm going to miss you more than I can say, but I'm too in love with you to be friends now, and I don't know how I'm going to bear not seeing you.'

The words were pouring out of him in a rush. Bella had never heard the self-possessed Josh sound so incoherent, and it took her a few moments to realise what he had said. When she did, she swallowed hard.

'Josh—'

But it only came out as a whisper, and Josh was still talking. Now that he had started, he seemed unable to stop.

'I haven't known what to do,' he was saying in despair. 'I was desperate to see you, but I knew that if I did I would just want to kiss you, and it's no good. I know you want us to stay friends, but I can't. I can't do it, Bella.'

'Josh—' she tried again.

'I'm sorry, I'm sorry, I don't want to embarrass you.' He hadn't even heard her. 'God, this is awful, but I have to tell you I love you. I *love* you,' he said again despairingly. 'I don't think I can manage without you, but I know how you feel about Will, and I know nothing is ever going to be the same again and—'

'*Josh!*' Bella had to shout in the end, and he stopped as if she had slapped him in the face. 'Will you please shut up a minute and let me say something?' she asked him.

He looked cautious. 'Yes.'

'I am not in love with Will,' she said very clearly. 'I do not want him. I want you.'

It was Josh's turn to stare. He kept opening and closing his mouth as if he couldn't decide which statement astounded him most. 'What?' was all he managed eventually.

'I only said that I was in love with Will because *you* were engaged to Aisling,' she told him. 'I thought it would be awkward if you knew how much I loved you then and it just seemed easier to let you believe that I was miserable about Will, but I wasn't. I was miserable because of you.'

'Easier?'

'Well, I didn't know that you loved me, did I?' Bella pointed out, exasperated.

They faced each other almost irritably until Josh finally registered what she had said.

'You're in love with me?' he said in disbelief.

Bella sighed. 'I think I've probably always been in love with you, Josh. It just took me a long time to realise, and when I did, it was too late, or it seemed that way.'

Josh was still having trouble assimilating what she was telling him. 'You *love* me?'

'Yes,' said Bella, going for the simple approach, which was all he seemed capable of understanding. She felt as if a huge smile had started inside her and was spreading out to her fingers and her toes and the ends of her hair and finally her lips. 'Yes, I do.'

'Bella…' Josh was still staring at her, but suddenly it sank in and he started to laugh. 'Bella,' he said again as he reached across the sofa and pulled her onto his lap and kissed her. 'Do you know how many years I've waited to hear you say that? Fourteen!'

'You're not going to try and tell me that you were in love with me all that time!'

'Of course I was! I fell in love with you at first sight,' he told her. 'You know perfectly well that you were gorgeous and irresistible, and you still are,' he said, kissing her again, and Bella wound her arms around his neck and kissed him back.

'Why didn't you tell me?' she mumbled against his throat.

'I knew you would never look at me,' said Josh, his hands moving hungrily over her. 'You were way out of my league! So I opted for friendship. I told myself that it was better than nothing, and I got used to the fact that you were going to end up with someone else. I didn't like it when I thought you were serious about Will, but you seemed so keen, there didn't seem much I could do about it.

'I think that's why I turned to Aisling,' he said. 'I thought she might be like you but the trouble was, she *wasn't* you. I was so relieved when she broke off the engagement!

'And you,' he said, pulling her down into the cushions and kissing her, long, deep, desperate kisses, 'you were so sympathetic, which was the last thing I wanted. You kept going on about being a friend and all I wanted was you. That's why I spent so much time with Aisling,' he told her. 'It was the only way I could think of to keep my hands off you!'

Bella sighed happily. 'For two people who know each other as well as we do, we seem to have got into a right old muddle,' she said. Her arms tightened around him. 'Is there anything else that I should know to avoid any more misunderstandings?'

'Only that I love you,' said Josh seriously, taking her face between his hands and looking deep into her eyes. 'I love you and I need you, and I want to come home every night and know that you'll be there. What do you think, Bella? Can we be lovers as well as friends?'

'Yes,' said Bella, pulling his head down so that she could kiss him again. 'We can, and we always will be.'

'This is all very mysterious!' said Gib, when Bella opened the door. 'All Phoebe will tell me is that we've been summoned to dinner and no excuses will be accepted. What are you girls keeping from me?'

'I've told you everything I know,' protested Phoebe, standing beside him. 'Tell him, Bella.'

'It's true. She doesn't know any more than you do. It's a surprise for everyone.' Bella smiled radiantly. 'Come in,' she said. 'Kate and Finn are already here.'

'Thank goodness you're here!' exclaimed Kate, hugging first Phoebe and then Gib when they went into the kitchen. 'Finn and I are dying of curiosity, aren't we, Finn?'

'I'm beside myself,' he agreed, deadpan.

'Well, *I* am,' said Kate when they all laughed.

'Me too,' said Gib. 'So come on, Bella! Don't keep us in suspense any longer. What is this big surprise?'

Bella looked at Josh, who smiled and took her hand. 'Bella and I are getting married,' he announced.

There was a moment's silence, then the four others burst out laughing.

'Well, we knew *that*!'

'That's not a surprise!' objected Phoebe.

'I agree,' said Kate. 'We've known for *ages*. I told Finn weeks ago that you were finally getting your act together.'

'I thought at the very least you were going to tell us you were having a baby!' said Phoebe.

'Well, it was a surprise to us!' Bella was inclined to be offended, but Josh was laughing too.

'It's no good, Bella,' he said. 'That's what comes of having good friends. They know you better than you know yourself!'

'But we're very, very glad you've come to your senses at last,' said Phoebe, making amends as she hugged them both.

'And about time,' Kate added, doing a swap. 'We were beginning to wonder if you would ever get round to it!'

'I think this makes it a hat trick, doesn't it?' said Gib

when the champagne had been opened. 'Three mock engagements, three happy endings!'

Josh put his arm around Bella and kissed her. 'Three happy beginnings,' he said.

Discover Pure Reading Pleasure with

Visit the Mills & Boon website for all the latest in romance

- 🌹 **Buy** all the latest releases, backlist and eBooks

- 🌹 **Join** our community and chat to authors and other readers

- 🌹 **Win** with our fantastic online competitions

- 🌹 **Tell us** what you think by signing up to our reader panel

- 🌹 **Find out** more about our authors and their books

- 🌹 **Free** online reads from your favourite authors

- 🌹 **Sign** up for our free monthly eNewsletter

- 🌹 **Rate** and review books with our star system

www.millsandboon.co.uk

 Follow us at twitter.com/millsandboonuk

 Become a fan at facebook.com/romancehq

...Make sure you don't miss out on these fabulous stories!

3 in 1 ONLY £5.99

featuring

THE MAN MEANS BUSINESS
by Annette Broadrick

TOTALLY TEXAN
by Mary Lynn Baxter

THE TEXAN'S
FORBIDDEN AFFAIR
by Peggy Moreland

featuring

HOUSE OF
MIDNIGHT FANTASIES
by Kristi Gold

FORCED TO THE ALTAR
by Susan Crosby

THE MILLIONAIRE'S
PREGNANT MISTRESS
by Michelle Celmer

On sale from 4th March 2011

*Available at WHSmith, Tesco, ASDA, Eason
and all good bookshops*

www.millsandboon.co.uk

We're thrilled to bring you four bestselling collections that we know you'll love…

featuring

THE MARCIANO LOVE-CHILD
by Melanie Milburne

THE ITALIAN BILLIONAIRE'S SECRET LOVE-CHILD
by Cathy Williams

THE RICH MAN'S LOVE-CHILD
by Maggie Cox

featuring

ALL NIGHT WITH THE BOSS
by Natalie Anderson

THE BOSS'S WIFE FOR A WEEK
by Anne McAllister

MY TALL DARK GREEK BOSS
by Anna Cleary

On sale from 18th February 2011

By Request